PRINCE OF SLAYERS

The Company of Slayers Series

Company of Slayers
Once a Slayer
Prince of Slayers
Empire of the Slayers (forthcoming)

The Kylnnar War Saga

Wolfsreach Academy
Dynamic (Forthcoming)

PRINCE OF SLAYERS

THE COMPANY OF SLAYERS, VOLUME 3

JUSTIN WAINE

Prince of Slayers

Cover copyright © 2025 Epsom Fantasy Press Limited
Cover illustration by: James Mckay
Cover Design: Benjamin Dickson

Published by:
Epsom Fantasy Press Limited
www.epsomfantasypress.co.uk

ISBN: 978-1-7391807-6-8 (ebook)
ISBN: 978-1-7391807-7-5 (paperback)

First Edition: March 2025

Dedicated to:
Erica, Paul and Oliver

CHAPTER ONE – COUNT OF CHAZANTRIA

Smoke drifted across the grassland, rising up and over the low rolling hills that framed a wide plain. The screams of the wounded and dying echoed across the battlefield. The clash of arms, metal on metal, pierced the air. Rain was falling and the field was a quagmire. The centre was a morass of infantry locked in hand-to-hand combat, fighting not just each other but the mud as well. The mud was such that skill at keeping one's feet had become more important than skill at arms. Soldiers drowned as their opponents wrestled them to the ground and forced their faces into muddy puddles, holding them down until their legs stopped kicking.

The crush in the centre was terrible. It seemed incongruous to those fighting to be so compressed together in the wide-open expanse of the Great Steppe. Not that many had time to think. Their task was simple: stab, cut, slash, punch, repeat. The first sound that stood out was not the shouts of men or the clash of swords, but the grinding of metal on metal, a slow piercing screech as armoured soldier struggled with opponent, hand to hand and body to body. The second was the sucking of boots pulling free from thick mud as the winner moved onto their next victim only a step away.

Spears were pointless at this range, as were the great broad swords still carried by some Sevains, swung in wide circles and a relic from the old way of war. A weapon that granted a fighter space was no use here. Short swords, daggers, single-handed axes, and stubby maces were what worked in this slaughter.

The two groups of soldiers were similar in appearance and dress; it was hard for them to tell friend from foe. Some wore tabards and badges to indicate their affiliation, but most did not. Still, those on the seething frontlines seemed to have some unconscious sense of which side they were on.

On the low hills above the battle, Kyrian Slayer, Count of Chazantria, sat watching the carnage impassively. His cold blue eyes barely moved as he surveyed the scene. The warrior's long black hair had been tied up with a leather thong in the manner of the steppe nomads. His head was uncovered so his men could see his face. He sat on the back of a hadan. The man-high lizard was a giant by the standards of its species. Its skin was a mottled collection of oranges and browns that stood out from the other, more usual, greenish hadan that surrounded it. Perhaps the creature was some hybrid, an outlandish mix of hadan and huffrin.

A dozen or so knights sat upon these lizards, fighting to control the truculent creatures as they snapped and bit at each other. Their lord's lizard seemed unaffected, too afraid or too respectful of its master to risk raising his ire. The knights' appearance differed from their Kanath count with his dark hair and pale complexion. Most were Sevains, white-skinned humans with hair the yellow of straw, partially concealed in conical metal helms. They wore chainmail covering the upper body, and simple leather breaches. Only one looked like his master and dressed in a similar fashion. His armour was a leather coat, covered with metal scales that stretched to the top of his knee-high boots. He was tall but rangy rather than hulking like Kyrian, his features still chiselled as he approached his fortieth year. His long black hair, showing hints of grey, was similarly tied up in a topknot. Unlike the Sevains, his head was uncovered. Marcus Romanch was a Kangorner and, indeed, a Lord of Kangorn. Not that the city on the Rock mattered much to him: it was on this battlefield that his wealth and position would be made.

"They have sent in their reserve," Kyrian observed.

The Lord of House Romanch surveyed the battlefield. The count was right; five hundred warriors were charging from a wooded outcrop to the east. They had thought to hide themselves there, but it was autumn, and the vegetation was already starting to thin, so only the evergreen spruce provided some cover. It had concealed their exact number but not their presence.

"Shall we deploy our own reserve force?" asked a knight flanking Kyrian.

Marcus gave a smile at that. *Very sensible; very traditional*, he thought. Not how Kyrian worked.

The Slayer was staring intently at the slaughter before him. His timing had to be exact: the enemy's reserve had to be committed so it could not change course, but not fully engaged or he would risk the lives of too many of his own men.

"My lord, the reserve?" pressed the knight, alarmed.

The Haydroners had almost reached the melee at the centre of the field. Kyrian waved his comment away irritably with a gloved fist.

"Now, Marcus," the Slayer ordered.

The Lord of House Romanch's hand dropped as a pre-arranged signal. A small group of soldiers stood on a nearby hillock, holding a large collection of coloured flags. Two of them stepped forward and each waved a pair of red and blue flags, large enough to be seen across the whole battlefield. Looks of confusion passed across the knights' faces. This was not the signal to the reserve. It was not any of the signals that had been agreed before the battle.

Moments later, cavalry appeared in the distance; they had been hidden in the lee of a small hill. They were moving fast, their mounts bounding across the open plain towards the charging Haydroners. The reserve had just made contact with the main formation in the centre, plunging into the bloodshed. Given time, their numbers should have allowed them to overwhelm Kyrian's soldiers. They did not see the approaching cavalry, but shouts started to rise from those to the rear of the attacking reserve, not yet committed to the fight. They could see the threat.

The Haydron commanders discounted the risk from cavalry. The few hadan-mounted knights that Kyrian's army had were on the far side of the battle around him, and no direct threat to the reserve, given the slow speed at which the lizards moved. The bird-like iribis, used as a mount for light cavalry, were common elsewhere but a rarity on the steppe. The wide-open nature of the terrain made the normally skittish creatures uncontrollable. Only one creature on the steppe moved at that speed: the oradar, a giant cat, five feet high at the shoulder and wide enough and strong enough to carry a man. Their fur was a variety of colours ranging from a pale brown to almost black.

PRINCE OF SLAYERS

"Fal'Gar, Lord Kyrian!" a knight with the Slayer shouted, tension clear in his voice.

Kyrian said nothing; he just continued to watch. Another broad smile had broken across Marcus' face. He knew the Count of Haydron and his men were likely to be as surprised as Kyrian's lords. Only one people rode oradar: the Gar, specifically the Fal'Gar, the ancient people of the steppe. Shorter and stockier than the Gar found to the south, they were still taller and thinner than humans. Their features were sharp and angular and their yellow skin was tanned to a dark brown by a lifetime riding across the windswept grassland. They lacked the translucent agelessness of their southern cousins, but it would have been impossible for anyone looking at them to decide which of them were old or young.

They wore coats of leather, covered with metal scales of alcidide, the Gar metal, stronger than steel, that never rusted. They sat in high-backed saddles, allowing them to manoeuvre their mounts with their legs alone and to fire their compound bows from the saddle. The bows were made of horn and wood glued together and reversed against the natural curve of the wood to create even more strain. An arrow from their bows could punch through almost any armour. A sheet of arrows was already falling from the cat riders upon the hapless reserve soldiery of the army of Haydron.

The Fal'Gar swept around in a large curve, circumnavigating the centre of the battle, keeping up a constant rain of arrows. A hundred yards out, the eighty or so Gar riders stowed their bows into specially designed wooden containers on the front of their saddles and unslung lances strapped to their saddles behind their backs. The lances were six feet long, with dark iron points and a counterbalance iron weight at the other end. Fifty yards out, the Haydroners broke and ran – not only the reserve, but also their main strength. They had heard the

11

shouts and screams of panic and decided they too wanted to be anywhere else but here.

The oradar cavalry caught the fleeing rear and set about it with lances. Giant cats batted men dead with a single swipe of their paws.

"Signal do not pursue!" Kyrian shouted.

Marcus looked to relay the order, but the flag wavers had already heard it and were busy with the combination of yellow and black flags that signalled the recall.

The Haydroners were fleeing to the east towards the collection of tents and fires that made up their camp. Kyrian's Chazantrian soldiers were milling around, watching their opponents flee as their commanders did their best to calm their animal spirits. This was helped by the block of Fal'Gar cavalry, which was partly interposing themselves between the two groups of Sevains. But this had created a new tension: the Fal'Gar had not been particularly careful about which Sevains they had killed. While their victims had largely been the Count of Haydron's men, a few of Kyrian's had shared their fate. The lack of heraldry among the two sides meant that such confusion was inevitable, but it only added to the historical antipathy between the Sevains and the Fal'Gar that went back centuries.

The Fal'Gar leader saw the problem and signalled to one of his riders. The Gar raised a long copper horn, a vertical tube ending in an open-mouthed falcon head. He blew a long keening blast that shrieked across the battlefield, making the humans present shiver. It was a common sound for them to hear before a Fal'Gar raid. The oradar riders pulled their mounts around and, avoiding the main body of Kyrian's force, padded off in the direction of the hill from which the Count of Chazantria was watching the confrontation.

"We could have run them down!" exclaimed Marcus, indicating the retreating Haydroners.

PRINCE OF SLAYERS

"I want to negotiate with Radnor Callico, not destroy him," observed Kyrian. "He's lost enough that he will talk now, but not so much that he will skulk behind the walls of Haydron. If Haydron is closed, then we'll never get the harvest surplus off the steppe. Then we all lose."

Marcus nodded his understanding. Kangorn depended on the farmland to feed the city. Almost all of those crops passed through Haydron. There were only a few beaches along the coast that could be used to land on, but loading a ship from them would be onerous. Loading the number of ships that usually traded the Haydron to Kangorn route would be impossible without a proper harbour, and that only Haydron possessed.

Kyrian gave his hadan a light kick and the beast started to move slowly forward down from the crest of the low hill. Marcus and the other assembled lords followed their count, wending their way down to the plain below. The oradar-mounted Fal'Gar had left the slower-moving infantry behind them and now approached Kyrian's group. The knights hefted their weapons as subtly as possible, readying themselves for combat, while trying to appear outwardly peaceful. There was no trust between the humans of the steppe and the Gar. The Fal'Gar were equally tense, watching the lizard-mounted warriors warily. They may have had the numbers in a confrontation at this moment, but the battle-weary infantry was closing the gap to their rear. Kyrian, by contrast, seemed unaware or at least indifferent to the tension filling the air.

"Well met, Falthar of the Skyriders," Kyrian saluted the Gar leader, choosing Westerly, the trade tongue. Westerly was a variant of Nerlinean with many words imported from both the Sevain and Kanath languages. It passed for a common language for those who traded around the Nerlinean Ocean.

"Kyrian Slayer," Falthar replied with the barest nod of his head.

Marcus was on edge, searching for meaning in Falthar's expressionless face. If Kyrian felt similar concern, he did not show it. To Marcus, the Slayer appeared nonplussed.

"Would you join us for dinner?" Kyrian enquired of the Gar.

Falthar's face broke into an uncharacteristic smile at that. "We could all eat," he laughed.

His humour was infectious – at least to his own people, who joined in their leader's merriment. It seemed odd on their normally phlegmatic faces. The Sevains did not join in the laughter, but the tension in the air relaxed a little. Weapons were grasped less tightly, and hands slipped from sword hilts back to saddle pommels.

Kyrian turned his hadan around, steering the irritable giant lizard in the direction of the camp, which lay out of sight hidden by the hills. The knights followed, still nervous at presenting their rear to the mounted Gar. The Skyriders dropped in beside them, the cats loping alongside the slow-moving lizards, visibly holding themselves back from overtaking. They had no desire to arrive at the camp first and alarm those protecting it. The infantry trailed behind.

The battle had lasted into late afternoon. Kyrian was pleased it had ended when it did, as night could come quickly in autumn this far north. No one wanted to fight in the dark or, for that matter, over multiple days. Such fights were messy, with high casualties and uncertain outcomes. It was cleaner and easier to get it all done in one day.

It had been nearly five years ago since Kyrian Slayer had come north to the steppe, not long after his colleague Balinor Slayer had become Prince of Kangorn. He had brought a few soldiers and more gold and started to carve out his own territory on the western fringes of the sea of grass. The Great Steppe framed the north of the Nerlinean Ocean connecting the Nerlinean Empire in the east to the kingdoms of the west.

PRINCE OF SLAYERS

Chazantria, an ancient name going back centuries, lay on the far west of the rolling grasslands where they met the lofty Daldara Mountain Range. Those peaks ran from the Nerlinean Ocean north into the icy wastes, where nothing but the hardiest beasts could survive for long. The main pass through the south of the range was the great fortress city of Hambledon. It had fallen to the Sevain tribes three centuries ago. Most of them had migrated south seeking better land, warmer climes, and to escape the constant raiding of the steppe.

A few had remained, clinging as they had done for centuries to the coast, where the windswept grasslands gave way to a land marked by low hills and small forests. This provided enough arable land to allow them to create their own agricultural communities. The only city on the steppe was Haydron, a small port surrounding the long coast's only natural harbour of any size. For as long as anyone could remember, the Counts of Haydron had laid claim to rule all the Sevains on the steppe, but in truth the territory was split into dozens of lordships, their borders fluctuating with wars, deaths and marriages. The real power of the Counts of Haydron ran only a little further than the fields that surrounded its city walls.

It was into this fractious environment that Kyrian had arrived, cutting deals with lords who needed money, buying crop surpluses to sell in Kangorn, and supporting the right lord in battle against the weaker opponent. The Romanchs, like several Lords of Kangorn, had for nearly a century ruled their own small swathe of territory here, paying deference if not allegiance to the Count of Haydron. Marcus could not really explain how a merchant company like the Company of Slayers, who had arrived apparently keen on trade, had instead in five years become a military force strong enough to challenge the Count of Haydron. For it was the forces of Haydron and their allies that they had just butchered on the field behind them.

Kyrian was a strong warrior, but more importantly an inspiring general, and each small battle had gone his way. Each victory brought more Sevain lords flocking to his banner. Marcus had seen which way the wind was blowing and thrown in his lot with Kyrian Slayer. His reward had been to already double his existing territorial holdings, and if today went the right way, as seemed likely, he would gain more. This battle had not been about conquest: Kyrian had no intention of besieging Haydron and laying waste to it. He did not have the soldiers to do that. Besides, he did not want to offend the Great Khan of the Mourn Horde, the ruler of everyone on the steppe.

The Slayer Count declared a victory on his return to camp, receiving roars of acclaim from the camp followers and those who had taken part in the fighting. The Gar had watched the celebration with the same detached disinterest that their kind seemed to treat everything.

Kyrian had ordered a number of adunel to be slaughtered, spitted and roasted to reward his followers. The giant bovines moved in small herds across the western reaches of the steppe, and were rare enough that their meat and leather were highly prized. No one had succeeded in fully domesticating the lumbering creatures, leaving the giant lizards – the huffrin and the hadan – as the beasts of burden and cavalry mount of choice for most. The giant cats of the Fal'Gar were unique to the ancient people of the steppe, and no human or Mourn had ever been able to ride them. The Mourn, like the Sevains and the Samath, rode hadan.

It was late in the evening when the Count of Haydron arrived. Night had fallen, cloud obscured the stars and Galvia's moons were dark. The camp comprised a number of large round tents; yurts built of wooden frames, covered with huffrin leather and adunel hide. Kyrian's tent was at the centre with the rest in concentric circles around. A wide alleyway ran from a wooden gate through the tents to Kyrian's yurt. The wooden gate was an

16

ornament; there was no rampart, no pitching of stakes or digging of a boundary ditch as there would be in a Nerlinean legionary camp. There was little enough wood on the steppe as it was.

The main thoroughfare was lined with braziers that guttered with flame from animal fat, throwing out a baleful orange light across the camp as well as a reeking stench, as the fat was often very old. Cookfires had been set up in the centre of the road, side by side, over which great chunks of adunel flesh were being roasted. The pleasant aroma of cooking meat offset the rancid stink from the braziers.

Kyrian sat in a curule chair placed in front of his tent. A number of rugs had been spread out on the ground, of bright red and orange patterns, although they looked almost black in the half dark. Marcus, Kyrian's lords and three Gar, one male and two female, sat cross-legged on the rugs, each holding a wooden plate laden with meat from the spits. The leaders of the Haydroners had come on hadanback. Radnor Callico led the way, followed by half a dozen knights. Behind them came another thirty men on foot. The Count of Haydron and his knights dismounted their lizards, tossing the reins to the accompanying infantrymen.

The Slayer assessed the Count of Haydron as he progressed through the gate towards Kyrian's tent. He was of medium height and lean. Long blond hair hung loose around his neck, and his beard had been trimmed to frame his angular face. His eyes, indeed his whole face, looked weary, giving him the appearance of a man in his late forties, ten years older than he actually was. Life on the steppe was hard and being a ruler here was even harder. Kyrian wondered if the last five years of war had resulted in a similar impact on his own features. It had been a long time since he had seen his own reflection in a surface good enough to allow him to tell the difference.

The Haydroners arrived at the edge of the rug, seemingly unconcerned to be in their enemy's camp. Laws of hospitality ran deep in the grasslands among people of the same race.

"My lord Radnor, welcome," Kyrian said politely. "Would you join us for food?"

"I can eat," the Count of Haydron grunted. "Your hospitality is welcome, my lord."

And there it was – the formula of words that meant there would be no killing tonight.

The Slayer signalled to his men to bring Radnor a chair. A curule chair similar to Kyrian's was brought forward and placed at the edge of the rugs. The Count of Haydron took a seat and a plate of meat was brought for him. He drew a knife and hungrily attacked the food. His accompanying knights took places cross-legged on the rugs and they too were brought plates of food and tankards of beer. The two groups watched each other and their lords warily. This was how it worked on the Steppe, at least among the Sevains, where rulers negotiated in front of their lords and knights. The Sevains who had crossed the mountains into the lands of the Kanath had adopted the more despotic rulership methods of those they had conquered.

Kyrian said nothing, but continued to eat. He wanted Radnor to make the first move.

"I saw you wrestle once." Radnor's tone was that of a man making polite small talk.

"Really? Where?" Kyrian's interest was genuinely piqued.

"Hambledon. Perhaps a decade ago. I was visiting the prince; I was not count then. You would have been a teenager."

"A long time ago," mused the Slayer.

"Kyrian of Kilon you were called then, if I recall correctly. Now you are Kyrian Slayer, Count of Chazantria. A Kanath ruling Sevains instead of being ruled by them."

So that was where Radnor was going, thought Kyrian. Appealing to the racial prejudices of his followers. The problem for the Count of Haydron was that, despite his Kanath ancestry and appearance, Kyrian had been brought up a Sevain. While his mother had taught Kyrian and his sister Dryana the old ways of the Kanath faith, they had also attended the church of the Sevain One-god, Caon. Kyrian had grown up speaking Sevain and been educated in the school of the Sevain church. After three hundred years of conquest, most of Kanath ancestry who lived in the four Sevain principalities to the south of the Daldara Mountains considered themselves Sevain. Kyrian had little interest in gods or tribes, and he did not think of himself as anything but Kyrian Slayer, but to his followers he could appear as much a Sevain as they were, as long he kept from voicing some of his more Kanath thoughts.

Kyrian said nothing, continuing to switch between watching the Count of Haydron and looking down to stab at his meat. He did not want to turn this into a confrontation.

Radnor realized he was getting no traction, so he tried another tack.

"I see you, Falthar of the Skyriders. What causes you to throw in your lot with the Slayers?" asked the count, trying to sound jovial.

The Gar looked up; a small smile played across his lips. He raised his hand and made a rubbing gesture with his thumb and forefinger.

"So, money," grunted the count. "You seem to have much of that, Lord Kyrian."

He turned back, his eyes resting on the Count of Chazantria. "One wonders if what you are buying in the steppe is worth the expense?"

He's fishing, thought Kyrian, trying to keep his amusement from reaching his face, though he had expressed the same sentiment to Saliana when she had first formulated this plan five years ago.

"I wish to confirm where the border between the County of Haydron and the County of Chazantria is," said Kyrian, done playing now.

"Borders mean little on the steppe," replied Radnor.

This elicited a chuckle from those seated on the carpet on all sides.

"Then you won't mind if it runs from the Rocks of Chaldor in a straight line south to the coast at the Headland of Mardin," responded Kyrian.

He had chosen physical locations rather than villages or hamlets to delineate the border, as even among the more settled, agricultural people of the western steppe, settlements tended to move decade to decade, even year to year. In the western grasslands the only constant was the port city of Haydon itself.

"That's a third of my county west of the city!" roared Radnor.

"Calm, my dear Radnor; I haven't finished yet," continued Kyrian. "All agricultural trade goods from the lands of Chazantria to be custom-duty-free through the port of Haydron."

"What?" Radnor barked angrily.

The Count of Haydron was raging inside, but he was also using his anger to give him time to think. "So, I give up land or I give up money?" Radnor demanded.

"I don't recall phrasing it as an either/or. I want both." Kyrian's tone was sharp.

"I can cut your access to the ocean trade. I can close Haydron to you," threatened Radnor.

The seated men and the three Gar watched the battle. All had much to lose if this went to a protracted conflict. Both counts were under pressure. Their warriors wanted this settled tonight.

PRINCE OF SLAYERS

"You can hold up in your city if you wish, but it will cost you all of Haydron. We have the forces to besiege and take your port if we need to. I have seen a city fall before; I have no desire to see it again," countered Kyrian.

The Slayer had been in Las Ma when the "city that could never be conquered" had fallen to the Sevain forces of the Prince of Setsonia, the Earl of Allakor and the Temple of Caon. The death and destruction had been seared into his memory, though he had escaped before the real slaughter and misery had begun. Had he seen that, then maybe the ever-reluctant Kyrian would not have threatened a siege. In truth, he lacked the forces to conduct a siege, but he knew the Count of Haydron had to weigh not only the forces before him but also the potential support of the wider Company of Slayers and possibly even the Prince of Kangorn.

"These men have been promised land." Kyrian's hand swept across the knights seated on the carpet in front of him. "I would hate to disappoint them."

"I may be able to concede on the territory, but I cannot compensate my followers for their lost land if I have no money," the Count of Haydron replied. "Besides, I care little if your followers are disappointed."

"You started a war, you lost it. You will give us territory." Kyrian's voice was as cold as ice.

"You began this conflict, Slayer, not me. You think we in the north are stupid. We see your plans and machinations," Radnor spat.

"You can lose something, my lord, or you can lose it all. Time to choose." Kyrian was mocking, his eyes boring into the Count of Haydron.

"You can have the land, but the custom duty stays," Radnor muttered angrily.

"Half duty," Kyrian countered, but his mind seemed elsewhere. He was no longer looking at Radnor, but over his shoulder towards the ceremonial gate.

"Agreed," Radnor replied, not realizing he had lost Kyrian's attention.

Kyrian was watching as three hadan progressed down the camp's centre aisle before fanning out to move three abreast towards the seated lords. Two moved to the right of the cooking spits, the third to the left. Men and women scattered from around the spits into the area around the yurts that lined each side of the thoroughfare. Spears were being grasped; swords grabbed up. The hospitable nature of the camp had suddenly turned more wary.

Kyrian stood up and felt a lurching in his stomach, the closest he ever got to fear. The hadan riders were much too tall to be human and far too heavily proportioned to be Gar, who avoided riding the lumbering beasts anyway. All the steppe warriors on the carpet were on their feet, hands resting on weapons yet undrawn. Even the Fal'Gar looked nervous.

The riders were Mourn. Each of the three cleared seven feet in height, making them look outsized for the hadan they rode. They were twice the width of a normal man. They wore long coats of leather armour that reached to their ankles, studded with steel ringlets. They wore pointed helmets with a face guard of chainmail and leather, leaving only their wide brow ridges and dark eyes showing. Kyrian knew what they looked like under those helms: skin the colour of light brown leather and as tough, lank black or dark brown hair. Pointed ears like a Gar, but small and flattened against the head, disproportionately small for their bulky frame.

The three pulled to a halt before the assembled lords of Haydron and Chazantria. The leader did not dismount, but instead looked down on them from his imperious position and removed his helm, resting it on the pommel of his high ridged saddle. The hadan pawed truculently at the ground, fetching the beast a heavy swat from its master. His face looked like Kyrian had expected, but it was heavily scarred, and the Slayer realized that the Mourn was missing his right eye. The Mourn eyed the men and Gar contemptuously.

"I am Harkon Lan, herald to his imperial majesty Lak Bok, Great Khan of the Mourn, Overlord of the Great and Mourn Steppes and Conqueror of Havagia. You are summoned to bring your banners three months hence to the slopes of the Mountain of the Moon."

The Mourn drew out a small flat piece of white-painted wood on which was carved a series of letters and numbers in black. He tossed this to the Count of Haydron, who caught it.

"You are summoned, Radnor Callico, Count of Haydron," said Harkon Lan.

He pulled out another wooden chit and tossed it in the direction of the leader of the Fal'Gar, who plucked it from the air. He did not look happy.

"You are summoned, Falthar Mrignandor, Chief of the Skyriders," the Mourn intoned.

Harkon pulled a third wooden chit from his leather sack and tossed it towards Kyrian. The Slayer made no move to catch it, letting it fall on the carpet at his feet. If the Mourn recognized this as insubordination, they gave no indication.

"You are summoned, Kyrian Slayer, Count of Chazantria."

The Mourn turned his lizard with a yank of his reins. Its tail swept round, sending a spit containing one of the roasting adunel crashing and embers from the fire skittering across the carpet.

Kyrian watched the three Mourn go before picking up the chit.

"What does this mean?" Kyrian addressed his question to Falthar.

"It means we are going to war." The reply came from Radnor, a look of sadness on his face.

"With whom?"

"With whomever the Great Khan chooses," Falthar replied.

The Haydroners were turning to leave.

"We have a deal?" demanded Kyrian of the Count of Haydron.

The count gave him a look as if such things mattered little.

"Callico, we have a deal," demanded Kyrian rudely.

The count laughed. "For all it matters, Kyrian of Chazantria, we have a deal." Radnor sounded weary.

Radnor turned and stalked through the scattered embers of the fire, leading his men to the gate.

Kyrian watched as they mounted their hadan and disappeared into the night.

"I don't suppose we can ignore this?" Kyrian held up the chit towards the Gar leader.

"If you do, the whole might of the Mourn Horde will fall upon you," Falthar stated.

Kyrian grunted acknowledgement of that.

"Will you stay in our camp tonight?" asked Kyrian of the Gar.

"Thank you, my lord, but no. You and I may be comfortable with our deal, but the enmity between my people and the Sevains goes back a long way. It is best we lodge in separate camps."

"My lord, a rider." Marcus Romanch was pointing to the ceremonial gate.

Kyrian looked up to see a thin figure on a brown striped oradar entering the camp.

"One of yours?" he asked Falthar.

"No," responded the Gar leader sharply, his hand falling to the scimitar at his side.

The cat rider picked its way around the displaced fire and the tumbled carcass to stop before the Count of Chazantria and the Chief of the Skyriders. They were dressed in simple riding clothes: black leather trousers and a shirt of alcidide mail shining over a purple blouse. A wide-brimmed hat of grey felt rested on the rider's head, and a dark purple scarf obscured their face. Slowly, the rider unwrapped the scarf, revealing her chiselled features, skin the pale white of polished bone, and tumbling white-blonde hair. She would have called herself Kanath, but something about her was not quite human: the hint of a point to the ears spoke of possible Gar ancestry.

A broad smile broke across Kyrian's face and warmth filled his heart.

"Who are you, human?" demanded Falthar.

What he saw was impossible: no human could ride an oradar, and it was a struggle for those Gar who were not of Fal'Dath. Yet here she sat, a human on an oradar, the binding of the saddle tied perfectly, her bearing as if she had been born in the saddle.

"Who am I?" The woman's bardic training allowed her to project her voice out across the camp. "I know you; you are Falthar Mrignandor, Dumech'Di'Fal'Gar," she announced.

The Gar licked his lips. That title was only used among the Fal'Gar and even then, not in such a public fashion. It was important that the people of the steppe believed that the Fal'Gar were split into tribes and did not look to a single war leader. It was what had saved them from total destruction during the Mourn conquest ten years past. Who was this woman to know such things?

She whipped off her wide-brimmed hat.

"I am Saliana Slayer."

25

CHAPTER TWO – PRINCE MORIANUS

The little boy stuck out his chin and gave his opponent a pugnacious glare. He waved his wooden short sword in front of him and tried unsuccessfully to mimic a fighter's crouch. At four years old, Prince Morianus of Kangorn already believed himself to be a warrior. He favoured his mother, the Princess Ascrina, in terms of looks: pink-skinned, with a mop of light brown hair.

The boy lunged out with his wooden weapon, trying to close the impossible gap to his opponent. Balinor Slayer sidestepped his infant son's thrust, batting away the sword with his own wooden blade, trying to do it lightly enough so as not to unbalance the child. Balinor Slayer – or, as he was now called, Balinor Strabo-Slayer – was the ruling Prince of Kangorn, the island city founded by pirates over two hundred years ago. In the centuries since, it had become the focal place for merchants, mercenaries and competing nobles in the northern Nerlinean Ocean. The Prince of Kangorn himself was the epitome of average: a regular build topped by a short-cut bowl of brown hair. He was pale-skinned; the deep tan from his younger years in Las Ma to the south had faded as he spent more time in colder climes and, in recent years, less time outside or at sea. He could not speak to his heritage except to say he was from the west. He had been born a slave among the Kanath of Las Ma, but his ancestry could have been Kanath, Sevain, Delenor, or a mixture of some or all of them.

Balinor's rise to rule the Rock had been a combination of his own scheming and that of many others, most notably his wife and co-ruler, Ascrina of House Strabo, the Princess of Kangorn. When the pair had taken the throne five years ago, she had been the last of the House of Strabo. Now there were four of them: Ascrina, her two children with Balinor, Morianus and Alisha, and of course the prince himself. He had taken the name of the royal house of Strabo, continuing its two-hundred-year control of the island city. To many, especially his enemies, he was Balinor Slayer of the Company of Slayers. His divided loyalties were still a subject of debate from the finest temple to the basest tavern.

The child prince made another sweep of his blade at his father, the wild swing missing by a wide margin. Balinor assessed his son. The boy was getting tired; sweat ran down his forehead, the wooden sword he carried looked comical to the man, and for the child it must have felt like carrying a broadsword.

"Balinor," came a woman's voice.

The Prince of Kangorn immediately knew who it was: only one woman would dare call him by his given name. Mentally he amended that. There were two, but he would have known if the other was in the city. Even someone as close to him as Dryana would address him formally in public, if not always in private. The Mistress of the Slayers by comparison felt no such obligation.

"Put up your sword, boy," he told his son. "Your mother wants me."

The princeling stuck out his chin and pouted, but dropped his wooden weapon on the floor. He was not foolish enough to gainsay his father.

Balinor turn and gave his wife an appraising look. She was beautiful. He had married her when she had been a pretty teenager, and he had been in his late twenties. At least that had been his best guess to his age, as the Kanath had never been overly concerned in remembering the exact age of their human livestock. Now the Princess of Kangorn was in her early twenties and had become even better looking as she matured into womanhood. She wore a long purple dress tied tightly with a gold belt. Her long black hair had been lifted into a complicated series of braids, which was the current fashion. On her right hip, she clasped a baby girl, their young daughter, the Princess Alisha. The child was howling mightily. The pair were flanked by a number of women of varying ages.

"Hello, my love." Balinor gave his wife a slightly mocking bow.

"Why are you wasting your time in the garden when there is work to do?" Ascrina demanded.

The child was continuing to howl and wriggle, which made the already irritated princess even more enraged. She detached the child and dumped her into the arms of a woman to her right. "Go to Madri," Ascrina instructed her daughter.

A young woman, of similar age to her mistress but blonde-haired and blue-eyed, willingly accepted the child. Gwen was the child's *madri*, a combination of wet nurse and nanny. The child started to nuzzle at the wet nurse's breast, and before she could start screaming in frustration again, Gwen took position on a nearby stone bench and started to feed her.

PRINCE OF SLAYERS

Balinor found it frustrating that Ascrina insisted on referring to Gwen by her position. 'Madri' could mean any of three people: either of the children's nannies, or the older woman who had performed the same function for Ascrina. It was a habit that the Strabo family had brought west with them from the Nerlinean Empire. Balinor thought of the nurses to the two children by their names, Gwen and Andar. He thought of Ascrina's own former nanny as Madri; if she had another name, he had never heard it.

"Surely Droma could be doing this?" demanded the princess, waving her hand at the scene before her.

Ascrina was referring to Captain Sliva Droma of the Prince's Guard, the head of Kangorn's limited military forces.

"I can spend time teaching the boy," Balinor replied testily.

The prince found his wife's disinterest in her own child odd and sometimes heartbreaking. Having been brought up with no memory of his own parents, he was particularly focused on spending time with his children. This confused his wife, who took the lessons from her own upbringing; she had been raised almost exclusively by servants even before her parents' premature deaths.

"Morianus will be prince one day; he needs to learn to fight," Balinor observed.

Ascrina favoured her husband with a look that could be described as mildly contemptuous. "The new Samath ambassador is here, waiting in the great hall to present himself to us," she announced.

"I didn't see him arrive," replied Balinor, looking up at the gatehouse to the palace complex that rested at the top of the terraces as if even now the new ambassador was arriving instead of waiting in the great hall.

"Well, you were busy trying not to lose a sword fight with a four-year-old."

Ascrina's waspish comment was not intended as a joke, but Balinor laughed anyway. The others surrounding them joined in, leaving the princess looking annoyed.

"Get me a robe and my crown," ordered Balinor, striding towards the palace.

The prince's palace was an ugly grey squat stone building. It rested on a low hill, the only real natural vantage point on the otherwise flat island. It loomed over the walled garden in which father and son had been practising. Balinor strode up stone steps that had been cut into the terraces that covered this side of the hill. He moved through the dark, forbidding, tunnel-like corridors of the palace, his wife and her followers struggling to keep up.

"Where is that bloody robe?" he snapped.

A servant carrying a long scarlet coat with an embroidered gold edging rushed up panting. He held it out, trying to dress his lord. An annoyed Balinor snatched it off him and put it on himself. The servant then held out a small gold circlet. Balinor took that from him too and placed it on his head, but it was too large and slipped down until it rested behind his ears. The circlet had previously been worn by his predecessor, the late Prince Karden the third, Ascrina's grandfather. He wore it rarely for official occasions and it had never occurred to the new ruler to have it resized.

Balinor stalked through a small door in the side of the great hall that led down a small flight of steps to the rushes that covered the flagstone floor. A wooden platform was at the far end of the hall, below narrow windows that stabbed light in long fingers across the centre of the room. On the raised dais were two curule chairs.

Balinor noted the three figures who stood in the centre of his hall. He passed around them, giving them plenty of space, before mounting the steps to the platform and seating himself in one of the curule chairs. Ascrina swept into the chamber behind him using the main entrance, rather than the smaller side door, before progressing up the hall and taking her seat next to her husband on the platform.

The three Samath stood in the centre of the hall, one, clearly the leader, slightly forward of the other two. They were over seven feet in height and heavily built. Their scaly skin was dark green flecked with brown, and long snouts protruded from their ugly faces, long rows of white teeth adding to their forbidding visages. A pair of small horns tapered back from their heads behind their ears. The lead figure wore a dark purple robe over his intimidating frame. His two compatriots were dressed in long leather coats over which hung a round metal plate protecting the chest and stomach. Chainmail epaulets completed the protection. Conical helms that tapered to a spike were clasped in their hands in front of them. They carried no weapons: their scabbards were empty, their swords reluctantly surrendered to the Prince's Guard at the gatehouse.

Balinor might be a Kangorner now, he might rule the Rock as a Prince of the House Strabo, but to the Samath he was still a partner in the Company of Slayers. The Samath's hatred for the Slayers dated back six years to the Battle of Syndion, when the Slayers, with Balinor's full participation, had defeated a combined Samath force of soldiers, sailors and marines. The Samath military had sought to take control of the archipelago of Syndion in the south of the Nerlinean Ocean. The losses to the lizardmen had been substantial, running into the thousands – almost the entire force that had been sent for the invasion. It was more the embarrassment than the actual losses that seemed to grate with the Samath. A sizeable expeditionary force had been defeated by a group of mere merchants. Balinor knew how it had happened. His fellow Slayer, the necromancer Dryana, had raised a Gar legion of dead to defeat the attackers. Many viewed this as an absurd story propagated by the Samath to explain their ignominious defeat, but those who knew Dryana knew the truth.

The incident had left the lizardmen with a deep hatred of the Slayers. This was particularly strong among the clans that served in their fleet and the marines, who had taken the loss very personally. The Samath army, which had lost more troops than the navy, seemed to view their losses more phlegmatically.

The Samath ambassador's gaze swept the room. The hall was small and rather poky for a prince's throne room. A few servants milled around, showing no particular interest in the lizardmen envoys. Aside from a pair of guards at the main doorway into the hall there was no sign of military presence. The Samath's eyes settled on the Prince and Princess of Kangorn seated on the platform in front of them. There were no advisers or councillors in attendance. The ambassador saluted, briefly considering leaping onto the platform and snapping the Slayer's neck, confident in his physical superiority. All he could see before him was one of the hated owners of the Company of Slayers, even if he called himself Prince of Kangorn.

The prince watched the ambassador with the predatory eyes of a venomous serpent.

Try it! he thought.

A hidden band of archers ringed the hall, bows nocked and half drawn ready to loose should the Samath try anything stupid. At the end of the concealed gallery, a pair of mages watched the three envoys intently. None of the Samath appeared to be a magic user, but the Kangorn mages were wary. Balinor was the first prince in several generations to actually prefer the palace for conducting the business of ruling as well as to live in. His last three predecessors had chosen to live in the manor house in the palace gardens, rarely if ever coming into the palace. They had preferred to conduct meetings in the manor's more comfortable hall or out in the palace gardens.

That had been in a more comfortable world, though. The palace had been built by Kangorn, the first prince of the city that bore his name, when the new island principality had needed to defend itself against a myriad of enemies. The palace had been constructed to provide a citadel that could act as a last bastion against attackers. It had also been designed as a place where enemies could be quietly disappeared. As Balinor had spent recent years exploring the palace, he had found complicated defensive structures, galleries and tunnels that had been covered over and closed off. He had set about opening them up. The concealed gallery had been closed off until a few months ago, but had now been cleared of the ancient, half-rotten furniture stored in it and put back to its original purpose.

The Samath ambassador restrained his impulses and gave the barest nod as a substitute for a bow.

"Your highnesses, may I present myself. I am Kolith Shardath, representative of the Samath Empire," the lead Samath hissed in harshly accented Westerly.

"Welcome, my lord," replied Ascrina politely. "We acknowledge your presence in Kangorn, and your position as the representative of your people."

Balinor was watching the ambassador carefully. He noted the clan name: Shardath, one of the warrior clans. The ambassador probably had an army background, rather than a naval one, which should make what was usually a testy relationship somewhat easier. Not that the relationship between the Samath and the Princes of Kangorn was ever easy, and that was before a Slayer had become Prince.

"You are welcome here, my lord," Balinor greeted the new ambassador.

The Samath gave the rulers seated on the platform another nod and turned to leave, not extending the prince and princess the normal courtesy of withdrawing facing them.

"A moment." Balinor's tone was a command.

The Samath turned back, fixing a hard gaze on the prince.

"What is the situation regarding the Anaror Strait?" Balinor enquired.

"The Anaror Strait?" The Samath's response sounded like a question, but it was hard to tell with his rasping voice.

"The Samath Navy is stopping ships in the Anaror Strait – merchant vessels and others. Why?" asked Balinor.

Kolith turned back, his eyes resting on the prince. Balinor would have said the Samath was annoyed or even angry at being questioned, but he found the lizardmen hard to read.

"The Anaror Strait lies off the coast of our newly conquered territories in what was once Las Ma. It is the main ocean-way for our merchant ships passing from the Tancree Islands to the Northern Islands. Why should we not monitor shipping in our oceans?"

Balinor was aware of the geography. And that meant he knew that Kolith was lying. The Isle of Anaror lay off the south coast of what had once been the Duchy of Las Ma. Five years ago, that territory had been conquered and split between the Samath Empire on the one hand and the Prince of Setsonia on the other. The strait was the ocean-way that lay between the mainland and Anaror and had been used as the main sea passage west since anyone could remember. It allowed ships from Kangorn and the Sevain principalities in the north and merchants from Nerlinea in the east to transit in relative safety to the Kingdom of Delenor and the Sevain Earldom of Allakor in the far west.

To go west of the Isle of Anaror required ships to go far south to avoid the storms that whipped around the small islets that strung out from the main island in an ugly tail. This area of open ocean to the west of the island was feared for its legendary sea monsters. There were reports of giant lizard creatures that appeared from beneath the waves to break merchant ships in half with their enormous jaws, and squid so vast that they could drag a vessel down to the deep with their mass of tentacles. This area of ocean had received the forbidding name of the Kraken's Wake. Balinor, ever a cynic, doubted these stories; one would expect to see similar creatures further to the east in the wide expanse of the Nerlinean Ocean. It did not matter in practice if it was storms or monsters: the ships that tried to sail west around Anaror did not return. Even the Nerlinean Imperial Fleet, which would normally sail anywhere, refused to enter those waters. Only one people seemed comfortable on the seas to the west: the Samath.

The two archipelagos the Samath ambassador had mentioned both lay to the west of Anaror: one to the south and one to the north. They had been conquered when the lizardmen had destroyed the Tancree, of which Balinor's colleague Slinker Slayer was one of the last. Slinker's people had lived primarily in the eponymous isles in the south, which had fallen to the Samath over a hundred years ago. Slinker and the other survivors of his people had fled to their remaining territory, a harsh rocky windswept collection of isles in the north. Here they had thought themselves protected behind the tumultuous western ocean with its storms and monsters. They had been wrong, however, as somehow the Samath had found a way to attack directly across the Kraken's Wake without using the Anaror Strait. Persistent naval battles and raids had worn down the Tancree, until a Samath armada had landed enough troops to conquer the Northern Islands and eradicate the Tancree. It had left Slinker as one of the few survivors, perhaps even the last of his people.

There was no need for the Samath to use the Anaror Strait to reach their territory. If anything, it made the journey longer for them. But now they controlled the Las Ma side of the strait, they had a vested interest in what happened in it, as Balinor was well aware. What worried him was their plans for the Isle of Anaror.

Anaror was surrounded by the Samath – as much as any island in the open ocean could be considered encircled by anyone. Samath islands lay to the northwest and southwest, their mainland conquests to the east.

"You have stopped ships of our Merchants' Guild. They have been turned back from Anaror. Why?" demanded the prince.

"It is important for us to ensure that foreign powers do not threaten us. We are in dispute with the Sevains in our new lands. The Order of Dawn uses Anaror as a base to foment dissent among our recently acquired subjects," the ambassador explained.

"The Merchants' Guild of Kangorn, the Company of Slayers, are traders, not foreign powers," Balinor retaliated. If he had known of another merchant that had been stopped, he would have highlighted them too.

"You control the Merchants' Guild of Kangorn, your highness. Are you not a prince?" Kolith responded with a leering smile that looked more to intimidate than reassure.

"A distinction has always been made between the state and commerce," Balinor replied testily.

"Among you humans, maybe, but not among us," observed the ambassador. "The Samath are clear: we will not allow the wizards of Anaror to threaten our newly acquired territories. Trade will have to wait, even for those of Kangorn."

"Such talk could lead to conflict?" Ascrina interjected, more a question than a statement.

"There is already conflict. War seems to be springing up everywhere," the ambassador replied with a shrug. "You Slayers are carving your own principality out of the steppe, yet we do not complain. You leave us alone, we leave you alone."

"I am not a Slayer," Ascrina replied, a hint of annoyance in her voice.

"He is," the ambassador retorted, nodding at Balinor.

PRINCE OF SLAYERS

Ascrina's face flickered towards her husband, momentarily creased in anger at him.

The ambassador had touched a nerve. He smiled inwardly, though his face remained impassive. He noted the princess's reaction in case it was useful later.

Balinor was also silently cursing his wife at her slip. *Never let your enemy know what you are thinking* – her grandfather had taught her that, just as Sali had taught it to Balinor. Not that it was a lesson that the prince really needed to learn. An upbringing in slavery had taught him to bury his thoughts deep where no one could find them. If that had not been the case, his relationship with his wife might be less fraught.

"I am Balinor Strabo and I am responsible for Kangorn. I do not control what the Company of Slayers do in Chazantria any more than I dictate the day-to-day trading operations of the Merchants' Guild."

Kolith noted the choice of language; Balinor had been careful not to tell a lie that could be held against him later. What he said was true. But what he did not reveal was how much influence Balinor had over the Company of Slayers or the Merchants' Guild. It was a subject of much speculation for those outside both, but particularly the Company of Slayers. Was the Prince of Kangorn a puppet of the Slayers, as some believed? Or was it more complex than that? The Samath did not know, and though he was keen to work it out, now was not the time. He had gained enough today.

"I am here simply to present myself to your highnesses. If there is nothing else, I would take my leave, with all due respect?" said Kolith.

Balinor watched the ambassador warily, suppressing his annoyance at how the audience had developed. A burning anger was simmering below his impassive face.

"It has been a delight to meet you, ambassador." Ascrina's tone was honeyed. Had the Samath been human he would have been charmed to the point of infatuation. The princess practically pouted at him.

Balinor was reminded how young his wife was and how wily she could be. She had been at this business a lot longer than him. She had been brought up learning these skills. She might not be able to fix her error, but she could at least rectify some of the damage.

"Thank you so much for providing us with your credentials and also your insights on the current trade situation," she continued with a warm smile. "Of course, you are excused from our presence. We look forward to our next meeting."

The ambassador gave a bow that was little more than a bob of his scaly head, but was still deeper and more respectful than the one he had opened with. He backed off a few paces before turning and leaving the hall followed by his guards.

The co-rulers of Kangorn let out a combined sigh of relief. Balinor could feel the archers hidden around the hall relax – or imagined it at least.

"Still a Slayer!" Ascrina observed icily at her husband.

The prince rolled his eyes. It was going to be one of those days.

CHAPTER THREE – PORT REN

The hot red sun glared down across the shimmering pale blue of the ocean. Gulls croaked and carped as they swung low across the water. The ship carved through the waves, taking advantage of the breeze and the turn of the tide. Slinker Slayer stood at the rail, looking out across the blue, feeling the burn of the sun across his face. Tall and lanky, with a mop of long grey hair framing his emaciated yellow skin, the Tancree was one of the last, maybe even the very last of his kind. At well past a hundred years of age, he reflected it would only be a matter of time before his people would be consigned to history, but his aged bones could enjoy the sun for now. It reminded him of his youth, when he had sailed these waters on a ship just like this, commanded by his mother.

"My lord!" The voice came from behind him.

Slinker turned from the rail and his moment of nostalgia to the young man behind him. Farmorl was an employee of the Company of Slayers, on the cusp of becoming a full-fledged agent. He was young, nineteen, thin and lithe, a Nerlinean from the western provinces with soft brown skin, black hair and deep brown eyes. Although clearly human, Farmorl still reminded the Tancree of himself. The thin, rangy figure was one reason, the sharp angular jawline was another. Most of all it was the armour. Leather with patches of chainmail, designed in the Tancree style. Slinker himself wore the same style of armour. His had been made by the finest manufacturers of his people, now long dead. Where the young man had got his the Tancree had no idea. He always meant to ask, but other matters would take priority and he would forget to do so. Farmorl's armour was clearly new, and lacked the precise finish of Slinker's, but still it was fair approximation. It must have cost him a fortune. On the human it looked archaic despite being new. Maybe it looked archaic on him too, the Tancree mused to himself.

Their weapons were different, though. Slinker carried a pair of Tancree fighting blades strapped to his back. When in use they were worn on the arms, a blade looping up from below the elbow and finishing in a sharp point past the fist. They were attached by a series of links to leather strapping worn on the arm and finished in a mail glove. The use of them was an ancient art unique to Slinker's people. As with many of their ways, it would die with him. He also carried razor-sharp throwing discs, a dagger and, on his hip, a loaded pistol crossbow. Farmorl was comparatively lightly armed, with a sabre on his left side and a long dagger on his right.

"What is it, Farmorl?" Slinker demanded, a little more harshly than he felt or intended.

A look of reprimand flashed across the young man's face before being replaced with his previous business-like visage. Slinker regretted his harsh tone. Of all the Slayer employees, this boy seemed to be one of the few who genuinely liked him; even looked up to him.

"We are in sight of the harbour. Do you wish to use the crown to manoeuvre us in or shall I fully deploy the crew?" asked Farmorl.

Slinker's hand absentmindedly strayed to his belt, where, wrapped in leather, a gold circlet was strapped to his side. It was a crown, a magical device through which a mage could control the movements of ship across the ocean.

Slinker looked over Farmorl's shoulder at the five other ships of the Slayer fleet strung out behind them. Though the rear castle of the ship largely concealed two of the following vessels with its mass.

"No. The Nerlineans may know we have it, but there is no need to rub their faces in it. Bring all six ships in under regular means."

"Yes, my lord. Who is meeting us? Will it be the Lady Dryana?" asked the young man.

Amusement played across Slinker's face. "I would hope so. What is it to you, boy?" he demanded, failing to hide his smirk.

"No reason, my lord," the young man tried to row back.

"She's a bit old for you, boy," observed the Tancree, enjoying his employee's sudden discomfort.

"I meant no offence. I was just wondering who would meet us," Farmorl's words tumbled out.

Slinker let out a rare deep laugh that sounded more like a whooping bark. Then his face turned serious. "Stay clear of her, boy, at least in that regard. She will use you and throw you aside, as she has done with many others. Then you will find yourself not welcome in the Company of Slayers. Worry about your career; there are plenty of beautiful women in Port Ren to have fun with," advised the Tancree.

Farmorl nodded politely, but Slinker doubted the boy would listen. Dryana had that effect on men, something that had only become stronger as she had matured into her twenties. It was a shame; he liked the boy. The Slayer went back to staring out over the ocean, where a dark line on the horizon was now taking form.

The south coast of the Nerlinean mainland spread out before him. The province of Ren was the richest and most populous region of the Nerlinean Empire. Its eponymous capital, Port Ren, was the largest city on the world of Galvia. It dwarfed the island metropolis of Kangorn. In the east, only the empire's capital of Nerlon came close in size, and that covered an area half as great. Port Ren was also older, pre-dating the Nerlinean conquest, though that had been more than eighteen hundred years ago.

The city sat at the apex of a triangle of sea routes. To the east, the island kingdoms of Amaland and others were bustling with commerce. To the south lay the province of Narazgon, a vast place of extremes, from seething hot jungles to icy tundra. To the west, through the straits of Nerlinea, lay the cities of the western coast and beyond that the teeming trade of the Nerlinean Ocean. It was along this western approach that Slayer vessels were arriving at the port city.

The cliffs of the southern coast of Nerlinea rose up before them. Buildings sprouted from the headland, palaces of blazing white stone that shone and sparkled in the harsh sunlight. They varied in style: some were low, boxy, flat-roofed structures, the traditional Nerlinean design, while others spiralled upwards, with interlocking towers and arching bridges in the Gar style. The Gar of Quil'Dath, the greatest of all their race's builders, paid reluctant homage to the emperor, and their twisting, turning structures could be found throughout Nerlinea – at least in the places where the richest could afford to build them. The cliffs dropped down to a large natural bay several miles across, which formed the harbour of the city. Here, ringing the bay, the buildings became smaller; simple dwellings of white-painted mudbrick. The warehouses of the great trading companies sat back from the coast raised up slightly on the low hills that rose up to meet the cliffs on either side of the bay.

Slinker had wondered about the layout of the city the first time he had arrived as a merchant several years back. He had been to Port Ren before that, but many decades ago, on a Tancree vessel, and as a warrior and a war mage, when such things had not mattered to him. It had been explained to him that the city was prone to flooding due to the infrequent but violent storms that would on occasion ravage the bay. With no protective stone bulwark, it was not unusual for the low-lying part of the city to be flooded at such times; therefore, the merchants had long ago relocated their warehouses and grander residences to higher ground. Port Ren spread out from the bay along the wide low valley framed by the gently rising hills to each side. Once there had been rivers running across this plain, but they had long ago been diverted through tunnels and culverts. This had allowed more space for building and, by happy accident, had reduced if not eradicated the insect-borne diseases that often ravaged the festering city during the summer. It still contributed to the port's feeling of sogginess, as water seeped into the silty ground.

Aside from a pair of watchtowers sitting on the cliff edges either side of the bay, there was no indication that the greatest city in the world had made any thought to its defence. There were no walls surrounding the city; no guard towers or bastions. The harbour had no wall to protect it from either attacker or weather. No chain was slung across its harbour entrance because it did not really have one. To a casual observer, the city was undefended, but such an observation would be a terrible mistake. For Port Ren was defended by a wall of wood and steel: the might of the Nerlinean Imperial

Fleet. Slinker could see its huge junks, a dozen at anchor, and three more sailing out of the bay as three more returned. A patrol changing over, he speculated. The fleet dominated the oceans of the east in a way that would be hard for those in the more tumultuous west to understand. The Nerlinean Imperial Fleet did operate in the west, patrolling the eponymous ocean, but with smaller junks both in terms of size and numbers. Junks the size of those at anchor would almost never be seen in the west. Indeed, the only time in living memory such vessels had come into the Nerlinean Ocean had been five years ago during the succession crisis in Kangorn. With no boundary except the water to its south, the city had spread out unconstrained, so it covered the valley and its surrounding hills to the horizon, a seething, boiling mass of Mankind, Gar, Samath and even Mourn.

The Lament of Las Ma, as the ship that Slinker was standing on was called, was closing now with the harbour. The Tancree could pick out other vessels beyond those of the high-masted war junks. The ships of the merchants spread out across from the left of the bay to its centre, where the stone quay gave way to a sandy beach on which were drawn up the fishing boats of Port Ren. The painted blue eye of the Goddess Daldara looked out from the side of each prow. Why the fisherfolk prayed to the Goddess of Magic rather than a weather goddess like Thytha or Sidarra was something known only to the boatmen. The war junks of the Imperial Fleet completed the semicircle stretching from the centre of the bay to its eastern edge.

Slinker picked out the flags of the trading houses; the House Caldric, the Company de Troville and others he only half knew or did not know at all. His lips curled in distaste as he saw the 'P' flag symbol that indicated the presence of the Imperial Pandus Trading Company, the largest and richest of the empire's trading companies. Its red and gold banners hung limply on their flagpoles, but still the Slayer found them threatening.

The Slayer ship was heading for its own quay. The wind whipped up, revealing the banner of the Company of Slayers, a gold broadsword pointing down on a black field. The Company of Slayers had purchased its own dock three years back as its business in the empire had grown. The seller had been the creditors of the now-defunct Sorrow's Point Company, a business over a century old that had found itself over-extended and badly managed. The Slayers had picked up the whole company, including its name, its two remaining ships and its port assets in Port Ren and Sorrow's Point. Once the company had stretched across Nerlinea, with dozens of ships plying their trade across the island kingdoms and the eastern coast of the Nerlinean Empire. It had once owned trading facilities as far west as Halfnight and Rastindor. For Slinker it was a salutary reminder of how quickly commercial success could disappear.

The Slayer dock was built of a combination of wood and stone. Pillars of rocks, held fast by cement, had been sunk into the sandy bay. On this was built a wide pier-like structure, made of wood thrusting out into the sea. It reflected the nature of the storms that would impact Port Ren. They were rare, but when they happened, they were so powerful they could tear apart a stone bulwark almost as easily as they would a wooden jetty. The rock pillars proved largely, but not totally impervious, leaving the city's inhabitants to rebuild the wooden superstructure after each major storm.

The Lament pulled alongside the jetty, coming in as close as possible to the coast. There were more ships behind it to moor up, after all. Slinker scanned the dock, seeing porters and dock workers wearing thin tunics that reached to their knees or others stripped to the waist in what to Slinker looked like short skirts. All were employees of the Slayers' company. Unlike the rest of the trading companies in Nerlinea and society as a whole, the Slayers refused to own or trade slaves, a legacy of the five Slayer partners' own experience of servitude.

The Tancree was not interested in his employees, but was looking for another figure. He spotted her as she was walking down the wooden pier towards the ship. She moved oddly, almost as if skipping. Dryana Slayer still looked young, almost girlish, despite being comfortably into her twenties. He knew she played up to it. It made people who did not know her well underestimate her, dismissing her for a lack of maturity. For those who knew her well, it was more terrifying, for Dryana was not just a merchant but a witch and a necromancer. Her apparent disengagement from the world made her terrifyingly unpredictable.

It had been a year since the Tancree had seen his fellow Slayer, and she had matured; the last vestiges of teenage years had faded away and a beautiful woman had replaced the girl. Dryana had come east four years ago to take over from the Slayer agents who had previously been running the business. Her brother Kyrian had started the operations more than five years ago, obtaining the initial permissions to trade from the imperial bureaucrats who controlled and interfered in the trade that criss-crossed the empire. Kyrian had not liked the place: too hot, too culturally different, too much intrigue for the plain-speaking Slayer.

The Council of Slayers, which comprised the five Slayer partners, had tried to control the burgeoning operation through agents, senior employees of the company who could be trusted to run the operations with limited oversight. That had worked up to a point. But as the operation grew and demanded investment it had become clear that one of the five Slayers needed to be present. The council had been loath to send Dryana – and for Slinker, the council meant Saliana, for it was she who really had come to have the final say on such decisions. Dryana had been controlling the operations in Kangorn back then, the

Slayers' most important trade operation. Sali had been reluctant to send Dryana east, but there was no other choice.

Saliana herself was too busy with the growth and reconstruction of the ancient Gar port city, Backistri, on the Isle of Syndion. Kyrian had already asked to return west. Balinor…well, Balinor was Prince of Kangorn now. Besides, the other Slayers did not really trust him – Saliana least of all. The five years since his ascension to the throne of Kangorn had done little to narrow the distance between the other Slayers and the brown-haired warrior. That had left Dryana the only option. Slinker had never been in contention. He had many skills, and many uses to the Company of Slayers, but they did not involve running a trading operation. He knew it and so did his partners.

So Dryana Slayer, the pale-skinned necromancer, just leaving her teens behind, had come east to command the operation. She had found something of a home in Nerlinea, a place where her belief in the old gods was not only tolerated but celebrated, though the Nerlineans called them by different names to the Kanath. She also found appeal in the different morals of the easterners, the very thing that had repelled her brother.

Slinker shimmied down a rope ladder and dropped to the dock with a creak of wood. He looked up to see the approaching woman. A little older, jawline a little sharper, stomach muscles a little more defined, but she still looked the same as she always had to him. Thin and fey-like, with soft white skin that had barely tanned in the burning sun. Long luxurious black hair that flowed down loose all the way to her waist. She wore her black silks, which combined a long skirt split either side almost to the waist. A second piece of black silk was wrapped around her breasts and tied tightly behind. On casual observation they were the same clothes that the witch always wore. He remembered with private amusement that Saliana had once managed to persuade the youngest Slayer to wear a dress. He noted a slight change, though: she no longer wore the silk around her shoulders, binding it under her arms instead, which told him that she did actually own more than one set of clothes. He could see the pale blue pagan tattoos that played across her upper arms and shoulders. At least here in Nerlinea her dress sense made both practical and cultural sense – something it had not in cold, windswept Kangorn.

"Uncle Slinker," Dryana declared, opening her arms to give the emaciated Tancree a hug.

He returned it, gingerly clanking metal against her soft body. If she noticed, she did not complain. He also noted the familiar honorific. Dryana had picked up some eastern customs.

"You are well?" he asked.

She gave him a broad smile and a nod. "Who is this?" she asked, stepping past the Tancree. She stopped in front of Farmorl, who had followed his commander, and eyed him up and down. The young man looked uncomfortable, and Slinker rolled his eyes.

"And you are?" she asked, sticking out her lip in a pout.

Farmorl licked his lips. Suddenly his mouth was dry.

"Far…Farmorl, my lady." The words stumbled out of his mouth.

"Are you sure?" she asked mockingly, eyebrow raised.

Farmorl looked at his lord, confusion on his face.

"Leave him alone, Dryana. Besides, you've met him before," interjected Slinker, coming to his protégé's rescue.

"Really? When?" she asked, turning back to Slinker.

"He was with me last year," the Tancree reminded her.

"Really?" Dryana looked to be accessing her visual memory.

She looked back. "That's the scrawny kid?" she demanded. "Wow, he grew up."

"If you were a man, Dryana, women would warn each other about you," Slinker observed coldly.

"Yes, well, I'm not a man, am I," she shot back, a dark look crossing her face. Then her face softened. "Did you warn him about me?"

Slinker gave a grin followed by a non-committal shrug.

"That's not very kind, Uncle," she proffered.

"Please stop calling me Uncle, Dryana, it is making me feel old," complained Slinker.

"What are you? A hundred years old, a hundred and fifty years old?" Dryana asked.

"Something like that," grinned the Tancree. "No need to make me feel my years, is there?"

Dryana laughed at that. "So, you all made it?" she said, changing the subject. The question was rhetorical – she could see all the ships she had expected mooring up. "No problems with pirates, Samath, others?"

"None," replied Slinker. "It would be a brave pirate that attacked a Slayer vessel. The Samath are too busy with Anaror to interfere with merchants going east."

Dryana nodded her understanding. "You didn't bring *The Spirit*?"

A hint of disappointment, maybe even sadness, entered her voice.

The Spirit of Summer was the Slayer flagship. It was their first and still their largest vessel, though several they now had under construction would be larger. It held a special place in all the five Slayers' hearts. It was more a home to them than the castle on Syndion or their fine residences on Kangorn. Dryana seemed to share the same love for the ship, which Slinker found slightly odd given the trauma she had experienced on the vessel at the hands of the Pandus.

"Dryana, we are hauling solinad shit. I am not sure Sali would have been terribly impressed had I used *The Spirit*," he laughed.

The witch returned his laughter with a broad grin.

"Solinad gold, more like, with the money we will make on this." She spread her hands to indicate the ships before her.

Slinker gave a nod of understanding. He had not told a lie. The six ships in his trading fleet had holds filled with the manure of the solinad. It had been dried and pelleted in Haydron, brought to Kangorn by third-party companies before being loaded onto Slayer ships to bring east. The solinad was a giant herbivore native to the steppe. Three times the height of a tall man at the shoulder and almost as wide, the creatures looked like giant hairy rectangular boxes. Their thick matted fur grew down almost to the ankles of their four legs. They had flat bovine heads with short stubby necks, and both males and females had large curling horns each side of their narrow eyes.

Solinads moved in two vast herds out of the icy wastes of the northern steppe. During the autumn months one progressed east to winter on the Plains of Havagia, while the second would move west, culminating its migration below the Daldara Mountains on the Plains of Chazantria. All the way they would graze on the hard steppe grass before spending the winter months in the relative comfort of the southern steppe. The manure that they defecated would cover the plains, creating inconceivably fertile soils. As winter gave way to spring, they would move back to the north, leaving behind more than enough manure to grow arable crops. It was these crops that had made Haydron wealthy and fed Kangorn. It was this food supply that had spurred Kyrian's ambitions in Chazantria. In the east it had made Havagia the breadbasket of northern Nerlinea.

The loss of Havagia to the Mourn a decade ago had spiked food prices across the empire, something that had only partially reversed in the ensuing ten years. The emperor found his people had less food than they were used to and were paying higher prices. He knew how restive that would make them – and if he failed to notice, he had an army of bureaucrats and advisers to tell him. Dried solinad dung had long been brought south from Havagia to fertilize the southern fields, so it was not a new idea. Dryana's idea had been to bring it across the sea from the western steppe. Every month, a convoy of six to ten vessels would arrive in Port Ren from the beginning of summer to the late autumn, bringing the manure that would fertilize the fields and stave off famine for millions of Nerlineans. It still amazed Slinker that so few ships could make such a difference.

The convoys were now the Slayers' most important operation. Dryana had made them all even richer. It was also the real reason for Kyrian's military activities in Chazantria: it was not just about securing Kangorn's food supply, but cornering the market for solinad dung. The Slayers had to walk a fine line, for Haydron was the gateway to and from the steppe, the place where such huge amounts of dung could be processed and shipped out. If they could, the Slayers would take the city itself, but such a bold move might attract the ire of the Great Khan, and even the Slayers could not stand against the Mourn.

"Did you bring the other stuff?" Dryana's voice dropped to a whisper.

Slinker glanced around him and nodded. "It's hidden in the dung, deep down," he replied quietly.

Dryana gave a tight smile. She was looking down the dock. A tall dark-skinned man in a long frock coat and a high round hat was striding down the jetty towards the two Slayers. He was flanked by half a dozen slaves of varied complexions wearing thin yellow tunics. Slinker's nose wrinkled slightly at the presence of slaves. Dryana seemed indifferent.

"My Lady Slayer." The man doffed his high hat, giving the Slayer a sweeping bow.

"Custom Officer Shan, always a pleasure." Her tone was calibrated to carry the weary tone of a merchant dealing with a bureaucrat. She was careful not to sound too friendly or too defensive, either of which might arouse suspicion.

"May we?" he asked. It wasn't a request; it was an order.

"Of course."

The six slaves clambered up onto each of the ships, disappearing out of sight.

"Lovely weather we are having," the bureaucrat observed.

Under the blazing sun, Slinker fought down the urge to point out the absurdity of talking about the weather in a country that did not seem to have any. Dryana, however, was used to this pantomime.

"It's lovely," she observed politely. "Dryer than last year."

The customs officer nodded his agreement. "The emperor's progress will reach the city tomorrow. All will be busy and chaos when he arrives," Shan observed.

Dryana was trying to work out whether Shan was making a complaint or was excited by the prospect of the imperial presence. It was hard to tell from his manner.

"The city will be honoured to host the emperor as ever," she replied blandly.

The customs officer seemed about to say something, but the slaves had finished their work and were now climbing down from the ships. Dryana hid her relief, fighting down the urge to let out a deep sigh. It was only the most cursory inspection.

"It seems all is in order," Shan said with a polite smile.

Dryana produced a small red envelope. Where she had been hiding it was beyond Slinker; it was like an illusionist's sleight of hand. She handed it to the customs agent. He accepted it with a polite nod and stowed it in the cavernous sleeve of his robe.

"Till our next meeting, my lady," he said politely.

Slinker and Dryana watched them progress down the jetty and out of earshot.

"How much?" the Tancree asked the witch.

"One aureus per ship," she replied.

"In that small envelope?" he demanded.

"Paper money," she explained.

"Nerlineans!" Slinker snorted a laugh and rolled his eyes.

"Are you complaining about the bribe or the use of paper money?" she asked.

"Both," he muttered petulantly.

The Nerlineans had taken bribery to the level of a fine art. First, when you bribed a Nerlinean they generally stayed bought as a matter of honour. Second, it permeated society so much that everyone had to be bribed to do anything. The bribe Dryana had provided to Shan had simply been to thank him for doing his job. To ignore what was hidden in the hold would have cost a lot more; perhaps an impossible amount more.

"Well, you can explain it to the emperor when you meet him in three days," she said with a smile.

"Explain?" The Tancree fixed his colleague with a hard gaze.

"We have been invited to the palace. The emperor is planning a great banquet, to thank the merchants for the prosperity that their trade has brought to the empire."

"He probably just wants to see who he can tax," Slinker observed sardonically.

"Almost certainly," the witch agreed.

CHAPTER FOUR – THE FAL'GAR

Kyrian wiped the sweat from his brow on the sleeve of his tunic. Nearly five years on the steppe and he had not got used to how the steppe peoples lived. He missed the solid stone of the buildings of the south, with their wide windows and largely fresh air. The movable wooden halls of the semi-nomadic Sevains of Chazantria and Haydron were bad enough. They were smoke-filled but at least the gaps in the wood stopped the festering heat from getting out of control. It was the yurts used by the true steppe nomads, be they Mourn, Gar or Men, that he really disliked. A wooden frame, lined with felt, over which lay layers of furs and leathers. Designed to keep out the harsh winters of the windswept open plains, they let in no breeze. A metal stove sat on one side of the hexagonal tent. Its small metal tube kept most of the smoke out of the yurt, but a small amount escaped into the living area, and the lack of through-breeze meant it lingered in the air.

The steppe people clearly disliked the cold and wind of their home, mused Kyrian. It was the only thing that could explain how they tolerated the fetid heat that contrasted so markedly with the outside world. This yurt seemed particularly well insulated. That did not surprise the Slayer, for this dwelling belonged to the Fal'Gar. Kyrian wondered if the Gar did things more efficiently simply out of their nature, or just the greater practice that their long lives afforded them.

Despite his elevated status – after all, he was now Count of Chazantria – the former wrestler sat cross-legged on one of the colourful carpets that lined the base of the yurt. Opposite him sat his Gar ally, Falthar Mrignandor, Chief of the Skyriders. The Gar leader sat cross-legged too, leaning lightly against a large hard cushion and holding a glass of white liquor. He had offered Kyrian a glass, which he had refused, reminding his host of the last time he had drunk alak. The laughter at the memory of the retching Kyrian removed any risk of him insulting their hospitality. On the steppe such things mattered and needed to be carefully managed. The Gar wore a light tunic similar to Kyrian's, with a pair of close-fitting brown trousers. Unlike the Count, he seemed unconcerned by the sweltering heat of the yurt.

There were other Gar in the tent. Kyrian counted a dozen of them, an equal mix of males and females. He recognized one of them as Caldimor, Falthar's wife. She had the sharp features of all Gar, but with a sour countenance rare among the normally expressionless race. She busied herself around the tent, ordering what Kyrian took for servants to various tasks. She seemed uninterested in what was passing between the Slayer and her husband.

A breeze swept into the tent, giving Kyrian a moment of fresh air. The tight door flap was swiftly reestablished, and

Kyrian felt the sweat settle over him again. He glanced up at two more Gar, both of them female, who had entered the yurt. They disrobed their heavy leather outer clothes until they were down to tunic and trousers similar to those worn by the two seated men. Instinctively, Kyrian looked across to Caldimor, who was favouring the two women with a sour look, particularly the younger one. For Kyrian it was hard to tell if it meant anything or if it was just her normal demeanour.

The two female Gar circled the Slayer before taking a seat with the Chief of the Skyriders. The older of the two sat next to him, whereas the younger squatted down on the rug behind the pair. It was then Kyrian realized that he could actually tell the difference in age between the two Gar, something that was nearly impossible for a human to do. Looking again, Kyrian discerned that the Gar squatting behind actually looked young, as if her youthful exuberance could not be contained by her impassive Gar face. He would have struggled to determine if the woman sitting next to the chief was younger or older than Caldimor, for example. There was a hint of gravitas about the seated woman, which hinted at a seniority of rank if not age to the chief's wife. Kyrian had seen neither of the women in his previous meetings with Falthar; by contrast, he was very familiar with Caldimor's sour glances.

The two women's hair was braided tightly in a complicated series of larger and small braids, not uncommon among the Fal'Gar for both males and females. It was their make-up that stood out. If Caldimor wore any, it was subtle to the point of non-existence. Among the Fal'Gar females that Kyrian had met that seemed the norm. The two in front of him were different. Thick grey colouring started at the hairline, darkening down as it progressed across the forehead until it finished in a black band across the eyes, stopping at the top of the cheek bones. Striking out from the band of black, curling, swirling loops of black created tiny circular patterns on the cheeks. They reminded Kyrian of the tattoos on his sister's shoulders; he shivered despite himself.

"You called this meeting?" Falthar pulled Kyrian from his thoughts.

"I am awaiting my colleague," replied Kyrian. "I'm sorry, I do not know where she is."

Kyrian looked over his shoulder, as if doing so would make Saliana miraculously appear. He was annoyed by her tardiness. It was not like her. Did she not know how easy it was to offend these elves with their odd views on hospitality?

"I am sure you can speak for yourself and your company?" observed Falthar. The Gar seemed bored by the meeting.

"Of course," Kyrian muttered. He was confused – this meeting had not been his idea but Sali's. Why had she sent him on ahead?

The tent flap fluttered, and wind billowed into the yurt. Sali's tall thin frame slipped into the dwelling. She had to crouch slightly to avoid hitting her head on the roof of the yurt. She had swapped her normal leather trousers for the cloth ones favoured on the steppe. She stripped off the leather jerkin she normally wore. It clinked as it hit the ground, concealing beneath the leather a thin sheet of alcidide chainmail. It left her in a purple blouse made of silk. It was her appearance from the neck up that was the most disconcerting. Her white-blonde hair, which normally flowed freely, was in a single long braid down her back with four smaller braids that hung down to the front across her face. It was done in the style of the Fal'Gar. It was not an unusual trick for Sali to dress like those she was meeting with, thought Kyrian, but it was the make-up that surprised him. It started at the hairline in a light blue before darkening to a bright blue in a band across the eyes. Like the make-up of the Fal'Gar women, it stopped on the cheekbone. It showed no swirling patterns on the cheek; instead, what looked like lightning bolts of blue arced out across her cheeks.

Kyrian realized his jaw had dropped. Then he looked back at the Fal'Gar; he wasn't the only one. Falthar had reacted similarly, though he covered it quickly, while the other Gar in the room looked bemused. The only two who were not were the two seated female Gar. The younger one stared intently, curiosity furrowing her brow. Was she insulted? Kyrian could not tell. The woman next to the chief just looked amused, a wry smile giving her normally impassive face an impish cast.

Saliana sat down next to Kyrian, crossing her legs. Falthar offered her a shot glass of alak. Sali downed it before Kyrian could say anything. She handed it back to the chief, her face unmoving as the alcohol burnt her throat. Falthar briefly considered offering her a second one, if only for the amusement of seeing what might happen, but a glowering look from Kyrian stayed his hand.

"Well, your arrival at least will save us making introductions more than once," the chief offered with a smile. "I am Falthar Mrignandor, chief of the Skyriders. This is my aunt and chief adviser, Hildamar."

Falthar waved his hand in the direction of the woman to his side. He made no attempt to introduce the young woman who sat behind or to include his wife in the conversation. They were both onlookers to what was transpiring. The chief used Westerly, the trade tongue.

"I am Saliana Slayer, Mistress of the Company of Slayers, High Lady of the Isles of Syndion. Thank you for welcoming me to your yurt and for the protection and help your people have extended to our company. Not only in the recent battle, but also in your forbearance in allowing our trade caravans to cross the steppe and the guards you have provided to protect them from raiders."

The chief nodded in acceptance of her thanks. He waited patiently for her to speak again.

"It seems we may well soon fight together?" Saliana observed.

"The Great Khan has called both myself and Lord Kyrian to war, not you, my lady. Syndion lies far from the steppe. Your ships are no use on the sea of grass," Falthar replied, seemingly unconcerned at being called to war by the Mourn.

"I would have thought that the Dumech'Di'Fal'Gar would not want to bow before the throne of the Mourn." It was a nasty jibe, and Sali knew it. It earned a look of warning from Kyrian.

The Fal'Gar tribes had been among the last of the steppe tribes to submit to the Mourn following their invasion of the Great Steppe some ten years ago. It had been Fal'Gar and the descendants of Nerlinean legionaries who had garrisoned the Falcongate, the pass that had kept the Mourn largely out of the Great Steppe. Its fall had been the catalyst for the Mourn army to rampage east from the Daldara Mountains to the plains and highlands of Havagia. On the steppe, the blame for the fall of the Falcongate largely rested in most of its inhabitants' minds with the Nerlineans. The Nerlinean Empire had failed in their undertakings to properly garrison the pass for over a century. However, this did not remove the shame the Fal'Gar felt for their own failure.

The Fal'Gar chieftain muttered some words in his own tongue to the woman next to him. He did not sound angry, but the atmosphere seemed frostier. He then turned back to Sali.

"Among all peoples, it is normally regarded as rude to point out their failures. Also, I would prefer if you avoided investing me with titles that are not mine. Others may not realize that you are clearly joking. There is no Fal'Dath; there is no

Dumech'Di'Fal'Gar. We are the Skyriders. That is all," he replied.

Kyrian let out a silent sigh of relief at the measured nature of the response. *What was Sali playing at*, he wondered? This Gar could kill them and disappear across the grassland, never to be found again.

"Not what you told your adviser," observed Sali calmly.

The chief fixed her with a glare, which suggested he thought she was bluffing.

Kyrian tried to keep his rising annoyance with his colleague from his face.

"Who taught you our language?" Hildamar asked.

"I'm a bard. I pick up languages with ease," Sali offered with a smile.

"Is this how you always negotiate? Bait your opponent, put them off guard, so they cannot really see what you are asking for?" Hildamar demanded.

"I should not have been so foolish as to play games with the Trendorn'Di'Fal'Gar," Sali replied in the language of the Fal'Gar.

That led to a sharp intake of breath from everyone in the room, except from Kyrian, who no longer had any idea what was going on.

"You are to be congratulated in your research, half-elf." Hildamar practically spat out the last pejorative. She had switched back to Westerly. "Tell us what you want and stop playing games. Your colleague has built a relationship on trust not on threats, but I sense you are a very different creature."

"Kyrian and I will be going north. We mean to secure more trade goods that are needed in the east," explained Sali.

"What do you need of us?" asked Falthar.

"I need a cat, big enough for Kyrian to ride," Sali responded.

"You are joking?" Falthar let out a very un-Garish laugh at that. "Humans cannot ride an oradar."

Sali spread her hands as if presenting herself.

"Your blood is not pure," observed Falthar.

Kyrian looked nervously at Sali. It was the second time that someone had commented on her Gar blood. It was an open secret among the Slayers, but usually elicited a volatile response from Sali herself. Her lack of anger about it now was most unlike her.

"I can convince the oradar, if you can find one that can take his weight," she replied.

Falthar looked at his adviser. She shrugged.

"Your funeral, Count Kyrian," he replied. "Why not use your hadan? It would be easier and safer."

"Because we will never make it back to the Mountain of the Moon for the muster if we take a hadan," explained Sali before Kyrian could say anything.

"How far north are you going?" queried the chief. He seemed genuinely surprised.

"That is the other thing I need from you: a guide," said Sali.

Falthar raised an eyebrow. "To where?" he asked.

"The lands of the Hunters," Sali replied.

"You think the Solinad Hunters will welcome you better if you have one of my people with you?" Falthar gave a laugh at that. "You will be going north against the migration, the time of the hunt. They will not welcome you; they have little love for anyone. Even the Mourn tread carefully with them when they mass for the hunt. What are you seeking? More solinad dung to sell?"

"You can leave the hunters to me. I need the guide for when I go further north. To provide an introduction, as it were."

"That is beyond the steppe, beyond the patrimony of the Great Khan," Falthar cautioned her.

"You think I am protected by the Great Khan?" queried Sali.

"Not that far north you won't be. The Great Khan is keen to protect merchants, and for one as important as you to turn up dead might raise his ire. That may restrain the hunters from their worst excesses. In the ice lands he has no power, and they are not welcoming of outsiders." The Chief of the Skyriders seemed genuinely concerned for their welfare.

"That is why I need a guide to provide an introduction," Sali said with a smile.

"One of my people will be nearly as unwelcome as a Kanath or a Sevain would be. I would be risking their life as well as dooming you. I have no desire for the Great Khan to hear I sent you to your death."

"I do not understand why you feel that the Great Khan would be so concerned for my welfare. We have never met. I doubt he knows who I am," said Sali. "You are right in one regard, though: one of your people would not be enough. I need a specific person. I need *her*."

Sali pointed past Falthar and Hildamar to the young Gar still sat calmly on her haunches behind him.

"That's impossible," Falthar stammered.

The young woman looked curious, but not afraid.

"Who taught you the blue of Daldara?" Hildamar demanded.

Sali's hand went to her face, touching the lightning bolt on her right cheek.

"She said she was my aunt, but I am not sure she was," Sali said, her voice unsure.

"Who are your family?" demanded the Gar. The tone of her voice seemed to contain a compulsion and she leant forward suddenly, eyes boring into Sali.

"I'm not sure."

Kyrian could not describe exactly why he thought what he thought, but those words seemed the most searingly honest and heartbreakingly sad words he had ever heard his normally unemotional friend utter.

Hildamar sat back, seeming momentarily tired. "You can have the girl. You will return her to us at the tents of the Mourn, below the Mountain of the Moon," she said.

Falthar seemed to be about to object, but a look from Hildamar gave him pause.

"Agreed," said Sali with a nod. A single tear had slipped down her cheek, blurring the lightning bolt. "Have her meet us tomorrow morning at sun-up."

"She will be there," offered Falthar, still looking at his adviser as if searching for an answer.

Sali and Kyrian stood, the latter giving a nod of a bow to Falthar. They then slowly strapped on their armour, weapons and outer trappings, which did somewhat spoil the image of their dramatic exit, and disappeared out into the cold windswept steppe.

"What in the name of the gods do you think you are playing at?" screeched Caldimor at her husband. "Sending our niece to the north with them? She'll be dead in a week."

Falthar looked at his wife, deciding on the merits of arguing with her when he largely agreed with her.

"It is not your concern, Caldimor. She is my granddaughter and Chosen of the Goddess. It is for me to decide," snapped Hildamar.

"Do I get a say?" asked the young Gar.

"No!" Caldimor and Hildamar both barked, but for very different reasons.

"I will speak to the woman before she leaves, impress on her the need to bring back Samarin unharmed." Hildamar's voice softened as she sought to reassure Caldimor.

"Who is she? Who is this half-blood who wears the blue of Daldara?" demanded Falthar.

"No idea," said Hildamar with a broad grin.

"What? And you are happy to send Samarin north with these two..." Falthar searched for a word, "Slayers?"

"I don't know who she is. Neither, it appears, does she. Her mind has been bound with weaves of blue and grey. Some, mostly the blue, have broken, some are still holding, but they are fraying fast. We must find out who she is. We will need her if we are to be free."

"How can you know that?" Falthar's tone was dismissive.

"Because I recognize that bitch Cliphine's handiwork when I see it. I may not know who she is, but I'm damn sure the Lady of the Crystal Ships does."

CHAPTER FIVE – THE SOLINAD HUNTERS

The oradar bounded across the open grass of the plain, oblivious to the light splattering of icy rain that fell upon it. The cat and its rider crested the small hill, no more than a rise in the open landscape, and came to a halt. The steppe stretched out beyond, undulating in a series of rising and falling prairies.

The young female Gar riding the oradar leant forward and around the high pointed saddle on which she sat and gave her mount an affectionate rub behind the ears. Then she gave a light tug of the creature's long hair on the top of its head. The cat purred contentedly. Samarin Mrignandor looked different from three days ago, when she had squatted patiently behind her uncle and grandmother. The make-up had been washed away, leaving her sharp angular Gar face tanned brown by the wind and sun of the steppe. She would normally have tied her hair back in a simple topknot, the most practical style for riding, but had chosen instead to maintain her braids. They were subtly different from those she had worn a few days ago, which would have told those who knew that she was a witch, a Chosen of the Goddess. Now they simply said that she valued form over function – not unusual for a Gar of her relative youth.

She looked back the way she had come, picking out the woman who had made her so conscious of her appearance. She was a couple of hundred yards back, though to her sharp Gar eyes she might as well have been just behind her. Saliana Slayer's braids remained in place, re-tied each morning in the same manner as those she had worn the night they had first met. Her make-up also remained in place. If anything, the combination of varying blues, offset with sharps dots of white and black, had become more convoluted.

A Chosen of Daldara, a mage, was a rare thing upon the steppe, rarer even than a witch, at least among the Fal'Gar. They had once had mages in similar numbers to the other Gar races; after all, magic seemed to flow freely for the peoples of the Aman'thy'Gar. The same had been true once for the Fal'Gar, but that had been centuries ago, outside the memory of even her grandmother. They had died in great numbers during the final fall of the Falcon Empress. Slowly their numbers were recovering, but the Gar were a long-lived people, with a slow rate of procreation, so it would take longer than the six centuries that had elapsed since the fall of Fal'Dath. The youth in her wanted to ignore the past. What did it matter to her? For her family, however, for as long as she could remember, it had mattered like breath itself. Now this strange woman had come among them, and her grandmother's eyes had glittered with hope. Hopes of revenge, hopes of resurgence.

Looking back, Samarin wondered again why they had brought the oafish human with them. He was the reason why Saliana lagged behind. Lumbering even on the back of an agile oradar, he was slowing them down. Saliana rode with him, though she could easily have kept pace with Samarin had she chosen to. The Gar found it remarkable this half-breed seemed to be able to control her oradar as if she were Gar, and a Fal'Gar at that. Samarin suspected she was using magic. If that was odd, the fact that a human like Kyrian had been able to mount the creature bewildered her. All she had been taught said it should not just have thrown him, but torn his head off.

Her uncle had selected the largest oradar in their tribe for Kyrian to ride: a cantankerous old male with a shaggy golden mane. Most Fal'Gar would have steered clear of it; it had reached the age where it should be left to run out into the night to join its wild brethren. She was unsure why Falthar had chosen the beast. Did he expect it to rip the human apart? Was it simple economics, to give up a beast nearing the end of its use? It may have been purely practical, as it was the only animal strong enough to carry the lumpen Slayer. The creature had come forward the morning of its departure, all irascible nature and gnashing teeth. It would have been a challenge for whoever had saddled the beast, but there was no chance that it would let anyone on its back, let alone a human.

Then Saliana had stepped forward, speaking soft words in a language that Samarin had found both foreign and oddly familiar. The cat had become docile; almost absurdly so. The Gar would not have been surprised had it rolled over and let the Slayer rub its belly. Luckily for the fate of the expensive saddle strapped to its back, it had not. It had then let Kyrian climb up on it and haul up his travel gear with no complaint at all. Something burned in the cat's eyes, or at least she thought so. She suspected its compliance was being forced by Saliana's magic. She wondered how long it would hold before the old beast turned on its rider. The thought brought out a nasty smile on her face.

"What's so amusing?" demanded Sali.

Lost in her thoughts, Samarin had not been aware that the two Slayers had closed the gap on her.

"Nothing. Just enjoying being out in the open after being among the tents," the Gar said with heartfelt honesty, even if it had not been the reason she was smiling.

"What's that?" asked Sali, pointing out across the plain in front of them.

Samarin scanned the horizon, her Gar eyes picking out the scene of what appeared to be a skirmish in the distance. A dozen or so Mourn on hadan were attacking a group of four carts that had been drawn up in a protective square. Humans were using them as barricades in an attempt to fight off the Mourn attackers. The huffrin that had drawn the carts had been cut loose and were grazing happily a hundred yards off, oblivious to the battle for survival that their owners were fighting.

"You can see that?" Samarin was surprised. "Looks like some Mourn attacking some humans."

"What men?" demanded Sali.

Samarin squinted hard, trying to see more. "No idea," she offered. "Doesn't look like a trade caravan; no outriders. Looking at the colour of the cart covers, they might be Solinad Hunters heading north for the hunt."

"We need to help," declared Kyrian.

Samarin looked at Saliana, the one she took to be the leader of their little band. "Why?" she asked.

"People are dying," roared Kyrian. "We should help."

The young Gar was genuinely perplexed. "It's not one of your trade caravans and they certainly aren't Skyriders," Samarin observed, seeking an explanation.

Sali watched Kyrian, who was quickly building up to an explosive outburst of anger. She was privately amused the two had been brought up with such different outlooks on life that they could not conceive of how differently each of them saw the world. Kyrian, ever the hero, believed in helping his fellow man. In his mind that largely meant the underdog and the innocent, regardless of race or species. For Samarin, brought up on the steppe, the idea of concerning herself with someone outside her tribe was absurd. Even another Fal'Gar tribe would have raised little sympathy from her. Humans raised none at all.

"We need to save them," ordered Saliana.

Samarin considered arguing, but her grandmother had instructed her to obey the Mistress of the Slayers. She gave a dismissive shrug of compliance. "There are twelve of them at least," she observed.

"You afraid?" said Kyrian unkindly. It was not like him; he was still annoyed by the Gar's reluctance to help.

The Gar bridled at that, her hand straying to the sabre blade of alcidide resting at her waist.

"Let's kill the Mourn, rather than each other," Sali interceded calmly.

"Twelve is a lot for three us, is all I meant," explained Samarin. "Any strategy for dealing with them? They are not little creatures."

"Usual plan, I think," Sali said with a grin.

"Which is?"

"Charge straight at them," replied Kyrian with a large smile.

Saliana took off down the shallow slope, her cat bounding forward at incredible speed. Kyrian set off after her, bouncing up and down on his creature. Samarin was unsure if it was his or the cat's decision to charge.

"They are miles away; you'll exhaust the cats!" the Gar shouted helplessly into the wind after them. "Oh, by the Goddess," she cursed under her breath and set off after them.

She passed Kyrian with ease, but she knew she wouldn't catch Saliana. Her cat was bounding hungrily across the steppe. It would take less than ten minutes for them to close the gap, enough to tire out the oradar at this speed. Saliana reached back to where two lances were strapped in a case against the hindquarters of the oradar. She unslung one and, bringing it forward, wrapped her arm around it, lowering it point first.

A mile or so out, the Mourn saw the incoming threat. Six of them broke off from their attack on the caravans and formed up in a loose line to face the oncoming charge. They started to walk forward, their hadan clomping against the grassland, then slowly they built up speed, until the thundering of six huge charging lizards echoed across the steppe.

Samarin spotted the incoming counter-charge and cursed. Oradar were fast, hard and deadly, but no match for the sheer muscular bulk of a hadan when it built up speed. Realizing that a lance was no longer an option, she reached instead for her bow, which rested on the left side of her cat's forequarters. It was a beautiful piece of Fal'Gar manufacture: wood and horn and stressed against the natural curve. She nocked an arrow to her bow, a thin shaft of wood topped with an alcidide arrowhead. Two hundred yards out, she used her knees to turn her cat. It barely slowed as it turned in a wide curve in front of the oncoming Mourn. Her arrow flew out, followed by a second and a third. They struck home, hitting one of the Mourn in his eye, chest and leg. The creature pitched from the saddle of his lizard. Samarin was already moving, turning away from the oncoming charge, sending another two shots out over the back of her cat.

Samarin watched Saliana continuing her charge and marvelled at her foolishness. This journey would be over sooner than she expected. Then she saw the Slayer was riding hands free, controlling her oradar with her knees like a Fal'Gar. Her left hand was clenched in a fist. Blue spiralling wreaths of fire were starting to form around it, growing and swirling. A moment before impact with the lizard-mounted Mourn, she flung out her hand and fire slammed into the Mourn rider to her left. Pitched from his saddle, he landed in a flaming heap on the ground. The blue fire then raked across his mount's back. It let out a high-pitched scream, uncharacteristic for such a vast beast, and danced sideways away from the oncoming attack.

This created a gap, which Sali moved into. It took her out of line with the oncoming Mourn to her right. Her lance thrust through the attacker's chest, the razor-sharp lance point penetrating armour and flesh, and bursting out the other side, leaving it hanging through the Mourn's chest. Then the second lance was in her hand. She spun it around in a long sweeping circle and decapitated another Mourn rider coming in from her left.

Kyrian bounced past Samarin's retreating form. He bore a weapon she did not recognize: a short piece of wood with three chains on the end and a spiked metal ball on the end of each chain; a flail. His cat passed the oncoming Mourn charge. Ducking under the creature's lance, Kyrian's flail slammed into the warrior's face; then, with a swift movement backwards, it cracked the Mourn on the back of his head. The Mourn pitched forward out of his saddle and landed in front of his own hadan. The oblivious creature dropped its large front foot on his head with a sickening squelch.

The wrestler wasn't finished yet. He flung his flail away and drew a long dagger from a scabbard on his cat's saddle. He climbed up into the saddle and leapt at the remaining Mourn warrior. Kyrian dropped on him, bearing him to the ground and knocking the wind from him. He slammed his elbow into the struggling creature's face. It was not enough; the Mourn was stronger and taller than Kyrian, and recovering quickly. He lifted the Slayer bodily upward, trying to wriggle out from underneath, and his left hand kept the hovering dagger from stabbing down even as Kyrian elbowed him in the face again. Kyrian, realizing he would be in real trouble if he did not finish this fast, redirected the dagger, cutting at the arm and hand of the Mourn. Desperately, he used the point to scratch through a gap in the leather bands protecting the creature's arm. It was enough to make the Mourn recoil for moment if not let go of the wrestler's arm. It closed the gap between them. Kyrian flung his face forward and headbutted the surprised Mourn full in the face. Then he did it again. He wrenched his dagger hand free and plunged the blade into the creature's throat, working left to right to do as much damage as possible. The Mourn stopped struggling and Kyrian slumped exhausted on top of him.

The other six Mourn had not moved to help their kin. One had picked up an injury from the caravan defenders, who had been emboldened by the Slayer attack. They had pulled back from the caravan and were putting it between them and the three oradar riders. Sali sent a lash of blue flames past the caravan and across the front of the six surviving Mourn. They turned their hadan and moved away as fast as the lumbering mounts could move. Samarin cantered her oradar to the side of the caravan to give her a clear line of sight. She let out a breath and sighted her bow on the closest rider. The arrow plunged through the back of his head, pitching him to the ground. She sighted on the next one and shot again. This time it glanced off the Mourn's helmet. She cursed and drew another arrow. A lance appeared in front of her before she could nock it.

"Let them go." Sali's voice was low, but her authority was unmistakable.

"They are heading west," the Gar declared angrily. "They will complain to the Khan."

Samarin tried to find a way around the lance blocking her from drawing her bow.

"I said let them go."

"You're a fool," Samarin declared, but she obeyed and thrust her arrow back into her quiver.

PRINCE OF SLAYERS

Assured she had been understood, Sali turned her cat around and the pair stalked back towards Kyrian. He still lay slumped on top of his opponent.

"Having a nice nap?" asked Sali with a smile.

Kyrian looked up and pushed himself off the opponent.

"Wow, these things are strong," he observed. "Any chance we can go back to fighting humans?"

"Not anytime soon," said Sali.

"Shame," Kyrian sighed, dragging himself to his feet.

Samarin had dismounted and was busy plunging her sabre into the throat, eye or other weak spot on the Mourn corpses.

"What are you doing?" asked Sali, curious rather than angry.

"Making sure they're dead," grunted the Gar.

"They're dead."

Samarin did not offer an opinion. She squatted down next to the first Mourn she had killed and started plucking out her arrows. She cursed when one broke. She unsheathed her dagger and set about digging the alcidide arrowhead from the corpse's flesh. She gave a grunt of satisfaction as her bloodied fingers pulled out the arrowhead. She wiped her hands on the dead Mourn, then mounted her oradar again.

"Where are you going?" queried Sali suspiciously.

"To get my arrowheads." Samarin nodded in the direction of the escaping Mourn she had killed.

Sali looked like she was about to countermand her.

"They are made of alcidide," the Gar explained.

The Slayer understood their value and gave a nod of permission.

"That was fun," said Kyrian, giving his arms a stretch.

Sali rolled her eyes. This was Kyrian all over: good in a fight, thrilled directly afterwards. Tomorrow he would be all

73

guilty thoughts and morose comments at taking another being's life. He never changed.

Saliana turned back to the caravans, where the defenders were slowly emerging from behind their wagons. All of them carried weapons: women, children old enough to stand, a couple of teenage boys on the cusp of manhood, but no adult men. Some held swords, which appeared to be archaic Nerlinean gladiuses. A couple of spears were held uncertainly. The rest had made use of tools to function as makeshift weapons; wood axes, staves, knives, and even shovels had been pressed into service. The lack of better arms surprised her: the steppe was a violent place and weapons were a priority item for a nomad. Then she saw the bodies, half a dozen of them scattered among the carts or just in front of them. It was hard to tell at this distance, but they appeared to have been holding better weapons, even if they did not wear much, if any, armour. Maybe they had been caught unawares and armour lay packed in their carts; maybe they were simply poor.

One of the nomads had taken the lead and was approaching them cautiously. He was round-faced, with skin tanned brown by the sun and wind. He had long black hair tied back in a topknot. Saliana guessed he must be in his early teens. He seemed unsure how to proceed. He slowly lifted his aged gladius, half threatening, half defensive. Saliana stowed the amusement she felt at the limited threat the boy posed. No reason to antagonize him with a hint of mockery; a blade was still a blade. A woman came up next to the boy. Gently she reached out and took the teen's arm and pushed the sword in a downward motion. Not out of action, but less threatening, less hint of imminent conflict.

The woman was old and her once-black hair had turned to a mix of white and grey. Her wizened skin had been baked the deep brown of saddle leather. She wore a pale green tunic over soft leather trousers, while a darker green cloak that reached to her knees was thrown around her shoulders and held with a bronze clasp. She clutched a staff, more for balance than defence.

"Thank you," she offered, her voice hard and confident.

It took a moment for Saliana to process the words. The woman had spoken Nerlinean, though an odd dialect of it.

"Thank you for your help," the woman expanded.

Again, the words were Nerlinean – or at least close enough to it to be understood.

"No problem," Kyrian supplied with a big smile, walking up next to Sali.

His arrival made the other humans shift nervously. Kyrian had spoken Westerly, but both languages were close enough to Nerlinean for him to catch the drift of what the woman was saying. She looked at him cautiously; something about his accent or appearance had worried her.

"You are Sevain?" she asked.

Kyrian wondered how best to answer. Brought up among the Sevains and now a count ruling Sevain tribes on the steppe, was he really one of them now? There was no such thing as a Chazantrian, and he could not really call himself a Kangorner. He really thought of himself as a Slayer, but explaining that would just complicate things. So, as he had done since birth, he used the ancestry of his family.

"I am Kanath," he informed her.

She looked perplexed for a moment, then gave a smile of understanding as if a memory had come to her.

"A child of Liones," she declared.

Kyrian looked at her. He had no idea what that meant; maybe the meaning was falling through the gap between Westerly and whichever dialect of Nerlinean the woman was speaking. He left it as the old woman now seemed more interested in Saliana. She had moved closer and was looking at the other Slayer's face. She then glanced either side of the Sali's head, taking note of the slight point to her ears. Sali's tolerance of the inspection amused her fellow Slayer. The woman's eyes widened as recognition dawned, and she gave another happy grin.

"A child of the Dragon," she marvelled quietly. "To think I would see one."

"I suppose it's better than calling you a half-elf," observed Samarin, cantering up on her oradar.

The humans moved back cautiously from the beast.

Kyrian was openly laughing now.

"What's so funny?" Sali shot him an evil look.

"Just waiting patiently for the usual denials about your ancestry," laughed Kyrian. "Though you seemed a bit more relaxed about it on the steppe. Must be the wind."

Kyrian doubled over at his own joke, which only he seemed to find funny.

"I am just a merchant. I am not the child of anything," said Sali politely in Nerlinean.

The woman took a moment to understand. There was definitely a difference in her dialect to the traditional Nerlinean that Sali was speaking. She grasped broadly what the Slayer was saying and nodded politely.

"What's a Liones?" asked Kyrian, tamping down his laughter.

"It's not a what, it's a who," replied Sali dismissively. "It's just another way of saying you are a Kanath."

"Like child of the Dragon is a way of saying you have Gar blood," replied Kyrian with an evil grin.

Sali ignored the dig and went back to the conversation with the old woman.

"What happened here?"

The old woman looked at her as if she was trying to get the correct response.

"We were attacked. It is the way of the steppe," she supplied with a shrug.

Sali was taken aback by the old woman's nonchalance in view of the bodies of what she took to be the woman's kin still lying in the dirt.

Samarin slipped from the saddle and approached one of the Mourn corpses on the ground. She gave it a vindictive kick; she had already made sure the creature was dead, so it served no other purpose. She squatted down and started inspecting the creature's body.

"White Skulls," she declared to no one in particular. "All of them."

"Does that mean something?" asked Kyrian.

"Just their tribe. It's one of the larger ones," she mused.

"You mean there are more of them?" The Slayer glanced around him as if they might be attacked at any moment.

"Don't panic," said the Gar with a smile. "They don't move as a single tribe except during time of war, more a series of families or groups. These could have been outriders or scouts for a bigger group, or more likely a group of male riders moving without caravans."

"How do you reckon that?" asked Kyrian.

"All the kit they are carrying." She gestured to the body. "It suggests no caravans. They are all males, and they attacked the caravan."

"Males, caravan?" Sali demanded, curious.

"Females, even warrior females, always move with caravans. A group made up exclusively of Mourn males are not gentle." That was the old woman walking up.

Samarin nodded agreement.

"They attacked the caravan because they were short on supplies," the old woman explained.

"They told you that?" Sali queried.

"They demanded food, other supplies. They said they were soldiers of the Great Khan, moving west to a gathering of tribes."

"And you refused to give them anything?" Sali nodded, understanding.

"We gave them what we could spare," the old woman said. "They said it was too little, but we had nothing more to give."

"The Great Khan has forbidden raiding on the steppe?" Samarin asked.

The old woman laughed at this. "This is the steppe. It will always be the steppe," she observed with a cold smile.

"What does that mean?" asked Kyrian.

"It means you can't change a way of life with a command," Sali muttered.

She squatted down and looked at the Mourn corpse as if searching for an answer.

"These White Skulls, they follow the Great Khan?" asked Sali to Samarin.

The Gar nodded.

"Will this be a problem, when we go to the Khan's gathering?"

Samarin shrugged but did not say anything.

Saliana swore quietly under her breath. She stowed her annoyance away. That was a problem for another day.

"You have a name?" Sali turned back to the old woman, her tone sharper than she intended.

"Amdon," the old woman supplied.

"The steppe is moving west to the Khan's gathering, yet you are moving east, why?" asked Sali.

"The hunt," explained Amdon. "The solinad are commencing their migration. Like the rest of the steppes, they are moving south, though not for your war gathering. At least some of them are moving southwest to the plains of Chazantria.

Other herds will migrate southeast to Havagia. We must take enough solinad to feed us through the winter. It is traditional for this to be done in one hunt as the creatures start their migration off the tundra of the northern steppe."

"And the Solinad Hunters have not been called to fight by the Great Khan?" asked Kyrian.

"How would he do that?" Amdon queried.

"Order your leaders to join him?" Kyrian explained.

She looked at him perplexed.

"Commanders?" Kyrian tried a different word for leader.

She seemed to understand the word, but her only response was to laugh, leaving Kyrian more confused. He watched the woman as she walked back to her caravans.

"I don't understand?" Kyrian asked Samarin.

"You will when we reach the wall," she said.

CHAPTER SIX – FIRESIDE

The small dung fire spluttered in the wind, belching intermittent blasts of heat and light across the seated figures. Kyrian watched the flames play across Saliana's pale face, giving her a ghost-like aura. He heaved a sigh at her beauty. She looked and gave him one of her rare smiles, before she went back to staring at the barely present flames. The steppe wind lashed at them despite being shrouded by a ring of caravans. They were simple wooden carts with a rear made of hoop and canvas resting on wooden-spoked, iron-banded wheels. The wind whipped between and under the gaps, with little respite. Kyrian almost found himself missing the sweat-inducing yurts used by the other steppe tribes.

He found it odd that the Solinad Hunters had not adopted them. Adoption of what worked seemed to be very popular on the steppe. How could one otherwise explain how peoples as different as the Fal'Gar, the Mourn and the Sevains seemed to share such similar attitudes to shelter, clothing and much else. Yet the Solinad Hunters seemed to be very different, as if they were not really a steppe people at all. The clustered around the fire wrapped in thick blankets, eating scraps of dried meat warmed over the fire. A bowl of porridge made from a coarse wild grain that the Slayer did not recognize bubbled in a black cauldron hung on a tripod over the fire. They had added some tiny bits of blood sausage and herbs dried until they were practically dust.

Kyrian had eaten a small bowlful of it. While it gave him some sustenance, it did not taste of anything. He had measured out his portion carefully. He could see how poor these people were. When the Slayers had saved the Hunters from the attack there had been six prone humans on the ground, all males. Only one had shown any signs of life, yet his wounds had been considerable. The old woman had dressed them with some moss and then bound them tightly. He suspected that the still unconscious man would be joining his fellows in the ground in the coming days. Kyrian wished Dryana was here; maybe she could have fixed him with her powers. He suddenly realized he had not thought of his sister in days. He wondered what she was up to now. He sighed, and the wind of the steppe felt colder for a moment.

He scanned the group around the fire. It had been two days since they had saved the family group from the Mourn attack, and they had stayed with them throughout. The Solinad Hunters had been initially wary of the two Slayers, and particularly of the Fal'Gar. That was not surprising as the Fal'Gar had almost as bad a reputation as the Mourn when it came to raiding the other steppe tribes. That had changed in the decade since the conquest of the Great Khan, whose laws forbade raiding. Of course, thousands of years of steppe behaviour could not be changed overnight, though the Fal'Gar tribes had been much more consistent in obeying the new edict than the other peoples of the grasslands. The general view was that the Fal'Gar feared the retaliation of the Great Khan. Certainly the long hatred between the two peoples made the Gar more wary than others of giving the Mourn an excuse to attack them. Kyrian knew differently, at least if Sali was to be believed, for she had told him that contrary to being a number of different tribes, the Fal'Gar were one people with one leader. As such, an order to desist from raiding could be given with the reasonable expectation it would be largely obeyed. Though maybe the power of the Great Khan was not so dominant if he could not even control the White Skulls from attacking the other peoples of the steppe, Kyrian mused.

The wariness of the Solinad Hunters had softened if not fully dissolved as they had grown more comfortable with their travelling companions. They had even let Kyrian sleep by the fire within the ring of wagons they formed each night. Sali and Samarin slept outside the camp next to their oradars, snuggling up to their giant cats for warmth. Kyrian's cantankerous older oradar had made it very clear that such an option was not open to Kyrian; apparently Sali's animal-charming magic went only so far. So he had found himself sleeping alone by the dying fire while the Solinad Hunters slept in their caravans. They would each take a small amount of the burning huffrin dung and store it in a metal receptacle that would provide just enough warmth to keep them comfortable through the night.

"We need music," declared Amdon, slapping a young lad in his teens on the shoulder.

He was the one who had stood forward to face the Slayers with a sword on the day of the Mourn attack. He lurched forward on his short wooden stool, spitting porridge as he did so. He looked back at the old woman, who was his grandmother or great aunt – Kyrian was unclear about the relationships – with annoyance. She returned him a steely but amused gaze. He disappeared off to his caravan, returning with two stringed instruments. One was a short banjo-like object; the other was longer, closer to a guitar. He propped the banjo against his stool, then proffered the guitar to the family matriarch. She raised her hand in rejection and pointed at Saliana. The lad shrugged and circled the fire to hand the guitar-like instrument to the Slayer. She regarded Amdon for a moment, toying with the emerald ring on her left hand, that she always wore, and a curious look played across her face. Sali took the instrument and plucked at it. She twiddled the tuning pegs at one end until she was satisfied. The instrument reminded her of her own hydakkar, though hers had a longer shaft and a triangular end. She gave the woman another look, questioning how the woman had known that Sali was a bard. She did not bother to ask. Amdon's penchant for ambiguous answers was already apparent to the Slayer.

"Any requests?" Sali asked.

"The Song of Liones, you know it?" asked the old woman, her eyes sparkling in the firelight.

"I know it. That's an old song," Sali observed.

"A very old song," agreed the woman.

"You want it in Nerlinean or the original Kanath?" asked Saliana.

The old woman chuckled. "Nerlinean. We do not speak the language of Liones."

"Which part? If I sing the whole thing we will be here until the morning," Sali said, with a smile lighting up her face.

"The beginning. I only know the beginning," the young man grasping the banjo interjected.

"The beginning would be wonderful," said Amdon.

"Try and keep up," Saliana said with a big smile.

The boy replied with a grunt.

The bard started to strum at her guitar and the banjo joined in. The sound carried far across the plain, thundering out so that Kyrian wondered if Sali was using magic to enhance it. Then Sali's voice joined it, lilting, rising and falling, spiralling upwards before dropping to sudden lows and spiralling up again. She told an old tale, the tale of Clovis Liones. A child confined to a monastic order in the lands of Kanath, before the Sevains, before Elian the Great, the Threefold Emperor. It was the tale of how his father the High King of Kanath was murdered by his brother along with all his siblings. Assassins came to the monastery, sacred to the god Tempor, Lord of Time. There was the escape of the warrior monk San Ja, and with him two novices, the young Prince Clovis and his friend Metus. They fled to Clovis' uncle Duke Volaran, only to discover his uncle was the murderer. Further rescues came about with the help of the three mysterious half-Gar Jeddera, Saska, and their sister Alluner. Then came the revelation that Volaran was a servant of the undying Death Lord Naron.

Wars and battles, daring escapes, marriages and lovers, kingdoms and empires. Magic and gods, history morphing into legend. Kyrian listened enraptured to a tale of his people told in the old way. He fought back tears. Some of the names he knew. Jeddera, but which one? Tempor, the greatest of the Old Gods, Metus the warrior, who some Kanath still invoked as a God of War. Naron, a name that gnawed deep down, a name to fear. Kyrian of Kilon, wrestler, merchant, Slayer, had heard many of those names, but many more were forgotten to him: Alluner, Clovis, Volaran, so many other characters tumbled out of Sali's story. People of legend and history, the tale of the Kanath as a free and independent nation. His face might be impassive, but his heart wept for all that had been forgotten; all that had been lost to his people.

***

PRINCE OF SLAYERS

Night bled into day and back into night again, and days merged together as the party traversed the endless sea of grass. Kyrian lost track of the calendar as one week blurred into the next. One night stood out in the memory. He had helped to bury the injured survivor from the attack. As Kyrian had feared the man had never recovered from the wounds he had sustained. He had died in the back of a wagon as it trundled across the steppe, he had never regained consciousness. The Solinad Hunters seemed to take the additional death in their stride, treating it with weary resignation rather than deep sadness.

They were going north, and east, was all Kyrian knew, moving at the speed of the huffrin-drawn caravans, which rolled at a fair pace across the open grasslands. It was still slower than the oradar-mounted Slayers and their Fal'Gar companion could have achieved had they moved at the normal speed of their fast-moving cats. It would have at least given them a small chance of returning in time for the Great Khan's Council, whatever its purpose. Whether it was for a war, as the other steppe leaders had speculated, or simply the Mourn ruler exercising his dominion, Kyrian was not sure. He had attended the Emperor of Nerlinea's own gathering of his nobility, the Amanthagan, five years before, and the Great Khan was known for copying imperial customs.

Kyrian had made his concerns clear to Saliana more than once. Each week they travelled east away from Chazantria was a week they would have to travel back. As the weather worsened, the length of the return journey would only increase, though at least he hoped they would be doing it without the encumbrance of the Solinad Hunters. Three months had seemed like plenty of time to bring his army west to the Mourn Khan, and now he was not so sure. He had left Marcus with orders to prepare supplies and his followers for the march to the Mountain of the Moon, but he knew that without being there himself that would be a struggle. A week away and he would return to disgruntlement; a month gone, there would be arguments between his lords; much longer than that and they would be fighting each other outright.

All this he had made clear to the Mistress of the Slayers. She seemed unconcerned. Rather, she seemed oddly uninterested. Odd, because it was Saliana's plan five years ago to use the Slayers' money and connections to carve out their own territory on the steppe, seizing the prime agricultural land that fed much of the steppe, not to mention Kangorn, during the tough winter period. Now, just as Kyrian had achieved their aims, she seemed willing to risk it all on a wild adventure across the steppe. He knew that his new principality's agricultural wealth and the Company of Slayers' current success in the east was dependent on the rich manure that the Solinad migration during the autumn brought with it. He did not understand why they needed to see it for themselves; after all, the migration had happened for as long as anyone could remember. Saliana seemed fascinated by seeing the great solinad hunt, a story told across the steppe. Kyrian had heard it many times, but not from anyone who had seen it first-hand. On the western steppe, the solinad was held sacred, at least among the Sevains, its value in the agriculture of the region so inculcated that the idea of killing it for its meat and fur would have seemed ridiculous.

The huge, thick-skinned beasts outdid the huffrin in both size and truculence. Kyrian speculated that part of the Sevain taboo on hunting them had come originally out of practical survival. Now the Sevains had the weapons and numbers to bring one down, but it would not occur for them to do so even in the harshest winter. He was fascinated to find out how the Solinad Hunters did it, but not so interested as to risk sacrificing five years of hard work.

The Slayer sat on the lead wagon of the caravan, a place he found more comfortable and less threatening than the back of his oradar. That was one advantage of Saliana's decision to travel with the Solinad Hunters, rather than make the journey alone. Sali's motivation for travelling with the Solinad Hunters was unclear, and Kyrian had not managed to get a straight answer from her. His fellow Slayer seemed strangely preoccupied with matters beyond their travel arrangements; matters she was unwilling to share. Samarin had speculated that perhaps Sali felt that they would be more welcome at the hunt if they arrived with Solinad Hunters, especially ones they had rescued. Yet Samarin could not say for certain that their presence would even be tolerated. Indeed, the Fal'Gar witch could not recall any recent story of one of her people attending the hunt, and despite her youthful looks she had lived on the steppe for several decades. The Solinad Hunters moved north into the coming winter, just as the rest of the steppe tribes moved south to reach warmer climes, so perhaps the reason was that. Yet Kyrian could not shake the niggling fear that there was some sort of taboo against outsiders and that they risked offending the leaders of the Solinad Hunters by their attendance. He had broached the possibility with Samarin, but she had returned him a blank look. That was better than the amused, almost mocking, smile he received from Amdon when he had raised the issue with her.

Kyrian's cat stalked alongside the wagon, giving occasional hisses at the yoked huffrin dragging the cart, and receiving an angry bark in return. Kyrian flicked the reins lightly across the lizard's back, seemingly to encourage, though it was doubtful that the great beast really noticed. He looked ahead at Saliana, who had cantered off ahead of the column of wagons. She had ridden up a small hill ahead of them and was standing up in the saddle of her oradar. Her white hair whipped in the breeze; her sharp pale features contrasted with the never-ending blue of the open sky.

"You are partners?" Amdon enquired politely.

Kyrian looked to his left on the wagon bench. The old woman had sat there silently for so long that he had almost forgotten she was with him. He struggled with Nerlinean despite its closeness with Westerly – not that his Westerly was much good. He much preferred Sevain, something that had only increased with five years living among them. The word she used had an ambiguous meaning, so he could not be sure exactly what she was asking.

"We are business partners," he answered in broken Nerlinean, hoping he wasn't using words from Westerly that she wouldn't understand.

"Only business?" she pressed with an impish smile.

He favoured her with a look of displeasure. "Just business," he clarified.

She chuckled at that. "You might want to tell your face," she observed caustically.

Samarin cantered down from the hill ahead of them. She brought her oradar to a stop, then turned the cat to pace along beside the wagon. Kyrian's older oradar gave an angry hiss as it was forced to move out of the path of the Fal'Gar.

"You have to see this, Kyrian!"

The Slayer and the Solinad Hunter shared a look of amusement at Samarin's excitement – not a normal response among the phlegmatic Gar. *She is young*, thought Kyrian, before realizing she was not only older than him, but not far off Amdon in age. He smiled at the thought.

"What's so funny?" Samarin asked, confused.

"Nothing. Show us." Kyrian smiled wider.

Samarin grinned like an excited human teenager and cantered back up the hill. Kyrian slapped the reins across the huffrin's back, encouraging the creature to speed up. It responded by doing nothing, as the wagon trundled resolutely up the hill.

PRINCE OF SLAYERS

When they reached the top of the hill, the land dropped away more than the Slayer would have expected. The steppe, which on occasion felt like a flat plain, was not really so. Instead, it undulated with long, shallow gradients, so it was possible to ride up a fair distance above sea level before the land dropped away sharply back down to the flat. Rocky outcrops would pockmark it in places; some larger, barrier-like monstrosities, others little more than a collection of pebbles.

From this hill, Kyrian could see for miles across open grassland, the long grass swaying back and forth in the wind. It had been nearly two weeks since they had fought off the Mourn and they had not seen anyone else in that time, not even from a distance. Only the odd wild herd of adunel or a small family group of feral huffrin moving south to avoid the coming winter. The occasional predatory cat breaking cover. No Mourn, no Gar, no Solinad Hunters, not even the creature they were named for.

So, it came as something of a shock to Kyrian to see the plain before him. Dozens of caravans made of hundreds of wagons were moving in unison across the grassland. They were heading for a long bank of rocks that cut the plain in a jagged line.

"The Wall of Sargon," declared Amdon from the bench.

From this distance, it looked to Kyrian like a natural phenomenon rather than a built structure. He assumed the name was more illustrative of its effective use than any real belief it had been constructed by someone. He did wonder why it had been named for a Kanath god, for the lands of the Kanath lay very far west of here.

"Hunter's Gap," the old woman pointed excitedly from the bench.

Kyrian followed her hand. The rocky embankment was not tall, sitting lower than the hill from which they watched. It

89

was hard to tell at this angle and distance, but the Slayer speculated that the wall itself was not that high, perhaps the height of a Kangorn townhouse, and fairly uniform in height. He could see why someone might think of it as a wall. A gap lay in the rocks, which he guessed to be a hundred yards in width. It looked almost like it had been cut into the stone, so sharp were the sides of the gap. In reality, he guessed it was probably as much a natural occurrence as the rock formation itself.

The caravans were heading for the gap, funnelling themselves into it from across the plain. Bright streamers tied to staffs whipped in the wind. The Slayer noted that the mass, while seemingly travelling as one, was not a singular group. Each group of caravans was separate, slightly distant from the next. The largest had maybe twenty caravans; the smallest was made up of perhaps two. There was no methodology or allocation. They all seemed to be slowly merging together as they approached the gap, while staying apart just enough to be distinct.

"Is it not a beautiful sight?" demanded the old woman. Her eyes sparkled with excitement and her face was beaming with happiness. "The time of the hunt has come."

CHAPTER SEVEN – MUSHROOMS

The House of the Four Stars rested in one of the less salubrious parts of Port Ren. To Dryana it sounded like a brothel. It was not, though a number of prostitutes, both male and female, plied their trade within its bounds. The five-storey wooden building was part tea house and part restaurant. It was built as a series of open wooden platforms, one above the other, with a large open atrium in the centre of the building that ran all the way to the top. Each floor was ringed with wooden rails on the outside and also on the inside facing the atrium. The roof was a hollow square surrounding the open space of the atrium; it was a broad pitched structure covered with carved wooden tiles painted a vibrant red. The wooden ends of the roof joists pointed out from the tiled area and were carved into stylized wingless dragons painted in greens and blues. The roof was largely for structural integrity than any attempt to keep the weather out of the building. This was Port Ren, after all; there were only two types of weather: blazing sun most of the year, then monsoon rain for one month. No one had worked out how to build a structure to keep out that downpour, so the people of Port Ren had largely given up trying.

Dryana strode up the steps of the tea house, the pliable wood bouncing under her light frame. She was followed by Slinker, his Tancree fighting blades strapped to his back. Two further Slayer employees, both men, both Nerlineans, brought up the rear. They were dressed in tunics with short-sleeved three-quarter-length robes over the top. Their short swords were half hidden by their coats. None wore badges of their company, though few in Port Ren would have identified them as the Company of Slayers had they worn such insignia. In Port Ren, the Slayers lacked the reputation or infamy that they had achieved in Kangorn or the other ports west of the Nerlinean Ocean. Here they were just one merchant company among many.

A woman dressed in a pink robe covered with thin lines of black flowers moved to intercept the new arrivals. Her eyes cast around at the square tables that were strewn across the ground floor of the House of the Four Stars. There was no need – she knew already they were occupied – but it was an indication to the approaching westerner and her strange companion that they would not be finding sustenance here.

Dryana's cold gaze passed over the woman, but in Port Ren she lacked the fearsome reputation that went with it.

The pink-robed woman barely noticed the look. "Sorry, we have no room," she declared imperiously.

Dryana had to concede that the ground floor was full, but looking up through the hollow atrium she could see empty tables on the higher floors. She had no idea why the woman had taken a dislike to them. Maybe it was the Tancree's presence. Maybe it was that they were all armed. Nerlineans were much less likely to carry weapons openly than was the norm in the West, though Dryana noted plenty of rough types in the tea house, some obviously armed, others likely to be carrying concealed weapons. Maybe it was just racism. Dryana's initial experience of the Nerlinean Empire had been an appearance of racial and religious tolerance, certainly by comparison with her upbringing under the Sevains. In reality, it concealed a complex web of relationships and hierarchies, religious, ethnic and economic, that were a struggle for most Nerlineans to fully understand and impossible for an outsider to grasp.

"We are here to see Lan Xian," Dryana replied.

The woman's mood changed from polite hostility to disgruntled acceptance. "Top floor," she said, turning away from them.

Dryana looked at the wide wooden staircase that snaked around the outside of the building all the way to the top floor. "Really," she muttered exasperatedly.

The woman turned back and shot her a look of malevolent amusement.

Dryana returned the favour and stalked up the stair trailed by her compatriots. When she arrived at the top, she was breathing hard and felt slightly dizzy. She looked out across the platform-like floor open on all sides and took a moment to enjoy the breeze. Her breath calmed and she took in the panoramic view of the city. Low, mostly single-storey, buildings surrounded the tea house, giving way to larger houses and municipal buildings in the distance. It was mid-morning, and the sun gleamed across the polished wooden surface of the floor. The room was a hollow square surrounding the atrium, with square tables, each framed by four chairs, spaced evenly across the platform, twenty in total. All of them where empty except for three diagonally opposite from the stairs. A dozen men sat at the tables positioned to leave the greatest gap between them and the top of the staircase while giving them a full view of it. Two tables had been moved imperceptibly so as to protect the third table, which rested in the corner. The men at the nearest table were clearly guards. Blades rested on the table in front of them, a mix of short swords and broad-bladed knives more akin to kitchen tools. They were already watching the woman at the head of the stairs warily. The four remaining men sat playing a game of Tonda, using wooden blocks that were painted black and marked with red writing. Shouts and laughter emanated from the group as they gambled.

Dryana waited for her colleagues to reach the top of the stairs. They were all puffing, especially Slinker, who stood at the top panting heavily, clutching the rail.

"Gods, I really hate stairs," he grumbled.

"Getting old," observed Dryana with a smile.

The witch circled the platform, weaving through the narrow gaps between tables. As she approached the four guardsmen, they pushed back their chairs from the tables and stood up. Blades rung on each other as they were picked up. The guards held them loosely at their sides, points down – not exactly threatening, but not welcoming either. As she approached closer, two more men got up from the game of Tonda and stood flanking the table furthest from the stairs. Another pulled his chair around so he was now facing the approaching Slayers, taking position next to the only one of the previously seated men who had not moved.

That man was Fatboy Xian. He was a corpulent mass, quite unlike most eastern Nerlineans. Large sausage-like fingers, wrapped in thick gold rings, played absentmindedly with the black tiles in front of him. He looked up at Dryana as she approached, before taking in the two men behind her, his eyes coming finally to rest on the Tancree.

"Your timing is terrible. I was just about to win big," he pouted with mock annoyance.

PRINCE OF SLAYERS

He pushed down the tiles in front of him, which clacked against the wooden surface of the table.

Dryana very much doubted that Fatboy's employees were brave enough to beat him, but she said nothing. She glanced either side of her to where the guards were blocking her way, then looked back meaningfully at Lan Xian. He waved them aside, creating a gap through which the Slayer could pass.

Dryana walked past them and took a seat opposite the fat trader. His hair and sharp little beard were still dark, indicating that he was in his late thirties, even if his weight and gaudy silks made him look much older. Fatboy was a trader: part wholesaler, part criminal. He had started out as a child pickpocket in one of the many gangs that preyed on the city of Port Ren. Making his way up to knifeman, he had garnered a reputation for ruthless violence if not martial ability. Smart enough to work out that such careers tended to be short and bloody, he had eschewed taking the chance of making gang leader. Instead, he had used his connections to become a trader, usually in goods that others did not want to be associated with. Lan Xian had received the nickname Fatboy in his youth, and it had never left him. Everyone referred to him by the moniker, albeit never to his face.

Slinker pushed past the guards who had moved to block him and perched on one of the tables that they had recently relinquished. Legs pushed out against the floor, arms crossed, the picture of bored insouciance. The guards looked at their master, who waved their concerns away. The two remaining Slayer agents stopped where they were, facing the guards.

"Sorry if you feel outnumbered?" Fatboy spread his hands in an expansive gesture of mock apology.

Slinker grunted with amusement.

"Is there a problem?" Lan Xian demanded of Dryana, ignoring the Tancree.

"Not at all, Mister Lan. He just finds the idea that you think we are outnumbered amusing."

Fatboy's nose twitched at that, but he changed subject. "What can I do for you, Dryana Slayer?"

By way of answer she reached to her side and detached a pouch from her belt. She cleared some of the tiles to one side and carefully tipped the contents on the table. It was a small pile of desiccated mushrooms, black originally, but now covered by a white dust from the drying process. Small amounts of the edges had crumbled to powder at the fringes of the small pile.

"Drun," Fatboy whispered reverently.

His fat finger poked at the edge of the pile, and he took a small amount of the dust and placed it on his tongue. A moment later a big smile played across his face.

"Wonderful, quite wonderful," he purred.

He pulled out a long white bone pipe and a packet of tobacco. He plucked some of the herb from the pouch and added a small amount of the dust from the desiccated mushrooms. He tamped it down into the end of the pipe and lit it. He took a big drag on the pipe and blew the smoke out.

An even more benign smile passed across his face.

"Amazing…" He let out the word as a big sigh.

Dryana smiled.

"Your product is perfect as always," he said with a broad smile. "How much do you have for me; your normal two sacks?"

"A little more than that," she replied. "My colleague brought it with him."

She indicated Slinker over her left shoulder.

The Nerlinean took another look at the Tancree, his lip curling up slightly in a hint of disgust. The Tancree tended to provoke one of two reactions among Nerlineans: disgust at the ugliness of the creature, or curiosity at what he was. The Tancree had never been common this far east, and even at their height, their presence would have been remarked upon. Now that Slinker might very well be the last of his kind, for a Nerlinean below the age of sixty, seeing a Tancree was almost as wondrous or terrifying as seeing a dragon.

"You smuggled it among the solinad dung," Fatboy observed.

"You are well informed," replied Dryana.

"That much solinad pellet arriving in Port Ren is well known to everyone. The farmers from here to Mahendra are buzzing at the news."

Dryana let the exaggeration go. It reflected the reality of how important those six ships were to the eastern harvest.

"Last time one of your ships came in, you had two sacks of drun. Can I hope the same multiple applies this time?" Fatboy asked greedily.

Dryana nodded politely.

"Twelve sacks!" His eyes gleamed.

The Slayer kept her face impassive and let the Nerlinean make his own assumptions. He did not need to know that they had actually brought in twice that amount of drun hidden in their holds of dried solinad manure. It seemed oddly appropriate that they had smuggled the mushrooms in such a fashion, for that was where drun was found – in the faeces of the giant solinads. Dryana did not know who had made the discovery, but she did know that the steppe tribes had long consumed the hallucinogenic mushrooms. No one knew for sure where the solinad consumed their fungi during their long annual migrations. The giant creatures would consume the mushrooms, letting them slowly digest in their cavernous stomachs. On the steppe, drun was considered a delicacy by the Solinad Hunters, taken half-digested from the stomach of a slain solinad. For the Solinad Hunters were the only steppe people willing to kill the beasts, and then only once a year during the great hunt. Drun was valued for its flavour and its interesting if limited hallucinogenic capacity. By the time the solinad completed the migration, either beneath the Daldara Mountains in the west or on the Plains of Havagia, in the east, the mushrooms had been largely digested, rendering any benefit from breaking the religious prohibition on killing the hulking animals moot. All that was left was a slimy black collection of threads laced into the creature's manure.

No one was really certain which lunatic had come up with idea of going through the droppings, pulling out the slimy black threads, washing them and then drying them. They dried the desiccated mushrooms to the point where they began to crumble into a dust-like substance. That had been a century and a half ago. The dust was highly psychoactive, as if the properties of the mushrooms had been concentrated down. It was the merchants and lords of Haydron and Kangorn who had first seen the opportunity to make money by selling it. Naturally, they chose the market with the most affluent purchasers: the Nerlinean coast. First they sold to the western empire and then to the wealthier, more opulent, eastern provinces and Amaland. It had made the fortunes of several of the noble houses of Kangorn: the Winterborns, the Hillers and the Brewers being the most notable.

It was only a decade later that the farmers of the plain of Havagia made the next leap. They were the main producers of the tobacco that was the Nerlineans' main source of relaxed pleasure up to that point. They discovered that when drun was combined with their tobacco and smoked the effect was truly mind-blowing. Havagia was at the time a Nerlinean province with easy land transit to the teeming affluent cities of eastern Nerlinea. Soon drun and tobacco sales from Havagia were booming and half the empire dropped into a drug-induced haze.

It took the Emperors of Nerlinea many years to truly appreciate the soporific blanket that had been thrown across the richest provinces. In part this was because the Nerlinean bureaucracy was usually uninterested in the lives of their citizens as long as taxes were paid. And in part this was because at least one of the emperors during the period had been addicted to drun himself. In fact, he eventually died from it, though his death would be officially blamed on a weak heart. His son and heir decided to react quite differently to the drun epidemic, though he was probably more concerned for the effect drun was having on his empire than due to any grief at his father's premature departure to his next life. As the ancient saying went: No one reacted as slowly as a Nerlinean Emperor; no one overreacted as much as a Nerlinean Emperor. Sumptuary laws had declared drun illegal, and consumer and seller had waited to see what would happen. Would the law, like so many supposed limits on luxury, actually be enforced or ignored as similar declarations on clothing and banqueting had been in the past. The crackdown when it came had been brutal; traders and merchants had been executed. Farmers were slaughtered and fields of tobacco burned, despite it not being illegal. Drying sheds for drun were smashed. The traders realized the Imperial Government was really serious when they started crucifying bureaucrats for the crime of taking bribes related to the trade in drun. Soon the supply from Havagia had dropped to a trickle and the Imperial Fleet sent ships east to Kangorn to impress on the prince and his lords that they should not seek to rebuild markets that they had lost over a decade before to the farmers of Havagia.

That had been over a century ago. For most of the period since then, drun had been covertly traded from both Havagia on the eastern steppe and Haydron on the western steppe to Nerlinea. Demand would flare up occasionally, only to be violently suppressed by the Imperial Government. Eventually a wary balance had been reached where the trade was largely ignored as long as it was kept quiet and did not affect too great a proportion of the population. Of course, such limits were arbitrary, which tended to keep the drun traders' operations small. It also remained one of the few areas where it was largely impossible to bribe Nerlinean officials – or, if one did, the payment had to be eye-popping.

This compromise had lasted until a decade ago. Then the Mourn Horde's conquest of Havagia had changed the whole picture, cutting off most of the empire's supply of both tobacco and drun. Far worse from the emperor's perspective was that it cut off not only the empire's supply of food from one its most fertile provinces, but the solinad manure that increased yields in the less fertile dumechates. Famine had wracked the provinces closest to Havagia, with wider food shortages felt across the Empire. That had led to civil unrest and rioting. The emperor, reeling from the loss of his notional overlordship of the steppe and, much more importantly, his very real dominion over the province of Havagia, collapsed into a slough of despond, leaving the Imperial Bureaucracy and Imperial Military both headless. Into this instability the emperor's most capable, though not eldest son, Nyandar had stepped. Taking swift control of the legions, he had sidelined or murdered his brothers. Then he had married his older half-sister, the daughter of the emperor's declared first wife and empress. Nyandar's mother was simply one of his father's concubines, rather than one of his four acknowledged wives. He had himself declared regent, then quickly after that co-emperor. His father died of despair a year later, leaving Nyandar as sole ruler of the vast empire.

This had made no difference to Mourn control of Havagia and little difference to the vital supply of agricultural produce from the lost province. When the Mourn had conquered the western steppe, the Sevain tribes living there and Count of Haydron had capitulated immediately. The Mourn may not have understood farming, but they saw no need to obliterate it if the people were willing to pay tribute and pledge fealty. They had not been so gentle in Havagia, where the Imperial Legions had stood and fought. The Mourn Horde had won in the end, but they had vented their displeasure by savaging the region. Farmers were butchered en masse, fields burned, irrigation systems smashed. By the time they had finished, the destruction was so great that half the population of the region had either fled or been murdered. It would likely take generations for the farming to recover, if it ever did. The nomadic conquerors were not concerned either way.

Now, a decade after the conquest, no tobacco was traded south, and there were no drying sheds for solinad pellet or for drun. Only a limited amount of fresh solinad manure was making its way south to the Nerlinean provinces adjacent to Havagia. It was too heavy in its wet form to carry further by cart. The western merchants of Kangorn and Haydron led by the Company of Slayers had stepped into the void, shipping dried solinad pellet from the western steppe to the Nerlinean Empire, rescuing its people from collapsing crop yields, and offering drun and a new opportunity to addict the empire.

To Fatboy this was all academic. He had been a drun seller from before the fall of Havagia, though only small-time, like all other such traders. That was before Dryana had come seeking someone who could move the Slayers' supply of drun. Their relationship had lasted almost four years, and it had made Fatboy rich and kept Dryana and the Slayers from coming to the attention of the Imperial Bureaucracy. Where Fatboy had got things wrong was in seeing himself as the senior partner in the deal. It was part Nerlinean arrogance and part a lack of appreciation for how powerful the Slayers were. It was easy for him to believe that the frail young girl in front of him needed him far more than he needed her.

"I can take all twelve sacks," he mused politely to Dryana.

He modulated his tone to sound like he was doing her a favour.

"It is a lot to move," he continued. "That will of course be reflected in the price I can offer."

That prompted a grunt from Slinker. For someone who did not know the Tancree, it was hard to tell if the sound contained amusement or contempt. Fatboy cast an assessing glance over Slinker, his face wrinkling in disgust at the alien creature in front of him. Clearly, he was one of those Nerlineans who found the Tancree's presence repellent rather than curious.

"I should have made an introduction," said Dryana, glancing back over her shoulder at the Tancree. "This is my business partner, Slinker Slayer, of the Company of Slayers."

Fatboy ignored the introduction, and his gaze passed back to Dryana. His irises were expanding under the effect of the drun.

"Are we dealing or are you just wasting my time?" Fatboy barked churlishly.

His men loomed closer. Intimidation and pretended indifference, she thought. Sometimes she hated dealing with men. It riled her, but Sali had taught her the secret was to always keep calm, no matter how much she wanted to scream and swear at the arrogant fool in front of her. She took a silent joy in the knowledge that she had imported twenty-four sacks this time, not the twelve that the man in front of her believed. It was unlikely that the unpleasant human she was negotiating with would ever discover it. A small part of her was disappointed that she could no longer sell the remainder to one of his competitors, but it had already left Port Ren by ship, destined for Amaland, the island kingdom across the ocean to the east.

"The price will be the same as before: a hundred aureus per sack," Dryana replied calmly, referencing the old gold currency of Nerlinea. "In actual gold, not paper equivalent."

"Twelve hundred gold? I doubt there are that many pieces in the whole of Port Ren these days. Paper is just as good," Fatboy observed.

He was exaggerating, of course, but not by much. It was a lot of real gold in a city that had long ago stopped using it.

"Gold," Dryana insisted.

"Also, twelve hundred. I need a discount. I've got to carry inventory." He sounded genuinely annoyed.

"A hundred and five per sack," the Slayer replied, staring coldly at the man.

Fatboy waved his hand to his men standing behind Dryana. She felt them closing in on her. Slinker and the two Slayer agents had not moved. The Tancree seemed to be looking out from the tea house across the city as if he had lost interest in the negotiation.

"Slinker, if they take one more step, please kill them," ordered Dryana.

"Sure." Slinker's gaze did not shift from taking in the view.

"One hundred and ten." Dryana's stare had never left Fatboy.

The Nerlinean looked genuinely angry, which slightly confused Dryana. Here in the East the Slayers may have lacked much of the ferocious reputation they had built in the West, but she still did not understand why Fatboy was being so difficult. She was about to make him very rich, after all. Maybe he was worried about the money, but her sources told her he should be good for it. If he really was struggling to buy all twelve sacks, why not offer to take less? Was it just pride getting in the way?

She picked up a hint of movement in her peripheral vision. The slightest shift of a shoulder. Slinker had seen it too; she could feel his wariness behind her. Fatboy had not moved – it was the thin man next to him, the one who had moved to that position when they had first arrived. The man relaxed again. Dryana realized what had happened. His hands were under the table. He had squeezed Fatboy's leg or perhaps poked him.

Fatboy looked at him and then back at Dryana. His angry mood seemed to soften if not fully dissipate.

"One hundred and five per sack in gold." He leant forward, the hint of menace returning as he pushed his jowly face in front of Dryana.

She could not be sure, but she thought she had seen a flash of annoyance on the thin man's face. Now as she looked at him from the corner of her eye, it had returned to the impassive visage that it had otherwise maintained throughout the negotiation. Who was he? Fatboy's numbers guy? Some sort of adviser? His boss? That made no sense; Fatboy was his own man. Was the thin man calling the shots or simply advising? There was something familiar about him, a nagging sense she had seen him before somewhere, just not any time she had met with Fatboy.

"Agreed," she declared perfunctorily.

Fatboy sat back with a smile of victory.

Idiot, she thought. She saw the barest flicker of satisfaction pass across the thin man's face.

CHAPTER EIGHT – A BANQUET

Dryana had to give the Nerlineans their due: no one did public buildings like them. Not that most other countries really did public buildings. She had grown up in the Sevain principality of High Ringstead, where the only government buildings were castles, designed to defend their inhabitants and keep the less compliant parts of the conquered Kanath population under the boot of their Sevain overlords. Kangorn had a few such buildings, like the public baths that she had frequented with the Princess Ascrina, back when she had lived on the Rock. She felt a sudden ache of absence, remembering her old friend. It had been years since she had last seen her. She tamped down her feelings and went back to staring at the ceiling of the monolithic structure in which she stood.

It reminded her of a temple, and a double-sized one at that. It had a double pitched roof with the edge of each span resting on a line of paired columns that ran the length of the long building. It bisected the room into two separate halls, though with a sufficient gap between the columns of the central colonnade for it to work as a single space. It was brick-built, with a façade of white stone covering the outside brick and red-brown tiles covering the roof. Inside, the walls had been plastered and painted white. Unusually, it had not been painted in more garish colours; the Nerlineans liked their interiors colourful to the point of vulgarity. Dryana assumed the reason it had been left bright white was to draw the eye to the suspended ceiling.

A plaster ceiling rode flat across the whole width of the double hall, disguising the wooden eaves of the roof. The fresco painted upon it was a mass of vibrant colours. Athletic figures of men and women fought and hunted through a series of scenes. Dryana suspected it told some old legend or story of which she was not aware; a Nerlinean tale she had never been taught. She could not recognize any of those depicted, though she assumed a figure dressed in purple might be an emperor. A large ship was shown cutting through the waves, or it might be clouds – it was hard to tell, as the artist seemed to have taken some creative license.

"The Voyage of the Ravenscar," a voice declared behind her.

She turned to look back at Slinker. "What's that?" she asked.

"Really?" Slinker chuckled. "The Voyage of the Ravenscar. That is Jeddera Summersword, Eron the Trickster, Denox the Sword Mistress, Far the Forgotten."

Slinker's fingers roved across the air, pointing out different figures depicted in the painted ceiling.

"Still no idea," Dryana said.

"You know who Jeddera Summersword is?"

"Sure: the Nerlinean emperor who became a god," the witch confirmed.

Dryana remembered her mother telling stories of the Lord of Morning when she was young; mainly his battles in the west against armies of monstrous creatures before the walls of Las Ma. She did not know any story involving him and a ship.

"And you never heard the story of the Ravenscar?"

Slinker was almost reproachful. He sounded like a teacher disappointed at a clear gap in a student's knowledge. His fellow Slayer bridled at his patronizing tone.

"Blame three hundred years of Sevain occupation," Dryana shot back petulantly.

"It's a shame; you would like the story. Jeddera Summersword led a crew of heroes across the Farthest Ocean, to fight in the war of the gods. His ship passed through the mists that lay there. He defeated Paschen's attempt to overthrow the gods, threw him down and took his place as the God of Summer and stayed in the land of the gods. It is a wonderful lyrical tale, and I am not doing it justice," the Tancree said with a smile.

"How did anyone know that it happened?" Dryana muttered contemptuously.

"Eron the trickster returned with the survivors of the crew and told the story," Slinker replied seriously.

"You mean he decided not to bother with a crazy voyage, thumped Jeddera, threw him overboard and sailed home with a good story," laughed Dryana.

Slinker's gaze shot nervously around the hall, which was starting to fill up with the great and good of Port Ren.

"Careful, Dryana: the Nerlineans take this stuff seriously."

The witch looked at her fellow Slayer and for a moment thought he must be joking. "Sorry," she declared, registering his annoyance. "But Far the Forgotten, please?" she went on, not quite willing to bow fully to his po face.

"Oh, you would like him," said Slinker with a laugh. "It is a misnomer, really; it should be something closer to Far the Forgetter or Far Who Could Not Remember, but that is not quite so catchy. He woke up in a prison in the Northlands, with no memory of who he was. The kind of story any bard might know."

Dryana gave Slinker her most baleful gaze. She recognized the dig at Saliana. While the other Slayers had long given up enquiring into their leader's background, accepting as true her contention that she could remember little to nothing of her past before they had first met on *The Spirit of Summer*, Slinker had not. Instead, it had been an increasing obsession for him, as if he were trying to piece some puzzle together. Dryana had tried to discuss it with him, but he refused. Despite that, it did not stop him digging for information or, for that matter, making jibes about it. Her baleful gaze wasn't working and Dryana started to wonder, between Slinker and Fatboy, if she was losing her touch.

"It's a nice picture," she said lamely, her eyes wandering back to the ceiling. "Do you really think the land of the gods lies beyond the Farthest Ocean?" she asked suddenly.

"I doubt it," said the Tancree with a shrug. "Just a lot of water."

"But where does it lead?" she demanded.

"Well, the Northern Isles and Delenor eventually," he observed. "We live on a sphere, after all."

"So, no one has tried to cross it?" Dryana's merchant nose was twitching at the possibilities.

"People have tried, but no human has made it," he replied.

"No *human*?" she pressed.

"The crystal ships of the Syn'Dion'Gar appear in the ports of Amaland and eastern Nerlinea but rarely. Tales tell of them coming from the east, not the west, but as we know, they travel under water, so who knows from which direction they really come from."

"I've never heard those tales and I've been here longer than you," she observed.

"I was here a long time ago, and I suspect it has been even longer since the crystal ships moored here," explained the Tancree.

Dryana shrugged and surveyed the hall. It had been set with long rows of low tables running down the length of the building, three rows of tables in each section of the building either side of the central row of columns. On either side, thick carpets were laid across the flagstones. Oblong cushions were arranged on the carpets in long lines either side of the tables. The guests could use them to prop themselves up as they ate. At the far end of one hall a raised dais had been set up, with a series of steps up running the length of the platform. A similar collection of tables and low cushions had been arranged along the dais.

"Who are you?" a woman demanded of the two Slayers, a short young Nerlinean with bony features and coal-black hair. She carried a wooden board on which papers had been tied, and a thin ink brush. A small inkpot with a narrow aperture dangled from a string attached to the board.

"Dryana and Slinker Slayer," replied the witch politely.

The officious young woman ran the end of her brush down the front page on her wooden tablet, a list of some sort. She flipped over the next page and then the next. Her frown deepened on each page. She seemed about to demand they leave. She reached the final page on her board and ran her brush down. It stopped halfway. A momentary look of surprise registered on her face before she carefully concealed it.

"My apologies, Lord and Lady," she said, her tone turning cloyingly deferential. "You are on table six just below the dais."

The woman pointed up the hall towards the platform.

The pair wandered up the hall until they were two tables down from the dais, in the far-right line of tables. A small gold six had been painted in the centre of the pale wooden surface. The pair took a seat, propping their backs against the hard cushions. Several men and women were already seated, all Nerlineans by dress, though they appeared to be of different ethnicities – several easterners and a smaller handful of western Nerlineans. The man in front of them was tall, close to six feet in height. His black hair was pulled back in a ponytail, with hints of grey at the temples and lines around the eyes that suggested he was older than he looked. His light brown face was smooth shaven. He was dressed in a loose-fitting expensive silk shirt that hung halfway open and, unusually for a Nerlinean, trousers.

"A Tancree! What a wonder. It has been a long time since I saw one of your kind," declared the man.

He thrust out his hand in the western fashion to clasp Slinker's emaciated claw and pumped it enthusiastically.

"Camlyn of Haldorn," the man announced. "Wonderful to meet you."

Slinker was so shocked at the man's behaviour he almost forgot to speak.

"Slinker. Slinker Slayer," he managed to get out.

"Dryana Slayer." The witch thrust her hand out.

Camlyn shook it, but he remained more interested in Slinker.

"Who thought I would meet the last War Mage of the Tancree?"

The man was beaming with excitement at a very confused Slinker. This was by far the warmest reception he had received from a stranger since arriving in Nerlinea.

Dryana got a sinking feeling. She had suddenly realized who was sitting in front of her.

"You are Camlyn Dumech of Haldorn." She bowed her head politely.

She was busy scanning the tables around her, realizing she was surrounded by Nerlinean nobles, and senior ones at that. Senior military figures from the fleet and the legions were seated further down from the dais. So were the bureaucrats. She was seated with the ruling class of Nerlinea, not the merchants.

"I think we may be seated in the wrong section." Dryana's voice had taken on a very uncharacteristic tone of worry.

She had meant to mutter it to Slinker, but it had come out louder than she intended.

"Not at all." The voice was female, confident with a touch of warm honey.

Dryana looked up at the woman standing on the opposite side of the table, next to where Camlyn sat. She was beautiful, thin, with copper-coloured skin. Her tight green dress laced with silver showed off her wiry figure. Curly black hair streamed down her back almost to her waist. On first glance she looked young, perhaps even younger than Dryana, but there was something in the eyes that suggested she was much older than she looked. There was also a gnawing sense of familiarity about the woman, and then Dryana placed it. The sinking feeling she was experiencing became plunging.

"My wife," indicated Camlyn, not really rudely but with a lot less interest than he had shown Slinker.

The woman took her seat next to her husband.

"Srias," the woman introduced herself. She did not extend her hand. "And no, my Lady Slayer, you are exactly where you should be. After all, where else should a Lady of Kangorn be seated but among the ruling class of Nerlinea? And the last of the Tancree – surely no guest could be more special."

Dryana gaped at Srias Halfnight Pandus. Suddenly she knew why she had felt such a sense of familiarity. This was

Charlotte Halfnight Pandus' mother, though in age she looked more like her sister. Charlotte was pretty enough, but had a rattiness to her features that seemed endemic to the Pandus family. Srias was the most beautiful woman – in fact, the most stunning human – that Dryana had ever seen. Her mouth felt oddly dry.

"I believe you know my daughter?" Srias observed.

"I do, my lady. We spent much time together on Kangorn, though it was some years ago," replied Dryana. Her tone etched with caution.

"Charlotte," grunted Camlyn. "Ludicrous name, stupid Pandus tradition, don't know why I agreed to it."

Srias shot her husband a malevolent look, which did nothing to dispel her beauty or to discourage Camlyn,

"I mean, Charles, Charis, Charlotte," the Dumech of Haldorn's mocking continued. "Where did you family get such ridiculous names. So much 'Ch' for one family."

Camlyn laughed riotously at his own joke, and a few of those around him joined in politely. The nervous Slayers joined in unconvincingly. Srias rolled her eyes in frustration at her husband's behaviour and swung her glance back to the Slayers.

"I met your brother, I believe," Srias informed Dryana. "That was some years ago too. We spent some time together at the last Amanthagan."

Dryana's nose wrinkled angrily at the implication; or at least what she thought Srias was trying to imply. She glanced over at Camlyn, wondering what his reaction would be to his wife hinting she had slept with another man. He seemed unbothered. In truth, he had grown bored with the exchange and was now speaking to the man to his right. Perhaps he did not care what his wife did or, lost in another conversation, he simply had not heard.

Dryana assessed the woman in front of her. She was beautiful all right, but hardly Kyrian's type – and her brother very much had a type. She decided that the woman was simply trying to goad her. She did not need a reason; after all, the Slayers and the Pandus were old enemies. She was surprised that anyone had been foolish enough to seat them in such close proximity.

"I wanted to meet, so I prevailed on the emperor to seat us together," explained Srias, as if reading Dryana's thoughts.

From another merchant such a claim would have seemed ludicrous, but from the operational head of the Imperial Pandus Trading Company it might just be true. Only one merchant stood higher in the councils of the Imperial Court: Srias' grandfather, Zem. Dryana doubted that the emperor bothered with anything as mundane as the seating plan at a banquet, but the fact Srias could influence whichever member of court did was impressive. The question was why. The antipathy between the two went back to the very foundation of the Company of Slayers. Charlotte Halfnight Pandus had formed a wary friendship with Dryana on Kangorn, but it never extended beyond the pair to their wider families and companies. Still, while things had been quiet between the competing merchant companies for the last five years, that did not mean things were forgotten on either side. Dryana knew Srias had a purpose in arranging this meeting.

"An odd desire. We are enemies, are we not?" Dryana observed. It was better to get to the point, she decided.

She could feel Slinker flinch at her candid response.

"So blunt. How very western. I wanted a meeting…"

Srias was cut off mid-sentence as a bellow of trumpets thundered across the hall. The collection of seated merchants, nobles and dignitaries all swivelled as one. Cushions were pushed back and everyone, from the lowest servant to the highest Dumech, placed their foreheads to the floor, fully kowtowing before the Emperor of Nerlinea.

"Nyandar the Ninth, Emperor of Nerlinea, Hadanan of Amaland, Ran'Dumech'Di'Gar, King of Kings, Overlord of the Oceans, Wellspring of Greatness, Lord of the House of Elian-Jeddera, Blood of the Dragon Lords of Old!" the voice of the Imperial Herald roared across the vast hall.

It echoed back from the far end of the building.

Guards in the blue and green of the Palace Legion, the emperor's personal guard, spilled through a door to the rear of the dais, circling around to take up position in front of it. A dozen men and women, dressed in robes of turquoise and amber, followed them out and took up position behind the guards: the emperor's mages. Then Nyandar strode through the door and mounted the steps at the rear of the dais. He wore a tunic of purple trimmed with gold; simpler clothes than many in attendance. His gaze swept the hall. Behind him, a group of dignitaries filed in and up the steps, taking their places either side of the emperor. The Dumech of Ren was among them, as were two of Nyandar's concubines, but none of his wives. The line stood in silence either side of the emperor, heads bowed. The emperor's piercing brown eyes continued to take in the scene of crouched subjects before him.

He took a seat on the dais, sitting himself on the carpet propped up on a cushion. He took one final look at the crowd and gave a nonchalant wave.

"You may be seated," the imperial herald declared.

The crowd crawled out of their supplicant positions and seated themselves back at the low tables. Heads remained bowed; eyes cast down for fear that they might look upon the emperor.

The emperor gave the herald another signal.

"A writ of vision is declared!" the herald's voice rang out.

A rumble of surprise filled the hall. Srias looked up. Dryana's eyes followed her.

"Stupid western custom," Srias muttered under her breath.

"It's a custom over a millennium old," her husband gently chided her.

"Stupid Kanath custom," she said a little louder, as if that was somehow worse.

That seemed to raise only a wry smile from the Dumech of Haldorn.

A spontaneous round of applause was spilling down from the back of the hall towards the emperor. The emperor gave a wave of acceptance as the Slayers and the surrounding nobles joined in the applause.

"A writ of vision?" Dryana whispered to Slinker.

"The right to look at the emperor," the Tancree explained. "For the duration of the audience."

Servants were bringing out food: wide platters of curried meat and vegetables; pieces of poultry marinated in a yellow spice on skewers; rice in vat-like bowls. They were served first to the platform and then working down the hall from the dais end to the great doors at the far end.

Now able to look up, Dryana took in the emperor. He looked younger than she expected; she placed him in his early thirties. He was the quintessential easterner with no hint of the mix of bloods that permeated his family line. His dark black hair was long, pulled back, and held up in a topknot that rose out of his crown then flowed down his back. Shrewd brown eyes, obvious even at this distance, played across the hall as he picked at his food. He sat like a coiled serpent waiting to strike.

Next to him chattering in his ear was the young Dumech of Ren, Pu Zin. Just out of his teens, he was a sallow, bony young man, who looked as though his skin had been stretched over his sharp frame. He had recently taken the position after his father's retirement. Like much in the empire, the way positions of authority were allocated seemed to be a mystery to anyone who was not born Nerlinean. A family might hold the title of Dumech through several generations, sometimes as many as five or six, and then suddenly be deprived of it, sometimes for good reason, sometimes for no reason at all. Dumechates would be broken up or merged together. An eastern family that had ruled an eastern Dumechate for three generations could find themselves sent north, south or west to govern a province they had never visited, often with a different culture and on occasions even a different language.

Dryana carried on down the line. At the far end was a young man, more a boy on the cusp of his teens, and the woman next to him was a surprise. She was Kanath, a stick-thin redhead with darting green eyes. She seemed to be deferring to the boy next to her.

"Who is that?" asked Dryana of Slinker, nodding at the far end of the table where the Kanath woman sat.

"The boy, Prince Anudin, Dumech of Las Ma," supplied Srias without being asked.

"I meant the woman," said Dryana.

"Oh, that's his wife," Srias replied absentmindedly.

"Bit old," Dryana observed quietly.

Srias shrugged. "She is the last Duke of Las Ma's daughter," she explained. "Samantha KalElian KalJeddera."

Dryana looked at the woman and a sense of sorrow filled her. She knew Leo, Duke of Las Ma, had died a year past in exile. Saliana had been insistent that the Slayers keep themselves informed of his sojourn in the east, and she knew he had daughters. She had just not expected to see one in the emperor's retinue. It seemed odd seeing the woman who should be ruler of Krenakealtron seated almost as a hanger-on at the emperor's table. Not that the title High King of Krenakealtron meant anything anymore; it had meant little for centuries.

Dryana was so lost in her thoughts, she had not realized everyone at her table was standing. She quickly rose to her feet to find that the emperor had come down from the platform and was standing among them.

"Camlyn Halfnight. How is my favourite general?" the emperor asked on sighting the Dumech of Haldorn. He gathered the shocked Camlyn in a bear hug, more like soldiers on campaign than absolute ruler and imperial subject.

"Good, sir; good, your imperial majesty," the Dumech stuttered out.

"And your wife. A pleasure, as ever." The emperor gave Srias the barest nod.

Judging from the shock on the nobles' faces, Dryana could only assume this behaviour was uncharacteristic for a Nerlinean Emperor. She tried to sneak behind Slinker.

"A Tancree. How fascinating," Nyandar remarked.

Slinker gave a head bow to the emperor.

"Zin, he's as cadaverous as you are, though taller," laughed the emperor.

The lanky Dumech of Ren had just arrived behind the imperial presence, trying to work out why the emperor had decided to ruin his carefully choreographed banquet.

"Very witty, your imperial majesty," said Pu Zin, trying for a smile.

"Tell your eyes, Zin, not just your face," the emperor rejoined with another smile, but with an edge of menace in his voice. "I'm an emperor, after all." He continued to muse. "The last Tancree," he said.

"It is an honour for me as a humble trader to meet you, your imperial majesty," Slinker responded.

"A humble trader," mocked the emperor. "The last War Mage of the Tancree. Did I bring enough mages?"

The emperor swept back, indicating the dozen or so figures still standing station behind the guards. All were focused on the imperial encounter taking place a few yards in front of them. Slinker could feel the power radiating from them.

Particularly the young man in the middle, his name was Ko Quan, Nyandar's favourite wizard, and one of the most powerful in Nerlinea. In this room he outmatched everyone for magical talent with the possible exception of Slinker and the Nerlinean had youth on his side.

"I am no threat to your imperial majesty. I am your servant." Slinker tried to pitch his tone between supplication and humour – not that the Tancree's leering smile was ever likely to set anyone at ease.

"And you. Who are you?" The emperor was staring at Dryana now.

"Dryana Slayer," she replied, taking an instant dislike to the man.

If Nyandar noticed the lack of any honorific, he said nothing, although the appalled faces of everyone around him spoke instead.

"You are a pretty young thing," the emperor observed.

Dryana's stony gaze was her only answer. The emperor seemed unperturbed by this unusual response.

"You will join us tomorrow at the Temple of Thytha." The emperor's tone was a command.

"It would be our honour, your imperial majesty," Slinker replied, trying to defuse the situation.

"Just the girl, just the girl," clarified Nyandar. "Until tomorrow."

Then he disappeared down the tables, the Dumech of Ren scampering after him introducing fawning dignitaries and citizens as he went.

"Gods, he hasn't changed," muttered Camlyn with a smile. "When he was a prince, he was after every woman he met. You'd think with the harem he has now, he would have calmed down. Guess not?"

Srias glanced at her husband with a hint of distaste at his far too approving tone. Dryana looked aghast. Her mind was racing. What had she just got herself into? More importantly, how could she get out of it? Despite her being an enemy, Dryana looked more to Srias than to her fellow Slayer.

"Men," grunted Srias despairingly. "Tomorrow is the Festival of Illthagan. I doubt he invited you to that for the sake of seducing you."

"Thank the gods," Dryana sighed.

Dryana was aware of the Festival of Illthagan. It was held to celebrate the transition from autumn to winter, although it lacked any real significance here in Port Ren, where differences between the seasons were minimal. It was an old Gar festival adopted by the Nerlineans. It formally started the next day and culminated a week later. Only the last three days were actively celebrated, and that was mostly around the temples of Cragon KalShon and Kay, the God of Autumn and the Goddess of Winter respectively.

"My understanding is the emperor wishes to make his obeisance before the Great Goddess and to view the Illth'Di'Gar. That is why he came here," explained Srias.

"Illth'Di'Gar?" Slinker sounded nervous.

"What is the Illth'Di'Gar?" asked Dryana, perplexed.

Camlyn shot her a look that implied she was an uneducated bumpkin. "It is a musical instrument, a flute; it is said that Cragon played it to send his sister Kay to sleep and bring on winter. In the spring Sidarra steals the Illth'Di'Gar from Cragon and uses it to wake the world from its slumber," he explained.

"So, it's a fairy tale?" Dryana was only getting more confused.

"A religious story about death and rebirth," said Camlyn. "We may be more tolerant in our faith than those from the West, but we do not like our beliefs being mocked."

"I apologize," said Dryana. "I am just trying to understand."

"Well, it has sat in the care of the priestesses of Thytha for the last thousand years, so I doubt the gods are using it to turn the seasons," the Dumech of Haldron said with a broad, friendly smile.

Dryana decided that Camlyn was playing with her and let out a breath. Slinker looked worried, while Srias seemed positively gleeful.

Dryana was missing something. "What?" she demanded.

"The Illth'Di'Gar," Slinker muttered.

"The Illth'Di'Gar," Srias repeated. "The Flute of the Elves. Do you want to tell her or should I?"

"Tell me what?" Dryana asked.

"What happened the last time that a necromancer stood in the presence of the Flute of the Elves?" Srias' smile widened to an evil grin.

CHAPTER NINE – THE FLUTE OF THE ELVES

They called it a Temple of Thytha, but in truth it was more like a large park. Dryana had first visited it when she had arrived in Port Ren, some years ago. After all, her powers were said to come from the Great Mother Goddess, although she had not felt the presence of the goddess when she had come here that time. Her mother had called the Great Goddess Lynidine, the Kanath name for goddess of earth and oceans. Lynidine had been praised in the woods at night when Dryana was growing up, for the worship of the old Kanath gods was forbidden by their monotheistic Sevain overlords. Dryana had attended Balinor's wedding at the Temple of Lynidine on Kangorn, expecting to experience the same sensation she had in those dark mercurial nights with her mother, but she had not. To her it was just another big building.

Only on Syndion had Dryana had the experience. Saliana had taken her to a small, wooded grove, not far from the port of Backistri, that the Gar had once held sacred to Thytha, the mother goddess shared by the Gar and the Nerlineans. The grove had been overgrown by years of neglect; its open centre choked with brambles and small shrubs. Nevertheless, for the first time since the death of her mother, Dryana had felt something of the brightness of the Great Mother, compared with the darkness that normally burned inside her. She had broken down in tears, sobbing like a child. Saliana had held her, saying nothing, just letting her young friend weep, releasing heaving sobs.

In the weeks that had followed, Dryana had cleared the centre of the grove, pressing her reluctant brother into service to speed up the process. The task had been half done when Saliana had informed Dryana she was being sent to Kangorn to manage the Company of Slayers' operations there. Dryana had argued with Sali about it, but the Mistress of the Slayers had been unmovable. Dryana had only agreed to go when Saliana had promised to bring in priestesses from Nerlinea to finish the job. Sali had been as good as her word. This had all been years ago, before Balinor's marriage.

The Temple of Thytha covered a large open expanse of grassland, sitting on the low hills that rose up from the shallow valley where the trading heart of Port Ren was located. Dryana suspected the park had originally been located outside the city, but as the urban sprawl had grown further across the landscape it had been subsumed, becoming a large park among the teeming streets of Port Ren.

The rectangular park was surrounded by a wide road. Originally designed as a religious processional, it had now become one of the main thoroughfares for cart traffic passing from one part of city to the other. It had effectively turned the Temple of Thytha into a roundabout for this part of the city.

PRINCE OF SLAYERS

Dryana and Slinker pushed through the crowds in one of the side streets heading for the temple-garden. They walked along unaccompanied by bodyguards or other hangers-on. Slinker had his fighting blades strapped to his back and Dryana wore her short sword at her belt. This alone was enough to raise eyebrows among the Nerlinean citizenry.

Dryana stepped into the large street surrounding the park, before leaping back as a huffrin-drawn cart trundled past, nearly crushing her. The lizard barked at her with annoyance. She heard a curse from the driver. She ignored it. Such was typical on the streets of Port Ren. She looked left and right as huffrin-drawn wagons continued to hustle past. The lizards may have been slow-moving compared to an iribis or an oradar, but they were not moving slowly enough to simply walk around, particularly when getting flattened was the punishment for making a mistake. The fact that couriers and the like, mounted on fast-moving iribis, were dodging with practised ease through the gaps in the cart traffic only made transit even more dangerous for hapless pedestrians.

Dryana looked for a gap and set off across the road, Slinker hot on her heels. The pair skipped into the park in the manner of people who had narrowly missed being run down but were trying to convince anyone watching that there had never been any real risk. They stood on one of the short sides of the park, half a mile in width, the rest of it lying before them running for two and a half miles before reaching the surrounding road on the other side. Ornamental lakes, rock features with small waterfalls and narrow streams were a feature of this end of the park. Officially part of the Temple of Thytha, it was used as a place of relaxation and exercise for the citizens on rest days and holy days. Today it was neither, and those moving through the park were largely those who wanted to get somewhere else.

Dryana and Slinker were heading for the centre of the park, dominated by a large expanse of grass. It was kept short and used for sports, athletic events and a martial arts practice area. It was mid-morning and Dryana would have expected to see a large number of people taking advantage of the open space. Instead, it was quiet. No, that was not right: it was empty. The pair circled a large lake that sat at the head of the grass plain. A few people were spread along the edge of the lake, trying to see across the lawn on the other side. The path passed into a small coppice of trees, and immediately they ran into many more Nerlineans. They were clustered in the wood, hanging from trees, crouched in the bushes, looking out over the open expanse of grass. Slinker and Dryana found they had to push past annoyed citizens. Shouts of "we were here first!" and similar filled the air.

Two guards in the blue and green robes of the Palace Legion used rectangular black wattle shields to thrust the protesting citizenry out of the path as they approached the two Slayers. They said nothing but, having collected Dryana and Slinker, they pushed back through the crowd on the path until they reached the point where it opened out onto the lawn. More legionaries stood in a group where the path joined the field. A few more were interspersed among the crowd in the wood.

A man with the badge of an officer on his breast stepped in front of them and gave them the barest of nods. He looked back over his shoulder to where a middle-aged woman, short, with long black hair, was standing. She wore a silk coat done up the front with silver buttons. Dryana could not work out whether she was a priestess or some sort of courtier. Her dress suggested status. Wordlessly she pointed at Dryana. The soldier nodded. He looked back at Dryana. He pointed her sword.

"You are chatty," Dryana observed sardonically in Nerlinean.

"Surrender the sword," he demanded.

His accent was strong, hard to understand, and Dryana wondered where he was from. He looked like an easterner, but his eyes were harder, the cast of his face more open and harsher than the average enigmatic Nerlinean. She pulled the scabbard out of the ring from which it hung on her belt and handed it to him. He handed it back to one of his subordinates. She looked to Slinker, knowing how attached the Tancree was to his fighting blades. Would he give them up, if only temporarily, she wondered?

Slinker looked unhappy but made his decision and started to unstrap the webbing that held them in place on his back.

"You stay here, breaker. Keep your arm blades," said the guard captain.

The Tancree's eye flashed angrily at the name 'breaker'. At least that was what Dryana thought the guard had said. Her Nerlinean was good, but it was a tonal language; small differences in inflection could change the meaning of the word, and his accent was really strong.

"Seems like this Narazgoner son of a whore won't let me accompany you," declared Slinker loudly.

The guards around the captain bristled at that, and the captain himself let out a laugh, seemingly unconcerned by Slinker casting aspersions about at least one of his parents.

"Not my decision, breaker; you just aren't invited," he grinned.

"Go on without me," Slinker said to Dryana.

"Breaker?" she asked.

"Long story; a hate from ancient times. He's from Narazgon, from the coast," replied the Tancree.

Dryana was desperate to know more, but she had places to be.

"Try not to kill them," she said in Kanath.

Despite Kanath being her native tongue, she had been brought up speaking mostly Sevain, only speaking Kanath with her family, so it was not that easy to use. She had no desire to warn him in Nerlinean, and the trade language, Westerly, which the Slayers normally used, was close enough to Nerlinean to risk her being partly understood. She would have preferred Sevain, but Slinker did not speak it, and she had no knowledge of Tancree. Slinker might be the last person alive who could still speak his native language.

"Sure, no problem. I'll do my best not to kill them." His reply was in Nerlinean and loud enough for everyone nearby to hear.

Dryana rolled her eyes at Slinker. She looked to the captain, but he just seemed amused. He made a gesture indicating she should go out onto the grass. The witch gave her fellow Slayer a last look of concern and with a shrug walked out onto the lawn. The sun blazed down on her face. The sun was baking, despite the time of year, and she wondered for the first time if this place had any seasons at all.

The grass was green; a triumph of irrigation, she mused. She set out walking across the field, heading for the altar, which she knew stood at its centre. Swishing across the grass in her black silks, she felt a thousand gazes upon her. She could see figures in the trees around the lawn, trying to keep out of sight. The presence of the legionaries among them would be sufficient to prevent anyone stepping out on the grass.

The central grove lay in the centre of the lawn, a fair walk from where Dryana had entered from the coppice. She had come the better part of a mile with the sun beating down on her, and sweat coursed down her face. It was wrong to call it a grove: it was too neat, too impersonal for that. There was a large circle of ten trees, and spreading out from this ring were five lines each of another ten trees, creating a sun or star-like pattern. They were vast, old cypresses stabbing up into the sky reaching ninety to a hundred feet in height. They towered over those assembled below them.

Dryana had a sinking feeling as she passed the first of the trees. They were all standing there waiting for her. Had she got the time wrong? She looked up at the sun and at the shadows cast by the trees, trying to guess the rough time of day. She had been told to arrive at this time, she was sure of it. Maybe she was simply the last to arrive, but the look of the crowd as she approached suggested otherwise. They had that sweaty irritable look of people who had been standing waiting for far too long.

The Emperor Nyandar was present, standing in loose-fitting robes of blue silk. Dryana stopped at the sight of him and moved to supplicate herself as was required.

"Please stop, my lady." His voice was gentle but commanding. "We are in your house, after all."

She pulled herself up straight, having been halfway to her knees. "My house?" she murmured. Her face was riven with confusion, an odd look on her normally confident visage. "What do you mean, your imperial majesty?" she asked warily.

"Are you not a child of the Great Goddess?" the emperor asked with a warm smile.

Dryana was still cautious. The warmth seemed genuine, but there were always layers, always complexities.

"Are we not all children of the Great Goddess, your imperial majesty?" she observed, more caustically than the polite tone she had been aiming for.

"'Sir' is sufficient; less of a tongue tie than the constant majesties," Nyandar replied. "But yes, we are all the children of Thytha – or, as you would call her, Lynidine.

Dryana held off explaining there were very real differences between the two goddesses despite the Nerlinean tendency to equate the two. Given the rapidly diminishing number of worshippers of Lynidine, she doubted it would matter much in the long term.

"Some of her children are more favoured than others, though," Nyandar observed.

"Who told you that?" She added "Sir" almost as an afterthought.

"They did," he nodded over his shoulder.

He looked past him. She recognized some of those standing in the group behind him, those she had seen when she arrived. Mostly older men, though a few women were scattered among the two dozen people. There were no guards, in the group or in the near vicinity, though there were at least two mages, judging by their robes. None of the group carried weapons anyway. Dumech Camlyn Halfnight was there, as was Pu Zin, Dumech of Ren. Another seven men standing near them were also Dumechs or similar nobles, judging by their dress and demeanour. There was no sign of Srias. Her eyes rested on Samantha KalElian, the daughter of the late Duke of Las Ma. She could not see the woman's youthful husband, and wondered why was she here without him. There were two who looked too much like Nyandar not to be relatives. A teenage boy was possibly a younger brother of the emperor; he looked too old to be a son, though it was just possible. Then there was a woman, eerily like Nyandar, despite the hairstyle and make-up. Was this the elder half-sister, the wife of the emperor? The one he had used to cement his power, but who was still denied the title of empress? She stared sourly at the Slayer witch. Finally, there were a dozen priests and priestesses, judging by their attire. Not just of the goddess Thytha, but also of the hunter god Rasmanor, Sidarra the Mistress of Rains and Jeddera Summersword, but oddly, given the nature of the festival, none of the god Cragon or the goddess Kay.

The leaders spiritual and temporal of the Nerlinean Empire were present; some of them, at least. They might know who Dryana was. They might know who the Company of Slayers were. Some of them might even care, but she doubted it. Her reputation as a witch and a necromancer had not made the journey east with her, and it was unlikely that they knew of it. Even those who likely did, such as Camlyn Halfnight, would know it only as a story, hardly something to vouch for her with the emperor.

Then she caught something in her peripheral vision, and cursed silently. Nyandar had nodded over his left shoulder, but she had looked over his right, because that was where the group of people had been. But they were not the only group. There was another. They had somehow blended in with the trunks of the cypress trees, which should have been impossible given the wide-open space between the trees and their lack of lower branches. The branches had long been trimmed off or simply fallen away as the trees had grown. There was nowhere to hide, except behind the trunks of the towering trees themselves, and for some reason she did not think that was what they had done. They had just stood next to them and become one with them. Was it magic or simply some deep understanding of nature that no human could match? Who knew with the Gar? There were six of them, all over six feet in height. They stood in distinct pairs one behind the other, as if afraid to come too close to each other.

The pair nearest were Quil'Gar, or Fire Elves, as the Nerlineans called them. They lived on a plateau to the north of the Nerlinean Empire, where it swept down from the Havagian highlands reaching the Farthest Ocean. Surrounded on three sides by mountain ranges and water to the east, the land of Quil'Dath had over the centuries fought off repeated attempts by its neighbours to conquer it. A token fealty was paid to the Nerlinean Empire as the least worst of its neighbours. There was one female and one male, with almost translucent pale skin and sharp features framed by white-blond hair. So much like the Gar Dryana had met before; so much like Saliana, she mused.

JUSTIN WAINE

The two figures behind them looked very different to their Quil'Gar compatriots. They were Debion'Gar, the Gar of the sands. They were a common enough sight in Port Ren and its surrounding provinces, though most still lived as nomads on the fringes of the great desert that scarred the centre of northern Nerlinea. Stories said that these Gar had once ruled Ren itself, before the Nerlinean conquest. Their skin was brown like deep burnished copper, their black hair, tied in tight braids, hung down to their waists, and their dark eyes surveyed the scene warily. Dryana wondered why, for the Debion'Gar had long been under the sway of the Nerlinean Emperor.

It took a moment for her to recognize the final two figures standing almost in hiding behind the Quil'Gar and the Debion'Gar. They looked much like their Quil'Gar cousins, though their clothes were a little different. It was the cold arrogance with which they stood, the confidence that marked them out as Syn'Dion'Gar. And she recognized them, for these two she had met before. They were both male, unlike the other pairs. On the left was a warrior dressed in shining armour of alcidide, though he carried no weapon. He stood unconcernedly in the sweltering heat, helmet clasped under his arm. The final figure was a male Gar, so old that he actually looked aged, a rarity among their kind. He was dressed in a simple green tunic over brown breeches. In his hands he clasped a six-foot staff, on which gnarled branches seemed to sprout from the head, curling around a large blue jewel. She knew them and they knew her, for they had stood behind the Lady of the Crystal Ships that day on Syndion. They had seen Dryana in command of the dead, an army of them.

Dryana licked her lips nervously. What had she walked into? Was it some sort of trap set just for her? She dismissed the idea; she wasn't important enough to justify this elaborate stage play. So why was she here?

PRINCE OF SLAYERS

"Some of these I believe you know?" the emperor addressed her with a knowing smile, indicating the two Syn'Dion'Gar.

"We have met once before, though we were never formally introduced, sir," she replied to Nyandar, her tone still wary.

"Well, we must change that. May I introduce my cousin Syndanor KalElian, Dumech of the Syn'Dion'Gar," announced Nyandar.

He was pointing at the younger of the two Syn'Dion'Gar. The Gar dressed in full armour showed no reaction at being introduced or, for that matter, being referenced as a cousin. Dryana's gaze wandered across to the pale, redheaded form of Samantha KalElian, another cousin. They were all so different in appearance it was impossible to believe they were related. They were all so keen to claim descent from a man nearly a millennium dead.

"And this is Greldin of the Way." Nyandar now indicated the Gar clutching the gnarled staff. "A priest of Thytha and a representative of the Trendorn of the Syn'Dion'Gar. Sadly, the Lady of the Crystal Ships cannot be in attendance for this rite."

So, the war leader of the Syn'Dion'Gar and a representative of the high priestess of the same people. Dryana's gaze played across the other Gar, stood in pairs. A male in armour and a female in the dress of a priestess. She leapt to the correct conclusion: a Dumech and a Trendorn, a male war leader and a female high priestess, the rulers of their respective tribes of Gar. Once, millennia ago, the Gar had been one people, their rulers matriarchal: a high priestess known as the Trendorn. When they had gone to war, the Trendorn had selected the best war leader from among her people and taken him as her lover. He would lead the Gar in war and was granted the title Dumech. Over time, the title Dumech had become the right of the

131

husband of the Trendorn, rather than being selected during each war. If the Trendorn was unmarried then the rank of Dumech would be held by a close male relative until the Trendorn married or a new Trendorn acceded to the position.

This had been the old way of succession, before the Gar had split into seven separate tribes, and the Syn'Dion'Gar had kept to it. For the Trendorn'Di'Syn'Dion'Gar claimed to be direct descendants from the ancient priestesses who had ruled the Gar as one united people. As they had spread across the world of Galvia, the Gar had adapted and changed with the environments they encountered. Customs had been abandoned; different cultures had started to grow up within a single people. Leaders had risen up who, if not challenging the Trendorn and the Dumech, competed with them for loyalty. There had been a great council, a Gathering of the People: an Aman'Thy'Gar, in the old tongue of the Elves. The council had decided that the seven greatest leaders of the Gar should have their own peoples, each ruled by a Trendorn and a Dumech, a priestess and a warrior. The Trendorn of the Gar became the Trendorn of the Syn'Dion'Gar, the people of the Summer Dawn. Perhaps to soften the blow or for fear of offending the gods, the Trendorn'Di'Syn'Dion'Gar was given the title Su'Trendorn, over-priestess, a term of precedence, veneration and respect, but with no real power except what the incumbent could make of it.

The Gar had resolved in peace to become seven peoples from what had once been one and to meet every decade in a gathering, the Aman'Thy'Gar, to resolve the differences between them. It had been the new Dumech of the Fal'Gar, a people who had already abandoned the matriarchal system of rulership for a hereditary male war leader, who proposed that the people needed a Ran'Dumech'Di'Gar. This Great War Leader could call the tribes to war when threatened from without by the Mourn or by the rising tide of humanity. The title could not pass to the Dumech of the Syn'Dion'Gar, or the council would have achieved nothing but changing the titles of its highest rulers. The Dumech'Di'Fal'Gar had assumed, as the greatest warrior of the Gar, that the title would be his for the asking, but the Dumech'Di'Den'Sar'Gar, another warrior lord, had also sought to be recognized as the Ran'Dumech.

The Trendorn of the Syn'Dion'Gar, realizing that all her efforts to resolve the disputes among her people peaceably were suddenly ebbing, reached a compromise. Using the rivalry between the two warlords to neuter each one's claim to military leadership, she resolved there would be Ran'Dumech'Di'Gar, but it would be the Dumech'Di'Dal'Ri'Gar who took the title. The others at the council agreed. For the Dal'Ri'Gar were not only the least numerous of the seven Gar peoples, but also the least warlike. The council's attempt to marginalize the position of Ran'Dumech had not succeeded. The threat from outside enemies meant that the Gar would have to fight on more than one occasion as a single people, and the position achieved greater political significance than the largely ceremonial position of Su'Trendorn, but that had been thousands of years ago. Now the Gar were standing in the presence of a human emperor awaiting his pleasure.

"Are you happy for us to proceed, Greldin?" asked Nyandar of the Gar.

"Of course, your imperial majesty." The tone was singsong, his Nerlinean accent odd, but his eyes were hard and cold.

"Bring it," Nyandar ordered to no one in particular.

The chief priestess of Thytha standing among the dumechs let out a keening wail. It pierced the air, moving out from the cypresses and across the surrounding field. It was taken up by the other priestesses. Dryana felt a prickle on her skin, a song in her mind, not something she had experienced for a long time, since she had worked with her mother. Someone else was using what her mother had called the Gift of the

133

Goddess, the power of the witch. She had never thought to use it in amplifying sound. That was what more than one of the priestesses present were doing. The mages shifted uncomfortably; they could feel the hint of power in the air, but it was not the power that they accessed, and she could see it made them nervous. That made her smile a little; it was a change for wizards to feel discomfited by the manipulation of unseen forces, especially when done with so much more subtlety than the mages usually managed.

A procession had started down a path from the far end of the park. Ten soldiers from the Palace Legion were leading the way, a commander out front and three rows of three guards, marching in neat formation. Behind them came more priests of Rasmanor, Thytha and all the other gods and goddesses. Next in the procession were four priests of Jeddera Summersword, wearing charcoal-grey cloaks over red tunics. They were Nerlineans but the clothing was designed in the Kanath style and looked odd on them. Hoisted between them on two long brass poles was a small wooden chest. Behind them came more priests and another troop of ten legionnaires.

Whatever was in the box must be important, speculated Dryana, to warrant the guards, given that the whole park was swarming with soldiers, even if they were trying to keep out of sight. She watched as the procession made its ponderous progress towards the cypress trees. It took nearly half an hour, and the baking heat was leaving her drenched with sweat. She could feel the skin on her shoulders starting to burn despite the cover of the cypresses. The faces of the waiting Nerlineans looked largely bored, while the Gar were impassive. The Emperor Nyandar was watching the procession with a borderline fanatical stare, almost bobbing from one foot to the other in excitement.

The procession finally arrived at the edge of the cypresses to be greeted by relieved looks from the Nerlineans and continued indifference from the Gar. The soldiers and the priests not carrying the chest filtered left and right of the grove and took up position on the edge of the tree temple. The four priests of the Summersword bearing the chest continued to the centre of the cypresses, where a small stone altar the height of a table rested. The priests had to manoeuvre the long brass poles on which they carried their charge around two large cypresses each side of the stone. Eventually they rested the chest on the stone altar and gingerly pulled out the brass poles from the rings on the sides of the box. They rested the poles either side of the altar and stepped back, performing a shallow head bow to the altar. They turned away and approached the six Gar present. Then they bowed to the Gar. Dryana registered a moment of confusion; there was something odd about the bow. Then she realized what it was: the priests were bowing in the western style, bending from the waist and sweeping their leg back. Except they had clearly never seen it done properly, so it looked wrong, a custom passed down through hundreds of years. Gar present, odd western bows at a Nerlinean ceremony... there was something peculiar about this rite, the Slayer decided.

Then it got stranger. The four priests crossed the grove until they were standing in front of Samantha KalElian, and gave the same bow to her. Her stoic face suggested she had expected this to happen. Dryana looked on in shock, wondering why the daughter of the last Duke of Las Ma was important to this ceremony. Then it occurred to her that it had been the Slayers who had been tasked by the Nerlinean Emperor with rescuing the Duke of Las Ma. The Slayers had assumed it was for reasons of political advantage; certainly the price paid was more than expected if based simply on a claim of distant family kinship. Was it at least in part so that the Duke of Las Ma could stand at this ceremony? she wondered. Leo of Las Ma was dead and now his daughter was standing here, but she was not the ruler of Las Ma, her husband having been granted that largely imaginary title on her father's death.

The priests of Jeddera Summersword moved around to Nyandar and made the same Kanath-style bow to the Nerlinean Emperor that they had made to the others, not the normal deep obeisance that his subjects were expected to make. Then it hit Dryana: the ceremony was some sort of holdover from the time of Elian the Great and his direct successors, the Threefold Emperor who had ruled Nerlinea as Emperor, Krenakealtron as High King and the Gar as Ran'Dumech.

The priests withdrew to the edge of the clearing.

"Dryana of Syndion, are you ready for the task ahead?" Greldin of the Way's voice was sharp and high.

Despite the tone, it contained a warning. She was not sure what it was.

She licked her lips suddenly, feeling the sweat on her brow from the burning sun. She nodded.

"Step forward," he ordered.

Dryana took up position next to the altar and looked down at the dark wooden box resting on it. The old Gar's face remained impassive, but something in his eyes indicated she should open the box.

She carefully lifted the lid; the hinges had been freshly oiled, and they moved easily. Inside was a lining of blue silk. It reminded her momentarily of the Amaland blue silk that had made the Slayers their first money. She did not know why that thought popped into her head. It seemed significant for a moment, then she shrugged it off. In the box was a flute: a simple, bordering on naïve, instrument, with five holes and no other markings. It was so white it might have been made of bone, but it was actually wood, aged by the centuries until it had lost all hint of its original colour.

"Take it out," the Gar commanded.

PRINCE OF SLAYERS

Dryana reached out and grasped the simple wood flute. Before she could pluck it from the silk something happened. She would struggle to describe it, because it was hard to tell where the burning pain she experienced ended and the searing pleasure started, the two were so mixed up. It reminded her of the time during the Battle of Syndion with the Samath, when she had refreshed her power by drawing it from the earth. Then she had used the hapless Saliana as a conduit, but now Dryana herself was the conduit. The power of the earth surged into her, roaring up from the hard sun-baked ground of the temple. It moved through her and filled the flute. Then it blazed upwards in a pillar of blinding white light, towards the heavens. All but Greldin and Dryana shrank back from the blazing, rotating column of roaring fire, despite the fact it admitted no heat. Dryana was frozen in place. Slowly she turned to stare at the old Gar. Calculating eyes answered: not surprised, more impressed. Of all those standing here, she knew he was the only one who had seen this before.

For the watchers it was only moments, but for Dryana it felt like hours, as if time was flowing differently for her. Soon the line between pain and pleasure dissolved, and she let out a scream as it became purely pain. She had to let go, but her hand would not respond. Life was flowing through her. If she could not control it, it would burn her from existence.

She did know how she thought of it, but it seemed the only way to counter it. She used the dark side of her power, and it sprayed out of her, so barely any more was flowing into the flute.

The column disappeared and instead tendrils of light sprayed out from her body. They moved relentlessly out across the park, avoiding any flora or fauna, searching not for the living but for the dead. She found hidden bodies, their murders long since forgotten, buried at the edge of the park, encased in forgotten cellars, decaying unmourned in the sewers. These she found first, but they were not enough, and the tendrils of light reached out beyond the edge of the city. There were no more dead. She cursed. The Nerlineans burnt their dead. She could feel piles of ash, long forgotten remnants of the dead – not what she needed.

She screamed. The power was going to rip her apart. She could feel it, more of it pulling back into the flute as she weakened. Then she found something with a tendril. It brushed a long-forgotten burial ground. It was centuries old, the bones almost dust in the dry earth. Were they Kanath who served the Threefold Emperor or some other people who had left their bones in the dirt? Was it the site of some lost battle? She did not care; it was enough.

Normally she would raise the dead by using the energy of the earth to imbue them with temporary life, but now she did the opposite. She drew death itself from the bones, the grey energy of entropy, and it gave her a feeling she had never experienced before. A feeling of glee, as if the dead of ages past were singing to her. The light at the end of the outstretched tendril turned grey, slowly darkening as if the light had been torn from the air. It swam back at the gathering place through the tendril. Other tendrils, those that had found hidden bodies, grasped at the dark energy of death and it flooded back towards Dryana. The shining tendrils became a dirty grey fog around the woman.

It reached the flute, and light exploded out from the instrument. Dryana was lifted into the air, slamming against the nearest cypress tree. She slid down, landing in a heap on the ground. She gasped for breath, winded from the impact. She winced, felt something. A broken rib, maybe. The grey mist that had shrouded them disappeared.

The flute leapt from the box unbidden, stopping in the air a couple of feet above the surface of the altar. It pulsed with a gentle light, spinning one way and then the other, as if held by invisible forces.

Greldin stepped forward and plucked the flute from the air and tucked it in his belt. He stepped back so he was now standing next to the Dumech'Di'Syn'Dion'Gar.

"Are we done?" Nyandar enquired of the Gar.

"We are, your imperial majesty," Greldin replied calmly.

"Well?" demanded the emperor.

Greldin turned to the other Gar and nodded.

In unison, the three Dumech of the Gar dropped to one knee before the Nerlinean Emperor. The two Trendorns dropped and held deep curtsies.

"Ran'Dumech'Di'Gar," the three Gar war leaders declared in unison. "We will come when you command."

Nyandar gave a narrow smile of victory.

"And you Greldin of the Way, do you not bow before the Ran'Dumech'Di'Gar?" said Nyandar quietly.

"The Su'Trendorn does not bow to anyone, not even the Ran'Dumech," the old Gar stated.

"You are not Su'Trendorn," observed the emperor calmly.

"She is not here, and I am her representative. Take your victory, child of Elian. It is enough," Greldin replied.

"You are not Su'Trendorn." Ice had entered Nyandar's voice. "She sent you to bow, so she would not have to bow."

A look of annoyance passed across the old Gar's face. It seemed for a moment as if he might refuse. He met Nyandar's predatory eyes. Slowly, Greldin of the Way knelt beside the other Gar before the Emperor of Nerlinea.

"Ran'Dumech'Di'Gar," the old Gar intoned.

"Good," said the emperor with a broad smile. "Now lunch, I think."

He turned away and strode out of the Temple of Thytha, mages and nobles trying to keep pace.

The Gar stood up, Greldin pushing himself to his feet with the help of his staff. The six made to follow, walking unconcerned past the battered Dryana. Greldin stopped in front of her. He glanced at his compatriots, watching them stride off after the Nerlineans.

He loomed over the witch, momentarily blocking out the sun. His face was inscrutable, as if he were thinking about something. He spat at her feet.

"Lyrn Tutharum," he muttered and stalked off.

Dryana lay there wondering if he was being rude, but she had not read contempt in his face. It was as if he were simply stating the obvious, but with the Gar, who knew?

A hand thrust down and grasped hers, pulling her to her feet. She coughed and winced in pain. Camlyn Halfnight gave her a smile.

"Thank you, my lord," she offered.

"The emperor wanted me to thank you for your service," he said.

She looked at the Dumech of Haldorn and raised an eyebrow.

"Next time it would be nice to have been told in advance what was going on," she said.

"Well, I'll pass that on."

"No, you won't," she retorted.

"No, I won't," laughed Camlyn. "The emperor in his wisdom has granted to the Company of Slayers a ship of the Imperial Fleet. It will be transferred to your quay by late afternoon. You will have to find your own crew. The Imperial Fleet were upset at having to part with it. Had you been given the crew as well, there might have been a riot."

"That is a very generous gift. They must cost a fortune to build," Dryana said, and she meant it.

"Good. I did well, then."

"It was your idea?" Dryana struggled to keep the surprise from her voice.

"Sort of. I asked my wife what she would like as a gift for great service to the emperor. After I knocked the more ridiculous ideas off her list, I got down to a ship," Camlyn explained.

"She's going to be angry when she finds out; she hates the Slayers," Dryana said, not sure what was going on.

"She does, but my daughter seems to like you despite all the bad blood, and I like her more than my wife," he chuckled. "Have the priestess of Thytha fix your wounds before you go, and I will see you soon enough."

Dryana brushed off her clothes and watched the Dumech of Haldorn disappear off in the same direction as the Emperor of Nerlinea.

"What do you mean see you soon?" she shouted after him.

"Oh, Slayer," he said, turning back. "My wife is your enemy; my daughter your friend: it is inevitable."

He turned and continued on his way.

Dryana screwed up her face, half in pain, half in frustration, and went to find a priestess who could heal her.

CHAPTER TEN – THE VALLEY

It had been several hours since the caravan that Kyrian was driving had passed through Hunter's Gap. It joined the end of the long line of Solinad Hunter wagons moving through the wide opening in the otherwise impenetrable rockface. The wagon had turned immediately right after passing through the gap, following the line of the Wall of Sargon. For a moment Kyrian did wonder if some ancient mage had maybe ruptured the earth, sending up a ragged line of stone to block the plain. Before meeting Saliana, such a thought would never have occurred to him, but now such ideas occasionally crept unbidden into his head.

He briefly wondered what had happened to his fellow Slayer. She had disappeared with Samarin into the slow mass of carts ahead of him as they had passed through the gap, and he had lost her in the surging group of Solinad Hunters. They all seemed to know where they were going, moving in a great crashing wave of humans, huffrin and carts. There seemed to be no direction, no orders shouted, and family groups seemed to somehow remain distinct even as the mass rolled inexorably forward. Kyrian suddenly realized that the caravans seemed to be disappearing off into the distance. It was another hour of movement along the side of the wall before Kyrian could see what was happening.

The plain gave way in a sharp escarpment, almost a cliff. The wagons were merging into a single file, with the front cart disappearing suddenly out of sight as it reached the edge. After some queuing, which the normally querulous huffrin tolerated with surprising equanimity, the wagon reached the edge of the cliff. Spreading out before them was a large crater; a vast semicircle. The flat edge of the semicircle was enclosed by the Wall of Sargon, which disappeared into the distance towards the horizon. The expanse stretched for more than two miles and was close to a mile wide at the apex of semicircle. There was a thirty-foot drop to the bottom from where Kyrian was seated, and the cliff-like corner of the pit rose higher as it completed the circle, reaching between forty and fifty feet in height at its highest point. A thin line of blue poured over the side of the cliff, before tracking the edge of the semicircle. The stream continued to flow along the edge of the pit before passing just below where Kyrian was waiting and disappearing through a narrow gap in the Wall of Sargon. In front of Kyrian was a steep bank down to the pit below, the only place along the sheer cliffs that a cart stood any chance of making its way down to the surface of the pit.

"The Valley," declared Amdon, seated beside him on the caravan's wooden bench.

Kyrian gave the old woman a sour look. It did not look like any valley he had ever seen despite the stream running through it, but he refrained from pointing that out. The stream they had just crossed carved its way around the edge of the pit. Now it was a flat trickle of water at the base of the wide shallow river channel, but come the spring it would be a raging torrent as the glaciers fed it with melt water. By the early summer, it would fill the full width of the channel. Once, long ago, the pit had been a lake, the water held in check by the stony mass of the Wall of Sargon, filled by winter rains and then swelled further by the spring thaw, before subsiding to a swamp as the long months of dry summer and autumn evaporated much of the water. Eventually, the river had found a small crack in the stone bulwark that sealed its southern side, the water widening it until there was enough space for the river to run through in all but the periods of greatest inundation, but that had been millennia ago. For the Solinad Hunters it had always been a dried-out pit. Only in the spring would the melt water occasionally overwhelm the banks of the river channel, turning part of the pit into an ankle-deep pond, a faint memory of the mighty lake it had once been.

This all mattered very little to Kyrian, who was genuinely puzzled how the other drivers had managed to get their carts down the steep incline into the pit without inverting them and tumbling head over heels.

"What are you waiting for? You are holding up the others!" Amdon's tone was long-suffering, but a glint in her eyes suggested she was enjoying his discomfort.

It didn't help that he had now noticed the presence of Saliana and Samarin, seated on their oradars at the base of the pit. Sali's leg was slung nonchalantly over the front of her saddle as she viewed the unfolding situation. Kyrian's own oradar, stripped of its saddle, wandered around its fellows, stalking back and forth in front of them. It flung occasional glares back at the cliff, where its erstwhile master was positioned. Kyrian was probably imagining it, but he was sure the odious creature was sending him contemptuous glances, daring him to fail.

144

Realizing that there was little chance of his audience dispersing, the big man made his decision. He lashed the huffrin hard with the reins. The beast leapt forward, bumping the cart upwards as it cleared the top of the slope, before bumping back down. Contrary to Kyrian's assumptions, the animal needed very little encouragement; it had made this journey many times before and Kyrian's attempt to overcome its reluctance was unnecessary.

The cart rattled down on the hard dry surface of the slope, scattering scree as it went. Kyrian silently wondered where all the detritus came from; surely the hundreds of carts that had already passed would have cleared it away.

Then the cart and the creature slipped and slid, and Kyrian struggled to keep control. He was terrified it would turn sideways, sending the whole rig tumbling. He hit the stream at the bottom of the slope, sending up a sheet of spray, before careering across the mostly dry riverbed and rumbling to a stop on the opposite bank.

Saliana treated him to a mocking clap.

"Phew!" Kyrian sighed.

Amdon patted his knee.

"Wouldn't want to do that in the wet," he muttered.

"It's impossible if the bank is wet," Amdon replied calmly.

"So, what do you do if it rains?" asked the Slayer.

Amdon looked at him oddly. "It doesn't rain on the steppe in the early autumn," she said, as if it were an immutable fact.

"What, never?" Kyrian was incredulous.

"Only very rarely; only in a dark year," she said seriously.

"What happens in a dark year?" Kyrian asked with a smile.

"We starve," came the very serious reply.

"You are in the way," Saliana declared, shifting Kyrian's concentration away from his conversation with the elderly hunter.

Kyrian stood up in his seat so he could look around the wooden covering of the wagon. Waiting at the top of the embankment, a line of other caravans was starting to build up. The Slayer reseated himself and gave the huffrin an encouraging slap with the leather reins. The beast's truculence had returned, and it seemed initially unwilling to move. It was already tearing hungrily if somewhat futilely at the short tufts of steppe grass. Another lash from Kyrian and the huffrin lurched forward. The other caravans in the family group followed, swaying down the bank and through the water.

The wagon trundled slowly across the basin, where the ground seemed slightly soft, giving a springy feeling to the wagon's movement; a welcome relief to Kyrian's backside after the hard surface of the steppe. In places, the wheels dug into the soft ground, but the huffrin dragged its wooden encumbrance free. Saliana pulled alongside the wagon, so she was keeping pace with it.

"It's impressive, isn't it?" suggested the Mistress of the Slayers with an expansive gesture across the basin.

Kyrian did not really think so. The basin was filled almost to bursting with wagons, neatly arranged in rings or star shapes. Small bender-style tents were set up between the carts, each group set up around a central fire. A stink of dung pervaded the whole place, partly due to the sheer quantity of huffrin, which were busily defecating across the basin, but also because the fires were largely fed with the very same dried faeces. With so many Solinad Hunters gathered in one place, the smell was truly noxious.

Kyrian struggled to find anything impressive about it. He could admire the teeming and towering cities of the East. He could equally enjoy the silence and emptiness of the open steppe. In the several years he had lived there, he had started to secretly love it, even if he would occasionally long for a city. For him, the sight before him was the worst possible compromise: a city on the steppe. And that was to dignify it, as the camp looked more like a slum.

The Solinad Hunters covered nearly three quarters of the basin with their wagons and tents sandwiched together. Kyrian was surprised that they had not used the space more wisely, but there seemed to be no one managing the process of setting up camp.

Amdon struck out her hand, pointing to an open space next to an established camp. Kyrian made to move in that direction, but he did not need to, as the huffrin already seemed to know where it was going. The Slayer dragged the protesting creature to a halt next to another group of caravans.

"No, closer," insisted Amdon, and her tone made her sound like she was reproaching a child.

Kyrian shot the old woman a look, which made Sali smirk.

He moved the cart further forward, until it was practically on top of the next-door camp. Children and adults appeared from among the neighbouring wagons and stood at the edge of the circle of the camp. Smiles and shouts echoed out from the watching Solinad Hunters.

"This is our space," declared the old woman, as if it was somehow obvious to anyone.

Kyrian could see no indication of why this was the case: there was no marking, no stones, no post to give any sign this belonged in even the most nebulous sense to Amdon's family. Despite this, the rest of the family wagons were now arriving and gathering slowly in a circle around a small open space.

"Ho, Amdon!" came a shout from the adjacent camp.

Kyrian looked up to see a man standing at the edge of an invisible circle that seemed to have suddenly surrounded

Amdon's tribe's carts. He was short and burly, heavy-chested with a slight paunch, and black hair, turning grey at the temples, pulled back in a ponytail. The Slayer judged him to be in his late forties. He was dressed in thick leather trousers, with a heavy padded tunic covering his upper body.

"Talnan," Amdon declared, returning his beaming smile with a toothy grin of her own. "Step in, step in."

The Solinad Hunter raised his hand in thanks and strode towards the caravan. He helped Amdon down from her seat on the wagon bench. They clasped hands like two old warriors meeting each other. His gaze swept across the camp.

"You have losses?" he asked, though he knew the answer.

"It has been a tough year," Amdon replied.

"Who?

"Mourn," she supplied.

Her own gaze swept his camp.

"You are missing a wagon," she observed. "Mourn?"

"Fal'Gar," he supplied.

Samarin on her oradar arrived at the camp at that moment and Talnan gave her a suspicious glare. The Gar seemed completely indifferent to the actions of her people. Such was the way on the steppe.

"Your mother… where is my old sparring partner?" the old lady demanded.

"Dead, three months passed," Talnan supplied.

He sounded more fatalistic than sad.

"Fal'Gar?" Amdon asked.

"Fever," he said.

She nodded in understanding but made no attempt at condolence.

Life on the steppe was hard, Kyrian thought; death a constant companion.

PRINCE OF SLAYERS

"Who are these?" Talnan asked, a sweep of his hand taking in Kyrian, Sali and Samarin.

"Travellers. They saw off some Mourn raiders. We would have not made the Hunt without them," she said.

"Strangers are not welcome during the Hunt," he muttered.

"Strangers never come to the Hunt. I am not aware of any prohibition on them being present," the woman countered with a grin.

The Solinad Hunters' society was based on traditions and customs. Lacking an overarching authority or even a single religion, there were no rules or laws that constrained them, though customs held the same weight. Amdon was right: no one came this far north to witness the Hunt. The Solinad Hunters were a tough, hardy people living on the windswept northern part of the steppe where they could live their nomadic lives largely unbothered by Sevains, Mourn and Fal'Gar tribes further south. Usually restricted to small family groups of at most a dozen caravans, they posed little threat to the more warlike steppe peoples. Here, all gathered together in the basin of a dried-out lake, they looked more like a large army encamped ahead of battle. For one of the Hunters' traditional enemies, such an agglomeration would be something to fear. For a traveller, it would appear a wonder.

Kyrian knew why no one would travel here to see such a sight: there was nothing here, no resources to exploit, no trade route to follow. The Solinad herds so important to the agricultural lands of Chazantria, Haydron in the west and Havagia in the east did not rest here for any length of time. They migrated through from their summer resting grounds in the north to their winter grounds on the western and eastern fringes of the steppe. It suddenly occurred to Kyrian that the Solinad Hunters lacked the herds of the other steppe nomads, such as the popular semi-domesticated adunel, the bovine creature that provided both meat and milk. The Solinad Hunters had only enough huffrin to draw their wagons, and a few younger creatures tethered behind the wagons. They were not food animals, not unless you were truly desperate.

What was the hard dried meat that the Hunters had been feeding them for the last few days? Kyrian suspected it was solinad meat.

"I am Saliana Slayer. We are travellers and merchants. It is an honour to see the Great Hunt first-hand."

Kyrian was brought out of his introspection. He looked over as his fellow Slayer dismounted and strode across to stand opposite Talnan. She had now stuck out her hand by way of greeting. The Solinad Hunter looked at Sali, his eyes wary. Kyrian was reminded of Falthar's warning that the Hunters would not be welcoming. In truth, that had not been their experience so far. Though the Hunters were wary of everyone, they seemed to save more of their dislike for the Fal'Gar than for humans. Talnan seemed to make up his mind and grabbed Sali's hand and pumped it.

"Well met, Saliana Slayer. It is rare to meet a merchant this far north; we are poor and have little to trade."

"You have furs. They are of great value to the south." Sali's hand spread wide, indicating the soft grey and white pelts that adorned the wagons of Talnan's people. She did not recognize the creature from which the skins had been taken.

Kyrian had not initially noticed them, and he had to congratulate his fellow Slayer; she was always spying a trading opportunity. Furs were highly prized further south, which meant most of the planet Galvia. The lizard creatures that predominated outside the steppe, the huffrin, the hadan and the bird-like iribis, were not creatures that provided warm pelts. Even the adunel lacked much depth of fur to provide the type of warm, soft pelts that graced Talnan's cart.

PRINCE OF SLAYERS

"They are prized possessions," Amdon interjected. "Talnan's tribe normally travel along the fringes of the Sul'Kirin, where such creatures can be found."

Sali had stepped past Talnan, around the invisible circle that enclosed the wagons of his family. She was fingering a large soft grey fur spread out on the seat of one of the wagons. Talnan's people had moved up, looking warily at the Slayer, and Kyrian wondered whether Sali had violated some tradition by stepping into the circle of their camp without permission. Kyrian's eyes played across Talnan's tribe, who had moved closer, but did not seem to be actively threatening his colleague. He forced his hand not to stray to the flail that lay tucked behind the bench on which he sat.

"Beautiful," Sali purred, stroking the fur. "You trapped this yourself?" she asked.

"Not that one; others," came the reply.

"One of your family?" asked Sali.

Kyrian was trying to read his friend. Was she just being polite, or was she trying to get into the fur trade? He had to concede the pelts would be worth a fortune if they could trade them further south.

"That one we traded; the small ones we trapped ourselves. That was not trapped, it was hunted, and we only are Solinad Hunters; we know nothing of hunting across the tundra," Talnan explained.

"So, who hunted it?" asked Sali.

"We traded it with the Grey Folk. They would have hunted it," he replied.

Amdon laughed out loud at that. "Stop teasing them," she said with a chuckle. "Talnan is playing with you, Sali. He is not brave enough to enter the Sul'Kirin, and the Grey Folk never leave it."

"What is the Sul'Kirin?" asked Kyrian. He had racked his brains, but the word seemed to have no meaning in the languages he spoke.

"The Sul'Kirin is the Sul'Kirin," Amdon offered unhelpfully, as if that explained everything.

"We are travelling further north to the lands of the Kyth'Dath. Is that what you mean by the Sul'Kirin?" asked Sali.

"I know of no Kyth'Dath," replied Amdon, looking at Talnan for confirmation.

He nodded.

"The city of Krynal, the Kyth'Gar?" Sali queried.

That elicited only blank looks from the Hunters.

"The only city in the steppe now is Haydron," replied Amdon. "If it still stands."

"Once there was Cularan," observed Talnan. "But now Cularan is a ruin."

He looked at Samarin. She seemed unconcerned by the destruction of her people's former capital. The city that the Mourn had looted and destroyed a decade past was a pale shadow of what it had once been.

"Krynal lies outside the steppe, in the lands of the northern ice," explained Sali patiently.

"Only the Sul'Kirin lies to the north, where the land turns to the white of snow and ice, and you are not welcome there," Amdon answered.

"That is where we are heading nonetheless," declared Sali. "Maybe we can trade pelts with the Grey Folk? We wish to see the summer grazing place of the solinad."

"You may not enter the Sul'Kirin," Talnan stated calmly.

He did not seem angry; he was simply stating facts.

"My uncle did warn you," Samarin interrupted.

She still sat perched on her oradar some yards away.

PRINCE OF SLAYERS

"The Kyth'Gar will not welcome you," Samarin observed.

"Who are these Kyth'Gar?" demanded Amdon, confused.

"We call them the Culimarin, but I believe you call them the Ice Lords?" offered Samarin.

Amdon nodded, understanding, and then started to laugh.

"What is so funny?" asked Kyrian.

"The Ice Lords have no interest in trade or anything else outside the Sul'Kirin," said Amdon. "You have wasted your journey."

The other Solinad Hunters were laughing. It was friendly, not mocking.

"You will stop us entering the Sul'Kirin or whatever it is you call Kyth'Dath?" Sali demanded.

There was an edge to her voice that Kyrian recognized, a hint of burning rage, which she normally kept so well controlled.

"We will not stop you doing anything. Enter the Sul'Kirin, try and go to this place called Krynal. You will not return," observed Amdon. "Anyway, enough of this foolish talk. We have a camp to fix and a feast to prepare."

The Slayers and Samarin left Amdon and her people to bustle about preparing things. They moved smoothly and the three made no effort to help for fear it would slow the process.

"My uncle did warm you, Saliana. None of us are welcome in Kyth'Dath," Samarin quietly observed to the Slayer as they watched the camp being prepared.

"Kyth'Dath is where the solinad rest during the summer," Sali replied stubbornly.

"You wish to make money from fresh solinad dung available in summer?" asked Samarin. "That far north from the

153

markets that need it in Nerlinea, how would you even transport it?"

Kyrian covered a smile. The priestess was smarter than he had given her credit. She was right: the dung was too heavy fresh to transport anyway; that was why it had to be dried. There might be some advantage to have an all-year-round supply, but that was not what Sali really wanted. Sali had a theory. The mushrooms, drun, had to be consumed by the solinad somewhere. It clearly wasn't in their winter living places in Chazantria, nor was there any evidence of the mushrooms on the open steppe on which they now stood. Saliana believed that they consumed it during the summer, while the creatures were in the far north. If the Slayers could get access to a summer supply of drun, then they could sell it year-round in Nerlinea. There would be a fortune to be made. Kyrian was starting to worry why no one had done it before. Maybe those who had had a similar idea had died trying.

"There is also the question of the furs, the pelts. We could make a fortune on those too." Sali's eyes sparkled with greed, trying to divert Samarin to a different train of thought.

"I am a guide for you both, because my uncle has no desire to explain your deaths to the Great Khan," Samarin said. "I draw the line at entering Kyth'Dath, I am not committing suicide so you can try and make some more coin."

"We'll see. I suspect you will feel differently when we get there," observed Sali sweetly.

"Don't get your hopes up," Samarin replied coldly, before stalking off.

Kyrian watched her go.

"Are you sure your plan will work?" he asked.

Sali shrugged.

"Have you heard the word 'Sul'Kirin' before?" he asked her.

"Yes and no," she replied. "There is so much I don't remember."

"Maybe you just don't know?" Kyrian grunted.

"Oh, it's there at the edge of my thoughts," assured Sali. "So close I can almost touch it. There is so much of my knowledge I still cannot access."

"So Sul'Kirin?" he asked. "It sounds Gar?"

"I speak a number of languages," she replied. "It does not match any word in Fal'Gar I know and there is nothing that makes sense in Westerly or Nerlinean. I think it means 'stockade'."

"Slightly worrying name," observed Kyrian. "Doesn't really make sense for a large area of icy waste. In what language is that?

"That's what makes even less sense," replied Sali. "It's in the language of the Syn'Dion'Gar."

CHAPTER ELEVEN – PREPARATION

Bleary-eyed, Kyrian pushed down the bed roll and stood up. His body caught the cold wind of the open steppe. The caravans and the natural bowl of the dried-out lake provided some relief, but not enough. He looked jealously at the wagons around him, suspecting they were warmer than the bed rolls he and his companions were using. The burnt-out fire next to him that had provided some warmth was now long dead, and he gave it a frustrated kick, sending up a small cloud of ash. He rubbed his temples. Gods, his head was stinging.

He strode off to find the latrine, a small hole that had been dug at the edge of the camp. Each family group had dug their own holes; not very practical and not particularly sanitary. Given the number of huffrin present across the camp and their willingness to defecate everywhere, he doubted it mattered very much. The morning after their arrival, his nose had not yet adjusted to the horrific stench of so many people and animals in close proximity. He took a long hard pee in the latrine hole and felt the pressure on his bladder relax. It gave him a moment of relief from the headache banging against his skull. He tied himself up and turned back. Sali was standing there waiting to follow him. For some reason he flushed.

"By Jeddera, you look worse than I feel," she laughed.

"Thanks a lot," he grunted.

He was regretting how much he had drunk. The Solinad Hunters had their own version of the white liquor, alak. If anything, it was even stronger than the Fal'Gar drink. The previous night's feast had been one great episode of gluttony. The normally meagre meals of the Solinad Hunters had been replaced by a feast, which, while not exactly opulent, had made up for the lack of diversity and quality with sheer quantity. It had involved huge amounts of tough dried meats, hard breads and animal fat, washed down by copious amounts of strong liquor.

Kyrian looked around for some water to wash his face and strode off in the direction of the stream that ran around the corner of the site. Sali trailed after him, saying nothing. The wrestler hunkered down and splashed water across his face and scooped up some into his hand. He glanced up the stream to where a pair of huffrin where drinking and defecating next to the water. He let the liquid drop from his hand and stood up with a sigh.

"You got anything drinkable?" he asked of his fellow Slayer.

Sali detached a flask from her belt and handed it to him. Kyrian took a long swig and handed it back.

"Gods, that stuff they serve is strong," he commented.

"Well, you did drink twice your own body weight. That might be a factor in your hangover," she replied critically.

Kyrian wrinkled his nose up at her, eliciting an evil smile from Sali.

"I didn't embarrass myself, did I? It's all a blur," he muttered.

"No, I don't think so," Sali replied slowly, as if trying to recall the previous night. "I mean, I'm sure Amdon was flattered."

Kyrian looked up at Sali, a hint of concern entering his face.

"What?" he asked cautiously.

"It's fine; she's a widow," observed Sali. "I mean, she's not your usual type, but it's a cold steppe, I get it."

"Please tell me you are joking?" Kyrian looked aghast.

"Surprising enthusiasm, from what I overheard," Sali replied.

"You are joking," Kyrian stated, though he did not sound fully certain.

"Am I?"

Yet Sali could not control herself, and her giggle became deep choking laughter.

"Getting bored on the steppe, are we, Saliana?" Kyrian observed caustically.

"Sorry," she responded with mock seriousness. "Besides, I think your dancing was more offensive."

Sali started laughing again.

"What's so funny?" Samarin was approaching them.

"Nothing," Kyrian answered grumpily.

"Just teasing our friend about sleeping with Amdon last night," Sali said trying to keep a straight face.

"Not sure why that would be funny?" Samarin observed, her tone curious.

"The age gap," supplied Kyrian. "And I didn't sleep with her. Did I?"

He turned to look at Sali, his look still questioning.

She gave him a broad grin.

"She's just winding me up," Kyrian barked angrily.

"Shame," said Samarin.

She stepped forward, so she was standing face to face with the Slayer. She ran the nails of her left hand down the side of the Slayer's face, her leg moving forward to touch his.

"I hoped you liked older women," she breathed into his face.

Kyrian stared back, shocked. His brain was trying to join up the fact that the woman opposite him, who he thought of as practically a girl, was not far off Amdon's age.

"Shame," she whispered in his ear, her soft lips almost brushing his lobe.

Sali doubled over with laughter.

"This is fun," Samarin declared, stepping back.

She flashed Kyrian a very un-Garlike mocking grin.

"I hate both of you," he muttered peevishly.

That only prompted more laughter from Sali and a wider grin from the Fal'Gar witch.

A cart was slowly trundling towards them. Its cloth and leather canopy had been removed and it was piled high with dried wood. Another caravan in a similar condition pulled out from its family camp area and followed the wood-laden cart towards the stream.

"Where did they get that?" Kyrian enquired, his curiosity piqued.

Samarin was also looking surprised, an expression that seemed out of place on her sharp Gar face.

"What do you mean?" Sali was confused.

"The wood – where did they get it?" replied Kyrian.

Saliana raised an eyebrow. "I don't get it?"

"Do you see a lot of trees around here?" Samarin supplied the answer.

"You make a fair point," said Sali.

The Fal'Gar witch looked at the Mistress of the Slayers. There was something very odd about this one, she thought. She could paint her face perfectly with the blue of a Fal'Gar mage – a rare thing among the Gar of the Steppe – but she did not think piles of wood were odd. Perhaps the right word was inconsistent, but she was not sure. Her aunt had placed great store in her finding out as much as possible about the Slayer mage, but the longer Samarin spent with Sali the more confused she became. Kyrian, by contrast, was an open book.

Further wagons stacked with wood were trundling past. The huffrin drawing them were straining to drag each vehicle up the steep bank, despite being encouraged by much whipping and cursing from the drivers. Once they climbed out of the basin onto the steppe, they moved off, following the line of the wall.

Amdon was striding towards them, accompanied by Talnan. The pair were chatting and smiling happily with each other.

"Don't get jealous," Sali mocked Kyrian, elbowing him to underline her point.

Kyrian ignored her.

"Well met, Amdon," Kyrian hailed her, stepping forward to greet the Solinad Hunter.

"You look better than I expected," she responded with a broad smile. "You were in impressive form last night."

This prompted sniggers from behind him. The Slayer shot his colleague and their guide an evil look. Amdon frowned, looking at the pair, then focusing back on Kyrian.

"What is with all the wood?" asked Kyrian.

"We are preparing for the hunt," replied the old woman, as if that explained everything.

"And your families are not contributing wood?" the Slayer asked.

"We are of the spears," Amdon said, again assuming that made sense.

"Amdon, your ways are not our ways. Things that are obvious to you are not obvious to us," Sali stated politely. "Please explain what you mean as if we are children, learning for the first time."

The woman nodded and smiled. "I'll show you," she said. "Follow me."

Amdon led them back to her family's circle of wagons, reaching her own caravan. She threw back the hard felt carpet that lined the base of the wooden cart to reveal a hatch at one end of the wagon. The cart had a false bottom. No, that was unfair, thought Sali, as she watched Amdon open it. There was no real attempt to conceal it; it was just a clever way of storing things.

Amdon pulled out a four-feet-long piece of dark wood and laid it carefully on the floor of the cart above. She pulled out a further two pieces wood of similar length. The poles were the thickness of a man's wrists with metal screws sticking out of them, one at each end. Finally, Amdon pulled out a green cloth bag and placed it on the floor of the wagon next to the three poles. She started to screw the three poles together, until they formed one single staff, pushing the end resting on the ground behind. Having completed the assembly of the pole, she rested the other end carefully against the back of the wagon. She stepped around it and picked up the bag, carefully rolling back the green, struggling a little with its weight. Something glinted in the morning sun as she pulled the green felt bag clear. It was a broad-bladed spearhead over a foot long, finely finished and polished. It blazed rather than sparkled.

"That's bronze!" Kyrian stated in surprise. "How old is that?"

Sali had stepped forward. She looked at Amdon for permission, receiving a silent nod in response. The Mistress of the Slayers stroked the spearhead gently, assessing it.

"It can't be sharp," declared Kyrian.

"It's razor-sharp," replied Saliana. "And immeasurably old."

"Never seen the like, have you?" Amdon said with a grin that spoke of rare one-upmanship.

"Never," Kyrian confirmed.

"Maybe not the blade, but the metal you have seen," Sali corrected him.

"Where?"

"In the tomb on Syndion. This blade isn't bronze; it's an alloy of copper and alcidide," Sali replied.

"You can't know that just from looking at it?" Kyrian grunted.

Sali ignored him, now looking at the shaft of the spear. She tapped the wood, so dark brown it was almost black. It felt more like hitting stone than wood.

"What wood is this?" Sali asked.

"I don't know its name," Amdon replied.

"How do you source more when it breaks?" queried Sali.

Amdon look confused. "It almost never breaks. When it is lost, it is lost," she explained with a shrug.

The Solinad Hunter picked up the spearhead by its base, a column of bronze as thick as the black wooden pole. She started to screw it on, struggling with the ungainly weight and shape of both parts of the weapon. When she was finished, she held up the fully formed spear with a wide smile. The weapon towered over her.

"What are you going to do with that?" Kyrian struggled to keep the derision from his voice and entirely failed to do so from his face.

"Don't be rude," Sali upbraided him – not that the old Solinad Hunter seemed bothered by Kyrian's reaction.

"Oh, but it's absurd, Sali," he protested.

"May I?" asked the Mistress of the Slayers, holding out her hand for the weapon.

Amdon handed the spear to Saliana, who almost lost her grip. The dark wood was heavy and smoothed by age. Despite that, the broad-bladed copper-alcidide spearhead was fighting to drag the weapon to the ground. It was so poorly balanced it was ridiculous.

"I apologize for my colleague's tone, but I have to agree it is impractical as a weapon," Sali stated.

Kyrian tried not to look smug and failed.

"It's not for you; it's for him," the old woman pointed at Kyrian.

She turned back to the wagon, seemingly indifferent to their criticism. She was pulling out another collection of poles and another green felt pouch.

She had two of these terrible things, thought Kyrian.

"This is for you." Sali thrust the spear into Kyrian's hand.

He held it, feeling the weight of the spearhead drag against the muscles of his arm. He put his foot behind the pole to make it easier to hold.

"I don't believe it; this is even worse than I thought," he said with a grin.

Sali shot him a look of annoyance. "It's like a sarissa, but I think it's too short for that and the blade is far too wide," she observed.

"What's a sarissa?" Kyrian asked, perplexed.

"The spear of the Kanath phalanx," Samarin said, joining the conversation. "I agree it's too short. Besides, that was a single piece of wood with a metal point at each end. This would not work as a phalanx spear – no way to embed it in the ground."

"How do you know about a phalanx and a sarissa?" Kyrian demanded. The military leader of the Slayers and warrior Count of Chazantria was feeling his lack of knowledge compared to his two travel companions.

"You have read Tren Ja's *History of the Kanath Civil War and Northern Invasions*?" Samarin asked.

"No."

"Odd for a general of your reputation," she observed, lending a Gar dismissiveness to the comment that she probably did not intend.

Sali intervened before her fellow Slayer lost his temper: "What I am saying, Kyrian, is that I haven't known of anyone using spears this length in battle for centuries. Besides, those spears were different and actually longer. I think these are for hunting?"

"Well, obviously!" declared Amdon. "We are of the spears."

She had finished assembling the second spear.

"So is that one for me?" asked Sali with a cheeky smile, half joking.

"No. You are a woman," Amdon answered, confused and even angry.

Sali was taken aback by the response. Gender roles were pretty traditional among all the peoples of the steppe, but she had never before detected that certain activities were taboo for women among the Hunters.

"I did not mean to offend." It was the Slayer's turn to be confused.

"Why would we waste last night's work by risking the life of the women?" Amdon replied.

Saliana thought back to the previous night. It had been a raucous night of feasting and drinking. The different small tribes had crossed camps, mixing together. She had definitely seen women from one group more than mingling with the men of another group. The feasting and the fornication, the very intermingling of family groups, was uncharacteristic, for what

164

little she had seen of the Solinad Hunters. Yet she had only a very limited experience with them, so who was she to draw conclusions? Maybe it was her bardic sense, but there was something that told her that previous night was different from the norm.

"What was so special about last night?" Saliana asked cautiously.

"It is the night before the annual hunt. We feast on the last of food, so we are well motivated," Amdon explained.

"You eat all your reserves of food, so that you have no choice but to be successful in the hunt?" Samarin was shocked. On the steppe such a course was the height of recklessness.

"When will the hunt take place?" asked Saliana.

"This afternoon. We were lucky not to miss it, but thanks to you we got here just in time."

Amdon then shouted over to her fellow Solinad Hunter. "Talnan!"

He was squatting by the dried dung fire at the centre of his camp, not far from where they were gathered. He looked up and walked over the invisible edge of Amdon's family camp. He took the same pause as before, then stepped over the imaginary boundary and strode over to where they stood.

Amdon thrust out the second spear, clearly intending that Talnan should take it. He stopped; his right hand held tightly at his side.

"I am of the gatherers," he said quietly.

"Now you are of the spears," Amdon replied.

"You know what this means for your family?" he asked. He made no move to accept the weapon.

"The Mourn slew our menfolk. We have none old enough who can stand forward for the hunt," she replied.

Saliana thought she detected a note of sadness in Amdon's voice.

"When this is done it, it is done?" It sounded as though Talnan was asking a question.

Amdon nodded. "One family," she said.

"And him?" Talnan indicated Kyrian.

"He stands surrogate, for my grandson. He is not one of us."

"Who holds the second spear will be my decision after dusk tonight. It may not be your grandson. Your family may never carry the spear again. You understand?" Talnan still held back from taking the proffered spear.

"After tonight, your family and my family will be one. Our family will carry the spears as you command. Maybe it will be my grandson, maybe it will not." She gave a shrug.

Talnan took a small step forward and grasped the spear. Amdon let it go and gave an uncharacteristic deferential bow of her head.

"It is done," he declared.

A rumble of thunder played across the steppe.

"I thought you said it did not rain in autumn?" asked Kyrian, staring up at the sky.

It was cloudless and blue, more like summer. Only the biting wind told what time of the year it was.

The rumble continued as it hit the stone wall and reverberated back on them.

"That is no storm," said Amdon. "The herd is here. The Hunt begins. Time for you and Kyrian to take your place on the Wall."

Talnan nodded.

"No longer am I of the gatherers. I am of the spears," Talnan declared.

He strode off in the direction the carts of wood had gone.

"You must go with him," Amdon told Kyrian.

"Sorry, what am I doing?" came his response.

CHAPTER TWELVE — THE HUNT

Kyrian rested his back against a slab of rock and tried to ignore the sharp stone stabbing into his torso. He had stripped down to just his trousers; his scale mail coat would give him no protection in the battle he was about to fight. The cumbersome broad-bladed spear was clasped in both hands and balanced against his shoulder. *This is insane*, he thought angrily. *What was he doing up here?*

The Wall of Sargon was only thirty feet tall at its highest point, and much of it was several feet lower than that. Kyrian decided that anyone foolish enough to still doubt it was a natural phenomenon should stand on top of it for a while. The erupting line of jagged rock was surprisingly narrow at the top, and variable. Where Kyrian sat near Hunter's Gap, it was slightly wider, which allowed him to half sit and half lean. Talnan was a few yards away, clasping his spear nervously, balancing precariously on a ledge barely more than a couple of feet wide. He had wedged the base of his spear into a gap in the rock to give him something to hold onto.

Two hundred Solinad Hunters stood, sat or perched along the rocky outcrop, spaced out as evenly as the unfriendly crest of the Wall of Sargon would allow. They clasped spears, similar to those held by Kyrian and Talnan, staring outwards north across the plain. Young faces were alive with fear and anticipation; older faces were wary and assessing. It was early afternoon, and the sun was directly overhead. Kyrian was sweating, but more from excitement as blood pounded through his veins than from the heat of the sun. That was offset by the wind snapping across the steppe, which stabbed and whipped at those atop the rocks.

The thunder of the approaching solinad herd had become a consistent low rumble that seemed to build as it reverberated against the Wall of Sargon. They could see the herd in the near distance: thousands of creatures, a mass of greys, light and dark, so tightly packed it was as if the plain itself were moving towards them.

Kyrian looked down to his left at Hunter's Gap. The hundred-yard gap in the Wall of Sargon was the only way for the solinad to get past the barrier without taking a detour of many miles. For millennia, the creatures had made their migration through this gap, and for centuries the Solinad Hunters had taken advantage of it. The gap was filled with wood stacked up to the chest height of a man and several feet in depth. Kyrian doubted that would be enough to hold back the solinad, but he had to assume the Hunters knew what they were doing. On the steppe, so devoid of wood, it would have taken all year to collect that amount of kindling. He had also watched them build a similar wooden barricade, but this time to twice the height of a man, at the entry to the camp.

"There are many, so many," declared Talnan.

For a moment, Kyrian thought his fellow spearman was nervous, but it seemed instead he was trying to impart some information.

"What do you mean?" asked Kyrian.

"They have bred well in the spring; this is the biggest migration I have ever seen."

"Is that a good or a bad thing?" Kyrian asked nervously.

"Both," chuckled Talnan. "More prizes, more danger."

"I don't think there is enough wood to properly block the gap?" Kyrian commented.

Talnan looked down and nodded with agreement. "I blame the gatherers," he said seriously.

"That's you, isn't it?" asked Kyrian incredulously.

"I am of the spears," responded Talnan with a broad grin.

Kyrian barked with laughter at that.

Kyrian glanced towards the gap, where several Solinad Hunters were hoisting wooden buckets and emptying out a black viscous liquid across the piled-up wood.

Coal tar or something like it, he speculated as he watched. He smelt the fumes being released as they wafted up and across the rock wall.

No, something more potent, he thought.

The Slayer looked back across the rolling steppe. The horde of grey-haired beasts were approaching in a thundering torrent, the sound getting louder and louder. It reminded Kyrian of standing on the cliffs of the south coast of Kangorn when a great storm had smashed into the rocks. The sound was the same: the sharp wind of the steppe mimicked the storm, only the lashing rain was absent. He found he missed it.

"Remember, aim for the back of the neck!" Talnan shouted out to next to him.

The tumult of the approaching herd was starting to drown out speech.

Kyrian ignored him; Talnan was as much reminding himself as he was instructing the Slayer. He could see the Solinad Hunter's nerves riven across his face. He wondered why the old man had decided to come up on the wall when he could have given the task to someone younger and faster if not necessarily fitter; a son or a nephew. Was he trying to save them from the danger? Kyrian thought that was unlikely: a riskless life was not something anyone on the steppe experienced. He suspected it was pride. He did not fully understand the elevation in status that Talnan's tribe had experienced in their move from gatherers to spears, but he could imagine that to stand on this wall was the ambition of most Solinad Hunters. Men particularly never really grew out of such dreams, the foolishness and risk-taking of youth was only hidden in old age, but never abandoned.

There were only men on the wall, and he wished Saliana was here. Her magic would have been a useful option in the face of the tumbling, rumbling sea of muscular, heaving creatures bearing down on him. It had been made clear that no female Solinad Hunter or otherwise could stand upon the wall, a taboo so long-standing that their presence was now considered unlucky. Stupidity, thought the Slayer. People would be injured, probably even die this day as a result of such outdated nonsense.

He was surprised that he was on the wall, such was its coveted status. He could not understand why the presence of a foreigner was not considered equally pernicious. He wondered why Amdon had insisted he take up the spear for her family group. No one had complained when he had done so and there were no overarching leaders of this strange people to gainsay the old woman. There was no tradition that made it taboo, probably because one had never been needed. He had asked the other hunters, those who had stood on the wall for previous hunts, the best way to kill the giant creatures that were approaching. He had been told to aim for a small weak spot at the base of the vast skull equidistant between the ears. He had asked how he was going to throw the massive spear and have any hope of hitting such a small target. That had resulted in gales of laughter from the hunters. *You will see*, was all they had told him.

"It would have been good to have some practice at this," he shouted over to Talnan.

The Solinad Hunter turned towards the Slayer with an amused grin.

"There is no practice, no way to replicate what we are about to do. You just hope you learn fast enough to live!" the Solinad Hunter bellowed back with a laugh.

"Great," muttered Kyrian.

"Stand ready!" the shout rang out around the wall.

It was taken up by all the spearmen and Kyrian joined the chorus.

The sound of the herd and its remorseless movement was deafening now. At its front it had formed into a flat-headed wedge of perhaps thirty creatures wide as the whole herd funnelled down, aiming for the gap in the wall. Given the width of the great beasts, the adult solinads were eighteen feet across on average, there was little chance they could make it through the gap thirty abreast, blocked as it was with wood. A small number – the younger and angrier, all bulls – had pushed out from the front group. Looking at the charging, snorting beasts, Kyrian thought there was no way the barricade would hold against the onrushing mass of meat. The leaders were yards away from the gap. Kyrian watched as Solinad Hunters bearing lit wooden torches were racing from behind the protection of the wall, heading for the wooden barrier that blocked the gap. They tossed their torches on the pitch-soaked wood. There was a whoosh of flame. Air was pulled in and the gap exploded into a sheet of fire.

Kyrian watched, sure that the lead creatures could not stop their rush before they hit the barrier, certain they would simply crash through it. Instead, the leaders reared up in the face of the roaring heat. The box-shaped creatures, thick heavy legs all hidden in matted pelts of hair, tried to scamper back from the fire. Two were half crushed against the side of the gaps, being driven part way up the jagged stone. They then rolled back down into the milling mass of their brethren, desperately trying to back away from the flames. There was nowhere to go: the vast swathe of the herd was still behind them, driving for the gate. Kyrian thought the sheer wall of solinads bunching up behind would push their hapless fellows through the fire, but they didn't. Instead, the main weight of the herd split like a river around a giant boulder. The boulder was the flaming pile of wood, and the rock wall each side became the banks of the river of charging meat.

Kyrian looked down wide-eyed as a heaving mass of creatures rolled along the wall, scraping and bumping against it. Angry roars and gravelly screaming emanated from the aggrieved solinads as they were sandwiched by their own kind against the stone, all of them trying to find safety from the flames. The animals were barely three yards beneath where the Slayer was standing, and he could smell the sweat of their matted hair.

"Hunt!" the shout echoed across the wall, reverberating from the men on the rock almost as one.

A Solinad Hunter in his early twenties jinxed his way along the narrow half path at the top of the rock wall and leapt out into the air, spear grasped in two hands pointing downwards. He plunged down, landing on the back of a creature, the broad blade of his spear thrusting into the back of the animal's neck. Its roar was cut short as its front knees gave way, crashing to a stop as it skidded across the steppe from its own momentum. The young hunter looked back, panic and terror on his face. The rest of the herd was coming on behind. They tripped and careered over their fallen brethren, crushing the hapless hunter still grasping the spear on the back of the slain solinad.

"Impetuous," declared an older hunter, who stood on the wall a few yards over from Kyrian.

He seemed indifferent to his fellow hunter's fate. Kyrian glanced across to Talnan, who looked more shocked. Maybe it was the realization that he might share a similar fate.

Hunters were leaping from the wall in numbers now, spears plunging down into the creatures that were moving past them. Kyrian noticed the solinads had slowed a little; some were caught up against the wall unsure which direction to go, milling about confused. Kyrian hoisted his spear, placing most of it against his shoulder, blade pointing downwards.

"This is insane!" he shouted to Talnan.

The Slayer leapt out into the void, his spear bearing down on the solinad below, aiming for its neck. As he jumped, the creature circled slightly to its left. The spear drove into the hard muscle of the animal's back. Kyrian slid down the wood of the haft, almost slipping onto the still exposed part of the spearhead. The Slayer found himself almost lying flat against the back of the giant creature, desperately grasping onto the spear in an attempt to stay on. The solinad was moving now – whether it had found direction, or was simply being buffeted by its fellows, the Slayer was too concerned with clinging on to care.

Kyrian pushed himself to a half crouch and grasped a large handful of the solinad's thick hair. The creature collided with the wall and then slammed into the side of another of its kind, almost tossing the Slayer into the rock surface. Kyrian clasped on tightly, left hand on the spear haft, right hand wrapped in the animal's hair. He started to work the spearhead free, and the creature barked angrily, tossing its shoulders, now trying to expel its unwanted rider.

Kyrian cursed but continued to work the wide bronze blade from the thick muscle of the animal's back. It came free, dousing him in a gout of blood so dark it was almost black. He swore louder, wiping the hot blood from his eyes with his shoulder.

The solinad had got free of the wall, though it continued to gallop parallel to it, heading in the direction of the camp. It had covered nearly half the distance to the valley in a matter of minutes, a journey that had taken them over an hour in the cart the day before. Kyrian looked forward: the creature's neck was a few feet away. He lifted the spear to his shoulder, resting it there with the blade pointing downwards. Blood continued to spurt over him from the creature's back, but he ignored it. The solinad raced ahead, Kyrian surfing its back. He calibrated himself with its movement. Taking a large breath, he released his grasp on its hair and leapt forward, bringing the blade down into the soft spot in the creature's neck.

It gave way surprisingly easily, sinking deep into the animal's flesh. Kyrian was so shocked by the ease when compared to the thick muscle of the back that he was nearly thrown forward by the excess momentum of his jump. He clutched to the spear as his feet flailed in the air. The animal's front knees gave way, and it skidded to a halt, falling dead on the steppe. Kyrian looked up at more solinad coming towards him, but the herd had spread out and there was space for them to move around rather than across their slain fellow.

The Slayer yanked the blade free; it came out easier than he expected. He looked across the steppe as more of the creatures barrelled in his direction. He clasped the spear and sprinted up the slope created by the slain animal's body. He reached the back and leapt, thrusting out and slamming his spear into another creature as it passed. Kyrian plunged it into the side of the animal's almost non-existent neck. It held and the beast carried on heading in the direction of the dried-out lake. Kyrian was left hanging from the haft of the spear, his legs kicking empty air as the solinad raced on. He worked his way hand over hand along the haft of the spear, reaching out for the animal.

He could see the dried-out lake ahead of him. The bank that led down to the river that provided access for the caravans had been blocked by piles of wood similar to those the Hunters had used to block the gap in the wall. They had also been doused in pitch and set alight; a blazing bonfire now filled the gap. The panicked solinad seemed to be heading straight for it at impossible speed. Alarm bordering on terror filled Kyrian. He grabbed onto the hair on the side of the animal, pulling himself up to its back. Clasping the hair that hung down the side, he scrabbled to retrieve the spear impaled in the side of the animal's flesh. He worked it loose, taking precious seconds as the panicked animal careered towards the fire or the steep side of the lake. Neither option suggested high survival prospects for the hapless Slayer riding the animal. Finally, the spear came free, and Kyrian pulled it up, desperately trying to manhandle the huge unwieldy weapon into position one-handed. He stood up on the back, watching the fire appearing in front of them. He plunged the spear down into the neck just as the creature tried to stop to avoid the flames. Its legs gave way just as it was turning. It sent the pair half tumbling off the sharp drop of the old lake edge and half sliding through the edge of the burning wood. The solinad part fell, part slipped into the stream below. Kyrian had launched himself in the opposite direction, using the animal as a barrier between him and the fire. He rode the side of the creature down the slope until it splashed to a halt in the stream below. The Slayer clambered off the solinad and yanked the spear out. He dashed away, heading in the direction of the wagons, fearful of the oncoming solinad herd behind him.

The solinad herd had reached the top of the dried-out lake, milling around its cliff-like sides. They were smart enough to know in their bovine brains that such a drop would kill them.

One had found the gap that Kyrian's actions had created in the wall of flaming wood protecting the bank down into the camp. It nosed through, roaring either at the fire or as if calling its brethren to follow.

Kyrian looked up as he ran from the stream, trying to get some space. Saliana was stalking across the soft soil of the old lakebed. She flung out her hand, and blue lightning sprayed out, aiming for the Solinad. It dissolved into a blue mist as it hit the creature. Nothing happened and the animal roared even louder, taking tentative steps down the steep bank, its fellows pushing in from behind, trying to break into the camp.

"Oh, crap!" Sali announced, shock on her face.

"What?" asked Kyrian, coming to a stop in front of her.

"Did you know solinad were immune to magic?" she demanded angrily.

"How would I know that?" he shrugged.

"Explains why they are so revered," she mused. "Oh well, time to get creative."

Saliana ignored the oncoming beast and instead targeted the solinad milling around on the ridge above them. She looked at the area and, with the barest flick of her right hand, the grass along the ridge erupted in flame. It did not hit the creatures directly but instead sent them into a panic, stampeding in the opposite direction away from the lake. One of their number, a calf, was caught in the confusion by its larger herd mates. It teetered on the cliff for a moment, before tumbling over it. It hit the ground below with a sickening crunch of breaking bones, sending a spray of water from the stream. It bellowed piteously, thrashing around in the shallow water, trying impossibly to get back to its broken legs.

Sali gave it the barest glance then flung out her left hand, as if trying to scoop up the burning wood pile that lay nearly a hundred yards away. It shifted, catching two of the solinads trying to get down the bank and hurling them sideways.

Matted animal hair caught fire, and howling and bellowing issued from the creatures. They bolted after the rest of the stampeding herd.

One solinad remained a threat. The truculent creature seemed to have thrown off its herd mentality and was angrily trying to reach the camp of its hunters. It slid and slipped down the bank, whimpering, then it reached the stream, splashing through its shallow course. It let out a great roar of victory, tossing its head back. Then it lowered it again and charged. Its huge forehead slammed into the nearest caravan, sending it toppling. Women and children scattered as the beast rampaged through the circle of wagons, and angry huffrin bellowed back, but wisely stayed clear of the mightier animal.

"Interesting," mused Saliana.

"What?" Kyrian demanded.

"Tell you later. Can you throw that monstrous thing?" Sali pointed at the spear clasped in her colleague's hand.

"Yes, but not that accurately. Won't do anything; it needs to go in the neck," he explained. "We need to do something quick or that thing will smash its way through the camp."

Sali glanced over to the bank, where several more solinad, recent arrivals driven along the wall or creatures returned from the panicked stampede, were trying to work out how to tackle the slope. Sali needed to stop them. She flung a ball of red and orange fire to hit one of the solinad full in the face. It screamed in rage and pain as its hair caught fire, crashing into its nearby fellows, and a smell of burning flesh filled the steppe. The creatures thought better of continuing and instead moved sideways, driving along the edge of the ancient lake to look for another way down.

Sali turned back to the rampaging animal, which was thirty yards from where she stood, smashing up more wagons.

Another family group was screaming in panic as their homes were crushed.

"Give me the spear," she ordered Kyrian. "I can make that jump."

"No!" Amdon's tone was firm. "It is forbidden."

"What?" Sali turned on the old woman angrily. "Children are dying."

"Female participation in the hunt is forbidden," Amdon declared. "If you kill a solinad, the gods will not bless the hunt, and all will have been for nothing."

Bloody stupid custom, thought Saliana, though she bit back the urge to articulate her opinion.

"What about that thing?" She thrust out her hand at the young calf she had sent crashing into the stream.

It cried piteously, still struggling vainly to regain its feet. It was slower and slower as time passed and death approached.

"It fell," offered Amdon, face serious.

Typical, thought Saliana, always a loophole when they wanted to find one.

"Well, what do you want to do about that thing?" Sali pointed at the adult solinad rampaging in front of them.

"It has happened before; it will happen again," Amdon shrugged defeatedly.

"What happened last time?" Sali asked.

"It wandered off eventually," Amdon replied.

"After much death and destruction," observed Sali coldly.

That elicited another shrug from the old woman.

"Kyrian, you'll have to make the jump," observed Sali.

"No w…" he started to reply.

"You can definitely do it," she cut in.

He looked at her and raised an eyebrow.

"Do it," spat Sali angrily as the solinad slammed a young woman against the side of a wagon.

Kyrian nodded and ran in the direction of the creature, building up speed. He was twenty yards away when the solinad spied him. It turned from its bloody work and bellowed. It faced the running man, ready to charge.

"Jump now!" shouted Saliana.

Kyrian knew as he leapt that he would struggle to reach halfway up the animal despite his strong leg muscles. He had experience, after all, having faced one of these creatures from the ground already today. He had contemplated doing the same as he had done with the previous solinad: using the spear to climb. This beast was a giant bull, bigger, angrier and warier than the one he had slain. That one had only wanted to escape; this one wanted to kill. He did not know what Sali planned, but it had better be something, because there was no way he was making this jump.

This was Slinker's trick, thought Sali, but he had taught her the mechanics of it. She had done it with lumps of fruit. Kyrian was just a bigger lump. The key was not to overcook the power, or you risked flinging the person past the target with potentially horrific consequences.

Kyrian felt the push, like a gust of wind up his backside. He had wanted to make this look controlled and dynamic, like when Sali did one of those jumps he had seen her make, over an impossible distance for the human she claimed to be. After all, there were a lot of women watching. There were also children who would tell this story for generations, assuming it worked.

He did not manage it. Instead his legs spiralled as he trod air, as if he were trying to run and failing. Then he was above the creature. He was passing over it. He was going to miss and land on the other side, probably crashing into the ground or a cart and wrecking every bone in his body.

He flung out the spear, trying desperately to arrest his flight. It carved a thin bloody line along the solinad's back before it dug enough into the thick muscle of its back to hold. It stopped his jump, and his arms screamed as he clung onto the beast's back. It flexed its muscles, trying to throw him off. It covered the gap to Sali and Amdon in moments. He saw the purple lightning Sali flung at the beast. Kyrian knew it would hit him too. What by Jeddera was she doing? He expected it to be his last thought. The solinad stopped as if shocked by the lightning, but the magic did nothing to it, merely puffing into a cloud of purple mist.

Kyrian took advantage of the creature's confusion. He wrenched the spear free and ran along its back before plunging it into the neck. The huge beast gave out a last piteous roar. Its knees gave way and the solinad slumped dead.

Kyrian slipped down, yanking out the spear. He stalked across to Sali.

"You nearly killed me," he muttered.

"You look okay," she observed quietly.

"I thought the thing was immune to magic, yet fireballs worked, and lightning didn't?" he queried.

"Immune to lightning, not magic," Sali explained.

"You knew that?" he asked.

"It seemed a reasonable supposition," she replied.

"You guessed. If you had been wrong, I would be dead," Kyrian snapped.

"Well, you're not," came her cold response.

Samarin approached them, applauding.

"Impressive, very impressive." She gave the Slayers a narrow smile.

Kyrian took the praise at face value. It was hard to tell with the Gar; they often seemed to mock with their observations.

"Look, I'm sorry and let's face it, it worked," Sali continued, ignoring the Fal'Gar's intervention.

"At least you've improved your application of Slinker's trick in the years since I've been away," he grunted.

Sali recalled the last time Slinker had tried to help her perfect his spell. She remembered the fruit splattered across the wall behind the table, instead of landing on it as intended. Slinker's non-stop mutters about too much power. That had been a couple of years back.

"Not really. Apparently humans are much easier than fruit," she grinned.

"Don't you have to go and collapse or throw up or something?" Kyrian demanded.

"No, I'm fine," Sali replied.

Kyrian looked at his fellow Slayer. She seemed completely unruffled at all the magic she had expended. Not even a bead of sweat marred her perfect features.

Something gnawed at him: a feeling of fear; the greatest he had experienced all day.

CHAPTER THIRTEEN – AFTERMATH

The General of the Slayers stood at the top of the bank and felt the deepest sense of self-loathing he had felt in his whole life. He had stood on many battlefields and he had always felt despair for the carnage he saw, and particularly for what he had inflicted. It was nothing like this. What he saw before him dug at the pit of his stomach.

The Hunt had ended an hour past, when the flaming wood blocking the gap in the rock wall had burnt down enough for the solinads to burst though. As more and more had flooded through the gap, the weight of meat had cleared the burnt wood from their path. The herd had formed a giant spiral as it gathered together and sought to push through the hole in the wall to the wide-open steppe beyond.

Thousands, probably tens of thousands, had made it through the gap, and they had left hundreds of their slain fellows behind. At a distance, Kyrian had found the huge beasts majestic, just as close up they had been terrifying. Looking now like great lumps of hair spotting the steppe, they seemed so much smaller.

Smoke from the fires set by the Solinad Hunters and those started by Sali continued to drift over the steppe, though most had been swept away by the racing winds of the grasslands.

The Solinad Hunters had not had it entirely their own way. A stream of makeshift stretchers bearing the dead and badly injured were moving off the battlefield towards the camp. Kyrian caught himself in that thought: it was more than just a hunt; it had been a battle. The survivors of those who had jumped from the wall stood, exhausted, leaning on their giant spears. A few squatted or slumped in the grass, trying to recover from their experience.

Kyrian shifted his position as yet another wagon crested the bank. The huffrin pulling at it squeaked angrily as the driver lashed it to drag their wooden encumbrance up the steep slope. Kyrian received a shout and wave from the driver, and he recognized one of Amdon's teenage grandsons – or whatever the relationship was.

"You said you killed one by the gate?" the young man was more confirming than asking.

Kyrian gave the barest of nods.

"Yana has run ahead to make the claim, but we'll need the wagon to carry it back," he shouted over his shoulder as he trundled by.

Kyrian had no idea who Yana was – maybe one of the women and children who had scattered out of the camp across the steppe. They seemed to have run ahead of the slow-moving carts to stand guard against the beasts claimed by each tribe. That said, he could see very little evidence of disagreement; it

183

was more a formality than a genuine fear someone might make an unjustified claim.

The Slayer turned around and scampered back down the bank towards the camp. Gravel scattered and spat from under his feet as he dug in his heels to keep from falling. He spotted his travelling companions on the other side of stream. Sali and Samarin stood watching the butchery before them. Amdon and several members of her family surrounded a beast languishing in the waters. It was the one that Kyrian had slain on the plain and then tumbled down the bank with. The Solinad Hunters were busy cutting at it, pulling back the skin and rolling up the great stinking strips of hair, before placing them on the dry surface of the desiccated lakebed and rolling them out to dry in the sun.

"Three kills, three kills," Amdon was muttering almost gleefully as she scurried around the great beast.

Kyrian sloshed through the stream, instantly regretting it as the red water, thick with animal blood, stained his boots.

"Are you enjoying yourself?" he asked a touch harshly.

Amdon looked up, grinning through her blood-covered face. "Three kills!"

"Four?" observed Kyrian, pointing at the young solinad that had tumbled from the cliff.

"It fell," she offered simply and went back to work on the creature before her.

Kyrian looked over in the direction of the great bull solinad he had slain. A young boy, perhaps six years of age, stood atop the creature with a proud look of defiance, as if he had killed it himself. It was somewhat comical in the otherwise blood-drenched scene.

"What happens to that, then?" Kyrian asked Amdon, nodding in the direction of the young creature.

The old woman stood up, a look of annoyance pervading her previously elated face. Clearly Kyrian was not going to let her get on with her work.

"It will go to a spear who failed to make a kill," she replied with a shrug.

"Who decides that?" he asked.

She looked confused and went back to work.

"What happens to the gatherers?" he pressed.

"What do you mean?" she asked.

"Well, what do they get? They don't seem to be claiming anything?"

It was true the women and children of the wood-gathering families sat quietly watching events with a bored disinterest.

"When we have taken half, they will take half," Amdon replied.

"Who decided that?"

She gave him another look of confusion. "Your life must be very complicated, always needing to be told what to do," she observed acidly.

Saliana stifled a laugh at the last remark.

Kyrian wanted to continue the conversation, but then saw a stretcher coming down the bank.

Talnan's body was crushed, a mangled mess, but his face was still recognizable. Kyrian surmised he had been crushed by a solinad or perhaps slammed against the great rock wall by one of them.

A man in his early thirties approached Amdon and thrust out the spear to her. One of its segments was missing, no doubt wrenched off in the hunt. The blade and other two wooden sections had survived well enough though.

Amdon stood there, covered in blood, watching the young man warily.

For the first time, Kyrian felt tension in the air among these normally placid people.

"Karn, son of Talnan," she said politely. "I mourn for your loss."

The man looked at her, anger in his eyes; rage, almost. "Take it," he said bitterly.

"You could be of the spears. My granddaughter has need of a husband," Amdon answered, leaving the weapon held outstretched.

The man looked over to where a teenage girl squatted by the creature, covered in its blood. She looked up warily, her eyes flitting between those of the man and her grandmother.

"No. Take it," Karn said, dismissing the young girl from his mind. "We are of the gatherers."

"Your father's kill?" she asked, still not taking the spear.

She had phrased it to suggest that Talnan had managed to slay a solinad before succumbing, but leaving his son room to explain otherwise.

"My daughter stands upon it, as your Yana stands upon the beast that one killed," he said, stabbing his hand out at Kyrian.

Amdon fixed him with a hard look. The man returned it equally hard, his eyes dark and hooded. Kyrian's hand strayed to the knife at his belt; he wished he'd not left his flail and armour in the camp. The man let out a breath, seeming to weigh something in his mind as tradition and custom held back the seething rage to which he wished to surrender.

"My daughter holds it for your family. We will yield it when claimed," he declared. "We are of the gatherers."

The last was said vehemently; he practically spat it.

"I understand," Amdon nodded, her tone kind. Any hint of hardness had evaporated.

She clasped the spear, and Karn let it go like a venomous snake. Amdon watched him leave.

"It seems we are a tribe again," she said with a broad grin.

A whoop issued from her family around her.

Kyrian looked over at the backs of Karn and his family as they walked away, fearful they might take offence against the celebration of Amdon's people, but they did not even look back.

"So, you will not be merging your tribes?" the Slayer queried.

"They have no wish to be spears – it is harder than they imagined," answered Amdon.

Kyrian searched her face for any hint of malice, but there was none. The old woman was simply stating things as they were.

"What will happen to this?" he gestured at the carcass.

"The skin and hair will be harvested for clothing, tents and wagon coverings. The bones will be used for tools and ornaments. The meat will be salted or frozen. There is enough here to see us through to next year," Amdon explained.

Now Kyrian understood the significance of the previous night's festival. While hardly an exercise in gluttony, they had eaten well compared to the normally parsimonious portions that passed for meals among the Solinad Hunters. The tribes had effectively eaten their last supplies. Had the hunt failed a whole people would have starved.

"Frozen?" Kyrian suddenly asked, wondering what the woman meant.

"You know," she countered, "Very cold, like ice."

"I know what frozen water is," he snapped, angry at being mocked. "How do you do it with food?"

Amdon looked at him as if nervous of revealing secrets. "We will travel north. The winter is coming. There are ice caves where the food can be kept good by the ice," she explained.

"You are going to the north?" Kyrian was surprised. "You must be the only people who migrate against the seasons rather than with them."

The Slayer had assumed that, with the hunt completed, the Solinad Hunters would travel back further south to warmer climes. It was a cold hard winter anywhere on the steppe, but in the north, it would be forbidding. Travelling into the ice was completely counterintuitive.

"Things will be hard further north as winter comes," Kyrian observed.

"We have enough for most of us to survive." She waved her hand across the beast she stood over. "This will feed us. In the south as winter arrives, things will be hard. Mourn, Fal'Gar and Sevain will raid each other simply to survive. We are not warlike; we would not keep this bounty if we travelled that way."

"And you have no enemies to the north?" he asked.

"Winter and wyrms, but no raiders," she replied.

"The Grey Folk?"

"As I said, the Grey Folk do not leave the Sul'Kirin. The Guardians forbid it," Amdon explained.

"The Guardians?"

"The Ice Lords," clarified Amdon.

"The Kyth'Gar?"

"That is what you say they are called."

Kyrian nodded. "We can travel with you. We are both heading north," the Slayer offered.

Amdon gave him a sad look. "That is not possible, despite the service you have done my family," she replied.

"You do not want to reveal your frozen caves to us; I understand," said Kyrian.

"That is part of the reason, but not the main one." Amdon seemed serious. "You intend to enter the Sul'Kirin, and we cannot be seen to have helped guide you. The Ice Lords are famously defensive of their patrimony, and we have no desire to incur their wrath."

"So Talnan lied when he said he traded with the Grey Folk?" the Slayer asked.

"Maybe?" she replied.

"Maybe? You were much more dismissive earlier."

"The Sul'Kirin has no barrier. You will see the bluestones, the marker stones, when you reach its edge. Maybe he traded across the border? Maybe he stepped within or one of the Grey Folk stepped without for a moment? The Grey Folk are bound to the service of the Ice Lords, but now they are seen more on the edge of the Sul'Kirin than once was the case. The Ice Lords are seen less than once was the case," she shrugged.

"And yet you still fear Ice Lords?"

"The children of Sargon may not be what they once were, but they are still to be feared."

"Sargon? Among my people he was a God of War. What is he to the Ice Lords? They are Gar."

"You will have to ask them," Amdon answered. "Here Sargon is not a god, but the greatest of the dragon lords, but those are old stories. Some older even than the ones your friend tells."

"And the Grey Folk; are they to be feared?" he asked.

Amdon did the strangest thing. She walked over to the Slayer's oradar, which was scratching the ground nearby. Before Kyrian could think to block her, she was standing next to the giant cat. The oradar looked at her beadily, more as if assessing food than a potential rider. She reached up slowly, then gently rubbed the cat on the top of his head. The cat let out a mewing sound.

Traitorous beast, thought Kyrian with a grin, though he was glad that it had reacted that way rather than biting the woman's arm off. Amdon slowly withdrew her arm so as not to alarm the creature and stepped back. Kyrian let out a breath he did not realize he had been holding.

"Does it have a name?" she asked.

"I don't know. I never thought to ask," he answered, a little chastened.

"Do you fear it?"

"No," replied Kyrian. "Well, perhaps a little."

The oradar gave its reluctant rider an angry look of warning, as if it understood. Though perhaps Kyrian imagined it; the creature was always giving him baleful glances.

"Maybe more than a little," he grinned with honesty.

"It is said that the Fal'Gar do not break the oradar as you might a hadan or an iribis. Instead, they are persuaded to accept a rider. Something only the Fal'Gar can do, and it would seem your friend and you. It is the wonder of my life to touch one," she said with a smile.

"Are you trying to make a point about the Grey Folk, or did you simply want to stroke my cat?" he asked.

Amdon gave him another smile, this one tinged with sadness. "I have seen the wild oradar tear down a fully grown adunel. I have seen a pride of them chase a solinad to exhaustion before feasting upon it. Here, all harnessed and saddled, it looks imposing, beautiful even, but still there is a sadness for the wildness it has lost. Yet that fierceness still lingers; it remains in all creatures. In some it is buried deep down, but with the oradar it remains, despite the centuries of domestication, close to the surface. That is why we find it terrifying, why even your Fal'Gar friend treats her cat with wary respect, even a hint of fear. Sometimes the wildness can only be tamed so much or for so long."

Kyrian wanted to ask more, but he was hit by the most overpowering smell. He gagged as the rancid smell wrenched through his nostrils and down his throat. Amdon's nose wrinkled up, but she seemed more used to it than Kyrian.

"What is that?" Kyrian spat.

He tried to hold his breath to squeeze out the overpowering stench, but it did no good. One of the Solinad Hunters had opened the slain creature's stomach, and its innards were spilling out across the ground. The water of the stream carried much of its thick viscous contents away, which helped a little, but the odour hung in the air.

Samarin had backed away from the macabre scene, her eyes watering. Saliana, by contrast, had stepped forward and was squatting down. She had drawn her knife and was poking at some of the contents of the Solinad's stomach that had not washed away. She speared a few black shapes from the mass. She walked upstream where the water was cleaner and washed them off. She held them up to the sun and a smile played across her face as she looked at the partially digested mushrooms. She stashed them in her pouch.

"Time to head north," Sali declared.

Kyrian looked at Samarin, who shrugged.

"Now?" he asked.

"We have wasted enough time here," replied Sali.

She was already stalking back towards the camp, where their oradars waited nearby.

Samarin waited the barest moment, seeing if Kyrian would countermand his fellow Slayer. When no such command came, she set off after Saliana.

Kyrian looked at Amdon.

"It seems we are going. Thank you for your hospitality," he said with a grin.

Amdon looked at him with a sad smile. She stepped to him and reached up her hand, touching his cheek. She brushed it gently, in a motherly fashion.

"We cannot thank you enough for your aid. Without you we would have gone hungry, though the other families would not have let us starve completely. Now we will grow strong through the winter, not weaker," Amdon replied.

"Happy to help." Kyrian flashed her another smile.

Amdon did not remove her hand. She looked serious.

"You are a warrior, they say; a prince of the western steppe. You have the mind and body of a fighter, but not the soul," she said quietly. "Your soul cries from the actions you take. It weighs on you. One day the weight will become too much to bear. When that day comes, come in the summer to the southern steppe where the grass turns blue-green, and the sun bakes the seashore. Find us, and you are welcome among my family."

"Thank you, Amdon, but I am on a different path," he said politely.

She clapped his cheek lightly and affectionately with her cupped hand and turned away.

CHAPTER FOURTEEN – THE INN OF THE PRINCE'S HERALD

There was a rap on the door. Balinor looked over his shoulder from the chair in which he was slumped. He ignored it and went back to looking out through the window. The third floor of the Inn of the Prince's Herald had been designed with the view in mind. Sited next to Lake Kangorn, the freshwater body in the centre of the island city, it was one of the few places in the city that could be described as having a view. It was the only one worth looking at in the teeming mass of streets sandwiched on the Rock.

Balinor stared out at the dawn spreading across the buildings and the water and took a swig from the tankard of ale grasped in his hand.

The knock at the door came again, louder and more insistent.

Balinor cursed under his breath and took another draw on his tankard.

"Come!" he ordered.

A man slipped into the room. The thin pale man, round-faced and of average height, looked nervously around as he clicked the door shut behind him.

The bedroom was opulent, the best in the inn, bigger than it needed to be. On the left-hand side of the room was a four-poster bed, its curtains pulled back and its sheets rumpled. Two forms rested quietly under the soft covers, occasional gentle snores coming from that direction. On the other side of the room was a desk strewn with scrolls and books. Between the two was a floor-to-ceiling window. The Prince of Kangorn sat looking out at it, his back to the door. The man who had just entered tousled his grey hair with his hand and considered what to say.

"Danzian. Finally my chancellor has deigned to return to his job," Balinor spat nastily.

"You saw my reflection, your highness?" queried Danzian Corinmount, Chancellor of Kangorn.

"I heard your breathing," answered Balinor, continuing to stare out of the window. "You are panting like a dog. Three flights of stairs and you are half dead. You are a Lord of Kangorn, Jeddera knows what you will do if you ever have to command a ship at war."

"If you need me to captain a ship in a war, your highness, you really are in trouble," observed Danzian with a smile.

Balinor grunted a laugh at that and looked over his shoulder at Danzian Corinmount, Chancellor and Lord of Kangorn, banker and merchant. Probably the richest person on Kangorn, with the exception of the Prince and Princess. Maybe

PRINCE OF SLAYERS

Lady Charlotte Pandus or Lady Dryana Slayer were richer, but they had a whole family behind them. Danzian was one man. He did not even have a child – at least as far as the Prince was aware.

"Bring the flask," Balinor ordered, turning back to watching the dawn through the window.

Danzian spotted the beer jug on the desk and picked it up, then walked over to stand in front of his ruler. Balinor thrust out his tankard and the Chancellor refilled it.

"You've been to the palace?" asked Balinor.

Danzian nodded.

"You've seen my wife?"

Danzian gave another nod.

"Bet she got more than a nod; the full bowing and scraping display?" Balinor asked waspishly.

"I did not want to wake your companions, sir." Danzian nodded in the direction of the sleeping forms.

"They are exhausted. It would take Dryana to resurrect them." Balinor gave a half proud smile.

Danzian glanced back at the covered figures, listening for their breathing.

"It's a joke, Danzian; they are alive," Balinor laughed. "I can recommend them, though. You could afford them with your vast wealth."

"Thank you, sir, but I'm not interested," the chancellor replied.

"Don't like women?" asked Balinor.

Danzian provided no answer.

"Always thought you might prefer men," the prince observed.

Getting no response, Balinor frowned. "What do you like?" he demanded.

"Money, your highness," came the urbane response.

"Now that I believe." Balinor slapped his thigh and laughed.

The two women in the bed briefly stirred.

"You don't approve?" demanded Balinor, waving at the sleeping women.

"Not my business, sir."

Balinor let out a loud breath of annoyance. His chancellor was apparently unwilling to rise to an argument. If only his wife Ascrina would be so accommodating.

"Where have you been?" he asked.

"The palace?" Danzian looked confused.

"No; where have you returned from? What have you been up to? It has been months since you have been in the city."

"I was most recently in High Ringstead and before that in Dimchurch," Danzian replied.

"Serving my interests or your own?" Balinor asked grumpily.

"I always serve the interests of the House of Strabo, my prince; our interests are aligned."

"House of Strabo?" grunted Balinor. "You're including me in that?"

"Your highness is the House of Strabo," Danzian replied, his face serious.

"Not sure my wife would agree," Balinor muttered.

Danzian said nothing and glanced over at the bed. He knew for sure that neither of the sleeping women would be the Princess of Kangorn. The prince's relationship with his wife, which had started so promisingly with their wedding five years ago and their ascension to the throne as co-rulers, had struggled over the last couple of years. Danzian speculated there could be any number of reasons for it: the arrival of children, which tended to chill even the warmest of marriages; the Princess Ascrina's close relationship with Lady Charlotte Pandus, or simply Ascrina's desire to assert the dominance of the Strabo family. Her family had ruled the Rock for the last two hundred years since its founding. Balinor had been useful in providing military prowess and then providing Ascrina with heirs. His position as a partner in the Company of Slayers had provided much-needed influence and, more importantly, money. Indeed, Danzian would never have persuaded the Bankers' Guild to provide the rulers of Kangorn with the loan they needed to survive had Balinor's share of the revenues of the Company of Slayers not underpinned it. As the wealthiest of the Bankers' Guild members, the Corinmount Bank was the biggest lender to the government of Kangorn. Danzian, every inch a banker, saw no conflict of interest in negotiating the loan with himself.

That had been then. Now the ship had been righted and the finances repaired sufficiently. Since then, Ascrina Strabo, hereditary ruler of Kangorn, had found it increasingly difficult to reconcile her royal heritage with the background of her husband, a man who had been born and had lived most of his life as a slave, for all he was now called Prince of Kangorn.

Had Balinor better preserved his relationship with his fellow partners in the Company of Slayers, things might have been different. His ascension to the throne had been achieved with the substantial aid of the House of Pandus, the implacable enemies of the Slayers. That had created a rift between Balinor and his partners, with only Dryana, who seemed to get on with both Balinor and Ascrina, providing a relationship that went beyond business to genuine friendship. Her absence in the last four years had only increased the distance between Balinor and the rest of the Company of Slayers. Saliana Slayer told Balinor she was still consulting him on major decisions, and he continued to receive his cut of the profits. Though what constituted a major decision, Danzian wondered. The Slayers had financed Kyrian carving out his own principality on the steppe. No one had bothered to tell Balinor, despite his island state's dependence on the agricultural produce of Haydron and the fact that the bank owned by his chancellor was one of those providing the financing. Armies did not come cheap.

The Slayers had not taken much interest in Kangorn since Dryana had left. Kyrian had stopped here briefly on his way back from Nerlinea to see his sister. He had then moved north to begin his conquest of the steppe, and had not returned since, despite his relative proximity. Slinker had passed through many times, but never stayed for long, and Saliana had not visited the island since just after the prince's ascension to the throne. Indeed, her confrontation with Balinor in his own great hall had only grown in its anger and violence as the story became legend with each re-telling. The Company of Slayers still maintained a considerable operation on the Rock, run by employees. Notionally, they should have obeyed Balinor's orders, but he had never tested the theory, knowing the likely outcome if he tried. This had only added to the prince's bitterness with his partners.

It had been a gradual process, but in the last year Balinor had found more interest in brothels and drink than in his wife and the business of ruling. Perhaps it was boredom. Life was good on Kangorn at the moment. The end of the war in Las Ma had led to a rebound in trade. Strong harvests across the west had resulted in cheaper food for the island principality. Kyrian's antics across Chazantria and Haydron had not really affected this, even if it occasionally impacted the timing of supplies. The influx of berthing fees and other taxes had reduced Kangorn's punishing debt, even if not to the extent that Danzian thought should be the case. It never ceased to amaze him how much the Princess Ascrina spent on seemingly pointless pleasures, operating as if the money she had access to was limitless. It was not a woman thing, Danzian had concluded, it was just part of being royal; her grandfather had had a similar attitude to money. Danzian had seen much the same from the Prince of Setsonia and the High Lord of High

PRINCE OF SLAYERS

Ringstead, both of whom the Corinmount Bank were now lending to. It was a precarious business lending money to princes: you had to walk the fine line between not lending enough and therefore not being considered of use and so not being repaid, and lending too much and finding yourself hanging from a gibbet because a prince might just decide you were better dead than repaid. A banker needed to lend just the right amount so the ruler in question would decide you were better kept alive so they could borrow more money in the future. Factor in the general irrationality and paranoia of the average prince and it became a constant balancing act.

"What news do you bring from your travels?" asked Balinor, dragging Danzian from his thoughts.

"There are rumblings of another war," Danzian answered disapprovingly.

Danzian did not like wars; they rarely proved to be as profitable as the poor seemed to believe. In his experience, princes went to war for vanity, glory and fear. Often these things were more imagined than real. Only the Nerlineans, with their constantly fluctuating borders and millennia of history, seemed to make war self-financing for their vast standing armies. The Prince of Setsonia, by contrast, with his conquest of half of Las Ma, was only now getting enough tax revenues from his new province to cover the interest he was paying the Halfnight Bank. It had been the Pandus-controlled Halfnight Bank that had provided the ruler of Setsonia the money to fund the war. It had disrupted the balance of power in the West, a place where previously money lending had been best described as nascent. It had cost the final Kanath Dukedom its freedom. It had also provided Danzian the opportunity to open his bank in the West in partnership with the Templars of Dimchurch, allowing him to circumvent the Sevain religious laws on usury. The Church of Caon had been surprisingly willing to connive in his plans.

They had been remarkably flexible in their beliefs for religious fanatics.

"War?" grunted Balinor, shaken slightly from the fog of drink. "The Samath?"

"The Mourn, sir," Danzian replied.

Balinor became more alert, stood up and poured another helping of ale from the jug. He placed it back on the desk and then took a swig of it.

"What have you heard?" the prince asked.

Danzian cautioned himself to be wary; his ruler was not as inebriated as he had first supposed. "The Great Khan has called a gathering below the Mountain of the Moon," he replied.

"How did you hear that?"

"My spies," Danzian said calmly. "Not that I needed them – it's the talk of every merchant, trader and mercenary from Setsonia to Hambledon."

"Doesn't mean war," Balinor observed, though he sounded as though he were trying to convince himself. "Who is going to be at this gathering? All the Mourn tribes?"

"All the steppe," the chancellor explained.

"Come again?" The prince was shocked.

"Not just the Mourn," Danzian continued. "The Fal'Gar tribes, Havagians from the eastern lands, the Sevain tribes of the western steppes, the Counts of Haydron and Chazantria."

"The Count of Chazantria…" Balinor chewed on the title. "Kyrian!"

The chancellor nodded by way of confirmation.

"Surprised the Great Khan hasn't demanded my presence," Balinor said with a laugh.

The Mourn Horde made intermittent claims to overlordship of the island city of Kangorn – an assertion that was treated with even more contempt in private by the Prince of Kangorn than the Nerlinean Emperor's similar claim. In practice, the prince was careful in his relationship with the

Mourn. After all, the island was dependent on Haydron for most of its food supply, and the Count of Haydron bowed to the Great Khan.

"Who would they march against? The Nerlineans? The Prince of Hambledon? Is there some enemy to the north?" asked Balinor.

"The north," laughed Danzian contemptuously. "There is nothing to the north but frost and forest. No: the Mourn are moving against either the Sevains of Hambledon or the Nerlineans. As they are gathering on the western edge of the steppe, that would suggest they intend to attack the Sevains."

"The Mourn can't take Hambledon?" That Balinor asked it as a question suggested he was seeking reassurance. "Besides, it's nearly winter. What fool goes to war in winter?"

Danzian understood Balinor's scepticism. The Daldara Mountains, of which the Mountain of the Moon was the highest peak, framed the western side of the Great Steppe, running in an arc from the Nerlinean Ocean to the icy north, to who knew where it ended. It had many small passes through which one might take a small war band or a raiding party, but only two large enough to allow one to take an army through. In the north was the pass that linked the Great Steppe to the smaller, inhospitable Mourn Steppe to the north-west. It was called the Falcongate after the mighty fortress the Nerlineans had built over a millennium ago to bottle up the Mourn in the icy waste that now carried their name. The Mourn had been held in this land, framed by mountains and thick forests, for centuries, raiding out through the smaller passes but providing little real threat.

Then the Great Khan had reunited the divided Mourn tribes. So much legend had grown up around Lak Bok it was sometimes difficult to distinguish fact from fiction. Certainly, his path to supreme leadership of the Mourn had not been smooth or obvious. What was known, was that he had become

Chieftain of the Snow Trees, the smallest but fiercest of the fourteen groups that the Mourn called the great tribes. Though rumour persisted that he had not originally been born of the Snow Trees. Within fifteen years he had united eleven of the great tribes into a single nation and destroyed the three others that would not submit. The lesser tribes which ranged in size from large family groups down to small warbands numbering less than a dozen had capitulated to avoid annihilation. The rest of Galvia had been unaware of the reunion of the Mourn tribes until Lak Bok had taken the Falcongate a little over a decade ago. His people had spilled out across the Great Steppe, destroying the Fal'Gar city of Cularan, before reaching the northern Nerlinean province of Havagia. There the Legions of Nerlinea had met an onrushing horde of hadan-mounted Mourn. Who had really won was still debated, but the Mourn's headlong expansion had been held, at the loss of northern Nerlinea's richest agricultural province, Havagia.

The second major pass through the Daldara Mountains sat at the south-western edge of the Great Steppe and led south into the Sevain principality of Hambledon. The city of Hambledon sat in the gap of the pass. Originally built as a fortress by the Kanath, it had grown into a town and then a city; a major trading centre between the steppe and the settled kingdoms of the Sevains and before that the Kanath High Kingdom. It had been taken by the Sevain tribes three hundred years ago, becoming the capital of the Sevain principality that now shared its name. It had grown in wealth since then as trade between the Sevains either side of the mountains had increased. Despite this, it had kept its walls maintained. Its great wooden drawbridge had been lined with the black stone that the Sevains had discovered repressed magical attacks targeted at it. The people of Hambledon might enjoy the richness that trade brought, but they did not trust the steppe tribes, even those they called cousins.

"He is going to attack Hambledon?" Balinor was incredulous.

"It seems the only obvious target," replied Danzian.

"Hambledon is no one's idea of an obvious target," observed Balinor. "You would have to put it under prolonged siege to have any hope of taking it, and that is the exact opposite of the steppe way of war."

"The Sevains took it three centuries ago," Danzian observed quietly.

"Yes, by treachery: Sevain soldiers pretending to be a returning Kanath patrol got inside the gate. Besides, that was at the height of the Third Kanath Civil War – the fortress's defenders had been stripped to the bone, and the Sevains had been infiltrating people into the city for months before the attack."

"You've been reading your history." Danzian was genuinely impressed, but he cursed that his tone was more patronizing than he intended. Born a slave, Balinor's ability to read was a recent accomplishment.

Balinor shot him a look of annoyance.

"They took the Falcongate," Danzian stated, trying to move the conversation on.

Balinor nodded in agreement. "They did after centuries of trying. The Falcongate was garrisoned by a combined force of Nerlineans, Kanath and Fal'Gar. The Falcongate was ordered built by one of the Jedderas, either Jeddera the Great or his son the Summersword. It was regarded as the most prestigious of postings. Even during the war between the Fal'Gar and the Nerlinean Empire, the fort remained fully garrisoned by a mixed force. Yet with time the Nerlineans lost interest in the threat from the Mourn, despite their claim to overlordship of the steppe. The Kanath were too busy with their wars, first with each other and then with the Sevains, to pay much attention. The Fal'Gar have declined since the collapse of their empire of

Fal'Dath. Word is that at the end the garrison was down to the inbred descendants of Nerlineans sent centuries before and a single troop of Fal'Gar cavalry. It had a tenth of its minimum required garrison when it fell."

"I stand corrected, your highness," replied Danzian smoothly.

"My only point, Danzian, is that Hambledon is well garrisoned and well maintained. You can't surround it so you can't starve it out. So, it has to be taken by storm, and I am not sure how nomads, even Mourn, can do that, given the height of the walls," Balinor said.

There was a knock at the door.

Balinor looked at Danzian and raised a questioning eyebrow.

"That's the other thing," Danzian answered the unasked question. "There is a messenger for you outside."

"Who from?"

"The Company of Slayers," Danzian replied.

"Come in!" shouted the prince, fixing his chancellor with an assessing gaze.

One of the girls sat up, the silk sheets falling away to reveal her small pert breasts. Her skin was a soft light brown, and her hair, black and luxurious, tumbled over her shoulders.

Danzian's first thought was *gods, that's Charlotte Pandus*, but then he realized his error. She was just a bit too pretty, her nose smaller and sharper. Despite that, the woman's resemblance to the Lady Pandus was uncanny. He hid a smile and noted that fact for later use.

The messenger stepped into the room, taking in the chancellor, half naked woman and prince. His face showed no surprise while he executed a deep bow. He stepped forward, performing another, shallower, bow. He handed over a small piece of black silk wrapped in a roll. Balinor had heard of this development: the Slayer mage Pendian had created it, but it was the first time he had seen it used.

Balinor unfurled the silk. Gold writing had been stitched into the black fabric. It read: *I am an agent of the Company of Slayers. None may hinder or prevent my progress or trading. To do so will incur the wrath of the Company of Slayers.*

Balinor rolled it up and handed it back. So arrogant, so Saliana, he thought. Magic tied the silk fabric to its bearer. Should it pass out of the hands of the designated bearer for too long, it would disintegrate. The owner carried it thrust in their clothes near the skin. Were another to steal it, it would not long survive in their hands. The system was designed to prevent messages from being intercepted.

"How long has he been outside?" Balinor asked Danzian, nodding at the messenger.

"He arrived the same time as me. We came from the palace," the chancellor replied.

Balinor nodded. *Should be long enough,* he mused. If the messenger was an imposter the fabric would have disintegrated by now, assuming Sali's new system worked.

The messenger stood, the fabric still clutched in his hand. Balinor did not recognize him. The man was a Nerlinean, an easterner.

"So, what is the message?" he asked.

"My Lord Slayer, her ladyship Dryana Slayer requests that you come to Port Ren. She and Slinker are engaged in a trade that will make the Company hugely wealthy. She needs the help of someone she can truly trust; a warrior, an honest friend. Enemies gather, most notably the Pandus family," declared the messenger.

"What trade?" asked Balinor.

"My lord," the messenger indicated Danzian and the women. "Not everyone here is of the Company of Slayers."

Balinor fixed the man with a harsh gaze. "Two things: first, I am Prince of Kangorn, so it is 'your highness' when you first speak to me and 'sir' after that, not 'my lord'. Second, last I heard Dryana was slinging solinad dung. Profitable, no doubt, but not as transformational as you suggest. So, I ask again, what is it? Before you decide your answer, anything beyond absolute clarity will see you whipped from my city, Slayer agent or not."

"Drun, your highness," the Slayer agent replied nervously.

Balinor nodded, trying to keep his face expressionless, but Danzian could see a smile creeping up on the prince.

Danzian had to congratulate Dryana: she had hit all Balinor's weak spots, reminding him of their friendship, then flattering his honesty and his martial skill. She had played him nicely.

"You cannot be entertaining this?" demanded an apparently shocked Danzian.

Balinor gave him a look.

"*Your highness*," Danzian added quickly, shooting an annoyed look at the suddenly amused messenger, who was enjoying the chancellor's error.

"Why not? My friend needs me; my company needs me," said Balinor.

"Your city needs you too, sir," observed the chancellor.

"Well, you are back now. You do the work you are supposed to do for once, instead of gallivanting around the Sevain principalities on your own personal business," the prince replied.

"What will the princess say, sir?" Danzian tried a new track.

"She will be the happiest of all: months, maybe a year, without me. She will be the happiest you have ever seen. She can finally do all the public works she wants to do, and you can have the fun of trying to stop her without me to run to."

"What about the Mourn?" Danzian asked.

"Well, if they start building ships we may have a problem. Until then we are fine. We live on an island. Look, Danzian, stop making up reasons to keep me here. I'm bored; I want to see my friends," Balinor declared with enthusiasm.

"But, sir…" Danzian seemed to be struggling with what to say.

"No buts. Get my ship ready. We make sail tomorrow morning."

Danzian stood silently for a moment. "Yes, your highness," he said.

"Oh, and this one – what's your name?" Balinor clasped the beautiful young woman's chin. "She can come with me."

"Shanti," the woman answered, confused.

"I'll talk to the Inn," Danzian replied.

"If she's willing. She's not a slave, what's it do with the Inn?" queried the prince.

"I will arrange everything. I am sure the lady with be honoured," said Danzian.

"Good, good," replied Balinor.

He turned back to the window, lifted his tankard and took a great swig. He stared out of the window, a large smile across his face.

Danzian looked at the messenger, and they nodded to each other. Giving a silent bow to the prince's back, they retreated from the room. The bleary-eyed young woman looked around for a moment, then she snuggled up to the warmth of her sleeping friend and joined her in slumber.

Chapter Fifteen – The Desert

The sand whipped across Dryana's face. She pulled her scarf closer against the hail of particles, blinking to clear her eyes. The sun glared down on them as the scrubby waste of low dry bushes gave way to the shifting sands of the desert proper. It had been two weeks on the river, starting on the River Kalshar, the mightiest river in Nerlinea – indeed, in the world of Galvia – which emptied out into the delta on which Port Ren was built. In the winter, swollen by rain, it would break its banks, inundating the surrounding land with water and rich soil, providing a strip of agriculture either side fertile enough to feed the surrounding provinces.

The two-week journey had taken them by river barge from Port Ren to the Fortress of Confluence, where the River Kalshar met the River Panon. The Fortress yawned over where the two great rivers met, its towering walls of brown-red bricks baked a dark yellow by the relentless sun. It was controlled by the Imperial Legions, its commander directly responsible to the emperor. The commander would always be a member of the royal family, close enough to be considered loyal, distant enough from the emperor to ensure no claim on the throne. The fortress was important, controlling two of the main arteries of trade. In any other society, a town, even a city, might have grown up at such a key location, but the Nerlinean Emperors had been ruthless about preventing that from happening. Only the Imperial Legions could moor up on the river dock below the fortress.

The Slayers had continued up the River Panon as it skirted the Desert of Debion. Both rivers were lined with jetties and docks for the transport of agricultural produce and other goods across the empire. They ranged in size from a mooring point to small way stations to large towns. The largest conurbation on the Panon River was Emperor's Crossing. It spread out from the eastern side of the river, lining the bank, but also surrounding a nearby lake, which was replenished every winter as the river flooded. Its original importance came from its proximity to the Amanthagan, the ceremonial heart of the Nerlinean Empire, where the emperor would periodically demand the supplication of his nobility. The river trade now sustained it. Here was one of the ferries across the river, vital when there were no bridges for hundreds of miles.

The Slayers had left at a way station just south of Emperor's Crossing, keen to avoid the attention they might attract in a larger town. The way station had an iribis stable, which would allow them to complete their journey over land. It was almost a rental system. The Iribis Company, as it was known, owned stables in way stations across the empire. They would sell travellers one of the bird-like creatures, used by humans as mounts. It would be at a premium to the value of the beast, but with the guarantee that the buyer would be repaid the amount less a fee for using the creature. The system worked: each creature came with a written paper that confirmed the deal and was always honoured by the way station at which the bird was returned. In a country used to paper money, it was just taken for granted.

Dryana pulled her brown and white iribis to a halt with a tug of the reins and stood up in her stirrups in a vain attempt to see more. The desert undulated out in front of them, dunes the size of small hills blocking a good line of sight. The wind whipped across their flat peaks, creating swirls and clouds of sand that obscured the view even further.

"We should have got a guide," she muttered angrily.

Slinker pulled to a halt behind her, his iribis chirping with annoyance. The creatures disliked the desert as much as they could tolerate it. Kept this close to the sands, they tended to shed the downy feathers of their chest and lower body, revealing gnarled greyish skin. It did not make the already ugly animals look any better.

"I know the way," Slinker declared.

"You sure?" Dryana snapped.

"Not enjoying the desert?" observed the Tancree with a smile.

"No-one could possibly enjoy this," she shot back. "This heat is terrible; aren't you hot?"

"Of course I'm bloody hot, it's a desert in Nerlinea," he laughed.

"What do you think?" Dryana demanded of Farmorl, who had just ridden up accompanied by two Slayer soldiers, not in uniform.

The young man looked from the war mage he idolized to the woman he was besotted with and tried to speak. Nothing came out, just a gurgle.

"This one is useless," Dryana grumbled caustically. "We should have brought a mage."

"We did," said Slinker with a grin.

"Another mage," she clarified.

"It's over the next ridge." Slinker indicated a sand dune maybe half a mile away.

"You said that three dunes back," she muttered petulantly.

They were trying to reach a small town, described as being on the fringes of the Desert of Debion.

"You are still worrying about what happened in the Temple of Thytha?" Slinker asked.

"No," Dryana replied.

They had gone through it a dozen times in the last couple of weeks. Slinker had been fascinated, but he had stubbornly refused to speculate on what had happened and what it meant. What was the strange flute that had used Dryana as a conduit? Slinker had told her the old legends about it. As usual, some were caught up with Jeddera Summersword, but some went even further back. The flute had been made by the Gar in the earliest of days when they had been one people. How had it come into the hands of the Nerlineans? Slinker did not know. He had never heard a story that adequately explained it; all the legends he knew spoke of them already possessing it. The flute was supposed to contain the power of the earth goddess Thytha, the Great Mother. It was supposed to give the user the ability to create life itself. Until she had been exposed to it, Dryana assumed that had been symbolic, representing the passing of the seasons and the return of new growth and life in the spring.

Slinker had told her older legends of the flute extending life, as if it might grant immortality; even bringing the dead back to life. Dryana knew from experience that did not work. You could raise the dead, animate them to do your will, use what of their soul, for lack of a better word, remained to imbue them with the smallest fraction of their previous existence. She knew it was impossible for a necromancer to create new life;

she had tried it with her own mother when she died. She knew because if the desire to bring her mother back was not enough, then no item, no wish, no power would be.

The Tancree had moved off, heading for the sand dune he had previously indicated, accompanied by the other Slayer employees.

Dryana kicked her iribis. It lurched forward and trotted to catch up with Slinker.

"There was something I forgot to mention," she offered.

He looked at Dryana sharply as her creature slowed to a walk to match Slinker's iribis.

"Lyrn Tutharum," she said.

"What does that mean?"

"I don't know," grinned Dryana. "That's why I'm asking you."

Slinker seemed to be lost in thought. She had piqued his interest.

"What was the context?" he asked.

"It was something Greldin of the Way called me. He called me Lyrn Tutharum and then spat as he walked past me," she explained.

"You didn't mention that before." Slinker sounded critical.

"I told you he insulted me and spat," she countered.

"You didn't tell me the words he used."

"I forgot," Dryana offered lamely.

Slinker gave her a sceptical look. Dryana ignored it.

"So, you know what it means? I guess it is the language of the Syn'Dion'Gar."

"Possibly; not sure," he replied. "Lyrn is an old Gar word for lord."

"So, what about Tutharum in Syn'Dion'Gar?" she queried.

212

"It's not a Syn'Dion'Gar word," he answered.

"Or not one you know?"

He raised an eyebrow at that. "Possible, but unlikely," he answered. "Besides, Lyrn is not really a word in Syn'Dion'Gar."

"You just said it was," she countered.

"It's an ancient word in Gar, the language that the elves spoke before they split. It's a dead language, but it influences the languages the various Gar races speak now. If words are commonly used, they morph over time. If not, they die out, but some cling on for a specific purpose," the Tancree explained.

"So why is Lyrn still being used?"

"Well, you know that Dumech is war leader and Trendorn is religious leader. Lyrn means leader or ruler. I guess that before the split, rulership wasn't so neatly allocated," Slinker said.

"So, he called me lord something?" she asked. "I would have thought he realized I was a woman."

"I don't think it is gender specific. You know the Gar now have a Dumech who is male and a Trendorn who is female, but I don't think things used to be that clear."

Dryana looked puzzled. "I don't think he was calling me Lord or even Lady something. It sounded more like an insult?"

Slinker shrugged. "Guess you need to find out what Tutharum means?" he mused unhelpfully.

"Thanks, Slinker, you've really helped," observed Dryana sarcastically.

Four dunes later, they crested a ridge and looked down at the small town of Omatko below. It surrounded a large oasis, shrouded by palm trees. The chattering of insects and screeching of birds replaced the silence of the desert as they approached.

A small village had grown up around the oasis, a single street of permanent buildings sprawled out from one side into the desert. A variety of tents belonging to the less permanent inhabitants of the way station surrounded the buildings. A wooden fence surrounded the oasis in an attempt to protect its precious waters from the animals nearby, which might contaminate it if allowed to get too close. A small culvert had been cut from one corner to a small pond, where a combination of gates protected the channel from becoming overwhelmed by water or draining too much from the oasis. A small herd of adunel were gathered around it, tracking back and forth through it trying to keep cool. The great bovines had never been truly domesticated, but herds could be driven or managed if the herdsman were brave enough. The adunel of Nerlinea tended to be smaller and lighter than the creatures that Dryana remembered from the forests of her childhood. They had longer, flatter horns 'but with the same viciously sharp points, which would dissuade anyone foolish enough to think that the creatures were not wild animals. No attempt to enclose them had been made – it would not have worked had anyone tried. The main job of the herdsman was to keep the pond sufficiently filled so that the mighty cattle did not decide to test the fences that protected the main waters. They were being driven west from the open grasslands that filled the gap between the desert and the coast. They would be driven to the river, which they would follow either south to the large cities of the coast, such as Port Ren, or north, where the river was narrower and could be bridged. The creatures were too wild to be put on the ferry or a river barge, and the waters of the great River Panon were far too deep at the nearest point for the animals to have any hope of surviving being driven across it.

Trapped as they currently were in the desert, a climate so contrary to their normal habitat, there was little risk of them running off despite their lack of enclosure. By comparison, two small fenced areas had been set up some distance away for iribis. The bird-like beasts milled around in groups, maybe a dozen of them in each area. Troughs of water regularly refilled were spaced evenly across the desiccated sandy paddocks.

The buildings on the main street were all wooden: eight single-storey structures, four either side of the wide hard sand road. Sand had been blown up against them, giving them an entrenched feeling that they had lacked upon their original construction. The wood had been brought here; there was little enough around the oasis, and the squat palm trees that did surround it would not have produced the right kind of timber to build the structures.

Originally, a small mudbrick settlement had stood on the far side of the oasis. It had been scoured clean by the desert many years ago and only the base of the walls, largely obscured by sand, were still visible, a hint of what once had been there. Even a seemingly permanent structure was temporary in the face of the rolling sands.

The eight buildings all served some sort of purpose. There were six shops of various sorts: a general store, something that might have been a herbalist, and the rest sold food of different descriptions. There was an iribis way station, the second largest structure in the village and the only one not entirely made of wood. A small rectangle of mudbricks formed the base of that building. The largest building was a bar. Dryana would have struggled to call it a tavern, as it lacked the homeliness that the name implied. It was a place for drinking and to get drunk. It was mid-morning and already the Slayers could hear the sound of raucous excitement emanating loudly from the building. They pulled their iribis to a halt outside the structure and dismounted, wrapping their reins around the wooden rail constructed for that purpose.

"Wait here with them," Dryana told the two soldiers.

They nodded their understanding.

"You want us to water them?" one of them asked.

"No; I don't want them uncomfortable if we need to leave in a hurry," she replied.

The iribis, normally docile creatures, chirped angrily as if they understood the instruction.

"Yes, my lady," came the soldier's reply.

Dryana strode up the steps to the open door of the bar, wood bouncing under her feet. The rest followed her, keen to get under the shelter of the awning that sprouted out from the front the building. The two soldiers took a seat on the benches arranged outside either side of the door. Dryana and Slinker stepped into the bar, followed by Farmorl. For a moment she thought about ordering Slinker's young ally to stay outside with the other Slayer soldiers. The idea of leaving the young man baking outside in the hot sun amused her. Recently she had taken a dislike to him. Initially she had been attracted to his good looks and easy manner, but he had proved unwilling to let her make full use of him. Dryana, who was not used to being refused, had taken this personally. She was feeling particularly stressed, caught up in the machinations of Emperor Nyandar and Srias Halfnight-Pandus, especially when she was trying to execute plans of her own. She found his reluctance to help her blow off steam grating. She did not understand it. She had caught the young man looking at her enough times. She suspected that Slinker had warned him off, which just annoyed her even more.

As Dryana stepped into the dark of the bar, it took a moment for her eyes to adjust to the gloom. Wide windows spilled light across the common room, so it was not really dark, except by comparison to the burning sunlight outside. She had expected it to be cooler inside, but the room was fetid and steaming, its air cloyed with tobacco smoke, laced with a hint of drun, and beer. Dryana wrinkled her nose and scanned the room.

216

PRINCE OF SLAYERS

A long bar framed the far end of the room. Rectangular tables with benches either side, built as a single piece, filled it. Two dozen people, all male, were seated at the benches, or perching on the tables, while two propped up the long bar. She noted a variety of long knives on belts, even one with a legionary short sword.

She found who she was looking for. He stood out as he was the only Gar in the room. The dark copper skin of his angular face was framed by glossy black hair that hung straight down, spilling past his shoulders towards his waist. The Debion'Gar had made no attempt to tie it back. He was dressed no differently from the others in the room. A dark purple tunic that stopped just above his knees was his only clothing, while a long dagger with a simple leather-wrapped handle was thrust through his wide black leather belt.

Dryana stalked across the room, heading for the bar. Interested gazes appraised her and the Tancree, and the man who accompanied them. She stopped at the bar and slammed her hand hard on the dark brown wood.

"Beer," she demanded.

The Nerlinean man behind the bar, an easterner, picked up a large porcelain vessel and drew down a draught of beer into it. It was the thin light yellow type preferred among the Nerlineans. He placed it down in front of Dryana and then poured two more for Slinker and Farmorl. Dryana drank it rapidly, throwing her head back as she chugged it down.

"This tastes like piss. Another," she demanded, as she slapped the porcelain back down on the bar.

"Money," observed the barman calmly.

Dryana reached into the pouch on her waist and tugged out a note in paper currency. The face value was far more than the beer was worth. She dropped it on the bar.

"Another," she barked. "And keep it coming until that is used up."

The barman picked up the note with a sweep of his hand and plunked down another beer in front of the Slayer. Dryana turned around and looked at the Gar sat on the bench.

"You Kcillit? she asked rudely.

She put down her beer on the Gar's bench, splashing some across the wood. She sat sideways on the bench, then slid her legs around so she was facing the Gar. The Gar looked at her appraisingly. He pulled up his right leg so his foot was resting on the bench. It looked to be a simple rearrangement for comfort, but it gave him the ability to push himself off the bench should he need to. The attachment of the bench to the table meant the option of pushing it away in a confrontation was not available to him.

Slinker and Farmorl waited behind Dryana, sipping slowly on their beers. They remained standing.

"Are you normally this rude?" asked the Gar.

His eyes darted around the room. The other men were watching the confrontation, but none made any movement except for a swivel of their eyes or a turn of their heads.

Dryana took another slug of beer before clanking it down on the bench, splashing even more.

The Gar watched the woman cautiously. Her boorish behaviour was not characteristic of what he had heard of her. Was it some sort of display, or had the hot desert sun driven her mad? Dryana was enjoying herself hugely; it was the first time she had managed to discomfort a Gar. She feared that her enjoyment would become too obvious and that he would see through her pantomime.

She reached into her pouch, watching the Gar shift uncomfortably. She fished out a smaller leather wallet and upended its contents on the bench. Threads of black fungus splayed across the wood, though some white dust puffed up and seemed to be held in the air by bars of sunlight. The Gar reached forward and prodded a single finger into the black threads. He put it to his mouth, then spat a great globule of saliva. It hit the floor next to him.

"This is what you wanted to discuss?"

Dryana gave a broad smile and took another swig of beer. Her cup was nearly finished, she raised it up above her head. "Another," she demanded.

The barman appeared, collecting the empty receptacle and placing a full one on the table.

"I have a supplier," Kcillit observed quietly.

Dryana was impressed by his Nerlinean; he had managed to almost completely remove the singsong tone that so many Gar imparted to human languages.

"Fatboy," Dryana stated.

Kcillit looked around nervously, as if Lan Xian could hear his unflattering nickname all the way from Port Ren.

"Where do you think Fatboy gets his supply?" the Slayer demanded.

Kcillit was not foolish enough to ask Fatboy where he got his drun from. Indeed, he had never met the big man, dealing only with his lackeys. He knew that Fatboy had found a new supplier – everyone in the business did – and it made sense that the ambitious western traders in front of him were providing it. But he could not fathom what that had to do with him. Drun was not big business for him; it was just one among many items traded across the desert.

"How did you find me?" he asked.

"Your directions to our messenger were very clear," observed Dryana.

Kcillit smiled at the misunderstanding. The Slayers had sent a representative to meet him two weeks ago, and the intermediary had arranged the meeting. That wasn't what he meant, though.

"I mean, how did you decide to approach me?" he clarified.

"Oh," said Dryana, a smile cracking her boorish display for the first time. "We asked around."

"Well, I am flattered by your interest," he said politely. "As you seem to already know, I have a supplier in the form of Lan Xian."

"Are you nervous of these men overhearing our business?" Dryana's hand waved at the men sitting silently at the benches watching the meeting unfold.

"Everyone in this room who does not work for you works for me," he replied.

"Is that a yes or no?" enquired the Slayer.

"You asked around," he countered. "Maybe Xian will ask around too." The Gar shrugged.

She understood the observation. He was implying that she had a spy among Lan Xian's people, which of course was true. She actually had two. The Gar apparently feared that Xian had a similar hook in his own organization.

"Well, we are here now, so I suggest you eliminate any spies you have among your number," she replied. "I have a proposal for you, and it does not concern my supply to Lan Xian."

"If you bring drun into Port Ren then Lan Xian will ensure it concerns him," Kcillit declared.

"And if I brought it in somewhere else?" she asked.

"Bring it anywhere else – Nerlon, any of the southern ports – he will still ensure it concerns him."

"What if I brought it into Mahendra?" she replied.

"Mahendra?" Kcillit was incredulous.

Dryana hid her amusement. She had never seen a Gar shocked before and was quite enjoying it.

Kcillit calmed himself. Mahendra was on the east coast of Nerlinea and fairly far northward at that – almost on the border with Quil'Dath.

"It makes no difference; any ship would have to stop at the southern ports. Xian will know what you are doing and demand his cut."

"We would need you to distribute it west from Mahendra to the central cities and across to the west coast," Dryana continued, ignoring his concern.

"What?" The Gar was getting annoyed. He leant forward as if trying to explain things to an idiot. "Why not land it in Rastindor or Halfnight, if you are bringing it from the steppe? You don't need me or Lan Xian."

"Those cities are under the control of the Pandus family. We do not expect them to be accommodating to Slayer ships," she replied.

Kcillit looked confused.

"If we land a Slayer ship or one of an affiliated company at the western ports, the Pandus will search it thoroughly and use the presence of drun as an excuse to seize the ship. It will be brought to the attention of the emperor, endangering our whole company," explained Dryana. "In the southern and eastern ports, the Pandus have substantially less influence. It's a matter of risk."

"The Pandus are powerful enemies to have," Kcillit observed, dismissing the idea.

Dryana cursed her misstep. There had been no reason for her to share why they could not land the drun in the western Nerlinean ports.

"Maybe you could recommend someone else who could distribute across the desert to the west from Mahendra?" she queried politely.

If it was made to sound like she had given up on him, it was the exact opposite. She could feel the men around her listening and watching the conversation. Eyes had started sparkling at the profits to be made. Now they would see it slipping away. One might even think Kcillit did not need to run things anymore; that they could do a better job. The Gar was more than aware of this. None of his followers' loyalty was so ironclad that he could be sure they were willing to walk away from the potential money the slight woman in front of him was offering. He tried another tack.

"There are gangs in Mahendra that control the drun trade," he observed.

"Let me worry about that," the young woman answered with irritating confidence. "There will be enough drun for everyone."

The men in the room moved restlessly. Their excitement was building at the potential on offer.

"Where is it coming from?" he asked.

She raised an eyebrow in query.

"The drun, where is it coming from?" Kcillit demanded.

"Why does it matter?" she asked.

"Because Mahendra is the least obvious place to bring in drun. Drun moving through the city has normally been on its way out, not in, going out to the island provinces or the Kasmeric Kingdoms. That was before we lost Havagia to the Mourn."

"So, the imperials are very unlikely to look for it," she replied.

"Not really answering my question."

"How so?" Dryana asked.

"Where is it coming from?" Kcillit demanded, his voice rising. "Your ships arrive east from the western lands. So, I assume you collect in Haydron. So far, so traditional. You can't land it in Rastindor or Halfnight because of your enmity with the Pandus family. You can't bring it through the southern ports because Lan Xian will demand he distributes it or at least gets a cut. It is not coming from Havagia, as that way is closed since the Mourn conquest. I would have known if that changed. So, if you are bringing it to Mahendra, it is not coming in from the steppe. That means you have a source other than the steppe."

"Maybe I do, maybe I don't," the Slayer replied with a smile. "It is not your concern."

The Gar gave a very human laugh in response.

"I would say you aren't very trusting, but then you came in here and spoke to me, a man you don't know, in front of people you don't know, in a place you have never been before. You seem open to the point of carelessness. I am surprised that you would not tell us every detail of your plans," he said.

He felt the room shift away from the presumptuous young woman in realization that she and her plans may not have been as clever as they initially appeared.

"*Man*?" observed Dryana with a cold smile.

"Male. I apologize for my use of the vernacular; too much time spent with your kind," he replied.

Dryana looked at him, her eyes calculating.

"Slinker, convince our doubting friend," she asked.

The Tancree smiled with his characteristic leer. He cleared his throat.

"Kcillit Taydas, of Clan Tiramor of the Debion'Gar, born eighty-seven years ago, in the city of Gromer – not in the great desert, as you claim. You grew up among humans, more than Gar, hence your excellent Nerlinean with no trace of Gar accent and your un-Garlike mannerisms. You grew up in a merchant household, a third child – a great rarity among the Gar. Your family fell on hard times when your father was murdered over a business deal, leaving your family destitute. You were fifteen at the time, young for a Gar. You claim that as a youth you ran with pickpocket gangs on the streets of Gromer, but in truth you were taken in by a senior bureaucrat of the Dumech of Gromer. He was sleeping with your mother and you left when you discovered he was also sleeping with both your older sisters," Slinker reported.

Kcillit was becoming visibly annoyed, hard eyes boring into the Tancree.

"Having left Gromer, you worked the river for several decades. Not the normal job for one of the Debion'Gar. You worked hard, saved up till you had your own collection of three barges. Making good money, you built yourself a new house in the river port of Halyn Station. You even started to use your family relationships among the Debion'Gar to start running caravans across the desert to Mahendra: mainly foodstuffs from Havagia, but also a little drun from time to time. More the behaviour of an affluent if morally flexible merchant than a gang leader. Then the Mourn invasion happened, nearly a decade ago now. Like many a merchant, you found the foundations of the house you had built were made of sand, appropriate for a desert elf. You owed moneylenders in Port Ren and Gromer. Serious people who could not be bullied or threatened to make the problem go away. You lost your barges, and you lost your house. Six years ago, you pitched up here, a small trading post on the edge of the desert, with an almost entirely transient population. You started to rebuild, but with little money and your old relationships largely useless after the loss of Havagia, you fell back on your family relationships, using your relatives and friends among the Debion'Gar to trade goods and a trickle of drun that still came from the eastern steppe to the cities on the coast. When that trade eventually all but dried up, you became a middleman for every raider and thief trying to move stolen and illicit goods around the fringes of the great desert." Slinker finished and favoured the Gar with a nasty leer.

"I'm impressed," Kcillit replied, and he meant it. "So, you know who I am, but that gives me no reason to trust you. The trade routes, be they river or road, buzz with the name of your company, but they have hummed with the name of other companies before and they came to nothing, many at the hand of the Pandus and their like. Why should I take the risk?"

"Money, position, fear. Take your pick; it matters little to me." Dryana was annoyed. *This was supposed to have been easier,* she thought. Why was the Gar being so difficult?

"Position?" the Gar demanded.

"With this deal you can make enough money to recover the position you lost; more, even. You could set yourself up in a big house in Gromer," she explained calmly.

"And fear?" he asked.

She looked at him – no, not at him, but through him. Kcillit felt cold, as if death were touching him. He looked into the eyes of this woman, who was barely more than a girl, and felt terror in the depth of his soul.

"And fear," she stated calmly.

Kcillit swallowed.

"Do we have a deal?" she pressed.

He nodded slowly.

"Good," she declared and stood up. "Now we need you to provide us with guides across the desert to Mahendra."

"I have some cousins who could guide you," the Gar offered grudgingly.

"Good," said Dryana, looking down at him. "Slinker will be staying here to ensure that things are organized correctly."

She strode out into the sun; the light was blinding after the dark of the room. She took a breath of the hot dry air, clearing her lungs after the fetid atmosphere of the bar. She enjoyed the change for a moment, but then the burning heat of the desert overpowered the temporary sensory switch. Gods, she hated this place, she thought.

"I am staying here?" Slinker whispered over her shoulder. He had followed Dryana out.

225

"I don't trust him," she explained quietly.

"Were we ever likely to?" he asked.

"I suppose not," she shrugged. "Kcillit may not know it, but this stinking little village is the lynchpin of the whole thing."

"Maybe." The Tancree did not sound convinced. "They are all links in the chain, none more important than any other and yet all vital. He makes a good point: where do we get the drun?"

"Sali has a plan," Dryana replied.

"Has she told you it?" Slinker asked.

"Of course."

"You are a terrible liar, Dryana," Slinker replied with a grin.

She shot him an angry look. She did not know why Saliana was keeping things from her; from them all.

"Just make sure this works, Slinker," she said, louder than she intended and stalked off.

"Yes, ma'am," he muttered at her back.

Chapter Sixteen –
The Debion'Gar

The tent was being pummelled by the hard grit of the desert, the blasting wind helping it find every gap in the overlapping layers of fabric. Dryana shivered under layers of clothing. This place made no sense: baking all day, almost freezing at night.

The had pitched their tents high on a sandy ridge, near what looked like a small outcrop of rocks. In reality, the rocks were the top of a much larger edifice almost entirely covered by the shifting sands. She had doubted their choice of location. They could have sheltered down at the base of the outcrop where the wind would be less biting, but her two Debion'Gar guides had laughed at that, declaring it unsafe. She had speculated to them that they risked being swamped by the sand dunes. They had laughed at that too; they had said there was a risk of being drowned. She had assumed they were joking, but no, apparently there was a risk of sudden rains filling up the gullies. It was absurd: out here in the desert, rain seemed like a distant memory, as all they did was bake during the day and shiver at night.

The two guides were Kcillit's cousins, Darinya and Koman Hellithan of Clan Tiramor. Dryana had assumed they were sister and brother, but Darinya was the mother and Koman her son. They were both in the time of a Gar's life where it was impossible to guess at their age, except to know they were neither young nor truly old. They could have been anywhere between fifty years old and well past a century or even two. Dryana's polite enquiries on the subject had elicited only shrugs in response. The pair looked much like their cousin, with coal-black hair and burnished bronze skin. The pair were taller than Kcillit, both comfortably clearing six feet in height. They were thinner, too; spindly by comparison with the other Debion'Gar Dryana had met.

Farmorl and the other two Slayer employees had stayed with Dryana, at Slinker's insistence. She had tried to leave at least one of them, preferably Farmorl, with Slinker, in case he needed the help. He had laughed at the idea.

Dawn broke and the six of them swiftly broke camp and rolled up the tents. They were of a Debion'Gar design used across the desert. They could be compacted down so that each iribis and rider was carrying what seemed to be little more than a bed roll. Dryana stripped off several of the layers she had worn through the night, so only a long white robe fluttered over her normal black silks. She shivered in the early-morning cold, but she knew she would be sweltering soon enough.

They had been riding their iribis from watering hole to watering hole for ten days now. The route was circuitous, determined by the need to access water rather than by distance. Dryana wondered if she should have taken the imperial road that ran east from the Amanthagan in an arrow-straight line. It crossed the desert in places, but mostly stayed south of the main expanse of the sands. Far to the east it would meet the Great East Coast Highway that ran from the south coast north to Mahendra before carrying onto Susak in Quil'Dath. It would be slower, taking the two short sides of a giant geographic triangle, but it would be on solid stone roads, with signs and way stations, rather than across the desert. Without the guides they would almost certainly be lost and probably die of thirst. Dryana struggled to sleep, fearful that the Kcillit's cousins might decide to disappear one night, leaving them to their fate. Life had not made her trusting.

The iribis were cantankerous that morning, snappy and grumpy, more like huffrin. Last night they had stayed in the open desert away from water. The beasts had to get by on the barest rations of water and meal. Dryana hoped the next waterhole was better than the last two. These had been simply a spring in the desert that created a muddy pool. Enough to service their needs but little else. Kcillit's oasis, as she had taken to thinking of it, now seemed like a paradise by comparison.

The group progressed along the ridgeline before dropping down to the desert floor and moving across the open sands. The sun was already cooking them. Dryana was drenched in sweat, and everything that could rub was rubbing. She appreciated the loose clothes kept that to a minimum, but still every juddering movement on the bird under her was unpleasant. The others were enjoying it even less, encumbered as they were with light leather armour and weapons. The two Debion'Gar seemed unconcerned; a life spent in this environment made it second nature.

"How many more days of this?" demanded Farmorl, to no one in particular.

"Same again. Another ten, I think, four more in the desert before it turns to scrub. Another day and it is grasslands and agriculture," Dryana replied.

"We could have gone by ship," he observed.

"You made this point," the witch shot back.

She had already explained it to him. To go by ship, they would have to go all the way back to Port Ren and then take the long sea journey north. It would take weeks longer than crossing the desert, though it would have been a lot more comfortable than either of the overland options.

They travelled until late morning and then stopped for three hours across midday, avoiding the maximum strength of the sun. They continued through the afternoon, and the sun was sinking in the sky when Dryana started to make out trees and low squat shrubs, their wood baked white with yellowed leaves. Behind were ruins, a tumbled-down medley of dark brown mudbrick walls, barely discernible as the buildings they once had been. Walls a brick or two high stretched across the sands, riven by gaps in so many places that there was more open space than barrier. As they continued to approach, streams of inviting blue speared out across the yellow earth, hinting at the oasis that lay beyond the wall.

Ahead of them, Darinya waved her hand, bringing their column to a halt. She dropped down from her iribis a few hundred yards from the ruins. Crouching down and toying with the sand, she scanned the oasis. She clicked her tongue as if assessing something.

"What is this place?" Dryana asked Koman.

"Our overnight stop," he replied.

He did not look at the Slayer. His eyes, like his mother's, were busy searching the ruins, though he had not dismounted. The iribis were growing restive; they could practically taste the water in front of them.

The female Gar stood up and scattered the sand in her hand across the desert floor. She looked at the ruins one more time. She mounted her iribis and, with another wave of her hand but with no word, progressed towards them.

PRINCE OF SLAYERS

It was getting dark when they reached the ruins.

The sun came down fast in the desert, reflected Dryana.

They camped in the cover of the collapsed buildings. Though largely destroyed, their sides were still higher than what remained of the ruined walls that had once surrounded this place. Dryana walked to the edge of the oasis, stepping over thin streams of water that bled across the desert floor before swiftly drying to nothing. At the edge of the water, the brown and yellow vegetation gave way to lusher, greener plants. Insects and small birds chirped and cooed in the evening air. The former clustered and buzzed around the burning brand that Dryana was using to light her way. She waved them away with her hand, but they just came back.

Surrounded as it was by plants and small trees, it took Dryana a moment to realize there was something odd about the oasis. She reached down at the edge of the water where it lapped against the stone. She hoped the motion of the water was created by the movement of the wind and not by some ancient monster residing in it. Not there would have been anything like enough animals in the waters or the foliage surrounding it to sustain such a creature.

She squatted down at the side of the oasis, where rivulets of water cut through the sand. The waters were spring fed, she surmised, new water constantly entering the basin at the bottom and causing it to overflow. A stone on the edge of the pool caught her attention. It had been finished in a neat line, now weathered by the passage of time, curving slightly to account for the bend in the edge of the oasis. Holding the torch in one hand, she used the other to move away wet sand. A thin layer of water rushed into the gap she had created, cleaning a piece of white stone underneath it. She brushed sand away to the edge of the pool. Standing up, she held up the torch so its light sprang out across the waters. It was hard to be sure in the failing light even with a torch, but if one ignored the vegetation then the pool was a perfect oval, as if man-made.

She walked back to the camp in the lee of the ruined building. A small fire of dried wood spat red sparks into the air.

"What was this place?" she asked Koman.

"It is an oasis," came his response.

"I know what it is; I want to know what it *was*," she tried to explain.

The Debion'Gar shrugged.

Dryana used the brand to light the corner of the ruined building and stared at a small carving on the wall. She ran her hand across the complex web of lines. It was a picture, more like an inscription, but she did not even recognize the alphabet, let alone the language.

"What language is this?" she asked.

Darinya, who was resting by the fire, stood up and came to stand beside Dryana, towering over the witch. She leant into the wall and squinted at the words.

"Kasmeric lettering," she said dismissively.

"Can you read it?" asked Dryana.

"No," came the terse response.

"But you recognize it?"

The female Gar fixed the witch with a beady gaze.

"They look similar to the letters of Kasem, used by several kingdoms in the east. It is said this was once a city of the Empire of Kasem," she said.

"A city in the desert?" queried Dryana.

"This was not always desert; once the Empire of Kasem stretched this far south," she explained.

Dryana had a sudden thought. "Why did you stop before letting us enter the oasis? Just caution?"

"Something felt wrong," replied the Gar.

"What?"

"I don't know," Darinya shrugged. "Get some sleep. We will start early in the morning; the next water source is a fair journey."

***

The creature emerged from the ruin and stretched its back, its muscles cracking. It took a moment to enjoy the cool of the night after the stifling heat of the tunnel in which it had hidden through the heat of the day. The collapsed buildings that surrounded the oasis were so reduced by the centuries they seemed little more than a clutch of mudbricks, but they hid a more complex world: a collection of tunnels and basements, some long filled with sand, but many more giving places to hide. The people who had once lived here had spent a part of their life underground to avoid the burning heat of the sun. Other buildings that had once been above the ground had been buried by the shifting sands of the desert, giving further places to hide.

It sniffed the air, its rat-like nose twitching, its long whiskers searching. Its beady eyes focused on the small fire flickering in the distance. It looked left and right. Despite its excellent night vision it could make out only the merest hint of its fellows in the dark amid the foliage, shadows hinted at in the limited light from the campfire. The creature was thin and rangy, all lean muscle covered with a dark grey fur. Its rat-like face was angular and sharp, halfway between that of a human and a rat. The peachy pink colour of its tail matched its ears and feet. It whipped side to side, hissing gently across the sands.

The wererat crept forward through the greenery until it judged the next step would reveal it. For while the only light for miles was the red of the low fire ahead, the sky was clear, and one of Galvia's moons spilled a white reflection across the ruins.

Two sat at the fire – a male and a female, from the smell, decided the wererat, one human, one Gar. They were sitting watch, though both were drowsy, struggling to stay awake in the quiet of the desert. The wererat extended his senses across the rest of the camp. There were six in total: the two he could see by the fire and another four slumbering in the tents beyond. Another three humans and a further Gar. This was going to be easier than he had been led to believe, the humans' mundane weapons would be useless against them. The Gar looked too impoverished to be carrying swords forged from alcidide, that would have been a threat to the five wererats. The five had tracked the Slayers to the village on the edge of the sands, quietly thankful that the group had left the mage behind before setting off into the desert. They had got ahead of the travellers the previous night, using the dark to steal past them and head for the oasis where they were certain they would go. They had seen the Slayers arrive, including their target, the young woman who implausibly seemed to be in command. The Debion'Gar, the old-smelling woman, had almost spotted them. They had been wary, and the woman seemed to have fully dismissed the warnings of her subconscious.

Still, the wererats had been cautious, waiting for them to fall asleep. Should the Slayers be forewarned, they would make it to their iribis and be away with the wererats unable to catch up. The lead wererat had considered attacking the birds and finishing off the iribis first, leaving their riders with no means of escape. It would be a risk, though: the carping of the iribis would certainly wake the slumbering party and allow them to prepare some sort of defence. He was fairly certain they had no magic, but who knew with the Gar. There was also the risk of alcidide weapons when the Gar were present. Also, his boss had been very clear to him not to underestimate the girl; that she should inspire fear. Having watched her across the desert, he found the idea that the thin, pale thing was any threat to his kind absurd, but he respected his mistress too much to fully discount her warning.

The camp was in the shelter of a tumble-down building protecting the humans and the Gar from the blowing sand and wind. It also created a barrier that could be defended should any attacker arrive from the desert. The iribis had been tied up to the side against an oddly angled palm tree, so one of his kind would be placed to prevent the Slayers from getting to their mounts.

The lead wererat leapt from the foliage, covering the twenty feet between his hiding place and the fire in seconds. He bounded forward on all fours, moving more like a racing wolf than a rat or a human. He caught the Gar as she moved for her sword, grabbing her hand before she got to it, and slamming his palm up through her chin. Her neck snapped with a sickening crunch and her eyes rolled upwards in her skull. He pulled the corpse forward and his slavering jaws locked onto the throat, ripping it out in a single vicious bite. Hot blood sprayed across his face. A sword slammed into his side. He grunted more in annoyance than pain and tossed the Gar's lifeless body away from him.

He turned on his attacker, the human who had been sitting watch. He noted the man's shock, for he had just stabbed the sharp length of his legionary short sword into the wererat with no effect. Where a gaping wound should have been, there was nothing. The wererat reached out with his bony clawed hand and seized him by the top of his head. The man continued to chop uselessly against the creature's body and arms with his blade, shouting with rage, but it did nothing. The wererat snapped the man's neck with a single nonchalant twist of his hand.

Dryana woke to the commotion, any grogginess swiftly dispelled by the shouts around her. She threw off her blankets and scrabbled to find her sword. The entrance flap was ripped back, and she turned around on her knees, weapon held desperately in front of her. In the half-light she could make out Farmorl. He grabbed her by the shoulder and yanked her bodily out of the tent. She took in the sight before her. The others were dead. The corpses of Darinya and the two Slayer soldiers lay strewn at odd angles across the camp. The other Gar, Kamon, lay on the ground. The lean form of a wererat squatted on top of his body, tearing great chunks of flesh from the Gar. She heard a howl from the iribis: a wererat was slashing and biting at the terrified creatures, cackling with glee at their fear.

Three wererats were advancing on Dryana and Farmorl. Slinker's protege waved his sword in front of him. He pushed Dryana behind him as he backed slowly into the corner of the ruined building. The witch glanced over her shoulder; there was nowhere to go. The wall was her head height; there was little chance they could get over it. Where would they go anyway? These creatures would run them down into the open desert.

She grabbed Farmorl by the shoulder and pulled the young warrior back, thrusting him behind her.

"Hey!" came his shocked response.

"That thing won't do anything to them," she declared contemptuously, meaning his sword. She wished her own blades were made of alcidide or were enchanted – the only hope against the wererats, who in their natural form were impervious to mundane weapons.

"Brave warrior, hiding behind a girl," came the mocking response from the lead wererat.

"Who sent you?" Dryana demanded.

That drew a laugh. "Who do you think?" came the growled response.

"The Pandus?" she asked.

She got no response. She needed none. She knew the answer anyway.

"There was a battle here once, long ago," she announced.

"There is a battle here now," the wererat laughed in response. "Time to die, little Slayer."

The wererat leapt forward. He slammed into the floor, careering through tents and landing against the side of the ruin. Darinya was ripping and tearing at him with no success. It took him a moment to work out what was happening: the Gar's head was at an odd angle, dead eyes looking at him. He tore the Gar free and tossed the animated corpse over the wall. He pulled himself up. His compatriots were laughing at him with deep-throated chortles. He shot them an evil glance and then laughed himself, as the two dead Slayers and the other dead Gar started attacking his fellows. They did little more than provide an annoyance. The wererat tore limbs off them and tossed them away.

The leader turned back to Dryana. "Well done, witch. I hope you enjoyed your extra moments of life?" he spat angrily.

"Just buying some time," came Dryana's cold reply.

"Time for what?" he grunted contemptuously.

"There was a battle here once," she repeated with an evil grin.

A skeletal hand, nothing but bones, thrust out of the dirt and grabbed the wererat's ankle. A look of shock covered its ratty features. He tried to pull free, but all he pulled up was the upper torso of a skeleton, still clutching his ankle. Another hand appeared from the dirt and grasped the other ankle. More were thrusting out of the dirt, grabbing at the wererats. They tried to stamp them away, but the dead were remorseless. The wererats heard something and looked back over their shoulders. Emerging from the foliage came skeletal forms, white bone devoid of even a hint of flesh. They were covered in bronze armour, and a few still had helms resting on their heads. Some still clutched the swords they had held in life.

There were dozens of them, and then there were scores.

Panic started to fill the wererats.

The undead attacked, bony hands, gnashing with ancient teeth, swinging swords of orange bronze. These attacks could not injure the wererats, but numbers meant something. The ratmen tried to throw the attackers away, pitching them over the wall, throwing them back into the greenery. It was futile, as more and more came forward, overwhelming the creatures, until all five were pinned to the floor, screaming and roaring with fruitless rage. Each attacker the wererats ripped apart was replaced by two more.

Dryana walked forward to where a semicircle ten undead deep had formed around the pinned-down wererats. One of the rats tried to reach for her, clawed hand scrabbling. She skirted it easily. She stopped before a figure at the front of the undead line. He wore a full suit of ancient armour. Clasped in his hand was a great two-handed bronze falchion, its point resting on the desert sand.

"Give me the blade," she demanded.

It was unnecessary: the skeletons were hers to command. They sensed her intent; they did not obey spoken commands. They had no ears to hear. Still, for a moment it looked as though the ancient battle leader might refuse to surrender his weapon. Then his skeletal hand opened, and he dropped the blade to the ground, missing Dryana's outreached hand. She squatted down and picked up the heavy blade. She hefted it in her grip as she stood up.

She walked to the nearest wererat and slammed the sword down on its face. It bounced off. She cursed. The wererat growled with rage but was otherwise unaffected.

"What was that?" demanded a shocked Farmorl.

"Leader," she indicated the undead commander. "I was hoping his weapon might be enchanted."

"Was it?" he asked.

"Obviously not," she replied, glaring at him. "Right, plan B," she declared to no-one in particular.

She picked up the Gar swords, first Darinya's and then Koman's, before tossing them aside with a mutter of annoyance. Then she stalked to where the pair had left their compound bows and quivers of arrows. She picked up the quivers and walked over to the fire. She sat down and emptied out the arrows on the floor.

"What are you doing?" Farmorl enquired. He looked panicked, watching the wererats as they struggled to free themselves from the mass of undead. Skeletal forms were tossed out from the group, before more replaced them.

She ignored him and their attackers.

Whatever she was doing was discomforting the wererats, who renewed their attempts to break free of the animated dead with even greater ferocity.

Dryana held each arrowhead up to fire, cursing as she tossed the first few aside. Then she found what she was looking for – a certain glint in the metal – the telltale sign of alcidide. She placed the arrow carefully to the right. She continued the process until she had four arrows on her right side and a larger pile on her left side. She got to the final arrow and checked it in the fire. A glint sparked off it.

"Thank the gods: one for each of you," she said with a nasty smile.

The wererats were raging now, writhing to get free.

Dryana stood up and looked at the bows. She shook her head, dismissing them. "You know that wooden hammer?" she asked Farmorl.

"The one we used for the tent pegs?" he asked, confused.

"Yes; you seen it?"

"It was over here somewhere," Farmorl replied. He started rustling through the destroyed camp, pulling aside tents and bedding until he found it. He lifted it up with a look of victory.

"Well done," Dryana replied mockingly.

She snapped each arrow over her knee, leaving an arrowhead attached to a portion of the shaft.

"Give it here," she said, holding her free hand out.

Farmorl passed it to her. "What are you going to do with it?"

Dryana stood over the squirming body of the leader. Always take out the leaders first, she had been taught. She wondered if it applied in these circumstances.

"One each, no sharing," she said with an evil smile, holding up the broken arrows.

The wererat spat at her, but she was too far away for it to hit her, and it landed back on its own face.

Dryana laughed at him, then took the arrow and positioned it above the wererat's heart. She took the wooden-headed hammer and slowly pummelled the arrowhead into its chest. The alcidide in the arrowhead penetrated the creature's esoteric protection. Pain shot through the wererat's eyes, and he screamed. Dryana continued until the barbed arrowhead and a good part of the shaft were buried in the wererat. She could feel the heart starting to fail, but it was still working. *Tough old things*, she thought grudgingly.

She stood up, leaving the remaining arrows and hammer by the side of the wererat. His body was flexing now, more an involuntary movement at the trauma that had been inflicted than any pointless attempt to escape. She walked over to the saddlebags of her travelling companions and emptied them out, looking for something she could use. She found a pair of pliers in one of the Gar's saddlebags. She walked back to the wererat. She squatted over him, standing on his naked torso, the only place there was space with the undead holding the beast down. She looked in his eyes. Already the life was fading, but not fast enough. She took the shaft of the arrow in the head of the pliers and yanked. On the third yank it came free, the barb taking a lump of flesh with it. Blood coursed from the chest rather than spurted, as the heart was already failing.

Farmorl watched with horrified fascination as Dryana repeated the same process four more times on each of the wererats. Each time the creatures seemed to be more accepting of their fate. The last one barely struggled, or so it seemed to the young warrior. Dryana tossed the pliers aside and stood up, feeling the life flow out of the last wererat. The skeletons holding them fast let them go. Some of the undead stood up, merging with the group that still stood in a semicircle around them. Others seemed to burrow back into the ground. After a moment the surrounding undead withdrew, disappearing into the foliage. Dryana watched them go.

"What do we do?" Farmorl asked.

The blood-covered witch looked at him, as if seeking more of an explanation.

"We are in the desert, our guides are dead, what do we do?" he clarified.

She sighed. "That is tomorrow's problem."

He looked as if he was about to say something. She stood in front of him and reached up, her bloody hand curling around the back of his head. She pulled him in and kissed him hungrily. Then she pulled him towards her half-collapsed tent.

***

She awoke to the hot sun blazing through the flap of the tent and reached out, patting the blankets next to her. He was gone. She sat up and rubbed her eyes. She needed to wash; she was covered in dried blood.

"My Lady Slayer!" Farmorl's shout came from outside the tent.

That was a bit formal after last night, she thought. She pulled on her bloodied black silks and pushed her way out of the tent, her sword held in her hand.

The fire was burnt out. The dead corpses of her colleagues, guides and the wererats were scattered across the desert floor in front of her. Skeletal remains were strewn among them. Her memory of the undead leaving or reburying themselves had been more comprehensive in the dark than the reality of the hot light of day. The foliage opposite was battered and scarred from the undead soldiers that had passed through it. She looked at the three surviving iribis still tied up by the palm tree.

"Farmorl?" she asked.

"Round here," he replied.

He was on the other side of the wall. She walked around, skipping over the wall at the end where it was low enough.

Farmorl was standing in the middle of the sands, his back to her. He was dressed, his sword in his scabbard at his side, but with his right hand resting on it, ready to draw.

She could see why.

There were twenty-one of them in all, perched on iribis. Tall, angular, with skin of bronze and black hair. Shrewd brown eyes assessed the pair. They were dressed in leather armour, dark brown in colour, swords resting at their sides. All but one clutched a short lance, more like a javelin, for throwing rather than charging. They were spaced evenly in two lines, every inch the professional soldiers they were. There was a female at the front. As with all Gar, age was hard to assess, but there was an authority to this one. Dryana recognized her from the Temple of Thytha back in Port Ren. This was the Trendorn'Di'Debion'Gar.

"What do we do?" Farmorl whispered urgently.

Dryana walked forward to stand next to him.

PRINCE OF SLAYERS

The Trendorn'Di'Debion'Gar slipped from the saddle and walked towards them. She gave Dryana a long appraising look, noting the blood splattered all over her. She continued to pass her until she reached the edge of the ruin. Her gaze took in the scene of carnage and destruction. She gave a nod that might pass for an acknowledgement of being impressed.

She strode back to the Slayers, stopping in front of the pair. She looked Dryana up and down again. "Lyrn Tutharum," she muttered.

"What does that mean?" demanded Dryana.

"I am Sconya Teldinar, Trendorn'Di'Debion'Gar," the female stated without answering the question.

"We met in the Temple of Thytha," observed Dryana.

"I remember," said Sconya perfunctorily. "Get yourself cleaned up; we need to be moving before the sun gets too high."

"Why are you helping us?" asked Dryana suspiciously.

"You know the way out of the desert?" demanded the Trendorn.

"No, but I'd like to understand why you are being so generous?" pressed the witch.

"We have been told to see you are protected," the Trendorn replied.

"Told! Told by who?"

"You ask a lot of questions," observed the Trendorn.

"And you don't answer them," replied Dryana.

The Gar gave a shrug in response.

"If you are tasked with protecting us, where were you last night?" demanded Dryana.

"We were too far back. Sorry," she offered in response. "Besides, it seems you coped."

"Two of my people are dead and two of yours," Dryana spat angrily. "That's hardly protecting us."

"You misunderstand: I am to protect *you*, Lyrn Tutharum. The fate of your people, your business and the other Slayers are of no interest to me," the Gar replied.

"Slinker? Is Slinker okay?" demanded Dryana, suddenly wondering if that was what she meant.

"As far as I am aware," said the Trendorn with a shrug. "Anyway, time is passing. Get ready: take much longer and we will tie you to an iribis and leave your lover to be a permanent resident here."

"Careful with the threats; you would be wise not to underestimate me." Dryana glanced behind her for emphasis.

"Oh, Lyrn Tutharum, one thing you can be certain of: none of us will underestimate you," replied Sconya.

CHAPTER SEVENTEEN — THE GREY FOLK

Saliana stared at the lump of blue-grey rock as if lost in thought. Then she reached down and brushed off the accumulation of moss and light snow from it to reveal a flat finished top at about her waist height. She squatted down in front of the block and cleared off further moss on the front and sides. She pulled out her belt knife and cut away a small amount of bramble that had formed around its base. It revealed several lines of thin spiralling script, which seemed to glow almost blue against the grey rock. It was a trick of the geology, the blue centre of the grey rock coming through where it had been carved. One of the bluestones that marked the boundary of the Sul'Kirin.

"You know what that says?" asked Samarin, standing behind her.

Saliana pushed herself to her feet and thrust the blade back in its sheath on her belt.

"Yes," she replied testily.

"Well?" demanded the Fal'Gar witch.

Saliana fixed her with a cold gaze.

"Anyone want to tell me what it says?" Kyrian queried, trying to break the tension.

"'Keep out'," replied Sali.

"Lot of lines for such a short message," the wrestler observed sarcastically.

"It says a little more than just 'keep out'," observed Samarin.

Kyrian looked at Samarin with a raised eyebrow and his gaze wandered back to Saliana. His fellow Slayer shrugged in response to his unasked question. The Mistress of the Slayers walked back to where her oradar waited patiently and mounted the cat.

"Let's get going," she ordered.

"In there!" Samarin practically screeched. "Not a chance."

Saliana fixed the girl with her most baleful gaze.

The Fal'Gar looked up at the Slayer, seated on the giant cat.

"You can stare at me all you like, Saliana Slayer, but I'm not entering the Kyth'Dath," Samarin said, using the Gar term for the land of the Ice Lords.

"You were informed this was our purpose when we began our journey. Your uncle, your grandmother, they both agreed."

Samarin was well aware what her uncle and grandmother had agreed with the Slayers. She also remembered what her uncle had told her; not to antagonize the Kyth'Gar and to follow their rules to the letter. If not, she had been told she would not return from the frozen lands of the north. Her uncle seemed oddly afraid of their northern cousins, given that, to her knowledge, they never left their icy fastness.

"It says it is death to enter Kyth'Dath uninvited. If we wish to treat with the Kyth'Gar we must wait here at the stone until we are given permission to enter," observed Samarin. "The instructions on the stone are very clear."

Saliana gave a sigh. "You have been ordered to help us."

"Help you, not commit suicide," Samarin snapped back.

"We cannot wait here," declared Saliana. "As it stands, we will be lucky to make it back in time for the gathering of the Great Khan. We cannot sit here hoping one of the Kyth'Gar comes by. We need to get to Krynal."

"We wait here," stated Samarin, brooking no argument.

She stalked back to the stone and sat down on its cold flat surface.

"I don't have time for this," muttered Sali.

She nudged her cat forward so she was towering above the seated Fal'Gar.

"I need you, Samarin." Sali's tone was pleading.

"Why? Because you think somehow I know the way to Krynal? Because with me there, the Ice Lords might pause before they execute us?"

"You have never been to Krynal," observed Sali.

"And you have?" laughed Samarin.

Sali looked at her, saying nothing.

"I'm staying here and waiting," Samarin scowled.

"Look around you. Look at the stone. It's possible no Kyth'Gar, no person, has been here for months, maybe years." Sali was angry.

Samarin gave a disobedient shrug and stuck out her chin stubbornly.

Kyrian stifled a laugh; it wasn't often that the Mistress of the Slayers did not get what she wanted. Especially from one she considered a subordinate.

"I haven't got time for this," muttered Sali. Then she said a word.

Kyrian heard the word. For some reason he could not have repeated it had there been someone to ask him, but other than that it had no effect on him. But the effect on Samarin was pronounced. The single word hit her like an electrical charge. She could feel it tearing into her mind, burning at her thoughts. She tried to fight it. Her gift came to her aid, witchcraft battling against the compulsion that the word contained. She knew the word was Fal'Gar, though she had never heard it spoken before. Despite never having heard the word before, she knew it meant 'obey'. It was a coercion to follow the orders of the woman in front of her. It was not simple magic, she knew. Instead, the compulsion sat somewhere deep inside of her. As if it had been sleeping in her soul since birth. How was that possible?

She used her gift, her witchcraft, to fight it, but the compulsion was unbelievably strong. She should have been able to resist. Some mages knew how to force the mind of the weak-willed, but against a witch, such an act was impossible, even for one as powerful as Saliana. The mind was the place of the witch, the place of the Gift. She pushed back hard. She would show this arrogant woman, this pompous mage, what a witch's mind could do. She sent out a savage blast of mental energy. On a normal person it might have done irreparable harm, but with a mage, especially one trying a similar trick, it would feel more like a good hard slap across the face. She felt it tear into the Mistress of the Slayers, unseen except in their minds, a scouring white light between them.

"Thank you." Saliana's voice, hard but amused, pulsed in Samarin's mind.

PRINCE OF SLAYERS

It was as if a skull, sharp and pale, devoid of flesh, laughed in her mind and Samarin realized the breadth of her mistake. Terror filled her. What had her aunt said? Saliana's mind had been bound with weaves of blue and grey. Some, mostly the blue, had broken, some were still holding, but they were fraying fast. She had assumed that whoever had bound Saliana had use weaves of blue to bind her magic and weaves of grey to bind her mind, to hide her memories. Now too late, she realized she had been wrong. Her blast of mental energy had burnt away the last of the grey weaves that had bound the Slayer but done nothing else. The word, the compulsion, slammed into her again, excoriating in its power, twice as strong as before, overwhelming her mind. It was then she understood. The word had been buried in the mind of the Fal'Gar, all of them, for decades, and maybe centuries: an order to obey the one who spoke it in all things.

Even that she could have fought, so strong was she with the Gift of the Goddess, had it been magic. It was not wizardry. The Fal'Gar had been bound with witchcraft. Samarin's mind screamed – it was impossible. For the gods never bestowed both the blue of magic and the grey of witchcraft on one person. Yet that was the only explanation, Saliana was not only a mage, but a witch. Sali's power overwhelmed her.

Samarin looked up. She could not remember how, but she was down on one knee in front of the stone. She had been looking down, and now she was staring up at the Mistress of the Slayers. The woman was standing above her. She did not recall the Slayer dismounting her cat or indeed herself moving from the rock.

"As you command, my lady," Samarin heard herself saying.

"Good," Sali said with a perfunctory nod. "Get on your cat and let's get going."

249

"You've got to teach me how you do that," said Kyrian with a chuckle.

Sali had forgotten her colleague.

"I couldn't if I tried," she said coldly.

"Hey, I know I'm a slow learner, but it's a great trick. Heard you played it on the Gar captain back on Kangorn," he observed.

Sali gave Kyrian an appraising look. She reminded herself that he was smarter than his wrestler persona implied.

"I wish I could," she said, giving a half smile.

"Take too long?" he asked.

Saliana mounted her oradar, watching Samarin cautiously as she mounted her own cat.

"I could teach your sister, but not you, no matter how long we had," Sali said.

"Shame. It's a great trick."

***

Autumn was giving way to winter, and the days were shortening noticeably. This far north light did not come until mid-morning and was gone again by the late afternoon. The constant snowstorms, varied only occasionally with lighter falls of sleet, meant that sometimes the Slayers had seen no sun at all for the whole day. On the rare occasions it broke through it was welcomed like an old friend.

The weather was not the only thing that had changed. The morning after they had crossed the bluestone marked boundary, Saliana had washed her face clean of the cosmetics that she had worn since the meeting in Falthar's tent. She had removed the complex web of braids in her hair, that until then she had been tying meticulously each morning. Her hair now hung loose across her shoulders, her wide brimmed hat resting firmly on her head. Samarin understood that Saliana had wanted to appear as a Fal'Gar mage, though whether it was to ingratiate herself with the Fal'Gar or to set them on edge she was not sure. Depending on the Fal'Gar in question she had achieved both. Saliana seemed to use the confusion she caused to get what she wanted, how you felt seemed to bother her less in Samarin's estimation. Now in Kyth'Dath, the Mistress of the Slayers had seemingly decided the appearance of being a Fal'Gar mage was of no longer of use to her.

It was getting colder. Today the snow was light but constant, a soft white drizzle. More than three days ride into Kyth'Dath, the landscape had changed. The open grassland of the steppe had given way to small coppices of woodland interspersed with swamps. Paths wide enough for two of the giant cats to move abreast curled and curved through the damp landscape. They were moving slowly, covering much less ground than when they had moved across the open steppe. Shifting mists and uneven, uncertain ground made them cautious. The further they rode, the thicker the forest became, but the path ahead of them remained clear of brambles as if it were in frequent use. It was hard to tell whether it was hardened earth or stone covered by centuries of mud. There were no ruts in it, which suggested the latter, but then they had seen no carts, so maybe that was the reason. Someone had kept it clear either by using it frequently or actively cutting back the vegetation that would have clogged it. Despite that, they had seen no one since they entered what the Solinad Hunters had called the Sul'Kirin.

Saliana was in the lead, the other two trailing slightly behind. She could feel her oradar's discomfort at the colder weather. She felt it too, though the whole party had wrapped themselves in additional layers against the cold and wind. The cats were hardy enough to endure the steppe, but here in Kyth'Dath it was different. Saliana was aware of Samarin's eyes boring into her back, or at least she imagined them. She had not wanted to force the issue back at the boundary, but she was running out of time.

"What's that?" Kyrian asked, distracting Sali from her thoughts.

She pulled her cat to a halt and looked over her shoulder at her fellow Slayer. He was pointing somewhere. She followed his finger, picking out what he was indicating. It was a small hut made from wooden planks, with a sloping roof. It was covered in vegetation and its roof looked as if it had been covered in turf. It blended so well with the trees surrounding it that she was surprised Kyrian had spotted it. A thin twist of smoke curled from the roof, which was what had given it away. She kicked her oradar into action and the cat cantered towards the hut. Her two companions followed her, trying to keep pace. When she got closer, she realized the hut sat close to the road, in a small grove of trees. It was obvious from the road when one got close enough, so for whatever reason it had become overgrown it was not to disguise it.

A figure stepped from the hut's small door. His eyes were wary, his face confused. Kyrian gave an intake of breath. He was Gar, over six feet in height, and thin: so much, so normal. It was the rest of his appearance that surprised the Slayer. His skin was a light grey, the colour of ash from burnt paper. His hair was darker but still grey. It reminded him of the white-blond hair characteristic of the Syn'Dion'Gar, but as if had lost all its lustre. He wore trousers of grey fur and a brown hair shirt. Solinad hair, unless Kyrian missed his guess. The Gar carried no weapon that Kyrian could see.

"Kyth'Gar?" he asked Saliana quietly.

She shook her head.

He looked to Samarin.

"Grey Folk?" she mouthed quietly.

Kyrian was about to observe that he had not realized the Grey Folk were Gar, but the odd-looking Gar said something. It was a harsh, clipped tongue he spoke, very different from the singsong tones of the Syn'Dion'Gar or even the lilting language of the Fal'Gar. Kyrian looked to Samarin for explanation.

"I don't know what he said," she replied, looking a little helpless.

She said something in Fal'Gar to the male, but he looked perplexed, clearly not understanding what she said. He looked even more wary, if that was possible. He spoke again and this time Kyrian caught the word 'Sul'Kirin' at the end of the sentence.

"He said, strangers are not welcome in the Sul'Kirin."

Kyrian looked at Sali. "You speak their language?"

"I'm a bard," she replied.

"That only covers so much of what you are not telling us," Samarin interjected.

Sali looked at Kyrian for support.

"She's got a point," he said.

Sali turned back to the male and said something.

"What did you tell him?" asked Kyrian.

"I told him to tell the boy to put down the bow," she replied.

Kyrian scanned the trees, picking out another male. A youthful Gar with a dark black bow of wood and horn clasped in his hands was hidden there. He blended almost perfectly with the wood. Kyrian's hand strayed to his flail.

"There are two others," said Kyrian quietly.

Saliana had already picked them out, but it was hard. They seemed to disappear into the foliage that surrounded the hut. Two Gar. A female, dressed in similar fashion to the man, but with a long grey cloak. The other was also female, but much younger; a child, perhaps around her tenth year. Both clasped bows, arrows nocked, pointing at the Slayers.

"You have children, two children." Samarin's tone was shocked, as if she was questioning her eyes. "I mean, they are both young, born close together."

Samarin was struggling with what she saw. Then she saw the papoose; the woman had concealed it with her cloak.

"That's a baby. You have a baby. Three, that's impossible," she declared.

Her tone was obviously agitated, and it was starting to alarm the Grey Folk.

"Calm yourself, Samarin," ordered Sali. "He does not understand you; you are making them nervous. And I for one have no desire to have an arrow through me."

"I don't get the big deal?" asked Kyrian.

"Three!" Samarin practically screeched.

Saliana knew the reason for Samarin's excitement. The Gar were not like humans. They did not breed children easily, though the survival rates meant those that they did produce usually survived, unlike humans. A Gar female might produce two children over their long life, usually decades apart. Three was not unprecedented, but vanishingly rare. To produce three in close proximity to each other, with less than ten years between each, was unknown. The great Cliphine, Lady of the Crystal Ships, was fabled for having two daughters close together. Yet Cliphine was not a pureblood Gar so maybe she was an exception.

"Please lower the bows; we mean you no harm," Sali asked the Grey Folk in their own tongue.

"Who are you? You are not Culimarin?" the Gar asked.

Kyrian looked on with confusion. Samarin caught the last word.

"He's asking if we are Ice Lords?" She looked at Saliana.

"No, he knows we are not. He wants to know who we are. He sounds afraid," explained Saliana.

PRINCE OF SLAYERS

Lightning flashed and then thunder rolled in the distance. The Grey Folk family turned in its direction, faces riven with terror. The man dashed back into the hut, emerging moments later with three backpacks. He tossed one to the woman and another to the boy. He hoisted the third on his back.

"Doto!" the little girl screamed in fear.

The man shot the mother an angry look before ducking back into the building. He reappeared, annoyance on his face, a toy made of wood and fur in his hand. It looked like some sort of cat, perhaps a bad rendering of an oradar. He rushed off the step, in front of the hut, and thrust the toy into the child's grasping hands. She pulled it close for comfort. He cursed at her and pointed at the bow she had dropped. The child looked chastened and stowed her toy, picking up her bow and swiftly wiping the damp string on the cloth of her sleeve.

The lightning sparked again. It seemed to be closer. The Slayers were looking at the direction it was coming from. It seemed to be on the ground, not coming from the sky. The Grey Folk were slipping away, melting into the forest and swamp that sat either side of the road. Flashes of white splashed from the mists.

"What is that?" demanded Kyrian.

"I think I have just worked out why the solinad is immune to lightning," replied Saliana.

"Huh?" Kyrian looked at her confused.

"A way to protect itself against a predator," explained Sali.

"That would have to be a very big predator," Kyrian replied nervously.

He loosened his flail from his belt. Samarin had taken her bow from the case on the side of her cat and nocked an arrow. The bow hung half drawn by her side, her eyes scanning the murk of the fog. The water caught in the air flashed as blue lightning electrified it.

Then they caught sight of it. A flash of movement, then gone, then another flash of movement. Whatever the creature was, it was huge. As it came closer, the beast became clearer. For a moment it looked as if it were moving like a snake, but it was an illusion – the animal was using its feet to scoot across the swamp.

"That thing has got to be fifty feet long?" Kyrian exclaimed.

A corona of blue electricity played around the head of the beast. It reminded Kyrian of a huffrin, a scaly mass of lizard, but it was much longer. It moved lower to the ground than the lizard beast of burden; its rear legs, powerful but squat, pushed its writhing form forward. Its front legs were small and scrabbling, more like claw-like hands than feet, but incredibly long, nearly half the length of the beast's body. A thin line of leathery skin ran along the side of the arms from just in front of the rear legs all along the body and down the front arms to the claws. As it lifted its front hands, the leathery skin caught the wind, sending out buffets of air.

What had Amdon said? Something about there being nothing to fear in the north except winter and wyrms. They had thought she was being poetic.

The giant creature was not alone. Roughly a third of the way back along its elongated body, behind the front legs, was a saddle. It was made of a mix of dark wood and leather, with a high-crested front and back to prevent the rider from falling out. The rider was dressed in shining silver alcidide armour. It was reminiscent of the armour of the Syn'Dion'Gar, but the plates that lay over the mail were cut in sharper, harder lines than those of the ocean elves. The helm was different, completely covering the rider's face. It was designed to intimidate as much as be practical, its front pointed out in a long angular shape. The rider was clearly Gar judging from their height and lithe frame, even wrapped in armour. Clasped in the rider's hand was a seven-foot spear, its central length made of alcidide, as was its thin point. Oddly, the rider held it with the point at the bottom, cradled in a mail basket attached to the high-backed saddle. The other end, which was held high and ready for use, was a noose of black leather. A further whip-like attachment of the same material was wrapped loosely around the haft of the weapon. It looked more like something used to control livestock than a weapon of war.

Saliana soothed her oradar. The creature was used to being an apex predator on the steppe, and now it was confronted by a foe that it could not outmatch in size or possibly even in speed. Some genetic memory had stirred within the cat and its was showing a desire to be somewhere else; anywhere else. Samarin was similarly struggling with her mount. For Kyrian it was worse. His oradar, recalcitrant with its human rider at the best of times, was trying to buck him off. The Slayer held on valiantly, slapping the beast into submission rather than using the calm words that the other two were employing.

The giant lizard slithered towards them. Kyrian looked to Sali, his hand ready to yank his flail from his belt and charge the potential attacker. Saliana shook her head sharply. Samarin had stowed her bow and unslung her lance, ready for combat, but made no move to charge.

"Have you ever seen such a thing?" asked Kyrian of Samarin.

"No! You think I would have come here had I known of such things?" she shouted over the roaring thunder.

Saliana refrained from pointing out that the Fal'Gar had been given no choice in accompanying them into Kyth'Dath.

The great serpent reached them and reared up, somehow using the muscle of its body so it was resting on its rear legs and tail. Its rear third propped up the front two thirds of the beast. Its rider hung from its back, tied in with a complicated collection of stirrups and straps. The noose-like end of the spear pointed down towards the Slayers. Samarin hefted her lance, but if she had expected the beast to reveal a soft underbelly, she was swiftly disabused. A series of overlapping plates of hardened scale lined the stomach and throat of the wyrm. Electrical energy, a corona of white and blue, roared around the creature, terrifying the oradars. Sali and the others wrenched at their reins as they skittered side to side, desperate to flee.

"Where is my prey?" The rider's voice was high-pitched but rasping. She also spoke perfect Nerlinean, not the archaic variant that the Solinad Hunters had used. It took the Slayers a moment to register that she was speaking the language.

"I am Samarin Mrignandor of the Fal'Gar." Not registering that the rider had spoken Nerlinean, she had announced herself in her own language.

"If you do not know Kyth'Garian, speak the imperial tongue, nomad, not your broken steppe cant," the rider dismissed her derisively. "Where is my prey? Your stinking cats are throwing me off the trail."

"What are you hunting?" asked Kyrian.

"Why are your slaves speaking?" demanded the wyrm rider.

"We are not slaves. I am Saliana Slayer, High Lady of Syndion."

The rider paused as if considering that information. With her face entirely enclosed in a helm it was impossible to read what she might be thinking.

"You should not even be within the Sul'Kirin," the rider declared harshly. "Only the presence of one of the Fal'Gar stops me from feeding you to my dragon. Where is my prey?"

"That's a dragon?" asked Kyrian, as Saliana shot him an angry glance.

"The Grey Folk, you are hunting them?" asked Sali.

258

"The boy! The boy must serve." The rider was raging.

Saliana dismounted from her oradar, handing the reins to Samarin, who was now left managing two of the fearful cats. She walked towards the wyrm, which recoiled as if ready to strike.

"I am Saliana Slayer, Mistress of the Company of Slayers and High Lady of Syndion, I seek an audience with the rulers of Kyth'Dath to talk trade."

She walked forward, her arms held open showing she had no weapon. Her cloak flapped on the breeze, and her wide-brimmed hat was pulled tight, concealing from the rider Saliana's mixed heritage.

"You are nothing to the High Lords," the rider hissed. "You are not welcome here. Tell the Fal'Gar what happens when humans trespass in the Sul'Kirin. You are food for my dragon."

The wyrm lunged forward, its sharp-toothed jaw heading straight for Saliana.

"Enough of this foolishness," Saliana announced.

Her hands slammed together. The wyrm's head was buffeted from either side by great flushes of blasting wind, so strong the creature swooned and recoiled, almost knocked unconscious by the invisible blows.

"Call this youngling a dragon?" screamed the Slayer. "What do you know of dragons, ice elf?"

Another blow of air slammed into the wyrm's face and then another, driving it back. It coiled backwards then uncoiled again and shifted its body down the road, reversing in an ungainly fashion in the face of the relentless blows.

It reared up again, seeking to avoid the invisible blows that hammered into it. The electrical corona swirled around its head. It let out a cry of rage, which came with a blast of lightning. It seemed to emanate from the throat, but in truth it was from special glands in the upper jaw. It bathed Saliana in a searing blast of blue and white. To the watchers it looked as if she changed: her human appearance eroded suddenly and she took on the thin, angular appearance of a pureblood Gar. Then that was gone, her face a skeletal mask, sharp white bones framed by the blue of the wyrm's attack. Sali's eyes were dark purple pits in her skull, blazing back at the serpent. The lightning exploded in a coruscating blast of white light that bathed the swamp and the forest around them.

"Dragon?" muttered Sali contemptuously, standing at the centre of the dissipating blast, apparently unharmed. "In a few centuries, maybe."

Blows of air rocked the wyrm, driving it upwards and forcing it to rear up in an attempt to escape. Then fire lashed out from Sali's hand. It was essentially harmless to the scaled beast in front of her, but not to the leather trusses that held the saddle in place. The flame erupted across the wyrm's belly, burning through the straps. Another blast of air hit the beast, and as it reared up again the damaged straps snapped, and the saddle and the rider were tipped from the wyrm's back. The spear skittered across the road towards Sali, landing at her feet. The rider hit the ground, landing with a heavy thump, armour slamming against skin. Her helmet protected the rider from the worst of the damage, but still she was knocked unconscious.

The rider lay on the road and the wyrm curled protectively around her. It eyed Saliana Slayer warily as she stalked forward. She picked up the spear and looked at it angrily.

"Nasty thing, slave grabber," she muttered angrily.

She put it over her knee and, focusing her magic on the hard alcidide, she snapped the spear in two. She threw it away with a look of disgust. Sali stalked towards the serpent curled around the prone form of its rider. The creature hissed at Saliana as she approached, seemingly fearful compared to its previous behaviour. Despite the creature being more docile, Sali still approached warily, suppressing the burning anger that was welling up inside. The wyrm's head rose from the ground, swaying from side to side, ready to attack should it become necessary.

"Leave!" Sali's words were unspoken, instead a pulse in the beast's mind. She used the same magic that wizards used to communicate across distances to speak to the creature.

Sali sensed confusion from the wyrm; it had never been spoken to in this way. So, its rider had no magical powers, Saliana deduced. In ancient times, the rider and their dragon would link themselves with magic, their minds interacting so as to move and fight as one. This young wyrm had no such experience. It was hardly a surprise – it was young, a couple of centuries old at most, Saliana suspected. It was a child and still thought and acted like one. It would be another century before it could use its own magic. It would be perhaps another century or two before its wings would have developed enough and its magic grown sufficiently strong for it to be able to fly. That would be if it lived long enough. The last dragon had flown in the time of the Jeddera the Great, over a millennium ago. Even the legends of his son, the god, Jeddera Summersword, contained no tales of the winged serpents among all the myths that swirled around him. In truth, Saliana had been shocked to see such a creature. She had assumed they had all gone. Some said they had died; some said they slept. Now with the evidence in front of her eyes she wondered if there was another possibility: maybe the creatures had sought a place away from civilization here in the far north. Something had given birth to this young wyrm, after all. She wanted to speak to it mind-to-mind to find out what had happened to its kin, but it was young, so it would be like speaking to a toddler, and a reluctant one to boot. It was best to focus on the matter at hand.

"Take your mistress and leave," Sali ordered the creature telepathically.

The wyrm seemed to be thinking, as its head swayed from side to side more rapidly. Sali could feel it wanting to attack, like the giant petulant child it was. She readied her magic, though she did not want to kill it; that would be an infamy. The beast made its choice. Its head slowed and then stopped moving. The jaws opened and slowly reached down; then the wyrm used one of its claws to carefully lift its unconscious rider into its yawning maw. With surprising gentleness, the teeth of the serpent closed on the armoured body of its rider, cradling it in its jaw.

In a great swooping motion, it turned the nascent wings along its front arms, creating a gust of wind that buffeted the Slayer. It turned swiftly, uncurling as it did so, back the way it had come. Its long tail lashed out, forcing Sali to duck to avoid it.

The last act of a petulant child being sent to their room, thought the Mistress of the Slayers.

She watched it go as it crawled along the road and then out across the swamp, moving faster and faster so it seemed to be slithering like a snake, rather than running.

CHAPTER EIGHTEEN –
DEN'SAR'GAR

Saliana waited for the wyrm to disappear before she let her eyes drop away from the horizon. She fought down the exhaustion washing through her; magic came easier to her now. The environment was rich with power, but that was not the only reason something had changed in her. Her ability to control and sustain magic was growing stronger. Still, she felt the drag on her body, an ache in her shoulders that spread to her lower back. She shrugged it off. Better than collapsing or vomiting, she mused.

She walked to the edge of the dirt-covered roadway to where the hut sat on the edge of the swamp. She squatted down on the muddy bank, struggling not to slip into the dark waters of the marsh. Her hand carefully brushed the surface of the ground. She could see the fungus just breaking the surface. The giant footprint where a solinad had stood to graze on the fresh mushrooms was visible on the water's edge. She looked out across the marsh and let out a deep breath. She slipped down the bank, letting the wet mud take her, hoping the waters were not too deep. Kyrian and Samarin watched, their faces curious at what Saliana was doing. To them she seemed to move almost as if compelled.

A feeling of victory swelled in Sali's heart. She had to be sure. She broke the water with her feet, sinking into the sludge almost to the top of her boots, which stopped just below the knee. She waded out, testing the ground. She cursed when it dropped away a little, sending her thigh-deep in the marsh. Dark swamp water rushed into her boots, and icy water froze her feet. Small lumps of ice floating on the surface bumped against her thighs, and she pushed forward. She stopped at a bunch of reeds sprouting from the waters. Thin lines of a withered black thread were caught in long strings across the reeds. Drun – the digested results of solinads consuming their favoured fungus. She looked out across the swamp; the threads laced out in a great wave across the reeds and plants of the swamps. She had found the summer resting grounds of the solinads. She had discovered the source of the fungus that, when passed through the belly of the solinad, created drun. Most importantly, she had found vast quantities of the hallucinogen, just lying across the landscape waiting to be dried. A vast storehouse of potential wealth, greater than that which was resting on either the western steppe of Chazantria or the eastern steppe of Havagia.

Saliana turned and waded back to the bank next to the road. She tried to climb up but slipped against it and splashed back into the water. She looked up to see Kyrian and Samarin grinning at her.

"You going to help?" she demanded.

Samarin looked at Kyrian, who smiled back and shrugged.

PRINCE OF SLAYERS

Sali cursed and worked her way around to the hut, where a small platform stuck out over the waters. She used a rope hanging from it to drag herself up to the wooden surface. She pushed into the hut; a fire still burned in the grate left by the fleeing Grey Folk. She tossed some lumps of wood from a pile by the stone fireplace and then used a small stick from the pile to poke the embers until the wood started to catch. Satisfied, she pulled off her knee-high black boots. Her socks squelched as she placed her feet back on the floor, and she grimaced. She picked up her boots and walked back out to the wooden pontoon. She emptied the water from the boots into the swamp and padded back into the room. She pulled off her socks and placed them in front of the fire.

The door creaked and she looked up to see Samarin enter followed by Kyrian. They dropped down their packs, Kyrian was carrying Saliana's as well as his own. Sali turned back to the fire and started to strip off the rest of her clothes. A leather jerkin, then an alcidide mail shirt, and finally the purple silk shirt underneath. She dumped them in a pile and stripped off her black leather trousers. She pulled a cloth from her pack and started to dry them off. She repeated the same operation on the boots, placing them close enough to the fire so they would dry but not crack. She stood by the fire and warmed her half naked body.

"What are you staring at?" she demanded, turning to Kyrian.

Her fellow Slayer was looking at her with an uncommonly assessing gaze. He shrugged and looked away.

"I think he was admiring the view," observed Samarin with a smile.

Sali favoured her with an unimpressed face.

"What? It's a nice view," grinned the Fal'Gar.

"You got anything to eat?" asked Saliana, changing the subject.

"Probably," confirmed Samarin.

She opened up her pack and fished out some grain, dried meat and some vegetables that had seen better days. She took a small black iron pot from her bag and disappeared out of the hut. She came back with the pot filled with water and a collection of herbs in her hand.

"Swamp water?" asked Kyrian sceptically.

"You see any other water? We are boiling it anyway," replied Samarin.

She sat in front of the hearth and built up the fire before setting up a metal frame above it from which she hung the small cauldron. Smoke billowed out across the room, the chimney not having been particularly well designed. Their eyes reddened in the polluted air. Sali coughed. It took time for the water to boil, but once it was at a rolling boil Samarin dropped in the meat, grains and herbs. The addition was enough to drop it down to a simmer. After nearly an hour, the vegetables were added. Their stomachs were audibly growling by the time it was finished.

Samarin ladled some into the small metal bowls they each carried. She opened a small pack of hard animal fat and cut off a piece, dropping it into the hot soup and stirring until it dissolved, giving the surface of the broth an oily sheen. She offered it to the others.

Kyrian rolled up his nose in disgust.

"Suit yourself," she replied with an amused shrug.

She offered it to Saliana, who let her drop a small piece into her bowl.

"Aren't you cold?" asked Samarin, looking at Sali still only wearing her underwear.

"Between the fire and the food, I'm good," replied the Slayer, slurping at her hot soup.

"You know, I think you are making him uncomfortable," Samarin nodded at Kyrian.

Sali shrugged. "When my clothes are dry, I'll put them back on," she said.

"Don't understand why you went for a swim anyway," observed Samarin. "It is freezing cold, there is snow everywhere and lumps of ice in the water."

"I don't know," replied Sali. She shivered at the memory, despite the warmth of the fire.

"And the dragon?" demanded Samarin.

"What about it?" asked Kyrian quietly.

"She just slapped a dragon around and you both sit here like it is the most normal thing in the world."

"It was a wyrm, not a dragon," said Sali.

"What's the difference?" asked Kyrian.

"A young dragon is born a wyrm. As it grows older it develops an inherent magic. This turns it from simply an animal to a sentient creature. It allows it to communicate with the likes of the Gar or Man. It is the magic that gives them their ability to fly; without magic the wings are insufficient to do it by muscle strength alone. Some wyrms never develop magic and, like the one we met, simply stay what they were born: a large predatory lizard," Sali answered.

"Yet this one had a rider?" queried Samarin.

Sali gave a shrug. "Perhaps it has the beginnings of magic."

"So, one day it could become a dragon?"

"How should I know?" replied Sali.

"In a few centuries, perhaps," muttered Kyrian.

Sali looked at him sharply. "What was that?" she demanded.

"Nothing," he grunted.

"I saw a dragon," Samarin declared with a smile. "And then I saw a mage slap it about as if it were some recalcitrant child. It will be a good story to tell around the fire."

JUSTIN WAINE

***

The morning sun spilled across the front of the hut. Saliana squinted as the white light caught the edge of her eyes. She had been on watch for the last three hours, since she had taken over the job from Kyrian. She watched the forest on the other side of the road where it covered a series of low hills. The oradar were close by, but out of view, splashing and gambolling in the swamp looking for fish or lizards that would feed them.

Kyrian stepped through the door; a mug filled with the liquid from last night's broth in his hand.

"You sleep well?" Saliana asked without turning.

"Not bad for a wooden hut with no pallets," he replied.

"A bed roll not enough for you these days?" she queried.

"I got rich, Sali: I want a large bed with silk sheets and curtains." Kyrian grinned at the thought.

"You and me both," she laughed.

"Maybe you could share," Samarin said with a grin, stepping out on the porch.

That was ignored, a silence that stretched out for minutes as they stood staring out across the woodland.

"Are they still out there?" Samarin demanded, looking at the forest.

"Yes," Sali replied quietly before pushing herself to her feet.

"How many?"

"More than four," replied Sali.

"They've been there all night?" asked Samarin.

"It would seem so," Sali said.

"And yet you both slept fine," Samarin nodded at Kyrian to include him.

The pair nodded back.

268

"You two are very odd," the Fal'Gar observed.

"Well, shall we get on with this?" Sali asked.

Kyrian nodded.

Sali stood up.

"Come out, we know you are there!" she shouted.

Her voice rung out across the forest.

"You think they will?" whispered Samarin.

Sali said nothing, watching the edge of the road where it met the forest.

A figure appeared, riding something. It looked like an oradar but smaller, perhaps half the size of the giant cats that the Slayers and Samarin rode. It was leaner, with thin wiry muscle rather than the bulk of the oradar. The fur was a mix of white covered with black spots, allowing it to blend perfectly with the snow-covered forest. From its clothes the figure that rode it was one of the Grey Folk. The rider practically lay on the beast; there was no saddle and instead feet were placed to grip just ahead of the creature's back legs. A grey cloak, hood drawn up, concealed any hint of gender. Only the wisps of hair escaping the hood indicated that one of the grey Gar rode the cat.

The beast came to a halt in front of the hut. The Gar rider unfolded itself from its crouched seating position on the back of the animal. Standing up, the Gar rubbed the head of the creature to reassure it. Kyrian marvelled how such a tall person could ride the cat at all. As the rider took down its hood its gender became clear. He was thin like all Gar and cleared six feet in height, closer perhaps to seven. He was dressed similarly to the other Grey Folk they had met: no hint of armour, just a simple shirt and trousers. His only weapon appeared to be a long dagger held in a belt. To Kyrian the mysterious Grey Folk seemed nothing more than bedraggled peasants. It was at once disconcerting but also comforting to see the normally confident Gar reduced to such a state. As if the effortless superiority the

Gar he had previously met seemed to have over humans was all just an illusion, that deep down the two races were not as different as the elves liked to pretend.

"The others?" said Sali simply in the language of the Grey Folk.

That raised an eyebrow from the male. "I can speak Nerlinean if you prefer," he offered in crisp, if accented, tones.

"The others," repeated Sali, this time in Nerlinean.

The Gar weighed in his mind the risk to his people of obeying, and, having seen the woman's display against the wyrm, of not obeying. His face showed nothing as he made his reluctant decision.

"As you wish."

He raised his right hand, palm open and pulled it down in a waving motion. Another two Gar riding white and black cats appeared from the forest, prowling across the gap to arrive behind the first. More Grey Folk appeared from the forest, until there were nineteen in total including the five that the Slayers had seen the previous day. These were all on foot, packs slung over their backs, most with bows clasped in their hands. A few had long daggers, the only other weapons they carried. What was most surprising was that fully a third were young, children and young adults, the flush of youth normally so rare among the Gar still on their faces.

"And you are?" Saliana addressed the one she took to be in command.

"I am Hynin," he replied.

"And you are the leader?" she asked.

"I am the eldest," he replied as if to explain himself.

"You speak Nerlinean?" she asked.

"I do," he replied.

His answers were cautious, giving little away.

"You speak our language?" he asked.

"I'm a bard; I pick up languages easily," Sali said with a friendly smile.

That prompted a laugh from Hynin. "That is a lie," he countered calmly. "The language of the Den'Sar'Gar is not something you simply pick up."

Samarin's blade came loose from its scabbard, her face fearful, the knuckles white wrapped hard around the hilt. Kyrian looked curious, but loosened his flail from his belt, nonetheless.

"You did not know who we are, or should I say who we were?" Hynin said, looking at Samarin.

"Sul'Kirin, the stockade. You are prisoners?" Saliana questioned.

"In a manner of speaking," Hynin replied.

"What did the Culimarin want with the family?"

Sali pointed at the group of four Grey Folk – five including the swaddled infant – they had first encountered the previous day.

"The Guardians wanted the boy," explained Hynin, using the closest Nerlinean translation for the word 'Culimarin'.

"Why?" asked Sali.

"It is a tradition: all male Den'Sar'Gar must submit themselves to the Guardians at Krynal on the day of their twentieth birthday. All females must do so on their twenty-fifth birthday. The boy turned twenty years of age a week ago. The family did not think it was wise that the boy submit himself. So, they decided to hide, and when they thought they would be discovered they tried to flee the stockade. The wyrm rider was sent to hunt them down."

"Why? What happens when you submit at Krynal?" demanded Sali, intrigued.

"That depends. In my day, most males were forced into military service. These days, it is the minority; most now simply return to their farms after submission. It is where I learned to speak Nerlinean," Hynin replied.

Sali raised an eyebrow at the last remark.

"The Guardians do not wish to speak our language, and we have no desire to speak the degenerate dialect of Syn'Dion'Gar the Kyth'Gar call theirs. So, we both speak Nerlinean. The Kyth'Gar still send their children south to the universities of the empire, so it suits them, and it is easy enough for us to pick up," the Grey Folk male answered.

"What had the boy to fear?" pressed Sali. "A short period of military service? Does he fear to fight?"

Hynin left out another laugh. He looked at the boy.

"Luckily, he does not speak Nerlinean or he might be insulted by you doubting his courage. No, he did not fear to serve, though if he was chosen it would be for at least two decades. Not a short time even for Gar. Myself, I spent five decades in the service of the Guardians. No, that was not what the boy feared. I will show you."

He waved the young Gar forward.

"Put out your hand," Hynin said in the language of the Grey Folk. "Show them."

The young male stepped forward and drew back his cloak. He then removed his glove and lifted his hand, cupping it palm up in front of his face. Saliana felt the barest surge of magical power. A lick of flame lit up like a small fire sitting in the young Gar's hand. It flickered there; he pulled his hand closed, extinguishing it. He stumbled back exhausted, sweat pouring down his face. His father stepped forward to catch him, in case he fainted.

"That?" laughed Sali, a little too meanly. "That trickle of power?"

"That is enough to ensure his death. Similarly, had he the gift of witchcraft he would also have been slain," replied Hynin.

Sali nodded. It made sense: what gaoler would allow their prisoners to have either the power of magic or the Gift?

"You said that fewer are taken into military service than in times past," Sali continued.

"Less as a proportion, a similar number in absolute terms," replied Hynin. "There are fewer Kyth'Gar each year, there are more of us each year. The Great Goddess has made us fertile in our captivity."

"Why not take more soldiers?" Kyrian interjected.

"If you wish to control slave-soldiers it is best to keep the ratios manageable, otherwise they get ideas," Hynin said with a grin. "Especially when they get bored, and no army of note has marched this far north in seven centuries and even then we were ordered not to fight. An army with no purpose must be managed carefully, lest it tries to find one."

"So, when did the Grey Folk last fight a war?" asked Kyrian.

"Not since we were sent here," he replied.

"Sent here? Who sent your people here?" asked Kyrian.

"The Summersword," said Samarin quietly.

"Correct, priestess," Hynin nodded.

"What will you do with the boy?" asked Saliana.

"He will be hidden as best we can," he shrugged.

He did not seem convinced that it was an achievable objective.

"You could smuggle him out of the Sul'Kirin?" offered Sali.

"Where to? We are a distinctive people; we cannot blend in with Nerlineans or Kasmerians even if we could get to their lands. And you can see how welcoming our closest cousins the Fal'Gar are." Hynin gave a tight smile and indicated Samarin.

The Fal'Gar witch seem nonplussed by the comment, and she hefted her still drawn sword as if to emphasize Hynin's remark. Saliana studied him quietly; she could not shake the feeling he was lying in that particular regard. Lying was probably a bit harsh – not telling her everything would be more accurate. Why should he, after all? He had no reason to trust them. Indeed, he had shown them remarkable forbearance.

Kyrian's oradar appeared from the swamp, ambling into the meeting. It gave the smaller cats ridden by the Grey Folk a contemptuous glare. The smaller animals bared their teeth and growled angrily. The other two oradar appeared from the dark waters, coming up behind Kyrian's mount. The three overawed their smaller cousins, which slunk back, but remained wary, willing to fight if it came to it.

"Beautiful animals," marvelled Hynin, a hint of jealousy in his tone.

"Larger than yours," Kyrian said with a grin.

"It will let a human like you ride it?" he asked.

"You saw us on the road. How many days did you follow us?"

"Only since you entered the Sul'Kirin," Hynan replied with a shrug. "How did you persuade it?

"She did," Kyrian indicated Saliana.

"Between that and scolding a wyrm, you carry strong magic," he observed to Saliana.

"You should have seen what she did to Las Ma," said Kyrian under his breath.

Hynan turned, and his hand dropped to the blade at his belt. He was not the only one. All the Grey Folk seemed suddenly angry.

"What do you know of Las Ma, human?" Hynin hissed.

He filled the last word with contempt.

Kyrian was so shocked by the sudden change in mood as a result of his throwaway comment that he struggled to process what was happening.

"We are leaving." Sali made it an order.

Hynan's gaze swung back to her. Some of the harshness in his eyes had dissipated, but only a little. "You are going to Krynal?"

Sali nodded.

"You will not be welcome. The wyrm rider will have gone there," Hynin said. He seemed more amused at the prospect than worried for the Slayers.

Sali ignored that comment. She picked up her saddle and started to carefully strap it to her oradar.

"How many days to Krynal?" she asked.

Hynin looked at her, his anger still boiling, but said nothing.

"It was a long time ago and you were not there," she said calmly.

He stepped forward, his eyes blazing. "What would you know of it?" he roared; his words flecked with spittle.

She fixed him with her most baleful gaze, the one that had terrified merchants, princes and mages. She finished fixing her saddle. Samarin and Kyrian had begun to strap on their own saddles and harnesses. Sali stalked back into the hut and returned with her pack. She went back in a second time and handed Kyrian's and Samarin's to them. They hoisted them onto their cats. She signalled wordlessly to Samarin and the Fal'Gar followed her into the hut. They returned with their weapons, the bows and quivers normally stowed on the saddles. The lances that they carried had been left with the saddles and strapped on with them.

The Grey Folk continued to glare collectively at Samarin, Sali and Kyrian. The three mounted up and kicked their cats forward, carefully navigating around the Grey Folk, who refused to move for them.

Kyrian looked into the cold darkness of their eyes. He remembered what Amdon had said that day on the steppe:

Sometimes the wildness can only be tamed so much or for so long.

"Any risk they shoot us in the back?" whispered Samarin to Sali.

"Some," she replied.

The cats bounded northward down the road, in the direction of Krynal. They travelled a mile before Sali pulled her oradar to a halt. She rubbed it between the ears, looking back down the road as her two companions pulled up their mounts beside her. She scanned past them looking for signs of pursuit.

"You think that puts us out of range?" asked Samarin.

"Depends if they followed us," observed Kyrian, scanning the forest.

"You think they are out there?" Samarin sounded nervous.

"They have no desire to get closer to Krynal; we should be safe," Sali answered.

"Still, don't know what I did?" muttered Kyrian grumpily.

"You mentioned Las Ma," explained Samarin.

"What has a city half a world away got to do with anything?" he asked.

"If they really are the Den'Sar'Gar, then they lost a battle there to Jeddera the Great and his son Jeddera Summersword," explained Samarin

"What do you mean, 'if they really are the Den'Sar'Gar'?" asked Kyrian.

"They are supposed to be extinct," replied Samarin.

"Not extinct, just imprisoned," said Sali sadly. "Kept in a stockade with very real, yet invisible boundaries. Culled and controlled by wyrms and Ice Lords. Given over a millennium to mull on their defeat, to warm themselves with their hatred in this cold place, while the world forgot them."

"Shame you haven't got a word to control them," the Fal'Gar muttered coldly.

"I didn't think of it back then," Sali grunted and kicked her oradar forward towards Krynal.

CHAPTER NINETEEN – THE CRYSTAL CITY

Vast ice-like shards stabbed upwards, their crystalline structure shining through the mists. Two days past, the swamps and forests had given way to tundra, great plains of mossy heath covered by a thickening sheet of snow. They had seen little sign of the Grey Folk in their journey north. The road had huts along the way, places for travellers to stay. It had hinted at their presence, but they had seen no signs of actual people. Occasionally they spied shadowed figures framed against the morning sun. They could have been Den'Sar'Gar or Kyth'Gar, but they were always far distant. No homesteads, no farms; a feeling of a people being present but hidden.

They no longer appeared on the tundra, where the land was too open to hide anything. Solinad tracks frozen in place by the harsh weather could be found under the snow. They spoke of great herds grazing across this land in summer. There were none to be seen now, only the occasional collection of bones from an animal that had not gone south with the migration. The moss was interspersed with a variety of fungus, including the one that produced drun – a hint that this land was not the wasteland it first appeared. On the undisturbed snow were the light tracks of smaller creatures, birds and small mammals. Under the white were the black threads of digested drun spider-webbed across a sea of frozen solinad dung. A light mist swirled across the tundra, catching the moisture in the air, as the near-constant snow had for a day at least switched to rain.

The ice shards in the mist were the towers of Krynal. It seemed more a fortress than a city, a collection of perhaps fifty thin structures piercing up into the sky arranged in a rough circle. Taller than the Dawn Tower that had once stood in Las Ma or the two towers in the Slayer castle on Backistri, they climbed impossibly high, spiralling upwards and wreathed in mist. The road was now paved, running arrow-straight across the open tundra towards the city. Only a light dusting of snow covered its grey surface, suggesting a level of activity that contradicted the total absence of anyone but the three companions. A wall a hundred feet high circled the base of the towers, connecting the outer spires into a defensive perimeter. It gave an impression more of fear-inspiring menace than practical defence, its remoteness more protection than the angular gothic fortifications.

Kyrian pulled to a stop a couple of hundred yards from the gates in the city wall. Saliana, who was leading the group, took a moment to realize he had stopped. She caught his absence in her peripheral vision and pulled her cat around. It padded back to where Kyrian sat staring at the walls. Samarin waited patiently and silently next to him.

"It's a crystal ship," he said with wonder.

"The same material, maybe," observed Sali.

"They look the same," he declared.

Sali looked at the city; it was certainly reminiscent of the crystal ships of the Syn'Dion'Gar, but the line of the Kyth'Gar city was somehow more complicated and baroque, lacking the clean lines, sweeping arches, and aesthetic clarity of Cliphine's people.

"Why are we waiting?" Sali demanded.

"You are in a rush to die," Kyrian muttered.

Sali looked at him and grinned. It turned into a laugh, a hard deep laugh that left her practically coughing.

"Something I said funny?" he demanded archly.

"Very," Sali replied, slowly gaining control of herself.

Samarin just stared at the pair, assessing their odd behaviour, wondering not for the first time how she had ended up in the cold north with two mad people.

"Shall we?" Saliana pointed at the city, inviting Kyrian to follow her.

The three set off, the wariness in their movement forward also affecting the oradar they rode. The cats and their riders rode gingerly, eyes raking the empty walls of the shining city ahead of them.

"There are no guards," observed Kyrian.

"There are," Samarin declared. "There is something, anyway. We are being watched. I can feel them."

Saliana nodded in agreement but said nothing.

The gate yawned above them. The arch was sharp and angular, peaking far above them. It was also surprisingly narrow, so they had to ride in single file. The gate was open, a single door of pale blue glass, translucent but not transparent. Kyrian looked up as they passed through, noting the lack of any murder holes that defenders could use to protect themselves. He caught a flicker of movement in his peripheral vision – a figure in grey moving from one tower to another across an open walkway.

PRINCE OF SLAYERS

Kyrian realized that the towers, far from being random as he first supposed, were arranged in three concentric circles. The first formed part of the outer walls in a ring of twenty-five towers; within this was a smaller ring of fifteen towers, then there was a final inner circle of ten towers. The two inner circles were linked by close-sided stone bridges between the towers, straight ugly things, practical and utilitarian ways of passing from tower to tower without using the ground.

The Slayers and their erstwhile guide passed through the final circle of structures. What then greeted their eyes Kyrian could only describe as an ice rink. A youthful memory arose of an icy lake, surrounded by a cordon of string and bright flags, knife blades strapped to boots to skate across the surface. Mainly that had involved him landing on his young backside. That had been a rarity. Only in the coldest winters in the lands of the Sevains had the lakes iced over, and not since Kyrian had been a young boy. It was a strong memory, though; one that stood out in the haze of a half-forgotten childhood.

Though the area before him had brought back the memory, in truth it looked nothing like the small ribbon-bedecked lake of his youth. The area of ice covered by a smattering of snow was acres in size, filling the whole centre of the city. It was ringed by a circular stone pavement, large grey flagstones hinting at their presence through the covering of white powder. The pavement was nearly a hundred yards wide, occasionally broken up by small squat structures, the only single-storey buildings visible anywhere so far in the entire city. Wooden hoists hung with rope harnesses surrounded the frozen waters. They looked the worse for wear; weathered, unused and in some cases broken. Kyrian struggled to fathom their purpose.

Saliana pulled her oradar to a halt at the edge of the pavement before it dropped away to the ice rink ten feet below. She dismounted and stared out across the ice. At the far end, the northern end, there was a break in the circle of stones surrounding the ice. The gap was more than fifty yards wide, and the ice stretched out in a channel passing between the ring of towers before it reached a gaping hole in the walls. It stretched beyond them into the distance, where the channel was lost in the snowy mists of the tundra.

No wonder they had left the gate open, mused Kyrian. What was the point of a defensive wall if it had a hole in it fifty yards wide?

He dismounted his cat, joining Saliana where she was standing next to the frozen water's edge.

"Pretty pointless wall," he observed, pointing out to the yawning gap ahead of them.

"This will work," Sali replied with a smile, seemingly ignoring his observation. "I think the sluice is still active."

She was staring at the gap in the wall and the channel through it, as if searching for something.

"If not, the harbour would have flooded," she mused.

"The *harbour*?"

She looked at Kyrian. "Of course the harbour. What did you think this was?" She gestured at the expanse of ice. "In spring, this melts; this is a port."

"A port?" Kyrian was incredulous. "We are a hundred miles inland. Where would a ship come from or go to?"

"The channel – it's a canal, it stretches for nearly that far north before it joins the river, the one Kyth'Gar call the Druminan. There the river reaches the Northern Ocean, and beyond lies the route to Nerlinea."

"Nerlinea? It's on the other side of the world," Kyrian declared, with a certainty that he did not feel.

"When you look at the map, yes, but we don't live on a map, we live on a globe. This far north, the distances between east and west narrow to nothing. The ocean to the north is not really worthy of the name ocean; it is not great in its expanse. Most of it is frozen all year round, but there are enough gaps in it in spring and summer for ships to pass through. This allows a ship to sail in one direction and enter the Farthest Ocean to the east of Nerlinea. Alternatively, you can go in the other direction and end up in the Kraken's Wake, the ocean to the west of Anaror and Delenor. Oceans on opposite sides of the worlds in your mind join here in the north," Sali explained.

"If we live on a globe then that implies that the two oceans are joined, not just here in the north, but at the equator. We could sail a ship around the world," Kyrian observed.

"That is what scholars have speculated. None who have tried it have survived except in legend," she replied.

"Legend?"

"The Voyage of the Ravenscar: Jeddera Summersword and his companions sailed east into the Farthest Ocean to fight in the War of the Gods," she replied.

"And he returned?" he asked.

"No, he became a god, but his friend Far brought the ship and some of the crew back to Nerlinea."

"But they never reached the Kraken's Wake?" Kyrian enquired.

"Not in the story," she replied.

"So, what lies out there?" he wondered.

"The isles of the gods, mists and tumultuous ocean, terrifying monsters such as giant kraken – that is what the story says, at least."

He nodded. "What is this, a harbour, then?" He indicated the frozen expanse in front of them.

"A shipyard," she replied. "This is where the crystal ships of the Syn'Dion'Gar were built."

Kyrian stopped himself before the inevitable question 'how do you know that?' sprang to his lips. A part of him was tired of asking; another part was reconciled to it. He had tied his path to the woman standing next to him, no matter who or what she was. Asking more questions would not change that.

Sali knew her history well. For it was here in the snowy north that the crystal mines lay. The Kyth'Gar were the miners and the shipwrights. Here in the harbour of Krynal they had built the great crystal ships for the Syn'Dion'Gar millennia ago. They had built smaller vessels for themselves, for once they had traded their wares – furs, crystal, and timber – across the oceans of the north, appearing in both the West and the East, only contributing further to the Kyth'Gar's mysterious reputation. The last time any vessel had come here had been centuries ago. The last ship to be built here had been decades before that. Yet the harbour and channel still remained working and open, even if the hoists and harnesses that surrounded it had fallen into decay.

"We have company," Samarin muttered.

She remained mounted on her oradar, but pulled it around so it was facing the oncoming party. There were three of them, all Gar but of two different races. The central figure was a female Kyth'Gar, with pale skin, soft yellow hair, and the angular, tall stature of all Gar. She reminded Kyrian very much of the Syn'Dion'Gar, but somehow seemed to lack the imperceptible aura that the Syn'Dion'Gar emitted. A feeling of coldness stood in its stead, as if the Kyth'Gar had taken on the nature of their northern home. She lacked the youth that marked Samarin, having reached the maturity that gave her the ageless quality distinctive of the Gar. She was flanked by two Den'Sar'Gar, ash-grey faces staring from black metal helms, dressed in plate armour of the same metal, spears grasped in hands. The Kyth'Gar by contrast wore a long white dress, which hung off her in waves of thin fabrics. It was cut almost to the waist with a slash in the side, so that much of the beautiful Gar's perfect skin was on display. This was deeply impractical for the frigid conditions in which they found themselves, but she seemed unconcerned. Bruises marred her skin, both her face and the parts of her legs and torso on display.

"It is good to see you again," said Sali, stepping past Samarin on her oradar.

The Fal'Gar rider's cat pawed the ground, picking up Samarin's nerves.

"You know her?" whispered Kyrian, too loud to conceal his question.

"We met earlier," grinned Sali, ignoring any pretence that the question was somehow disguised. "You have recovered well from our earlier encounter."

"The Fal'Gar is not the only witch in the north," the Kyth'Gar replied.

"No, she isn't," said Sali with a wide smile. "Do you have a name?"

"I am Pynathin of Krynal, daughter of Esselindanor, High Lord of Kyth'Dath. My father requests an audience with the High Lady of Syndion." Her tones were clipped, and her face indicated she was not happy to deliver the message.

"You are much more polite without your wyrm," observed Sali.

Kyrian realized who the woman was: the Culimarin, the Guardian on the dragon. Now he understood the comment about witches; there was no way that Pynathin would be walking around without the healing craft.

Pynathin's gaze wandered across the three of them. "You cost me my prey," she replied. "We have a task to keep to, and you interrupted it. Had it been my decision you would not have entered the city, but my father wants to speak to you. He is oddly intrigued by you."

She turned away and strode off, accompanied by her guards. A few yards on she turned back, noting that the Slayers still stood by the harbour.

"Come or don't: it makes no difference to me, but it will to my father. Besides, you came all this way for something."

She walked off.

Sali looked to Kyrian. He shrugged.

The three set off after Pynathin, Kyrian and Sali leading their oradars, Samarin still mounted padding along behind. The Kyth'Gar female led them to a tower on the innermost ring. It was indistinguishable from the others, and in fact the uniformity of all three rings was slightly disconcerting to the Slayers, who were more used to a variety of contrasting buildings and architectural styles. Samarin felt similarly, though for very different reasons. Like all nomads she found cities, especially walled ones, deeply alien. It was part of the reason she had remained mounted on her oradar; it gave her a feeling she could ride off anytime.

She was forced to dismount as they reached the door at the base of the tower. It was narrow, wide enough for a single person only to enter. Grey Folk grooms appeared seemingly from nowhere to take the three beasts.

"They will be fed," explained Pynathin, before she pushed through the door and disappeared inside.

Kyrian gave Saliana a querying look.

Her face said, *this is what we came for, isn't it?* She did not have to articulate her confirmation out loud.

The pair entered the tower, a reluctant Samarin bringing up the rear. The entrance hall led to a flight of stone steps, one leading down into a dark subterranean room, the other leading up to a brightly lit room, more a raised mezzanine floor than a first floor. Pynathin had disappeared from view, but the sound of conversation was coming from the floor above.

The Slayers and Samarin progressed up the stairs, through an open doorway again only wide enough to allow a single person to enter at a time. It was narrower than the approaching stairway. This was because of a second lower but equally narrow doorway to the side of the main door. Through it, Sali could see a spiral staircase leading up the tower to the higher levels.

PRINCE OF SLAYERS

The three squeezed through the door into the brightly lit room. The doorway was designed for Gar, tall and thin – easy for Sali and Samarin, but more of an issue for the broad-shouldered Kyrian. The room was windowless; not even arrow slits let in any natural light. On the wall to the left, a large stone fireplace was built into the wall. A fire burned in the grate, with almost all the smoke taken away by an efficient chimney flue. A small amount created a slight haze in the air reflected by the bright white light that filled the chamber. It came from a ring of white illumination that circled the top of the tower wall just below the ceiling of the next floor above. Sali could sense the magic used to generate it.

That was the most impressive thing about the room. It was spartan, undecorated, with bare walls of grey stone, the floor a simple wooden surface, not recently polished but darkened by age. The only furniture was perhaps a dozen wooden chairs scattered along the sides of the room and five throne-like seats set against the wall directly opposite the entrance. Kyrian only assumed that they were thrones because they were higher-backed and sturdier than the other chairs. He could see flecks of gold in the crevices of the wooden scrollwork on the sides of the back panels, a hint that they had once looked more impressive than the simple wooden chairs they resembled. Their throne-like quality was ephemeral; they rested as if they had sat in the same position for centuries if not millennia, contrasting with the other chairs in the room, which seemed, from their careless dispersal, to have been moved regularly.

Kyrian looked at Sali and his face said it all. If this was the throne room of the High Lords of Krynal, the rulers of Kyth'Dath, it was deeply unimpressive.

The were five Kyth'Gar in the room including Pynathin. Her Grey Folk guards had disappeared, leaving only the three travellers and their Kyth'Gar hosts. A male Gar stood by the fire, tall even for one of the ancient people, his head bowed in conversation with Pynathin. The other three Kyth'Gar, two females and one male, watched the new arrivals cautiously from where they sat. All had the same ageless quality that Kyrian expected of the Gar. They were dressed in similar light clothes to those worn by Pynathin. It took a moment for Kyrian to register how hot the room was. No wonder they were so loosely attired.

He heard a crash behind him and looked around, alert for attack. Samarin had stripped off her cloak, outer layers and kit. She had just dumped them on the ground, as she would have done on entering the warm interior of a Fal'Gar yurt. The crash had been her armour and weapons hitting the ground. It then occurred to the Slayer that no one had thought to disarm them. His flail still rested in his belt, and Sali's pair of short swords rested either side of her waist. Kyrian removed his cloak and tossed it on the pile Samarin had created, but kept on his arms and armour. Even after his few years living on the steppe, he had still not become comfortable with its customs of hospitality, which guaranteed the sanctity of the guest. He did not know if Samarin knew the steppe customs applied among the Kyth'Dath, or she had simply assumed it. He noted the juxtaposition with her wariness earlier. She might dislike cities and walls, but a warm room was a warm room. Sali followed her fellow travellers' lead and stripped off her cloak and hat, adding them to the pile by the door. Like Kyrian, she remained armed and ready.

The male Gar by the fire stopped talking to Pynathin and walked over to the empty five thrones. He took a seat on the central throne. Old eyes assessed the three travellers who stood before him. Pynathin took her own seat on one of the simpler chairs in the hall. None of the other Kyth'Dath sought to sit on one of the four empty thrones.

The silence started to stretch. Sali was about to step forward and say something.

"Samarin Mrignandor, what brings the future Trendorn'Di'Fal'Gar so far north?" he asked coldly.

She struggled to say something, somehow confused by his description of her. Instead, she nodded nervously at the Slayers, at a loss for words.

"Taking orders from humans; how very Fal'Gar?" he grunted contemptuously. "They are not even Nerlineans."

"Yet you are speaking a human tongue," observed Sali.

Indeed, they were; he had addressed them in Nerlinean.

"Well, my Fal'Gar is terrible, and I doubt any of you speak my language. Since the time of the Jedderas we have sent our children south to learn and be educated at the University of Nerlon."

"As in, know your enemy," observed Sali.

"Something like that," replied the Kyth'Gar, warming slightly.

"You speak the tongue of your enemy with the Grey Folk," asked Kyrian, curious.

"Well, our charges refuse to speak Kyth'Gar even after all this time, so Nerlinean seems to be enough of a compromise. Make them speak the language of their enemy, if they won't speak that of their jailor," he said with a sharp laugh.

"You could speak their language," Kyrian suggested.

"Speak the dark tongue?" the Gar laughed. "That would be the height of foolishness."

"They are the Den'Sar'Gar," observed Samarin, finding her voice.

"Well done, Samarin of the Fal'Gar. Had your uncle not spoken to you of what we guarded?"

"You know my uncle?"

"Of course. Sorry, I should introduce myself: I am Esselindanor, but you may call me Essel. Gar names can be a mouthful, especially the more ancient ones. I came south maybe seventy years ago, acting as representative of my people for the crowning of the Dumech'Di'Fal'Gar at the tent city of Cularan."

He gave a long sigh. "All gone now. Cularan, I mean, and that Dumech too. He was your other uncle, Tolemar, Falthar's older brother. Dead now in the Mourn conquest. I would have sent my daughter south for Falthar's crowning had there been one. Cularan was gone by then; Fal'Dath too."

"Fal'Dath endures," replied Samarin fiercely.

"If you say so." His response was polite, his tone conciliatory, but underlying this he sounded unconvinced.

"The Den'Sar'Gar," she pressed. "How are they still alive?"

"The same way your people endure, and Fal'Dath does not. When they were defeated, those that would not bow were sent here, our punishment," he replied.

"This makes no sense. The Den'Sar'Gar were destroyed, obliterated before the walls of Las Ma when Jeddera Summersword defeated Naron," Samarin declared with a certainty that she could feel slipping away.

Kyrian was taken back by the name 'Naron' to the song Sali had sung for Amdon on the steppe. She had sung of wars and gods, the Gar people: the children of Naron, she had called them. They had to be the Den'Sar'Gar. He looked at Sali, trying to catch her eye, but she was staring ahead focused on the ice elf.

"I have a proposition," declared Sali.

Samarin shrank back as if reprimanded. Essel's gaze swung to Sali, his eyes assessing. He had noticed Samarin's reaction to Sali's interjection. He took in Kyrian and Sali.

"You interrupt your betters, human," he muttered.

Then he raised an eyebrow. "You wear a glamour," he accused Sali, thrusting out his finger.

PRINCE OF SLAYERS

His hand swirled and a gust of magical wind blew across the room. The wind ruffled Sali's hair, but nothing else happened. She stood there, staring back with a small smile on her face.

Essel sank back in the chair, the ineffectiveness of his magic giving him pause for thought.

"The Company of Slayers, Prince of Chazantria, Prince of Syndion – even Prince of Kangorn, I hear," he observed, changing the subject from Sali.

"*Count* of Chazantria," corrected Kyrian.

Sali said nothing.

"But which is Prince of Slayers?" Essel queried, ignoring Kyrian's comment.

Sali said nothing, her unblinking gaze meeting his.

"Prince. Interesting title: it was the Nerlineans who used it, but it's not originally a Nerlinean word," Essel announced to the room, ready to lecture on the etymology of the word. "One of the kingdoms they conquered, I believe. They liked it for its clarity; it just meant 'first'. Now it is used for those who would be first, who think themselves first, and who might one day be first."

Sali dropped her gaze, her eyes sweeping across the others in the room, focused on Essel.

"You blocked my magic with the barest of your power. I felt it. Who are you really? What are you? What is hiding below that glamour?" Essel asked.

"I am a merchant, sometimes a warrior, on occasion a bard," replied Sali calmly.

"You are modest. I know of you, Slayer. Even in the far north we hear things. What your people did on Syndion against the Samath is known to me. I hear talk of what happened in Las Ma: they say you brought down the walls with magic doing what Naron could not. Now you stand here in my hall," Essel observed.

291

"I didn't bring down the walls of Las Ma: that was the Sevains, apparently with the help of the Pandus family," replied Sali.

"Magically?"

"Chemically," clarified Sali.

"And Syndion?" he asked.

"I don't know what you've heard?"

"I heard that you took Davyn KalEron and his army from the crypt of the ancestors and destroyed a Samath force trying to take the isles," Essel said.

"I had the help of a witch, but that is essentially correct," agreed Sali.

"This one?" Essel indicated Samarin.

"Another one. My colleague Dryana Slayer; my friend here's sister." Sali indicated Kyrian.

"But under your command?" Essel demanded, leaning forward in his chair, his gaze penetrating.

"Yes," confirmed Sali.

"So, *you* are the Prince of Slayers," Essel declared, sitting back with a look of satisfaction on his face.

"Not a title I would claim. I am titled Mistress of the Company of Slayers and High Lady of Syndion," Sali replied, her eyes searching his face for meaning.

"Semantics?" the Kyth'Gar muttered.

"Does it matter for my proposal?" enquired Sali.

"I don't know. We shall see. Are you speaking as a merchant or a prince?" Essel asked.

"A merchant."

"Well, we have little need of trade up here in the far north, but you have come a long way so we will listen," he replied.

"You know what drun is?" she asked.

"Of course," he nodded in response.

PRINCE OF SLAYERS

"During the summer months, the solinad graze in your land within the Sul'Kirin. It is here they consume the mushroom fields. Through the summer months, they graze and defecate, producing huge quantities of the half-digested mushroom. Before the coming of the winter in the late autumn they consume the last of the mushrooms, carrying it in their stomachs to survive on while they journey to their warmer winter grounds in Chazantria in the west and Havagia in the east. Having reached it, they graze on the ample grass and defecate, turning the otherwise harsh steppe plains into fertile agricultural terrain for the spring and summer until they return north. A small amount of mushroom is not fully digested by the solinad in its journey, and they crap this out when they first arrive in Chazantria. There it is dried in sheds and taken south to be added to tobacco and smoked. The same was true of Havagia before the actions of the Nerlineans put a stop to it, something that has only got worse since the Mourn conquest resulted in the Havagians returning to the steppe way of life," Sali finished.

"So much I know. What is your proposal?" Essel replied.

"Here in the lands of Kyth'Dath, the land lies thick with drun. The black threads hang across the landscape ready to be collected and dried. I want to set up an operation for drying it and sending it to Nerlinea," Sali proposed.

That provoked an amused chuckle from Pynathin.

"You have something to say, daughter?" Essel's tone made clear that the question was rhetorical.

"The Nerlineans are very opposed to the trade in drun. They would soon detect caravans coming south filled with drun and where it comes from. I have no wish to have a Nerlinean army at my gates. Besides, the Great Khan of the Mourn will likely block the drun going south, or at least expect a tribute for letting it pass," continued Essel, switching back to looking at Sali.

"You cannot have it both ways, my lord: either you fear that Nyandar of Nerlinea will cross the steppe to fight you, or you fear the Great Khan will block the passage south. Only one of those fears can be true. The Nerlineans have lost Havagia to the Mourn, so they can hardly march an army against you, and the Mourn are not interested in drun or they would sell it from conquered Havagia," countered Saliana.

"I can have it as many ways as I like, Prince of Slayers: I rule in Kyth'Dath. The Mourn leave us alone, and I have no reason to offend them. The Nerlineans are blocked for now, but my people remember when they last marched north and the humiliation we experienced," replied Essel.

"Six centuries ago. That is a long memory," observed Sali.

"We are a long-lived people. It was in my grandfather's time, recent enough that he could tell me the story as he saw it as a youngling, My great grandfather was one of the High Lords. We were punished, this city looted, for the crime of not taking sides. You are well informed, I will concede." Essel's tone was calm, but his eyes hinted at annoyance if not quite anger.

Saliana doubted that Essel's grandfather remembered it. Three hundred years was a good life for the Gar; most died early in their fourth century. A few lived closer to four centuries – an eternity compared to a human. Sali suspected that Essel was approaching the middle of his third century, but still looked ageless, no hint of the visible age that would have marked his features had he been approaching his fourth century. Working back, that meant his grandfather would had to have been around four hundred years of age when he told him the story, old enough to have been there as a babe, but unlikely to have remembered it. He had probably imbibed the stories himself and retold them as a first-hand experience.

PRINCE OF SLAYERS

It was a half-forgotten history. There had been a war between the Falcon Empress, the ruler of Fal'Dath and the combined forces of the Empire of Nerlinea and the Syn'Dion'Gar. The half-elven Nerlinean Emperor, as Ran'Dumech'Di'Gar, had called all the Gar to war. He had done so with the full support of Cliphine, the Su'Trendorn'Di'Gar, the high priestess of all the Gar. The Kyth'Gar had refused to take sides. They had argued that their historic duty to guard the Grey Folk trumped the war between different Gar peoples and they could not spare the Guardians for battle. The truth was more complicated: the sympathy of the Kyth'Gar had lain with the Falcon Empress. For they too believed that the Gar should not bow to a mostly human Ran'Dumech, no matter his lineage, but they also knew that the Falcon Empress would likely not prevail against the combined forces arrayed against her. Their neutrality had not protected them when the Nerlineans had marched north, following their defeat of the Falcon Empress.

Knowing they had no chance against the enemy approaching them, they tried to surrender, but the Nerlinean Emperor, the man who called himself Ran'Dumech, wanted to prove a point. They made no attempt to give battle to the approaching army. The Grey Folk had melted away into the dark forests and swamps, so the Nerlineans never saw them. The Kyth'Gar remained in Krynal, but they did not attempt the impossible task of defending the city. The Kyth'Gar had sent their Grey Folk slave-soldiers from the city and opened the gates.

They had thrown themselves on the mercy of Zedian VIII, Emperor of Nerlinea. At first it had worked, despite the emperor's violent reputation. Then one night, three days after the army's arrival, the Nerlinean army had looted the city and slaughtered many of its inhabitants. The emperor had been drinking with the high lords, and in his inebriation, demanded to see where the dragons slept. They had protested that the dragons were gone, but it was to no avail. Drunk, angry and unwilling to be refused, he had imprisoned the high lords, executing two of them and unleashing his army upon the city. Only the arrival of Cliphine and her Syn'Dion'Gar the following evening had persuaded him to stop. The Kyth'Gar population had never recovered. It had left them with a burning hatred and engulfing fear of the Nerlinean Empire.

"We will pay you for the drun," Sali stated.

"You think we are so interested in money?" Essel replied.

"Most rulers are. If not, do it for revenge," she said with a shrug.

"Revenge? What is our revenge to you? Our problem is the Nerlineans will find out where it has come from – you cannot hide the caravans," Essel said.

"That's why I intend to use ships," replied Sali.

"What?" Essel looked confused.

"Ships. Big wooden things with sails," she explained facetiously.

"Oh, Father, this is absurd. Can I kill them now?" Pynathin demanded.

Sali looked over at her and raised an eyebrow. So, the woman had not taken her recent beating as well as had first appeared.

"Ship?" Essel mouthed quietly, leaning forward and waving his daughter to silence.

"We will bring our ships over the Northern Ocean, down the canal and into the shipyard. We will load up here and take the drun out over the ocean to Ravangia and the east coast of mainland Nerlinea," Sali explained.

"Even in the summer there is floating ice. It will be very dangerous for wooden ships," Essel observed.

Kyrian could see his resistance was fading. Money and a way to damage the Nerlineans with little chance of repercussions: the temptation was building.

"We have crowns for our ships; the ice won't be a problem," the Mistress of the Slayers reassured him.

Kyrian watched the look on Essel's face. They had him. He would agree.

"And one other thing," said Sali.

Kyrian looked at her, trying to keep the annoyance from his face. What was she doing? They had him.

"I will also need three crystals of milky amber," she announced.

Pynathin laughed, and she was not the only one. Kyrian had never seen a group of Gar laugh like that; it was a deeply odd experience. He looked at Essel hard to tell if he was amused or angry, but the mood had changed.

"Greedy, like all merchants," Essel observed coldly. "All you offer could not buy one such jewel, let alone three."

Kyrian was incredulous; he could not keep it from his face. He was staring at his colleague. What had she done? Years of planning, work, ending with a journey to this cold wasteland, and she had thrown it all away at the last. The vast wealth they had been moments from making had been lost.

"I have a sweetener," Sali declared, raising her gloved left hand.

She pulled off her glove. On her left hand was a ring, a gold band, set with a large emerald of radiant green. She tugged it off her finger. Kyrian remembered well the day when she had obtained it. It had been the same day his lover, Lana Levacic, had been executed on Sali's order. They had taken the ring in part payment for rescuing Leo, last Duke of Las Ma, from his defeated city. Kyrian remembered now how insistent Sali had been on receiving the payment in the box of jewels she had demanded, rather than the paper the Nerlineans would have preferred. He had been tired at the time, too busy revelling in their escape and the success of their mission to register why Sali was insisting on being paid in a particular way. He should have: Saliana never did anything without a reason.

She tossed the ring to Essel, who snatched it out of the air. He examined it. His eyes widened. He looked at Sali, his eyes searching her face, then back to the ring. He breathed out and Sali felt a rush of magical power. Light blazed through the emerald, turning the harsh white ambience of the room to green. The other Kyth'Gar, even Pynathin, were staring at the ring clasped in the high lord's hand. A bead of sweat rolled down Essel's pale face, the only sign of the magic stressing his body.

"Where did you get it?" he asked quietly, his formerly confident voice now a whisper.

"In payment from the Imperial Treasury," Sali replied.

"Did they know what it was?"

"I doubt it," she observed.

"Do you?" Essel asked.

"Yes."

"Get out. I need to sleep on this. I need to think." Essel seemed flustered.

Saliana turned, grabbing up her hat and cloak, and walked out. Kyrian, shocked by the change, took a moment to register their dismissal. Then he picked up his kit and chased after Sali. Samarin was unsure what to do. Trying to ignore the baleful gaze of her hosts, she decided not to bother rearming. Using both arms, she loaded herself up and used her chin to steady the unwieldy pile of clothes and armour. Almost dropping it, she gingerly walked from the room.

CHAPTER TWENTY – DRAGONS

Kyrian sat by the dock, wondering if it ever got light around here. It was mid-morning, and he could detect only the barest hint of dawn, not helped by the swirling mass of grey cloud that covered the sky. He sat on the edge of the shipyard, his feet dangling from the stone quay. He imagined skating across the icy surface of the water, but dressed in leather armour, he was not going to test the theory it would hold. He felt the cold damp of the snow permeating through the cloth of his trousers. He knew he would soon regret seating himself on the snow. The adult in him told him it was foolish, but where was the fun in life without being a little foolish?

He heard footsteps behind, soft pads on the snow-covered flagstones. Kyrian turned, recognizing the approaching form of Esselindanor. Tall and lithe like all of his kind, he moved catlike across the dock. Kyrian suspected that the Gar could have crept up behind him with ease, so the sound he had made was not to alarm the Slayer. Kyrian went to push himself up.

"Stay seated; no need to stand up," Essel instructed.

His voice was high-pitched but lacked the singsong quality of the other Gar that Kyrian had met. Instead, it had a cold hardness, as if the Kyth'Gar had taken on the nature of the icy northern home in their speech as they had in much else. The Gar took a seat on the dock next to Kyrian, as equally unconcerned by its damp snowy surface as the wrestler.

Kyrian gave a nod of his head, the closest he could manage to a bow. "Morning, your highness. If you wish to negotiate further, Saliana should join us," the Slayer declared.

"Not sure I've ever been a highness. Essel is fine," mused the Kyth'Gar High Lord. "And no, our negotiations are over. Only the decision remains."

Kyrian gave a polite shrug of understanding. He wanted to ask why the High Lord was being so informal. Did he see Kyrian as an equal? The wrestler doubted that. Still, he let it go, deciding it wasn't the time to enquire.

"I love it here," Essel continued. "The clear air, the quiet, all within the walls of a city."

The Slayer said nothing. For him it was a cold, dead, forbidding place, lacking the vibrancy of a city or the relaxing natural life of the forest or the plain. Besides, he disliked the cold.

"How did you meet?" Essel asked.

"Pardon?" asked Kyrian.

"How did you meet the..." Essel was grasping for a word. "How did you meet her, Saliana?"

So, Kyrian told the story: how they first met as slaves of the Pandus, their escape and flight to Kangorn. Soon it all flooded out: his mission to take a crown to Lana Levacic; the battles with the Pandus and the Samath; the siege of Las Ma;

Balinor's rise to Prince of Kangorn; Kyrian's years building his own principality in the steppe, and most recently their journey north. The Gar asked question after question, narrowing down the story, always focusing on Sali and her role, especially on her magical powers. Kyrian left out much, partly for time, partly out of caution, but the Gar was easy to speak to, and he probably said more than he should.

"What do you know of Saliana Slayer before you met on the ship?" asked Essel as Kyrian finished his tale.

"Not much," Kyrian answered, his tone cautious.

"Not much?"

"Nothing," the Slayer amended, under Essel's penetrating gaze.

He had left out the moments when she had revealed unexpected knowledge on Kangorn, on Syndion, among the tents of the Fal'Gar, and on so many other occasions, too many to count.

"So where did such a powerful mage hide for so long?" Essel mused.

"Slinker always wondered that," grunted Kyrian.

"The man you spoke of, your colleague?"

"Yes," confirmed Kyrian. "Well, he's a Tancree, not a man, a war mage, but yes."

"Ah! A Tancree," Essel gave a beaming smile. "He must be among the last of them. It would have been nice to meet one before they passed from the world."

His tone turned sad at the last.

"Why do you wish to sell drun to the Nerlineans? Why do you wish to intoxicate an empire?" asked Essel, changing the subject.

Kyrian kicked his heels against the stone, saying nothing. He did not really have a clear answer; it had been Sali's idea.

"You are a good man," Essel observed. "You must have a reason."

"Do I need a reason? Trade is trade. Is it any business of mine what a working man chooses to do with his spare time? How he chooses to relax?" Kyrian replied, his tone sharp.

Essel nodded. "So, your reasons are altruistic?" His tone was mocking.

"Money is my reason, what is yours?" Kyrian shot back. "You have decided to give us the drun, haven't you?"

Essel did not answer for a moment. He fished into a pouch at his side and produced the emerald ring and held it up. In the grey light it seemed very ordinary, still somehow larger than when it had rested on Sali's finger. Kyrian had gotten so used to it over the years, he was long past noticing it. The stone looked larger too held in the Gar's frost-pale hand. In reality, it had not changed; it was purely in the presentation.

"You know what this is?" Essel asked, staring at it.

Kyrian considered lying. He was still annoyed that Sali had not told him about this last part of the plan. Assuming it was something she had planned. No, she had definitely planned it – the Kyth'Gar reaction told him that. Why had Sali not shared it with him? Why could she not trust him with the last inevitable twist of her plans?

"No, it's just a ring to me," shrugged Kyrian.

Essel took a deep breath. "Nations, peoples, are defined by their wars," he declared.

Kyrian fought down a sigh. It was going to be one of those wandering explanations. Why could people never get to the point? If Essel detected the Slayer's frustration, he ignored it.

"The wars they fight define them," continued Essel. "They remember the ones they choose, forget the ones they don't. Consign those that don't define them to the history books. There are certain wars that define us and they need not be great victories; agonizing defeats do the job just as well. We pretend the Culimarin has been unmolested for hundreds of years, since the Nerlineans marched north six centuries past. It is not true. Mourn tribes and the Fal'Gar empire have raided here, attacked and demanded tribute. I suspect that, one day soon, the Great Khan will send an expedition north to demand our fealty. If it is small enough our Grey Folk soldiers and wyrms will destroy it; if it is too large, we will pretend obeisance. Whichever, it will be forgotten by us with the turn of time. The Kyth'Dath, unlike others, are delineated by two wars we did not fight. The second was the war between Zedian, Cliphine and the Falcon Empress, and for that you already know our punishment: to be brought to the edge of extinction."

"People are always telling me history as if it matters," muttered Kyrian. "It does not feed a man or put a roof over his head. Kings, princes, high lords... so much history weighing on you, only because what weighs on the ordinary person is already taken care of for you."

"You are a philosopher," observed Essel with a smile. "It is always amusing to hear a rich man and a purveyor of hallucinogens champion the common man. There is nothing more hypocritical to hear, especially for one whose family has held status through the generations, than the whining of the newly arrived for the common folk they have so recently left behind."

Kyrian gave the Gar a hard look.

"You will listen to my meanderings because they matter to me and one day you will realize they matter to you. Right now, they matter to you because that is how you get your deal, so you will listen with polite interest and one day I suspect you will remember, but only when it is too late," barked the Gar.

"I apologize. Please continue," Kyrian replied cautiously.

JUSTIN WAINE

"I shall tell it to you as a legend, rather than a history. Maybe that will appeal to your commoner's mind," Essel declared waspishly. "There was a warrior king of your people, the Kanath. His name was Jeddera the Great, and he had become king by right of his wife, for his blood was not of the House of Liones, but of the Dal'Ri'Gar. He was the last heir to the Dumech'Di'Dal'Ri'Gar, despite his half-elven blood, and so Ran'Dumech'Di'Gar. The warlord who could call all the Gar to war. For an ancient enemy had arisen, one he believed that his father had slain. Naron the Death Lord, Dumech'Di'Den'Sar'Gar, who had for centuries claimed to rule all the Gar as high priest and war leader. His armies of Gar, their human allies and monstrous slaves prepared in the Daldara Mountains ready to march south and to finally destroy the alliance of Kanath and Syn'Dion'Gar. So Jeddera sought allies everywhere for the battle he knew was coming. He sent his second son and namesake, who would one day be called the Summersword, to Nerlinea to marry the empress and bring their legions west. He sent others to call the Fal'Gar, the Debion'Gar, and the Quil'Gar to war, and even though all three were involved in wars in the east they sent forces to the west to help. To Kyth'Dath Jeddera sent as his envoy his closest friend and most gifted warrior, Sargon. For though the Kyth'Dath were few in number, they had one thing that could turn the war: they had dragons. Yet the Kyth'Dath rejected the call to war, partly out of arrogance, partly because they had always been close to the Den'Sar'Gar, and perhaps hoped they might win. The greatest reason was they knew the truth and it frightened them. The dragons had started to sleep. Only five were still awake, barely enough to defend their own land. They were not willing to strip their land of its only defence to fight a war half a world away. The High Lords of Kyth'Dath had not reckoned with one of their number, the High Lady Irimindor the dragon keeper, for she had fallen in love with Sargon. She conspired with him to take the five dragons that did not slumber to the aid of Jeddera. She rode one, Sargon another, and the other three chose as their riders Jeddera the Great, his wife, the Queen Zara Liones, and Simon the Archmage. Together we call them the last dragon lords," Essel stated.

"This is all ancient legend; I have heard a version of this tale before. Even among the Sevains who have no love for old pagan stories it is still recounted," interrupted Kyrian. "Except the dragon keeper is called Erindar and there is no mention of the Kyth'Dath in our version of the story."

"In your version how does it end?" asked Essel politely.

"Jeddera the Great is unknowingly betrayed by his eldest son Rodan, who conspires with Naron to wrest power from his father. The kingdom of Kanath is overwhelmed. Jeddera the Great loses half his kingdom. There is a great battle where the Kanath face certain defeat. Naron personally destroys two dragons, slaying Zara Liones and binding Simon with magic. Sargon and his dragon are slain and Erindar is overwhelmed by grief and flees the battlefield. Then the legions of Nerlinea appear, led by the King's second son, Jeddera Summersword. He uses a magical flute to defeat Naron, who just disappears into thin air, due to the tune it plays. The Summersword saves his father and the Kanath and the combined armies of Naron flee the battlefield," said Kyrian. "All very heroic, all very implausible."

"What, you don't believe in dragons?" Essel asked mockingly.

"Until I met your daughter on the road, I didn't," Kyrian said with a smile. "If that is a dragon, then maybe the story is exaggerated truth rather than simple fantasy."

"Maybe one day you will see a dragon," said Essel with a grin.

"Maybe one day I will meet the Summersword," Kyrian shot back with a chuckle.

"Maybe," Essel countered, smiling at the joke.

"What has this to do with our deal, even with your people?" asked Kyrian.

He had enjoyed the tale more than he would admit, but he still did not see why it mattered. Rather its importance to Essel, as it did not matter to Kyrian at all. Essel reminded Kyrian of Leo of Las Ma; another ruler obsessed by the past while his kingdom mouldered around him.

"In our version of the legend it is Irimindor and her dragon that is bound with Naron's power, not Simon. He is by contrast slain outright, his dragon fleeing home to Kyth'Dath. Irimindor is forced to watch as Naron tortures and murders Sargon, before Naron mounts Sargon's dragon to battle Jeddera the Great. She is broken by the experience. Riven with grief, her dragon takes her and the body of the broken Sargon back to Kyth'Dath, where she buries him in the mountains. When she returns to Krynal, she is imprisoned, but Jeddera and his children bring their armies north and free her. Jeddera is about to lay waste to Kyth'Dath for the failure to answer the call to war and for the treatment of his war companion. Irimindor begs for mercy for her people and her jailers. So, Jeddera decrees that their punishment for refusing to take sides in that war is to become the jailers of the Den'Sar'Gar. Over the next decades, many Den'Sar'Gar are sent north to their prison. In truth it was only a part of their number that were transferred, for they were the most numerous of the Gar peoples. Many were killed, most were subsumed into the other races, some into the Syn'Dion'Gar, most into the Fal'Gar. Only those that would not bow before a Dumech other than Naron were sent here. Once the greatest of the Gar peoples, they were reduced now to servants and guards to the Kyth'Gar. They are called the Grey Folk by those of the steppe who have seen them close to our borders. The mystery of who they are causes fear or pity depending on the viewer. Or maybe the fear is simply a subconscious memory of a time long past when the Den'Sar'Gar were conquerors."

"You encourage such stories about the Grey Folk?" Kyrian asked.

Essel gave a little smile.

"So, Samarin has Den'Sar'Gar blood?" asked Kyrian.

"Possibly; probably," Essel answered with a shrug.

"But not the Kyth'Gar?" asked Kyrian.

"We were once close to our dark cousins. When we became their jailers, we chose to see them as less. Perhaps that was the only way it would work; perhaps that was Jeddera's intention," Essel said with a sigh.

"And what happened to the dragonkeeper?"

"Irimindor went into the mountains, where she died of grief. She was brought back and buried in a new temple to the god Sargon, the Dragon King, the human who had been her husband. The emerald ring he had given her as a symbol of their matrimony, of their love, was placed on the altar. Our most sacred object, a token of passion, a symbol that at least one of us was brave enough to fight at the side of legends. This ring!" Essel stated, shaking the gold band in his hand for emphasis.

Kyrian nodded. Now he understood. He kept it from his face, but his mind was whirring. *How had Sali known*, he wondered?

"It was taken by the Nerlineans in their loot when they invaded. Zedian VIII wore it on his hand till he died, but then I suspect it was lost in the Imperial Treasury until your friend demanded it. We still send our children to be educated as he insisted. It is a chance for us to know our enemy, for they have long forgotten why we come. Human memory fails so quickly, a punishment for being short-lived." Essel stood up as if about to leave.

Kyrian followed suit. He looked up into the Gar's eyes. He would never get used to these lanky creatures being so much taller than him. Essel reached into his pouch at his belt and pulled out a small grey bag with a drawstring. He dropped it into Kyrian's hand. The Slayer untied it and shook out three stones. They were small round jewels, smooth like beach-rolled pebbles. They initially appeared to be orange, but white threads swirled through them, the colour changing as if the stone writhed underneath its smooth surface. One moment they were dark orange, another milky white, another almost gold.

"What are these?" the Slayer asked.

"Things of magic; rare and valuable," Essel said quietly.

"Worth more than an emerald ring?" Kyrian asked.

Essel smiled at that. "Incalculably more. Each one is worth far more than the ring, except to us," he said with a gentle sigh.

"Why does she want them?" asked the Slayer.

"If you don't know, how should I?" came Essel's amused response. "Besides, the question you should be asking is: how did she know?"

"And do you know the answer?" asked Kyrian.

Essel smiled. "We are protected by mystery, sheltered by legends of Guardians, wyrms and Grey Folk. Few come into these lands and even fewer leave. You have crossed our land; you have learned our weakness. In our heyday, we abandoned the offices of Dumech and Trendorn that our kin, even now, cling to so determinedly. Instead, five High Lords ruled us. They sat in the chairs in that tower."

Essel pointed back to the crystalline building in which they had first met.

"Now only my family remains. I am the last of the High Lords of Kyth'Dath."

"Then why let us leave? You would not give us this unless you intended to let us go?" Kyrian asked, lifting his palm to show the stones, sounding nervous that Essel was simply toying with him.

"We are a fading people; our enemy will come for us soon enough. There is no need to speed up the process," said Essel.

"Your enemy?" asked the Slayer. "The Mourn? The Nerlineans? That makes no sense. How does letting us leave slow your enemy?"

Essel gave Kyrian a sad smile, and turning, walked away.

"We have a deal?" Kyrian shouted after him.

Essel looked back over his shoulder. "Yes," he answered before carrying on his way.

Kyrian watched the figure disappearing among the towers. He looked down at the amber jewels in his hand. He made a decision. Had someone been there to ask him, he could not really have explained it. He carefully shuffled two back into the small bag and drew the string tight, slipping the bag into his belt pouch. He palmed the third. With a furtive glance he looked around, then, crouching slightly, he dropped it into the top of his boot. Time to tell Sali they had a deal, but he had only been able to get them two stones.

CHAPTER TWENTY-ONE – THE DOCKS

Dryana wrinkled her nose with pleasure at the smell of crispy meat and pulled some more off the wooden skewer on which it had been cooked. Being back in a city was so much better than being on the road, she mused. She finished the skewer and chucked it on the cobbles. She grabbed up a couple more from the grill on the stall in front of her, tossing the vendor a small coin. The Nerlineans may have moved over to paper money for larger transactions, but old-fashioned metal was still required for small purchases.

They had been in Mahendra for nearly three weeks now and the novelty had definitely worn off – grilled skewered meats marinaded in a sugary sauce aside. They had spent almost as long travelling with the Debion'Gar. That had been a long couple of weeks as far as Dryana had been concerned. The desert had given way to scrubland and eventually plains pocked with forests. After ten days, they had reached the main road connecting the city of Gromer to the west to Mahendra, which lay on the ocean shore in the east. Dryana had expected and hoped to be rid of the Debion'Gar at that point, but the Trendorn of the desert elves had been insistent on joining them for the remaining three days of the journey. This was despite the direction being very obvious, simply a matter of following the monotonous, if somehow now comforting, stone path of the arrow-straight Imperial Highway.

Sconya would not be argued with. She had insisted on guiding them all the way to the gates and beyond. The Trendorn and her fellow Gar had only agreed to leave the Slayer pair after they had found them a boarding house to stay in – one of the better ones in the city, with soft silk sheets and well-stuffed pillows. After weeks on the road and in places worse than that, Dryana had luxuriated in them. Now she just found them sweaty and slippery, something that lost its charm after a couple of days. Having made such a grand entrance, it was well known she and Farmorl were in the city, although few of the inhabitants of Mahendra had ever heard of the Company of Slayers, either as merchants or for any less salubrious reasons. The Slayers' reputation for good or bad had yet to make it this far north and east, at least in terms of the general populace. The arrival of the Trendorn'Di'Debion'Gar was another matter. In a city used to the presence of the desert elves, a column of twenty-one led by their supreme priestess had generated a buzz of excitement. The two dishevelled humans with them only added to the mystery and thus the intrigue and ensuing gossip. Soon their arrival was discussed in every teahouse, drinking den and brothel in the city.

Once Sconya had arranged their accommodation, the Gar and her fellows had disappeared from the Slayers' lives. Dryana was not sure whether the Trendorn and her followers even remained within the city, but the sense of someone watching them nagged at her. Was it the Debion'Gar or someone else?

She strode out onto the harbour wall. *Always on a dock*, she thought, and took in a breath of the sea air. She closed her eyes, feeling the salt sting her nostrils and the late autumn sun warm her face. A beach of large pebbles spread out in a wide semicircle nearly two miles in partial circumference. A wide promenade of worked stone sat behind the beach, forming a firm road above it. It extended out into the sea at each end of the semicircle like a pair of horns. The horn on the left was for the exclusive use of the Imperial Fleet; the horn on the right was for merchant shipping. The beach in between was where the fishing fleet drew up, filling much of its pebbled surface with their smaller boats. Now it was largely empty, only a couple of boats being repaired still on it. It was mid-morning, and the rest had left much earlier with the dawn and a favourable tide.

The docks of Mahendra were different from those Dryana had seen in the other Nerlinean cities she had visited. If anything, the place reminded the Slayer witch most of Dimchurch, though the harbour lacked that city's extensive defences. The similarity lay in the city being located separately to the dock. In the case of Mahendra, the city lay on the plain several hundred yards from the harbour. Oddly for a Nerlinean city, it was walled. Dark stone, a grey that was almost black, provided thick towering walls, and decagonal towers not much higher than the battlements were spaced evenly on the corners around the city's dodecagon shape. Whoever had designed it had liked their polygons. Against one wall a large citadel, comprising a dark keep, prodded out above the city's other towers. It was still used by the Dumech of Mahendra as their official residence, though in reality the current incumbent spent most of his time in a villa far outside the city.

The walls, towers and keep were very different from any Nerlinean style that Dryana had seen before, because

PRINCE OF SLAYERS

Mahendra had been built by the Kasem, or perhaps the Kalygon – it depended on who you asked. Indeed, the original city of Mahendra, a Nerlinean frontier town, had lain thirty miles south. It had been completely destroyed in one of the many wars between the Nerlinean Empire and the Kasmeric peoples. When the Nerlineans had taken this city, they had renamed it, and the ruins of the original border outpost that had first carried the name had blown away to dust long since.

The Empire of Kasem had long ago collapsed, but still the walls stood, maintained fastidiously by the new owners. To the north lay Quil'Dath, and the fealty of the Quil'Gar to the Nerlinean Empire was reluctant at best. The human successor states to the Empire of Kasem, which lay further north, were also no friends of Nerlinea, so a walled city made sense. Still, the people who lived here were too many to be constrained by the city walls. A slum of squat wooden buildings had grown up around the city, lacking the sanitation and planning normally characteristic of Nerlinean construction. Between the city walls and the docks were low single-storey warehouses, with flat roofs, making up in area what they lacked in height. Workshops, kitchens and small food outlets surrounded them. Cart-like stalls pushed by hawkers filled in any of the gaps available. Streets of mud, polluted with sewage, provided a maze through which to move around the collection of buildings. Only the Imperial Highway into the city and the stone road to the dock and the cobbled surface of the harbour wall itself were kept clear.

An ordinance from the Dumech of Mahendra had decreed centuries past that buildings should be single-storey and made solely of wood. This was supposed to make it easier for the buildings to be removed by demolition or fire, allowing defenders on the walls to have clear fields of fire, as well as denying any attacker the benefit of cover. It was a hopeless ambition, as the sheer volume of construction meant that any attempt to clear the detritus of buildings around the city walls would take at least weeks and probably months. Despite this, the Dumech and his garrison of legionnaires would sally out into the slum to destroy any building deemed too high or using unsanctioned materials. It was about the only time that the Dumech did bother to enforce imperial authority within the wooden hodgepodge that enveloped the beachfront of his city. Instead, power rested in the hands of criminal gangs who controlled a shifting collection of invented streets. Everyone from the lowest hawker to the great trading companies had to cut a deal with someone for protection.

Even Dryana found the slums of Mahendra intimidating, and she had lived much of her recent life in Port Ren and Kangorn, two cities with colourful reputations. Indeed, Mahendra ran Port Ren close in terms of its renown when it came to criminality and violence, despite being a fraction of the size of the vast metropolis to the south. Dryana was glad that Sconya has arranged for them to stay in a boarding house within the walled city. At least at night the city gates were closed, locking out the seething mass of humanity that surrounded them.

She watched Farmorl appear from one of the myriad alleyways that passed for streets within the slum, crossing out onto the open stone of the dock area. Despite herself, Dryana gave a little smile on seeing the man. He crossed the space between them, stopping in front of her. Before he could say anything, she thrust out a meaty skewer with one hand while shoving one in her mouth with the other.

Farmorl gave the meat skewer a look of fastidiousness bordering on contempt and shook his head to reject the proffered food.

"You should try it; it's good," she protested.

PRINCE OF SLAYERS

Farmorl watched the woman he considered the most beautiful in the world as she spat flecks of grilled sugary meat in his direction, and briefly doubted his judgement.

"I don't know how you can eat that stuff?" he grunted.

"Cause it's yummy," Dryana declared, sending more threads of dead animal his way.

"Do you even know what creature it is from?" he asked.

"No idea," she said with a grin. "Did you find somewhere?" she demanded, suddenly serious.

"I think so," he said with a nod. He did not sound convinced.

Dryana tossed her cleaned skewer of wood on the floor and sized up her lover and employee with a frustrated look. "What's that supposed to mean?"

"There is a warehouse. It is slightly smaller than our requirements, but it meets your other demand," he replied.

Dryana's other demand was their choice of partner. It was an odd way to describe the criminal gang that controlled the particular district of the slums in which they would base themselves. She had sounded out Fatboy Xian for his view on the most reliable gangs in Mahendra. She had used the excuse that the Slayers were looking to create a trading operation in the city. She had let him assume it was for solinad dung brought up from the south. He had happily provided a couple of names. She had immediately rejected those as possibilities, as she had no desire to partner with someone who might share their activities with Fatboy. She had become even more distrustful after the attack in the desert.

"It will have to do," she declared.

"There are empty warehouses of the size you ask for, bigger even, but they sit within the territory of those you suggest we avoid," he explained, his tone seeming slightly truculent.

"You disagree with my decision to avoid Fatboy Xian's recommendations?" she asked.

Farmorl took a moment to think about it. He wanted to calibrate his answer such that it did not create an argument over nothing. Dryana had been increasingly on edge since their arrival. She had expected a Slayer ship and crew to be waiting for them when they arrived. There had been none, and as the ship's arrival was increasingly delayed, she had become more and more worried. Were it to have been lost at sea then their plans would be sent substantially awry.

"I don't disagree with your decision. To be honest, I am tired: three days of trudging around a slum looking at warehouses, avoiding being stabbed ten times a day, takes it out of you," he said with a small smile. The hard look he got from his employer suggested he would have been better keeping his complaint to himself.

"I don't get it," he continued. "Why do we need such a large warehouse?"

"What do you mean?" she queried.

"The drun." Farmorl's voice dropped to a whisper. He noted the annoyance on Dryana's face. She scanned around them as if searching for someone who might be listening to them on the busy dock.

"The *stuff*," he amended quietly. "It won't take up even a fraction of the warehouse that we are renting, let alone the size you originally requested."

She pushed him towards the wall of a wooden building – the back of a sail master's workshop, from the look of it. She glanced around, partly to look for listeners, partly to give her time to think. She considered holding off this conversation until they got back to their lodgings, but that might be just as risky. It was more likely someone who wanted to hear their plans would be listening through the wall of a boarding house than trying to eavesdrop on a crowded street. She considered keeping him in the dark, but Slinker trusted the young man, which said a lot.

"The *stuff*, as you put it, will need to be brought in hidden among other cargo to prevent discovery by the Imperial Customs," she explained.

"They are hardly going to be looking for it in Mahendra," Farmorl grunted incredulously.

"They still check the ships, so we need to hide it in something. Besides, when the stuff being brought into the empire increases exponentially, they will eventually work out which port most of it is coming through. The Imperial Bureaucracy is not that stupid," she muttered.

"If we are using solinad dung as a cover the warehouses will not be big enough," he replied.

"We won't be using dung, we will be using fruit," she explained.

"Fruit!" he said a little too loud.

She shot him an angry glance of reproach.

"I mean fruit? Where are we going to get fruit?" Farmorl was struggling to contain his incredulity.

"Fruit, grain, other foodstuffs," Dryana replied, slightly enjoying her colleague's confusion. "We will be bringing in the stuff through the summer with the Ravangian fruit harvest."

"What? That makes no sense," Farmorl said.

"What, that fruit comes south from Ravangia?" she asked with a grin.

To be fair, she had struggled with the idea when this plan had first been developed by the Slayers – the four of them excluding Balinor, though Sali had really been the driving force behind it. As with everything, Sali had told them all different amounts, probably sharing with Dryana more of her plan than she had with Kyrian or Slinker. The witch suspected that as ever her friend was leaving much of it secret even from her. With Saliana there was always another angle, another level to her schemes.

JUSTIN WAINE

The Isles of Ravan lay to the north, appearing on the map as two large islands sitting off the coasts of the Kingdoms of Kasem and Kalygon. In reality they were a collection of many small islands connected by channels of both seawater and freshwater. Despite their northern latitude, they had an odd microclimate more suited to the equator. A territory that should be covered with snow was instead clogged by steaming jungle and marked by air so thick with humidity that it was said you could drink it. Some said it was a natural phenomenon, others a magical accident. Nerlinean histories maintained that their invasion of the isles had changed the climate. It had been the Emperor Jeddera Summersword who had conquered the isles, completing a string of conquests that had secured the north of the empire. In doing so, his use of sorcery had been so pronounced that it was said it had permanently changed the ecosystem. It may have been legend, a way for the Nerlineans to explain the odd islands they had just conquered. For so unknown had they been, that an imperial bureaucrat had confused the conquest of the Isles of Ravan with the annexation of the highlands of Havagia in the campaigning season the year before. So, the Isles of Ravan had become the Nerlinean Dumechate of Ravangia. Despite the bureaucratic error, the name had stuck.

"No, I get Ravangia and the fruit," Farmorl muttered. "It's the timing on the drun that makes no sense. You want to bring it in during summer. It won't be ready. The solinads rest on the southern steppe in the winter, and the threads are collected in the early spring, when they migrate north again. You need at least a couple of months in the drying sheds to get it perfect, then you have four months' voyage to Port Ren without a crown, and another month to six weeks to bring it up the east coast to Mahendra. Depending on the wind, how much time you stay in port, how many detours you have to take to avoid pirates, the Imperial Fleet and our various enemies, you are taking nearly six months to bring it to Mahendra. If you go further north to Ravangia that is at least another month, maybe more, though less time back due to the currents. So, you won't reach Ravangia even with the earliest shipment until the height of winter, when the oceans in between are filled with ice. More importantly, the fruit will have been shipped south at the end of summer. I don't care how odd the climate is in Ravangia, there aren't fruit harvests in the middle of winter."

"The stuff, as you call it, will be collected, dried and ready to be brought to Ravangia. It will be brought south with the fruit harvest in the late spring and summer," she replied in a tone suggested that was the end of the matter.

"It's not coming from the steppe," he said, his eyes searching for clues.

A stony gaze was the only thing he got in return.

"But there must be solinads to digest the mushrooms," he whispered. "Why not bring in the solinad manure at the same time?"

Dryana said nothing, her gaze fixed on his face, her own betraying little as she watched him speculate.

"If you have another drun supply you have another solinad dung supply, but you cannot hide ships full of solinad pellet the way you can drun. You don't want anyone to know you have an alternative supply. Where is it coming from?" he asked.

"You will see soon enough, and as you have worked it out, you can captain one of the ships we send to collect it. Just make sure you wrap up warm when you go there," she said.

"What, in summer?" he asked.

"Even in summer," she said with a grin.

He looked confused, which amused Dryana. Then a look of worry crossed his face.

"Well, I hope you don't want me to captain that ship," he said pointing out across the bay.

A large wooden junk was limping into the harbour. Its front mast had been destroyed and was lying broken across the front of the vessel. Even from this distance there was visible damage along its sides; great gouges dug in the wood. Black burn marks scored the decks. On the central mast, a flag hung limply despite the breeze. It had been caught in the rigging when the top of the mast had been partially torn off, leaving the crest of the mast and flag dangling beside the wood that had once been below it. The pair could not make out any symbols, but the black with a hint of gold told them their ship had arrived.

Dryana cursed. Could nothing go to plan? She tamped down the anger, which was more frustration than real rage.

"When they dock, get a full damage assessment, then bring Kanjar to me," she ordered.

"Where are you going?" asked Farmorl, less deferentially than he should have.

She gave her lover her frostiest gaze. Farmorl did not seem to notice, more concerned for her than intimidated.

"I need to secure the warehouse. Enough has gone wrong without losing that; we have lost too much time already," she explained.

"You are going into the slums alone?" he said, shocked. "I should come with you."

"You think I need your protection?"

"Well, it would make a nice role reversal," he commented with a smile.

The icy gaze she returned chilled his attempt at charm. "Do as you are ordered!" she shouted.

She stalked past him, heading into the slums.

CHAPTER TWENTY-TWO – THE WAREHOUSE

The lecherous old man looked her up and down for the tenth time since they had been speaking, lingering on her flat stomach and pert breasts, before making the clearly onerous effort of meeting her eyes. Dryana contained her raging annoyance and favoured him with a sweet youthful smile.

She widened the gap between herself and the man by walking further into the warehouse, leaving him standing in the doorway. She had to congratulate Farmorl on his optimism when he said the place was usable. It would need a lot of work. She felt the old man's eyes burning into her rear. Maybe she had imagined it. She glanced over her shoulder. She noticed the sudden shift of his eyes as the lingering gaze moved up to her face. No, she had been right.

She reached out with her mind, searching for the feel of the dead around her. It was not a graveyard, but there were a few corpses to be found. Murdered adults buried under floors, parts of bodies resting at the base of rubbish pits where they had simply been dumped. Even a collection of human bones resting on a cold stone slab – a makeshift altar, she speculated. She also felt the presence of abandoned babes, their tiny skeletons left when their parents, unable to cope, gave them up. They would not be useful to her, she thought coldly, but the others might be if it came to it.

She looked over her shoulder again, this time catching the man staring at her backside. She doubted he would try anything more than look; he was old, and she probably matched him for strength. But who knew with men? She nearly spat as her thoughts churned through her mind.

She continued into the wooden building. Her attempt to widen the gap from the lecher felt even more futile as he ambled after her.

Dryana stalked across the wide-open space in front her. The roof of the warehouse felt close above. She suspected that had her brother been here he would be smacking his head on the low beams that supported it. As she approached the far side, a smell of rotting food stung her nostrils, and she fought down the urge to vomit. Stepping sideways and backwards, she knocked into the old man. She fought down her normal reaction, fixing him with another benign smile.

"What is the smell?" she enquired politely.

"What smell?" the old man replied with a convincing lack of understanding.

She sighed. Maybe his olfactory senses had deserted him. The she spotted the mould, lying on the edge of the roof, a white layer covering the beams. A bit further along on the roof boards, she spotted black threads.

"You've got a leak," she observed.

"Huh?"

"The rain is getting in," she clarified, raising her voice slightly in case the man was hard of hearing.

She got a shrug by way of a response.

Her eyes scanned the wooden roof, walking around. It was too close to her head to get a panoramic view of it from one location. Instead, she had to go panel by panel to check. The damage seemed to be mainly in one corner She suspected that was why the fruit had been left in that location; it had gone mouldy and the previous tenant had simply left it when he had finished using the place. The warehouse would need repairing. Its flat roof design was more suitable to the hot, dry climate of the south, where, when it did rain, it did so in such a volume that no trick of architecture would really protect the buildings. Here in the north, with much more frequent, if less fearsome rains, a pitched roof made all the difference, but the regulations that defined construction in the outer city removed that option.

"So, are you taking it then?" the old man demanded. He was finally getting impatient with her inspection.

Dryana heaved a deep sigh. It would have to do.

"How much?" she asked.

"Two gold aureus a month," he said with a polite smile. He referred to the gold piece that had once been the main currency of the empire. Now it was the primary unit of account for largely paper transactions.

It would have been fair, had the warehouse been sat in a prime position in front of the docks of Port Ren. It wasn't. She also knew that whatever she paid the old man for his property she would be paying the same to the criminal gang for the right to operate in their territory.

"Are you taking the piss?" she demanded, her previously demure persona dropping away.

The old man looked at her, slightly taken aback.

"It's a prime warehouse," he declared, sounding meeker than he intended.

"It's a leaky pit," the witch retorted.

"Make me an offer," he replied.

Dryana looked at him, saying nothing.

"Okay, I can do it for a single aureus a month, but only because you're pretty," he leered.

Dryana's gaze grew frostier. His attempt at charm, if it could be called that, was not helping his cause.

"I'll give you half an aureus a month," she stated.

"Let's split the difference," he said with a broad smile, thrusting his hand out.

"Let's not," she replied, looking at the proffered hand with a face bordering on contempt.

The old man looked annoyed but gave a nod.

"Agreed, but you pay the first four months in advance."

Dryana smiled, not like one of her earlier sweet smiles, but something much more predatory. The man was clearly badly in need of two aureus, and she wondered for a moment whom he owed.

"Agreed," the Slayer confirmed, though she did not take the hand that still wavered in the air.

After a moment he took back the hand, realizing he was not going to get a handshake. She reached into her pocket. A crackle of paper sounded, and she made to pull out the notes to cover the forward payment.

"Metal," he pronounced.

She looked at him and raised an eyebrow.

"Shaking hands, paying in metal? I thought we were in Nerlinea," she replied jokily.

Her mind was racing; she knew the few coins she had on her would not amount to close to the gold he was demanding. She only carried them for food and nightly accommodation in more out-of-the-way places.

"Well, you are Kanath, so you should be used to it," he replied snarkily.

She bit back her own response; it would have been unnecessarily rude and would have lacked the pithiness to give her even the feel of a verbal victory. The old man was clearly an easterner, what would be considered a pureblood Nerlinean, if there was still such a thing. He did not have a hint of the Kasmeric blood that marked out many of the citizens of Mahendra.

She caught sight of something in her peripheral vision. She turned towards the main door and saw four figures standing in it. The light spilling through it meant it took her a moment to recognize them. Farmorl was in the middle, and standing next to him was Pendian the mage and Slayer agent. What was he doing this far east? Where was Kanjar? The pair were flanked by two men, heavy-set and dark-skinned. They looked like Southern Kingdomers. She did not know them: they wore no uniforms, but swords hung at their sides; Kanath-style swords such as were often issued to the Slayer soldiers, longer than the short swords preferred by the Nerlineans. Their demeanour suggested bodyguards.

"Pendian, pay the two aureus the man is demanding. He wants metal for some reason." She pitched her tone haughty, a way of indicating her leadership status to the old man.

She hoped Pendian had the money in metal. She knew Farmorl didn't.

The mage stepped forward, unfazed by Dryana's perfunctory tone. He slipped two gold aureus from his pocket and plopped them into the old man's waiting hand. His fist closed around them, and he smiled. He slipped them into his tunic. Dryana did not want to think where he had stowed them.

"You settle with the Lodge of the Golden Key; they will want the same," the old man declared, looking with trepidation at the armed men blocking the doorway.

The Lodge of the Golden Key. Dryana wanted to laugh at the name. A criminal gang pretending to be some sort of friendly society. A community organization that in reality preyed upon the very community it claimed to represent. *Wasn't that the nature of all governments*, she pondered.

"I understand. Now get out of my warehouse," she ordered.

She watched the old man scuttle away. He stopped nervously at the looming forms of Farmorl and the two bodyguards but negotiated his way around them before disappearing out into the sunlight.

"Sorry about that," she said, her gaze falling back on Pendian. "Now where in the name of the gods is Kanjar?"

"We have a big problem!" came his half answer.

"I prefer straight answers," she retorted waspishly.

"He is unfit to travel," came Pendian's reply. He looked testy.

Dryana glared at him coldly. She had never been close to the man, but he was one of Saliana's favourites, if not her favourite agent. Sali's devotion to him was returned slavishly. Dryana did not trust him. He had been recruited by Saliana and Kyrian in extreme circumstances, during the fall of Las Ma to the Sevains. Dryana had never been fully convinced of his loyalty; her upbringing among the Sevains had left her wary of mages, something she conveniently overlooked when dealing with Sali or Slinker. She also could not fully dismiss the possibility that he was a spy. He had worked for the Slayers for five years now, but that was the blink of an eye to his former masters, the Order of Dawn. His decision to abandon the Order and join the Slayers had felt very sudden to her. She could not shake the idea that he still served the mages of Anaror. Normally he was stationed on the Isles of Syndion, shadowing Saliana. When she left the isle she would put the Chancellor Tandral in charge, but Pendian would be tasked with its defence,

326

particularly in magical terms. Sali had taught him how to operate the Tancree mirrors, so Saliana could travel in moments between the mirror in the Slayer trading house in Kangorn and its twin in the Slayer fortress on Syndion. Pendian needed the support of two less powerful mages to perform the task, but he could do it. Only Slinker and Saliana among the Slayers were capable of opening the portal alone. Dryana wondered why Sali still kept the second mirror in Kangorn. She should have moved it Port Ren, where the Slayers now made most of their money, but Saliana was insistent it remain in the pirate city.

Given that Sali was in the north, on the steppe, Dryana was surprised that she had let the mage leave Syndion. It was far from undefended, but still Pendian was a major loss to its protection. Not only that, it meant that Saliana had lost the option of returning quickly to Syndion from Kangorn, leaving the isles they had captured even more at risk.

"Hang about," Dryana said, a thought occurring to her. "How did you get here so fast?"

Pendian looked at her perplexed. "My understanding is we are at least two weeks late – a touch longer, maybe?"

"No, I mean here," Dryana's brain was whirring. "How are you here, in the east?"

The clarification helped the confused Slayer employee. "I was sent east by Sali," he replied.

"But how did you get here so quickly. Do you have the crown?" Dryana demanded.

"Slinker has the crown?" Farmorl supplied.

"What?" Dryana's voice came out as a shout. "He didn't tell me."

Her lover shrugged and he looked down, not meeting her eyes.

"Surprised that Sali gave it up even to him." It was an observation, not a question.

"She doesn't need it?" said Pendian.

Dryana looked at him, her eyes narrowed. "She doesn't need it, or *she doesn't need it?*" she asked.

"I am not sure how you would like me to answer that, my lady?" came Pendian's amused response.

"If you had no crown, how did you get this far east so quickly?" she asked.

"Oh, I left Syndion some months ago. I arrived in Port Ren, not long after you went upriver to the desert," he explained politely.

"Why?"

"To aid the Slayer operations in the east. Saliana told me I was to replace Kanjar as agent in Port Ren when he came north to Mahendra. Under your overall direction, of course," he answered carefully, though the last words came out slightly as an afterthought.

That was all she needed, Dryana cursed internally. Sali's little minion, looking over her shoulder. It was also unlike Saliana, who normally trusted Dryana implicitly. What had she done to lose her friend's trust? She could think of no reason.

"So why are you here? Why are you not in Port Ren? What is wrong with Kanjar?" The Slayer witch was getting angry.

That was enough to make them all nervous.

"We have been betrayed, my lady," explained Pendian. "Lan Xian has turned on us. Kanjar arranged the delivery of the drun, but Xian had not brought the gold. Instead, his gang set upon our people. Two were killed, and Kanjar was beaten unconscious. We lost the goods with nothing to show for it."

"And Kanjar?" she asked.

"He is still unconscious – at least he was when we left," Pendian explained. "We waited a week before we sailed, hoping he might recover, but when he showed no signs of recovery I took his place."

"And you haven't spoken mind to mind with our mages in Port Ren since you sailed north?"

"I'm sorry, my lady. It did not occur to me. I can do it now?" he offered.

"No; later," she ordered. "I need to think."

The witch paced up and down, the four men staring at her cautiously.

"Slinker could be back in Port Ren by now?" she speculated.

The others decided the question was rhetorical.

"But it's unlikely," she continued to herself.

Her mind was racing, plans conflicting with her own anger, as she tried to get her thoughts under control. She was raging internally. How had she made such a blunder? She had been so sure Fatboy Xian would keep to the deal that she had been happy to leave it to Kanjar. She had miscalculated; she had forgotten that the Slayer reputation, so terrifying in the west, did not carry the same weight in Nerlinea. Still, four years of trading and building wealth here should have been enough to prevent him from taking such an aggressive step. Simple business sense should have made him keep the deal. Why take the one-off gain, rather than years of future business? Even if you ignored alienating the Company of Slayers, which was a fairly large thing to skip over, it still made no sense financially.

Unconsciously, she was clutching her hair. She took a breath; she had been on the point of tearing it out. She dropped her right hand to her side and flexed it as if convincing it to obey her. It didn't make sense, but then it didn't have to. She just had to work out how to respond.

"The ship – how was it damaged?" she demanded suddenly of the waiting men.

Pendian was taken aback for a moment, glancing at Farmorl, before looking to Dryana.

"We were attacked. That is the other reason we were delayed. We lost a week sailing round the Graci Isles, trying to lose our pursuers," he explained.

"Attacked? Who by?"

"The Pandus, we think," Pendian replied.

"Why them? Why not pirates?" Dryana shot back.

"I don't know; a feeling," Pendian offered with a helpless shrug. "They carried no banners or other indications of their allegiance, but they were remarkably persistent. They pursued us for days, even after we sank one of their ships, but two more continued to stalk us. Pirates would have cut their losses."

"Unless they knew you were carrying gold?" interjected Farmorl.

"Except they aren't carrying gold, are they, you idiot, because Xian didn't pay!" she shouted angrily.

The young warrior looked crestfallen and then angry.

"You didn't bring any gold, did you?" She looked at Pendian hopefully.

"Some, but not enough. Certainly not what was planned, as Xian didn't pay," he shrugged helplessly.

She should have kept the gold she had been paid for the solinad dung, though mostly they had been paid in paper, bills of exchange and the like. She had sent that west in a convoy of ships the day before she had left to go upriver. Fatboy's gold was supposed to pay for the Mahendra operation. Gold, unlike paper, had a permanence that mattered with this kind of deal.

"How can you be sure it was the Pandus?" she pressed.

"I can't," replied Pendian honestly. "But who else is our enemy this far east?"

"Well, it's not Xian; Fatboy knew there was nothing worth stealing," she observed angrily.

Pendian nodded, accepting that her acknowledgement was likely to be the closest he got to agreement.

PRINCE OF SLAYERS

She was thinking about Xian, an image of the fat fool sitting in his tea house. Had he always planned to double cross her? She remembered the man next to him – his accountant, his adviser, whatever he was. The lingering sense of memory tugged at her. Three years ago, in Nerlon, a deal with the Tooze and Omay, a matter of trading semi-precious stones from mines in Amaland to the Samath. For the Slayers were not welcome among the lizardmen. Her friend Charlotte Pandus, the owner of the Tooze and Omay, had come from Kangorn to negotiate the deal. It had been a happy reunion. In the year after Balinor's ascension to be Prince of Kangorn, Dryana had become close friends with Balinor's wife the Princess Ascrina and with Charlotte, like Dryana a bearer of the title of Lady of Kangorn. The three young women had been thrown into a world of politics and money at a young age, finding friendship and commonality that others their age had little chance of understanding. It did not matter that Charlotte was a member of the Pandus family.

Dryana searched through her memory of that day, trying to remember Charlotte's entourage. They had been a dozen of them, all men. Some acting a little too paternal for the young merchant's liking. She picked him out from the picture in her mind. Sat at the back, non-descript, silent, attentive but not excessively so, unremarkable, plain. The man who had been sitting next to Xian in the tea house. Fatboy had done a deal with the Pandus, or he was their creature, it did not matter which. The effect was the same: they had walked into a trap. They were out of position and short of money. She had been so busy calculating the threat from Srias, she had not factored in the threat from her daughter Charlotte.

Dryana knew she was not foolish enough to trust her friend – the bad blood between Slayers and Pandus was too great for that – but she had not expected her to be the one to attack the Slayers.

331

"How long to fix the ship?" Dryana asked Pendian.

He looked at Farmorl, whose face indicated he had no intention of getting involved.

"Four, five days at a guess?" the mage responded.

"Get it done in two," she ordered, pushing past him. "Then get to work on getting this warehouse fixed. Farmorl, come with me."

"I don't understand," Pendian offered.

"Are my orders in any way unclear?"

"No, but why are you giving them to me?"

Dryana gave the wizard her most baleful gaze. He worked for her; she did not have to explain her decisions to him.

"I am making you Slayer agent in charge of our operation in Mahendra," she pronounced.

"But Sali?" Pendian muttered.

Dryana thrust her face into the agent's face, standing on tiptoe to do so.

"This is Sali's plan. You want me to explain to her how you derailed it?" she hissed.

Pendian shivered and shook his head.

"Come on, Farmorl," ordered Dryana, stalking past the pair of bodyguards, heading for the light of the door.

"Where are we going?" It came out as a yelp.

"The Lodge of the Golden Key. Let's hope the criminals in Mahendra are more progressive when it comes to payment than their warehouse owners," she spat over her shoulder.

CHAPTER TWENTY-THREE – A LOAN

Charles Pandus stood at the rail of the ship tapping his fingers, the only sign of his growing impatience. His face was impassive, his shoulders relaxed. He looked at the back of his hand, where the once lustrous brown skin had faded to a paler colour, more a dark cream. Too much time spent in northern climes, he mused, the temperate lands of the Sevains, mostly Hambledon and High Ringstead. Where summer seemed to last a month if you were lucky and, in the summer just gone, they had not been so favoured. Too much rain, not enough sun; the harvest had been poor if not disastrous.

"Where is she?" The question was rhetorical, a verbal articulation of his musing.

"I don't know, my lord," came a voice from behind him.

Charles glanced over his shoulder. Espand Dani, one of his employees, an agent of the Imperial Pandus Trading Company, stood there, hands clasped calmly in front of him. He was tall and thin, contrasting with Charles' squatter but more muscular frame. His skin was a warm brown and his hair jet black; a western Nerlinean, born in Rastindor to a family that had served the Pandus for three generations. He had come west to the Sevain principalities a year ago. The weather was yet to leech the healthy colour from his skin, as Charles felt it had done for him. Gods, he missed the sun. Gods, he missed saying 'gods'. He had spent five years among the monotheistic Sevains, and their religious inflexibility grated almost as much as the horrible climate.

He was in a bad mood, and he was also distracted. That was the only way he could explain not hearing Espand's approach. The man was slippery, moving with a silent ease that was disconcerting, especially to a wererat like Charles with his finely tuned senses. It was the nerves that were making him so inattentive. His ship had arrived at Kangorn three hours earlier and it now rested beside the wharf of the Imperial Pandus Trading Company. The new wharf, he thought, the one they had taken over when his niece, Charlotte Halfnight-Pandus, had restored the company's fortunes on the island city, seeing her created a Noble Lady of Kangorn in the process.

Charles glanced over the harbour, the high ship giving him a vantage point to see over the low-slung merchantmen that made up most of the ships resting against the jetties. In the distance he picked out the dock of the Company of Slayers. Three ships were at anchor: two small merchant vessels used on the route between Kangorn and Haydron and the third a full-sized galleon. A fourth vessel, another small merchantman, was sailing out of the harbour, wallowing in the water, the combination of a weak wind and a heavy cargo.

PRINCE OF SLAYERS

Charles briefly considered putting to sea and hunting down the smaller vessel, waiting until it was out of sight of the Great Watchtower of Kangorn. A nice bit of piracy, a bit of fun for a change. He dismissed the idea; there was no benefit to it. The value of the raid in seized cargo and ship was insignificant in the greater scheme of things. Hardly worth shattering the fragile and wary peace that currently pervaded the relationship between the Imperial Pandus Trading Company and the Company of Slayers.

Still, the sight of the Slayer wharf annoyed him, and the bustle of ships around it rankled. Once it had belonged to the Imperial Pandus Trading Company. Once they, not the Slayers, had been the most powerful trading company on the Rock. The fall of the Pandus family had cost his cousin Alorn his life and left Charles and Charlotte barely escaping with their own skins. Since then, Charles had avoided Kangorn despite Charlotte partially restoring the family's position in the city five years ago.

"Where is she?" he muttered, quiet enough to avoid further unwanted comment from Espand.

For all Charlotte's assurances about his safety, he was not so trusting. A guarantee from the Strabo Princess of Kangorn was about as valuable to Charles as one from the Slayer Prince of Kangorn. The fact it came through his niece did not improve the situation. He did not trust her either. So, he had insisted on staying on his ship, where there was at least the option of an attempted escape. He wanted to be away from this place as soon as this business was done. Frankly, he would have preferred it if Charlotte had taken a ship to meet him in High Ringstead. Her insistence that the meeting was here reflected the delicate nature of the forthcoming negotiation. It made it harder for him to reject what she was likely to ask. He intended to make the most of her dragging him here.

"Sir," Espand interrupted Charles' thoughts, pointing down the dock.

A group of ten people were marching down the dock towards the ship.

"Calm down, Espand. Let's not convey our excitement to our guests," Charles instructed quietly. "I'll be in the captain's cabin. Allow only her on the ship, not the others. Understood?"

"Yes, sir," Espand returned with a nod.

Charles strode off towards the cabin. Espand started issuing orders to the guards on the dock, using hand signals rather than shouts.

A woman strode along the dock, leading the party. She was in her early twenties, a western Nerlinean with hints of eastern and even Kanath blood. She was pretty, if not quite the beauty her mother Srias had been at the same age. There was a Pandus rattiness to her features that had skipped her mother. The obvious anger on her face wasn't helping. She was dressed in tight-fitting black leather trousers and a red blouse. A sabre hung at her belt. The cold autumn wind was blowing across the harbour, but it showed no signs of bothering her. Whether she was warmed by her anger or her wererat heritage made her more resistant to the cold did not really matter. The figures trailing behind were more sensibly dressed for the weather, in long grey cloaks, some with their hoods drawn up against the drizzle. The clank of metal indicated that at least some of them were armed.

Charlotte watched the man on the vessel signalling to the guards below. It only made her angrier. Her uncle was game playing as always and his idiot servant was so stupid as to think she could not understand Pandus hand signals.

"Wait here!" she shouted over her shoulder at the retinue.

She stalked towards the ship. It was new, one of twelve built in Halfnight for the company. Only three had left the dockyard to the best of her knowledge, so clearly Charles was in Zem's good graces to have been entrusted with one. The side of the galleon towered over the low wharf. Two guards stood either side of a scramble net thrown down the side of the vessel. A small lift platform rested to one side on a pulley system. Porters waited patiently to pull her up to the deck.

"My lady!" Espand shouted down. "Step on the platform and we'll winch you up."

Charlotte looked up at the man and imagined throwing him off the ship onto the wharf below when she got up there. She rushed up the scramble net and in her anger moved at a pace that even the most athletic human would struggle to match. She reached the rail and vaulted over it in one swift motion.

Espand covered his surprise.

She fixed him with an angry glare. "Where is he?"

"The captain's cabin," he said, pointing down the deck towards the rear of the vessel.

She moved to follow his direction.

He stepped in front of her. "The sabre please, my lady," he demanded.

"It's not enchanted," she grunted and shrugged past him.

He scooted back and blocked her path again.

"I'm sorry, but the sabre," Espand insisted.

She gave him an odd look. The wererat secret of the Pandus family was not something that they would ever confirm, even to their agents. They did their best to avoid open displays of it, her angry display on the scramble net notwithstanding. Within the company it was so widely rumoured that most senior agents acted as if it were an established fact, even if it was not discussed openly. Only a magically imbued blade could harm a transformed wererat, combined with the fact that they were family, meant that giving up her blade was both insulting and mostly pointless.

She undid her sword belt and dropped it into the agent's outstretched hands. "You are a moron," she declared.

She stormed down the deck, stepping through the door into a small corridor. She walked down, reaching another door at the end. She threw it open and stepped in.

Charles was sat in a large high-backed chair, his hand resting on a square table to his right. He was drumming his fingers.

"You could knock," he offered.

"Where did you find that fool?" she demanded, not bothering to respond to his barb.

"Espand?" Charles replied. "He is a Dani. Your mother sent him to me. Trustworthy agents are hard to find among the Sevains."

"He is a mage?" Charlotte asked with an evil grin.

"No," Charles countered testily.

"Mother's still angry with you." Charlotte's grin widened to a mirthless smile.

"She very reasonably believes that mages are too precious a resource to risk in the west, given the Sevain attitude to them."

"So that would be a yes," Charlotte guffawed, enjoying her uncle's annoyance. "I mean, still no new mages sent west after five years. I know Mother can hold a grudge, but that is some going even for her. I mean, you only got two – no, three – killed."

Charlotte counted on her fingers to further annoy Charles.

"Still, nice ship. Mother might be angry at you, but at least you are back in Zem's good books," observed Charlotte.

Srias was operational head of the Imperial Pandus Trading Company, with overall control of its extensive operations in the east. Zem largely left matters to her, but the allocation of a brand-new vessel was something he might have

338

got involved in. There was no way Srias would have trusted her little brother with such a prize had it been her decision. Charles and Charlotte had come west to represent the eastern branch of the family at the wedding of Antonnin Pandus and Ascrina Strabo. The wedding had never happened, as Antonnin and his father Alorn had both been slain by the Slayers. Charles and Charlotte had barely escaped with their lives. Charles' attempts at salvaging the family honour had largely backfired, leaving the Slayers in control of Syndion and as the dominant trading company on Kangorn. Still, the loss of the western branch of the Pandus family had left a void that they both realized they could step into. The fact that it put them at a distance from Srias' oversight was also a positive.

"Zem is pleased about my success among the Sevains," Charles observed with a tight smile.

"So, he gave you a big ship. Sweet." Charlotte's tone was mocking.

"You dragged me here. I can leave if my big ship offends you," Charles replied calmly, eyes assessing.

Charlotte's ratty nose twitched. She took a breath, pulled up a chair and slumped into it. "Sorry," she muttered.

"No problem. Always good to see my dear niece," Charles replied.

Charlotte searched his face to see if he was mocking her, then for a real sense of sentiment, but she found neither.

"You dragged yourself here, not me." Charlotte's tone was matter of fact. "All you had to do was agree."

"It is a big ask," he replied.

"It's a smaller loan than you have out to either the High Lord of High Ringstead or the Prince of Hambledon. Slightly more than you have with the Setsonians," she observed with a shrug.

"You are very well informed about the books of the Halfnight Bank," he replied. "I think I may have to reassess some of my employees."

"It is the family bank. Should I not have access to it? Besides, I don't know for sure, because, as you correctly observe, I don't get to see the books. I do, however, have spies among the Sevains. Also the westerners talk," she lied. "Gods, do they talk."

She rolled her eyes to emphasize her point.

"I shall remind my borrowers to be more circumspect," he replied. "Doesn't change the fact that I want to see the whites of the eyes of my borrowers, especially when it is this sort of money."

"You were invited to the palace. The princess was happy to give you a private audience, but you refused," she said.

"For very obvious reasons, I am not comfortable with meeting Ascrina Strabo in her own palace. If she wants the money she can come here and ask for it," he observed.

"Well, aside from the fact she is the Princess of Kangorn, not some impoverished merchant, such an action would raise the interest of every spy in the city. The Slayers would know, and so would the Corinmounts."

"The Slayers have spies in the palace, and so does Corinmount," Charles replied with a shrug. "Slayers spying on Strabos, other Slayers, the Corinmounts and everyone returning the favour. It's a wonder the servants get any work done. Where is your lover in all this?"

"My lover?" Charlotte looked at him, confused.

"Prince Balinor. With you and Ascrina both keeping him company, why has he decided to tour the east?" he replied.

"Charles, you are absurd – he's not my lover," Charlotte shot back.

That was true enough: nothing had transpired between her and Balinor. One night he had drunkenly propositioned her, but she had managed to avoid the entanglement. The next day he had been too embarrassed to mention it, or had simply not remembered.

"The woman he took east with him apparently bears an uncanny resemblance to you – bit prettier, maybe," Charles replied nastily. "You're sure the princess knows that he is making do just with her?"

"Yes, and I don't see why it matters?" she asked.

"Well, if you are standing here, guarantor for the loan, then you should worry. How likely am I to be paid back if the introducer, that is you, has their head stuck on a pike for screwing the princess' husband?"

"Well, first, I'm not sleeping with Balinor. Second, I'm not the guarantor, I'm only providing the introduction. Third, Ascrina is not planning to kill me," she pronounced angrily.

"Because a Strabo has only killed two members of this family in the last six years," observed Charles sarcastically.

"And you were so close to Alorn and Antonnin," observed Charlotte briskly, choosing not to point out that it was in fact the Slayers who had killed their cousins and that Strabo complicity was only assumed in the death of the former.

"Hardly the point," Charles shot back. "You know, niece, you have a very un-Pandus-like sense of forgiveness."

"Not really; I just don't let it get in the way of making money," she spat back, a touch more petulantly than she had planned.

"I think you confuse your short-term interest with the long-term interests of this family," Charles said calmly.

Charlotte took a deep breath, trying hard to disguise she was doing exactly that. She realized he was trying to bait her. Charles was in no position to speak for the whole family; that was reserved for Zem and possibly her mother Srias. It was also deeply hypocritical on her uncle's part; he was the most likely of all of them to disregard family interests when they conflicted with his own. He was trying to rile her, and frustratingly she had fallen for it. Why? she asked herself. Was it for a good reason or was he simply amusing himself?

"Uncle," she pronounced politely, favouring him with her sweetest smile. "Let's not argue over matters past. Let's focus on the present subject: an opportunity for us all to make money and advance our interests – yours, mine and the family's."

Charles' nose twitched in a decidedly ratty fashion, and he observed his niece beadily. *She was no fun*, he thought, suppressing the evil smile that wanted to creep across his face.

"You can be as sweet as you like, but it does not change the situation. There is a good possibility that our borrower, the Princess Ascrina, suspects you of sleeping with her husband." Charles raised his hand as Charlotte moved to protest. "Let me continue. It doesn't matter whether it is true or not; it matters that she might *think* it is true. Your relationship with the Slayer girl does not help the situation."

"You mean Dryana?" demanded Charlotte. "I am capable of being acquainted with someone without sleeping with them. I am surprised you haven't accused me of sleeping with the princess."

"She doesn't strike me as the type," observed Charles, based on nothing; he had never met her, after all. "I just worry that your closeness to Dryana Slayer might further exacerbate things."

"You are clutching at straws, Uncle. I've not seen her for three years. I doubt she has been back to Kangorn in four."

"So, you are not concerned that your mother plans to have her killed?" Charles observed.

He caught her momentary look of concern; genuine feeling, perhaps. Charles' eyes glinted at the small victory.

"What do I care?" declared Charlotte. "My mother will do what she feels is best for the family. This diversion does nothing to resolve our problem. How can I get you the sureties that you require if you won't come to the palace and the princess can't come here?"

"Can't or won't?" asked Charles.

"Can't," confirmed Charlotte. "As I have already said, Danzian Corinmount."

She said the last as if the name itself explained everything.

"Then we have an impasse," replied Charles. "One that is not my problem to resolve."

He finished the last with a shrug of indifference that sent Charlotte's blood boiling. Doing business with family was always the worst, she mused. She thought the money he would make would be enough to persuade him, not to mention the enemies and competitors the loan would injure.

"I have a possible solution," offered Charlotte.

Charles leaned forward, interested. So, he wanted to do the deal, thought Charlotte, but he was genuinely worried about getting the money back. Maybe he was not using meeting the Princess as an excuse to avoid a deal. It also told her that he was genuinely fearful of what might happen to him if he disembarked the ship into the city of Kangorn.

"I need someone from the group that accompanied me, if you are willing to let them up," she continued. "I think that will be enough to set your mind at rest."

"Espand!" shouted Charles.

A moment later the door opened and Espand stepped in. "My lord," he enquired politely.

"Charlotte would like you to collect someone from her entourage on the dock. Please do so," ordered Charles.

"Who, my lady?" asked Espand.

"They will know," she replied.

Espand looked at Charles as if seeking confirmation, but all he got from Charles was a shrug. The Pandus employee disappeared out of the door, which clicked shut behind him.

The two members of the Pandus family sat in silence. Charles started to tap his right foot against the leg of the table. Charlotte shot him a look of annoyance. He stopped tapping. The silence continued to stretch.

"So, you've been keeping well?" he asked.

"Shut up, Charles," she answered waspishly.

The male wererat flashed his niece a grin.

The quiet of the cabin seemed to envelope them, such that they could hear the worms in the wood. After what felt like an age for both of them, there was a knock on the door and Espand stepped into the room, followed by a cloaked figure.

Charles pushed back slightly in his chair, watching the figure warily. They were tall and thin, their head close to scraping the low roof of the cabin. Male or female, Charles could not be sure, but he knew a Gar when he saw one.

Tallyn Hanath pulled down her hood, her long white-blonde hair spilling out across her shoulders. Charles could see the hint of alcidide mail under her cloak. He looked for her famous rapier, which was missing, as Espand had disarmed her. Charles unconsciously let out a sigh of relief. He had never met the Gar, though he had seen her from a distance during his escape from Kangorn. He knew her by reputation: the former Captain of the Palace Guard under Prince Karden who had become the first non-human Lady of Kangorn under his granddaughter. First non-human known publicly at least: the Pandus family were wererats and so they were truly the first non-human nobles of Kangorn.

Tallyn Hanath, mused Charles. The princess' closest adviser, the one who was loyal to her and her alone. She had stood with Ascrina when most others had switched their allegiance to the de Havillands or simply stood by as Jon de

344

Havilland had tried to take the throne of Kangorn. Was she enough to guarantee that he got the money back? What Charlotte did not know, what Charles had not told her, was that the Halfnight Bank's position was stretched – just the right side of being precarious. It was a good deal, if the princess paid the interest and was good for the principal in the long term. He just had to be sure. Was the Gar standing in front of him enough?

"You asked for me?" Tallyn's singsong voice enquired, her high tones dancing off the cabin walls.

"The loan," Charles started cautiously. "The princess has the means to repay?"

"Of course; she is Kangorn," replied Tallyn.

"Is Balinor Slayer not also Kangorn?" asked Charles.

The Gar said nothing, but the frosty gaze she returned spoke volumes.

"You know what I am asking?" pressed Charles.

"Your lien is with Kangorn as agreed with the Princess of Kangorn, its ruler and sovereign. You will be paid."

Charles nodded and stood up. He unfurled two scrolls on the table next to him, using an inkwell and two books to hold them down. He needed something else, and cast around. Charlotte removed a hidden dagger from her boot and plumped it down on the table. Her uncle picked it up and used it to hold down the second scroll. He gave Espand a hard look, and the agent who had been ordered to disarm their guests dropped his gaze, looking chastened.

"Sign here?" Charles offered Tallyn an inked quill.

Charlotte stood, quickly perusing the short loan documents, checking Charles had not changed the agreed wording. There was little point in choosing such a dishonourable path, as enforcing against princes was notably difficult. Giving them an excuse to claim you had tricked them worked more against the lender than in his favour. Charlotte nodded to Tallyn. The former guard captain signed with a

345

flourish and a long curling signature. She repeated the process on the second document. Charles quickly countersigned them, his spidery writing crawling across the manuscript. He dusted some sand over the wet ink and, after deciding they were dry, rolled up the scrolls. He handed one to Tallyn.

"Odd to think that Alorn signed similar documents with Prince Karden once," Charles observed, a smile playing across his lips. "Different times, different conditions, I guess."

"He asked for too much," observed Tallyn cooly. "You are smarter."

Charles raised an eyebrow.

"You didn't ask for a princess," she replied, turning and striding from the room.

***

Charles watched his niece, the Gar and their followers as they disappeared off the wharf, heading back to the city, no doubt going to the palace to the tell Ascrina the good news.

"Get the gold and silver offloaded," he ordered Espand.

The agent nodded.

"Take it to the palace yourself with as many guards as you need. Use our people, not Charlotte's," he instructed.

"They will insist on helping," replied Espand.

"Dissuade them," Charles replied, his voice hard-edged. "Now get to it."

Charles strode down the ship.

"Captain, as soon as the cargo is off the ship, get us back to sea," he ordered.

"Yes, my lord!" came the answering shout from a woman on the bridge.

"You are leaving me here?" asked Espand.

Charles turned back to the Pandus agent, who had a look of confusion on his face.

"Of course I am. I'm not leaving that amount of metal without someone to look after it. Charlotte will let you lodge at our trading house." Charles' tone was offhand.

"Surely I am of more use to you back in High Ringstead," Espand countered. Being stuck on the Rock looking after a pile of money he did not control and would be blamed for when it was lost was not his idea of a good way to spend his time. Especially as the blaming part would likely cost him his life.

"Do as I order." Charles' utterance brooked no disagreement. "Oh, and try and avoid being bewitched by my niece. Apparently even witches aren't safe."

Espand nodded and scurried off to collect his gear and complete his task.

CHAPTER TWENTY-FOUR — THE DARK ELF

The milky orange jewels shone in the firelight. Saliana played with the pair in her hand, rolling them around so the light emanating from them changed as they caught a glint of fire at different angles. She was lost in thought. Despite that, she felt eyes boring into her back.

"You are supposed to be asleep," she observed without turning.

"I thought I would share the watch with you," Kyrian's voice rumbled in response. "Besides, I can't sleep, and the dawn will be upon us soon."

Kyrian circled Saliana, seated himself opposite her on the other side of the fire and crossed his legs.

"Samarin?" asked Sali.

"Still sleeping." Kyrian looked past the Mistress of the Slayers, to where the Fal'Gar and the three oradar slumbered.

PRINCE OF SLAYERS

Behind that lay a small stone that marked the borders of Kyth'Dath, invisible in the darkness. He did not really understand why Sali had made the decision to camp here: they could have ridden for another hour, maybe even two if the light had held, deeper into the steppe and further from the boundaries of the Sul'Kirin. Instead, Sali had decided to break their journey here, on the edge of the ice elves' domain. They had not stayed long after Essel had agreed the deal with Kyrian, leaving the same day and heading south.

"What are they for?" Kyrian asked, looking at the stones.

"Pardon?" Saliana looked up, momentarily confused.

"The stones. What do they do?" he asked.

"They focus magic, amplifying it," she replied, slipping them back in her pouch.

"How so?"

"When you cast a spell, you draw power from the world around you. Some places have more than others, some lots, some a little," she explained.

"Like the difference between Syndion and Las Ma," the wrestler nodded in understanding.

"Precisely," replied Sali.

"So, the stones have magic in them?" he asked.

"No: you can bind magic into an item, to create an effect, a magic totem or a weapon. The magic rests in the item, imbuing it with an ability. The magic can be drawn from the item, rendering it mundane, but to do so is extremely wasteful. Magic wants to escape, so the process of binding is long and complex, or it will seep from the enchanted artifact. The stones by contrast contain no magic. Instead something in their makeup means they amplify the power of the spell as it is cast. So, a weak mage in a place of weak magic will appear to be far stronger than they are, but in a place like Las Ma, where there is almost no magic, the effect would be fairly muted," she said.

"What about a strong mage in a place of power?"

"It would be a thing to see," replied Sali with a smile.

"Why did you need three. Surely one would be enough?"

"Once you direct magic through it, it changes the structure of the jewel, altering it permanently. It cannot be used again," she explained.

"Shame. I can see why you wanted three," Kyrian replied.

"But we only got two," she muttered. "I was sure he would part with three. Odd that was where he decided to negotiate."

"Well, he probably wanted a small win," Kyrian shrugged. "Shame you can't find a way to make them reusable?"

"The knowledge to do that was lost when Far the Forger died," she replied.

"Digging up another legend, Sali," said Kyrian with a grin.

"A mage and a smith from the time of the Jedderas. He worked out a way to bind the stones in the pommel of four swords. The stone enhanced the magic of the sword without exhausting the crystal," she replied.

"Four swords?" Kyrian asked. "Never heard that legend, or of Far the Forger."

"He was the demi-god of smiths among the Kanath before the coming of the Sevains. Sometimes he is called Far the Forgotten."

"Still never heard of it," Kyrian grunted.

"You have heard of the sword Othrys?" she asked.

"No."

"Othrys, the sword of the summer, the blade of Jeddera, the Summersword? It's where his name comes from."

"Okay," Kyrian shrugged, indifferent.

350

"It is why it is wrong to call him Jeddera Summersword when he defeated Naron because Othrys had not been forged at that time. We only do it to distinguish him from his father," she declared proudly.

Kyrian gave her a look of boredom.

"Well, it's interesting if you are a bard," she observed, feeling somewhat unappreciated. "We sing these songs and tell these tales."

"We got to see a dragon," said Kyrian with a big smile.

"Hardly," laughed Sali. "A wyrm at best."

"So do you think there is a cave of sleeping dragons?" he asked, his eyes shining from the fire.

"It was just an animal, a mount, like an oradar or a hadan," said Sali quietly.

"Why do you do that?" Kyrian asked, his tone sad.

"Do what?"

"Lie to me," he said. "I heard your comments on the road when we faced the dragon and its rider. What was it you said – 'Dragon? In a few centuries, maybe'?"

"I'm sorry, I'm not really lying. It is hard to explain," she answered, genuinely troubled by whatever she was struggling with.

Kyrian's heart flexed and he wanted to hug her. His feeling for her was fighting against the long accumulation of distrust that had come between them.

"How did you know about the ring, the one you gave the Kyth'Gar?" he demanded.

"How I know I'm not sure," she answered.

Kyrian gave a disgruntled sigh and started to stand up.

"Wait," she pleaded. "I am explaining it badly. I think something was done to me long before we first met on *The Spirit of Summer*. Then Slinker unblocked my magic and slowly memories came back to me, memories that weren't mine. The more I used my magic, the more they came flooding back. My recent confrontation with Samarin seems to have released the rest."

"Who are you, Sali?"

"I am Saliana. I am a bard. I grew up in High Ringstead, like you a Kanath among the Sevains, and at the age of seven I was apprenticed to a bard to begin my own training."

"'I'm a bard', your go-to excuse for how you speak a language or know a people or a story of a city half a world away. Your master could not have taught you that, no matter what secrets you minstrels and storytellers still keep," replied Kyrian.

The wrestler did genuinely believe that Sali's bardic training was part of the source of her own knowledge. Once, before the coming of the Sevains, the bards had been one of the three orders of the priesthood of the Kanath old religion. They had their own place of learning, the College of Bards in what was now High Ringstead, long since used as an administration building by the Sevain rulers of their renamed city. The Sevain Temple had violently suppressed the other two orders: the priests and the seers. The bards had survived the initial conquest, even if their buildings and much of their status had been lost. The Sevains had equated the bards with their own minstrels – musicians and storytellers rather than religious figures. So, they had lingered on, largely surviving the slaughter of their fellows. Their religious aspect had dwindled to nearly nothing; at least it would have done by the time Sali became an apprentice, thought Kyrian. Still, they would have old stories to pass on, ones that the Sevain Templars would prefer forgotten. Assuming that Sali was the age she appeared, then it occurred to Kyrian that if anything Sali had become more Garlike in the time he had known her. The agelessness that came with that made him wonder. He tried to remember back to that first time he had met her on *The Spirit of Summer*. She had been different then, not quite human, he had thought, but still largely human. What age had he placed on her then? Late twenties, maybe; it all blurred in his mind. Back then he had never seen a Gar; they were not welcome among the Sevains.

"How old are you?" he asked.

"Thirties, I think," she replied, in a slightly offhand fashion. "You know you are not supposed to ask a woman that?"

"How old exactly?

"I don't know. Thirty-two."

"Not very precise," he muttered.

"So, you know exactly when you were born?" she barked back.

Kyrian grunted at that. She had a point; knowing and celebrating your birthday was something reserved for the nobility. He remembered being booked for a wrestling match to celebrate some lord's birthday and being surprised such a thing was worthy of a celebration. Kyrian knew that he been born in the autumn. He might even have a stab at the month but could not give the exact date. If asked he would have said he was twenty-eight, but the answer could be a year past that or even two years before. His family was from a small village, and no one was keeping records. His parents were gone, and there was no one to remember his birth. His main benchmark was Dryana, who he thought was four years younger than him. He had the vaguest recollection of her being born.

"It must have been tough growing up in High Ringstead. You don't look Kanath or Sevain?" Kyrian decided to dig, as this was the most open Sali had ever been.

"Not really. I think most people assumed I was Sevain because I had blonde hair, so I had an easier time of it than most Kanath. My parents were dark-haired like you," she replied.

"You've never mentioned them before, not in the years we have known each other. What were they like?" he asked.

"I don't really remember them. I was seven, or thereabouts when I was apprenticed to a bard outside the city, so my memories of them, such as they are, are before that," she said.

"Wait – your parents apprenticed you and then never saw you again?" Kyrian was shocked.

She nodded.

"And that seemed normal to you?"

"At the time I guess so. Now of course not, but by the time I was old enough to realize that they were gone. I travelled to High Ringstead, across the lands of the Sevains, to Las Ma even, plying my trade. In the early days I would enquire after them, but eventually I gave up," she said.

Kyrian tamped down the sadness he was feeling for his friend, but he could now understand the hole that seemed to exist in her connection to people. He had lost his parents, though his father he barely remembered, dying not long after Dryana's birth. His mother had told him it was in battle, but in truth the battle had been with disease. She had lived longer, long enough to watch him achieve fame as a wrestler, long enough for him to watch her be murdered by the Sevain Templars.

"Chaza is not a common family name," he commented. "You would have thought someone would have remembered it."

"How did you know that name?" she asked, surprised.

"Danzian Corinmount called you by it, when I first met him on Kangorn," he recalled.

"Good memory," Sali congratulated him. "I had forgotten that. It wouldn't have helped – that was a name I gave myself. I don't remember if my parents even had a family name."

Kyrian nodded, for unlike Sevains or Nerlineans, many Kanath did not have family names. Instead they had largely followed the Gar tradition of placing 'Kal' in front of a parent's name, to mean 'child of'. That had changed with the coming of the Sevains, when what remained of the Kanath nobility had been the first to adopt a surname. The rest were now slowly following suit, using their professions, so there was now a profusion of Carters, Smiths and Brewers. Others, like Kyrian, had used a place. He had chosen the nearest large town where he had initially made his name as a wrestler, so Kyrian of Kilon.

"Why did you pick Chaza?" he asked.

"I needed a name, and it gave me a bit more flare than simple Saliana. It matters when you are telling stories to make money. I prefer Slayer, though," she said with a smile.

Kyrian returned the smile. "So do I."

"I still haven't answered your real question, though," she observed.

"No, you haven't," he confirmed. "I was wondering if this heartfelt meander was an attempt to avoid it."

"Perhaps a little. I don't have a great answer, not that one that makes sense. And if it doesn't make sense to me, it will make even less when I explain it to you," she offered lamely.

"Try," Kyrian grinned wolfishly.

"I can remember my parents, but only vaguely. I can remember my apprenticeship as a bard; my master's house. It is all clearer now, my time as a travelling bard to Hambledon, Las Ma, Kilon, Kangorn and always back home to a rented room in a tavern in High Ringstead. The tavern in which I was drinking the night that I was drugged and kidnapped. The next day I woke up, chained opposite you, a prisoner of the Pandus. My memory of everything but the night before had been expunged, until it started to slowly return," Sali said.

"So, you can't explain what you know?" he responded, annoyance creeping into his voice. The suspicion he was being lied to was returning.

"You are not listening," Sali's voice raised.

Kyrian was surprised. He looked over at Samarin, who continued to sleep in the protective embrace of her giant cat.

"I can remember learning to ride an oradar on the Great Steppe, taught by my father. I can remember being in the caves of Syndion praying to Sidarra and Thytha the entwined goddesses, next to my mother," she declared.

Kyrian leaned forward, intrigued. "But you said your parents left you when you were seven," he said, seeking an explanation.

"I can remember standing next to Zedian VIII, when he took the emerald ring from the altar in the Temple of Sargon," she continued. "That's how I knew."

"That must be some sort of magic; something Slinker did to you?" Kyrian postulated.

"I don't know, but I can remember so many lives. I can remember acts of magic by me and against me. Different fathers and mothers, prisons and torturers, cities I know I've never been to." Sali sounded almost desperate, which was very unlike her.

"Zedian took Krynal centuries ago. It must be some sort of magical curse. Maybe Slinker triggered something and that combined with all the bardic tales resting in your mind," he suggested, attempting to comfort her.

"Kyrian, I can remember dragons in the sky," she pleaded, on the point of tears.

"That would be amazing to witness," Kyrian replied, his mind taken away by the wonder of the image, and momentarily overlooking his friend's pain.

"What's that?" he then asked, suddenly alert.

Kyrian was on his feet, his flail pulled from his belt and hanging loosely from his side. Saliana stood up turning around to see what was happening behind her. The three oradar were awake and facing in the direction of Kyth'Dath. The largest, Kyrian's cat, stretched and shook its mane before letting out a low growl. Samarin stood partially sheltered by her own oradar, still half-dressed from her bed roll. Even so her bow was in her hand, arrow already nocked.

PRINCE OF SLAYERS

Six pairs of eyes, human, Gar and oradar, scanned the edges of Kyth'Dath, which lay just beyond the small stones that indicated its boundary. The cats growled louder as a rider emerged from the darkness of the trees still within the Sul'Kirin. The firelight picked out only the barest shadows of movement.

The cat seemed to pause at the stones, as if considering the magnitude of the act it was about to commit. It growled lightly as if something held it back. Then it stepped across the line and into the edge of the firelight, revealing its rider. The red light of the dying fire flickered across the ash grey of his skin. Charcoal eyes stared intently at the three companions. The rider pulled down the hood of his grey cloak, shaking his lank grey hair free. It was the young Den'Sar'Gar boy that they had saved on the road. Sali scanned the dark behind the boy and his cat, searching for signs of his family or the other Grey Folk they had met. She found none, though anything could be out there in the dark.

The boy dismounted from the snow oradar, dislodging his feet from the small wooden stirrups and making the awkward job of climbing off look easy. His feet touched the ground, and he straightened to his full height. It was only then in the firelight they could appreciate how young he was. He genuinely looked like a youth. Had he been human, he would have looked like a teenager – all gangly long limbs not fully under his control. He was of a height comparable to Kyrian, though rake thin. Either he still had some growing to do or he was going to be short for a Gar.

The Gar stepped forward and held his hand out palm up, presenting it to Saliana. A blue light started to build slowly in it, swirling and curling in the darkness. Samarin pulled her bow tight ready to let her arrow sing. Sali reached out her hand to her side, waving as if to calm the Fal'Gar witch.

"It's alright," she said quietly to Samarin.

The Fal'Gar looked unconvinced, keeping a wary look on the youngling in front of her.

"He is offering service," Sali explained to her companions, though she did not sound entirely sure.

The ball of blue light continued to grow in his hand, where now the light was flecked by colours of teal and aquamarine. Sweat was pouring down the Grey Folk boy's face, his jaw was clenched, and his eyes darted nervously between the three.

"You can put that away now. Your offer of service is accepted," Sali told him in the language of the Den'Sar'Gar.

The boy nodded, and as the blue light vanished, he collapsed to the ground, panting for air.

"What did you say?" asked Kyrian.

"I accepted his offer of service," replied Sali.

The Den'Sar'Gar looked up from where he was slumped, cautious eyes trying to fathom what they were discussing now the pair had switched to Westerly. Even Samarin was watching them, straining to follow the conversation as she translated the words in her head.

"Is that wise?" demanded Kyrian. His eyes had moved from the recumbent mage to the darkness of the Sul'Kirin.

"What are you looking for?" Sali asked.

"The dragon lady and her giant lizard," he muttered.

"I doubt she is out there," Sali reassured calmly.

"Based on what?" her fellow Slayer observed coldly.

"Nothing really; just a feeling. I think we would have heard a wyrm coming, I don't think this one would be foolish enough to come into our camp if he was being followed by a Guardian," Sali said, nodding in the direction of the Den'Sar'Gar.

Kyrian chuckled. "That is pure wishful thinking."

"Not really," she observed. "Samarin, are there tales of wyrms rampaging across the steppe in pursuit of escaped prisoners?"

Samarin looked embarrassed to be brought into the argument, but she shook her head.

"And are there stories of young Gar of unknown origin seeking a home among Fal'Gar tribes, especially the more northern tribes?" she asked.

"The occasional story," conceded the Fal'Gar.

"There you go," replied Sali with a slightly too condescending smile.

"This one drew her blade when she heard the word Den'Sar'Gar," Kyrian pointed at Samarin. "Yet you think her people have been taking in Grey Folk refugees."

"The Skyriders are a tribe of the western steppe," replied Sali. "Before our journey here Samarin had never been this far north, for all she was acting as our guide. I suspect that the northern Fal'Gar tribes have been taking in Grey Folk for centuries. Mages and witches fleeing execution at the hands of the Kyth'Dath. Maybe they don't know their origin; maybe they suspect but don't care. The Fal'Gar have lost many of those so gifted in their wars, be they against the Nerlineans in centuries past or the Mourn more recently. They would not readily turn away a strange Gar with such powers. Samarin, are there more magic users and witches among the northern Fal'Gar tribes?" enquired Sali.

The Fal'Gar shifted uncomfortably at the question. "It is possible," she acknowledged. "But not all tribes were impacted equally down the years. So that is another option."

Sali's face flashed momentarily with a look of annoyance at her theory being partially challenged.

"I think the Grey Folk have been sending their gifted children out of the Sul'Kirin for centuries. I suspect that most are killed by the Guardians, but the rest escape. Both outcomes are suitable for the Kyth'Dath. Dead or gone, it's all the same," she declared.

"And this won't screw our deal if they find out we helped one of the Grey Folk escape?" asked Kyrian.

"What do you want me to do? Send him back to die?"

Kyrian laughed, not at the idea, but at Sali and the fact she was judging his human decency. "Not what I said," he barked.

"It will be fine," Sali replied, forging on. "First the Kyth'Dath have to find out, then second they have to decide to sacrifice a load of money, over something I am guessing they don't much care about."

"Well, he is here now," Kyrian grunted.

"Let's break camp and get going. For all my nonchalance, I think we should be a bit further south and west," she grinned in the firelight.

"It's still dark," observed Samarin.

"We will go slowly. I will light the way with magic," Sali proposed.

"That should help any pursuers," offered Kyrian.

"There aren't any pursuers," she replied.

Kyrian grunted something under his breath.

"We have to be at the Mountain of the Moon in slightly over a month, and it has taken us nearly two to get here. We will need to ride hard and long to stand any chance of getting there in time. I suspect the Great Khan of the Mourn is planning a war and it would be a shame to miss it," Sali reminded them.

"Samarin, you are a steppe native," stated Kyrian. "What is the chance of us getting to the Daldara Mountains in a month?"

Samarin kicked the frost off the frozen ground with her booted foot. She could feel Kyrian's gaze boring into her.

"Zero," she replied quietly.

"You hear that, Sali, zero!" shouted Kyrian. "Might as well stay here and wait to be eaten by a dragon than go to certain death at the hands of the Mourn."

Sali gave him a grin. "Trust me, I have a plan."

"Of course you do," he muttered and stormed off to collect his kit.

The Mistress of the Slayers chuckled and followed her fellow Slayer in sorting her gear. Samarin relaxed her bow and walked over to the Den'Sar'Gar, who was still sat on the cold ground. He looked up at her nervously. He looked less tired; the sweat was gone.

"We are leaving now," she told him in Nerlinean.

He looked at her perplexed and Samarin heaved a big sigh.

"Going," she said in Nerlinean, raising her voice as if that would make a difference, and she pointed at Sali and Kyrian.

The Den'Sar'Gar seemed to understand something, either from the gesture or the word and pushed himself to his feet.

"You got a name?" she asked again in Nerlinean.

The look of confusion returned.

She thought for a moment, searching for an older word, one from a more ancient Gar tongue that she had some vague recollection of.

"Name?" she demanded in the old tongue.

He paused for a moment, and seemed to understand what she was asking.

"Rayllor Duth," he answered.

"Well, welcome, Rayllor. Your chances of dying have changed from nearly certain to almost certain, so I am not sure that is progress," she laughed.

He grinned back at her, an attempt to mask the total confusion on his face.

She sighed; he clearly had no idea what she had just said.

CHAPTER TWENTY-FIVE — A RAID

Dryana Slayer pushed her way through the wooden bead curtain and out into the sunlight. She felt the warmth on her face and briefly closed her eyes against the midday sun. She kept them shut for a moment longer than she needed to, then let out a sigh and opened her eyes. She adapted to the sudden influx of light, squinting. She turned around to see Farmorl push through the bead curtain that shaded the door, wood clacking against wood. He also took a moment for his eyes to adjust to the sun. The shack that the pair had just exited was surprisingly cool and dark. The Lodge of the Golden Key was more of a wooden shed, Dryana had thought when she had entered it. Her opinion had not changed by further exposure. Despite the grand name, the criminals she had negotiated with still did their business in the less salubrious end of the slums that surrounded the mighty walls of Mahendra.

"Well done," Farmorl said quietly.

"Thanks," she replied. "At least we got the deal we needed."

He nodded, though he seemed concerned.

"Something I missed?" she asked a little too archly.

"Nothing," he offered. "Really nothing."

The cramped windy street they had exited into was alive with people, pushing and shoving. Some commotion was the norm, but this was something more. Forcing his way down the narrow avenue was Pendian with half a dozen Slayer sailors. The mage shoved aside an old woman to get to Dryana. He did not bother to listen as the outraged crone hit him with a stream of invective before tottering down the street.

"We need to go," he insisted as he stopped in front of Dryana.

"What? What's going on?" she demanded.

"There are ships in the harbour, black wood and black sails," he responded. "I don't recognize them, but these people do."

He cursed as more pushed past him, seemingly unconcerned by his presence and steely gaze.

Behind them a group of the very criminals with whom they had just negotiated appeared through the door before pressing on up the street without even a glance at the Slayers.

"Are the black ships a threat?" she queried.

"I don't know, but the population of the slums is moving out of them and heading for the safety of the walled city," he replied.

Dryana craned her neck trying to see through the mass of people that now thronged the alleyways and crowded curving streets, seeking a view of the harbour. She could not even see the sea, though she could smell it. Even with all the people gone, the maze of buildings blocked any clear view.

"How many ships? How large?" she demanded.

"What? Hardly the point. We need to get into the city proper."

"Gods, will you answer the question!" she barked at him.

"Five that I saw; could be more. Big things – not quite the size of an imperial war junk, but still big," replied the mage.

Dryana looked up to the mighty dark grey wall of the city that loomed over them, her mind calculating.

"So maybe two thousand enemy, if they are enemy?" she replied.

"If there are only five," Pendian shot back.

Gods, the man's very voice grated, thought the Slayer. How did Sali put up with him? That said, he was no fool. If she could get over her irrational dislike of him, it might be worth listening to his opinion.

"Our ship. Is it repaired?" she asked.

"We have had a matter of a day since we got here – there have been some repairs, but nowhere near enough," he replied.

"The crew, have they been given shore leave?"

"No, you ordered rapid repairs," Pendian answered.

"Good," she muttered, deep in thought.

A flaming ball arced through the sky before slamming into a nearby wooden building. The ball, which was some sort of large jar, exploded on contact. It bathed the area in burning propellant, sending the wooden structures up in flame like so much tinder. Acrid black smoke filled the air, along with the screams of the panicked populace.

"We have to go!" Pendian grabbed Dryana by the shoulder, trying to pull her in the direction of the city gate.

Dryana shrugged him off with a look of burning rage. "Enough! Get to the city, and take these others with you. Farmorl and I are going for the ship," she declared.

"The ship?" Pendian shouted across the expanding tumult. "Damn the ship, the company has others."

"Not enough, not this far east," she shot back. "I am going for the ship."

"We'll come with you," Pendian insisted.

Dryana half liked the man for his obvious desire to protect her. His loyalty to the Slayers trumped whatever personal animus came between the two.

"No!" she shouted. "We need you here, to get the operation set up and rebuild it if that becomes necessary."

"But what if they intend to take the city?" Pendian exclaimed.

"With two thousand men, even double that against those walls, don't be ridiculous – it's a raid," she roared over the shouts of the people. "Now get gone."

Pendian looked like he was about to argue, but another flaming jar of burning oil slammed into the slum. He made his mind up.

"You're the boss," he grunted. "Good luck!"

"Good luck," she shot back.

She watched as Pendian and the sailors headed for the citadel, then with a nod at Farmorl they set off in the direction of the ship. The pair struggled against the mass of citizenry flooding through the winding, curving streets of the slum. Eventually, they gave up trying to fight the oncoming wave of humanity and instead cut down towards the bay, where the wide promenade separated the wooden expanse of buildings from the ocean. They reached the promenade and realized why it was relatively quiet.

Two black ships had dropped anchor in the bay and disgorged a collection of small boats towards the shore. Two had reached the beach and soldiers in dark metal armour decorated with sweeping sharp curves were already on the quay. They were capturing the citizenry of Mahendra, in nets large enough to ensnare a man, and hooped ropes on the end of long poles that could enclose a person's neck before being pulled tight. Not that they seemed very interested in targeting men – they were going after the women, the younger and prettier the better.

Dryana spat out a curse, but there was nothing she could do to help. She had to get to the ship. She and Farmorl ran along the promenade towards the merchant dock at the far-right-hand side of the bay. She glanced across the bay; on the other side she could see the naval dock. Two ships of the Imperial Fleet were burning at anchor, belching a grey wood smoke across the bay. Blue flame, magical in nature, arced out from the walls of the city, slamming into an invisible shield above the enemy ships. The sky above the ships flickered red as the blue flame hit, revealing the ward, and then the attack dissipated in a cascade of purple.

Three of the black ships were attacking the Nerlineans at anchor, but they seemed close to completing their task. One was already turning. Where would they go next? Dryana suspected it would head straight for the merchant dock. The ships there were less of a threat than those of the Imperial Fleet, but still had to be dealt with, particularly the largest: the Slayer vessel.

Someone on the ships in the harbour had spotted them and sent a scattering of arrows in their direction. They missed, clattering across the stone of the harbourside.

Why were they bothering to fire at them? pondered Dryana.

The pair reached the merchant dock, dashing down the stone quays towards their ship. They passed smaller ships bobbing at anchor. On them she could see desperate crews getting ready to sail. The Slayer ship, as the largest, was the furthest out, framing the far end of the pier. Luckily it was pointing out to sea rather than in the direction of the bay. Well, it was not really luck, more a sensible position in the face of any incoming swell.

The sailors on the ship were already hard at work, striving to get the vessel under sail. The other ships on the dock were doing the same. One had just cast off and a second merchant junk followed suit moments later as Dryana and Farmorl dashed past. Smoke was drifting across the bay from where the attacking ships had fired at the junks of the Nerlinean Imperial Fleet. The pair searched for the black vessels to see where they were moving to target the merchant harbour, but the great mass of the Slayer ship obscured their view.

The pair continued their rush along the stone bulwark of the dock, reaching a narrow wooden gangplank that connected the ship to the harbour. Dryana danced across it, barely slowing, and ran onto the main deck of the Slayer junk, using the central mast to stop her sprint. She stood clutching it for a moment, panting for breath. Farmorl had slowed his run as he approached the gangplank, and he skipped across it more gingerly than his leader, stepping onto the deck.

Dryana looked around. She had caught her breath. "What are you waiting for? Get us underway!" she screamed angrily.

Slayer sailors leapt to obey.

"Yes, captain!" came the shout from the nearest officer – when a partner of the Company of Slayers was on a Slayer ship, they immediately became captain of the vessel by default.

A pair of sailors quickly dragged the gangplank in, letting it crash to the deck with a thunderous bang of wood on wood. Poles ten feet in length were brought forward by half a dozen sailors, who used them to push the ship away from the dock and out into the bay. Sails were being unfurled.

Dryana pushed away around the mast and the wooden crates on the deck, heading for the side of the vessel where she could get a better view of the attackers. A second black ship had made the turn now, and the two vessels were heading in their direction. She licked her finger and tested the wind. There was enough. She thanked the gods.

The sails caught and the Slayer junk surged in the water. It was now far enough out from the harbour wall to have a chance of making an escape. As a larger vessel with many more sails than the merchantmen that had already put to sea, it soon gained on them. The steersman went for the gap between two light vessels – the quickest way to make open ocean. It was tight, but the Slayer vessel was much larger and heedless of its effect on the merchant junks. The wooden side of the Slayer vessel sheared along the side of one, tearing off rigging and railings with a sickening crunch of screeching wood. Sailors on the smaller vessel screamed as they were thrown to the deck as the Slayer ship rocked by. A hapless sailor was caught and flung into the non-existent gap between the two ships, releasing a hideous scream as his life ended.

Dryana did not notice; she had run down to the end of the ship, perched on its rear, hanging off the rail and staring out at the oncoming black ships. They were moving out into the channel, pursuing the Slayer vessel. She cursed loudly.

A blazing ball of orange fire spiralled out from the closest of the two black ships. It arced through the air, its destination a horrible certainty. Dryana was caught watching it, its horrible beauty fascinating her for a second, so she did not fully register the danger. Suddenly she realized it was going to hit, and flung herself off the raised stern of the ship. She pitched herself down half a dozen steps, arms outstretched, reaching for the wood of the main deck. She slammed into it, rolling as she did so, taking the impact of the landing on her shoulder and avoiding her neck. She flipped over, hoping to come up in a neat roll, but she had too much momentum. She tumbled over, landing on her back and sliding along the rough deck to a stop in a tangle of mast ropes.

"Ow!" she observed gingerly, checking to see if anything was broken.

A hand reached out and grabbed hers, dragging her to her feet. She looked at Farmorl's concerned face and was actually touched for a moment. Then she saw the red raw scrapes down the back of her legs. She reached back and realized there was matching damage on her half-naked back. She winced in pain as she touched the fierce red skin. For once she regretted her clothing choices.

"It's just a scrape," Farmorl observed dismissively as he assessed her in the least erotic manner possible.

She shrugged away his hand, which was still clasped with hers, and looked back. Flames were licking across the raised deck at the stern, and the crew had rushed forward with buckets to put out the fire. Luckily, it largely hit the deck itself, missing the sails and rigging, where it could have done real damage. Soon the fires were out, leaving nothing more than scorch marks.

A second fireball spiralled through the air. The Slayers watched nervously as it passed in a large arc across the sky. It disappeared out of sight, hitting the water just beyond the junk with a fizzing hiss. It was followed by arrows. They peppered the deck, most catching in the sails and rigging. A few made it, though, thudding into the deck, and one caught a sailor through his calf muscle. A particularly unlucky deck hand was caught through the eye as he looked up at exactly the wrong moment. Dryana and Farmorl ducked against the mast, trying to take cover from the incoming rain of death.

"They are after us," she declared angrily.

"It's just a raid," Farmorl replied. "Once we are further out into open ocean, they will go back to attacking Mahendra."

The Slayer witch fixed him with a hard stare. She could tell from his face he was hoping that was the case rather than truly believing it. She raced back up the stairs to the stern, taking in the sight of the harbour behind her. They were well clear of the harbour now, out into the open ocean, and she could feel the wind in the sails propelling them forward away from the city. The two black ships had ignored the commercial dock and were heading out into the broad expanse of water after the Slayer junk. The intermittent fireballs had stopped. Was the mage too exhausted or simply preparing something nastier? She did not know. The withering fire of arrows continued. Most were falling short, though the odd one embedded itself near her in the deck or the rail. The wind and waves meant that the gap between the ships was constantly changing, making it nearly impossible for archers to accurately target even something the size of the ship.

Half a dozen Slayer sailors had come up to the stern deck armed with bows and were sending a small number of arrows back in the direction of the pursuing ships. It was an attempt to get the enemy archers to keep their heads down, but the attackers clearly had the greater numbers.

A Nerlinean man joined Dryana on the deck dressed in a stripped-down version of the uniform that the officers in the Slayer service wore. He was bulky rather than fat, and he'd removed the arms of his black and gold jacket, allowing his large biceps room to move. His calm brown eyes assessed the two ships pursuing them. He ran his hand through his short black hair, cut in an unflattering bowl shape. He looked like he wanted to say something, but then thought better of it and instead stood silently looming over Dryana. Chan Shal had been in the Slayers' service for a little less than a year, though he had already spent six years as a merchant sailor, and he had spent another decade before that in the Imperial Navy. He had jumped ship to the Company of the Slayers from the House Caldric for the chance to finally reach the rank of captain – something he had temporarily had to surrender with Dryana on the ship.

371

She looked back at him, as if acknowledging his presence, before her focus returned to the pursuing ships. A third black ship had now crossed the bay, fresh from firing at the Imperial Fleet vessels. It had moored up against the commercial dock and disgorged its raiding party onto the harbour wall. She could hear the screams even from this distance. The ships not lucky enough to make it to sea were being boarded and seized. That was what she would have expected. It was the behaviour of the two other ships that worried her. Larger and with more sails than the ordinary merchant vessels, they should have easily caught the two smaller merchant junks that were now in open water. Instead, they were ignoring them. The two black ships seemed focused on hunting down the Slayer junk. It was the largest of the merchant vessels in the dock, certainly, but there had been other prizes they could have seized with ease rather than pursue the Slayer ship. Why were the raiders obsessed with them? As a Slayer she was used to collecting enemies, but she did not recognize the black ships as one of them.

"Who are they?" she asked Shal. "Pirates, slavers?"

That elicited a laugh from the Nerlinean, but little else.

"Who are they?" she barked again. "Kalygon, Graci?"

"Kasem, my lady," Shal replied, suddenly registering that an answer was required.

"Kasem slavers?"

"Sorry, my lady, I was not being clear." In truth, Shal was struggling with the western woman's oddly accented Nerlinean. "Those are Kasem Naval vessels."

"Is it normal for them to being raiding here?" she demanded.

"Raiding, taking slaves, it is their way," he observed with a shrug. "But to attack Mahendra – that is bolder than they have been in a long while. Such an escalation is likely to draw the attention of the Imperial Fleet, especially with their ships burning at anchor."

"And Nyandar?" she asked.

The merchant captain looked at her, confused.

"The Emperor Nyandar? How is he likely to react to such an invasion?"

"Who knows, my lady?" he shrugged.

"Those vessels are larger and have more sails. They will catch us at present speed and yet you seem unconcerned?"

"They will break off," he declared confidently. "There is easier prey for them to take."

The Slayer ship overtook another merchant junk – one that had left harbour just as the attack had begun, and probably the largest of the merchant vessels after the Slayer ship.

"So, they should take this one," she waved her hand at the ship now to their rear. "Assuming it is just a raid."

Her Nerlinean colleague nodded confidently.

Another fireball, magical rather than chemical, arced out from the lead black ship. It slammed into the water just behind the stern, sending up a cloud of steam. The Slayers recoiled in shock.

"What are they doing?" Dryana pointed towards the lead vessel. Five men seemed to be manhandling something that looked like a ballista onto the front of the ship.

"Steersman, hard right, change sail now!" Shal screamed.

The Slayer ship lurched right.

"Get down, it's a cutting chain!" he shouted.

Dryana flung herself to the deck. She did not see what hit them, but it crunched through the left handrail, smashing through the wood and sending up showers of splinters that caught sailors too slow to move. It ripped rigging ropes clear from the sails before wrapping itself around the forward rail on the prow. Dryana looked around nervously and pushed herself to her feet. It was a pair of ballista bolts with a large metal chain suspended between the two. Had Shal not given his order it would have gone down the centre of the ship, taking out at least one mast if not both of them. Then they would have been easy prey.

"Captain, I apologize for not clearing my order with you first," Shal said.

"Sure, no problem," Dryana replied quietly, still shocked by what had happened.

She looked back; they did not seem to be reloading. The first black ship passed the other merchant vessel, ignoring it completely, and the second one followed suit a few minutes later.

"So, they are after us." She was certain now.

Shal nodded his acceptance.

She walked to the edge of the upper deck and spotted her lover pacing the boards below.

"Farmorl, get up here!" she shouted down to the main deck below.

The young man's head swivelled around as he was dragged from his thoughts. He turned and ran up the steps to the deck, covering the stairs in a couple of bounds.

"Take your time, why don't you?" she muttered petulantly. "It's not like we're being pursued."

Farmorl ignored the barb. He knew she was not one to be won round by arguing; besides, they had bigger problems to worry about.

"We are being pursued," she stated blandly.

"And?"

"Any suggestions?" Her request took in both Farmorl and Shal.

"We can't fight," Shal stated.

She looked at him; not that she disagreed with his assessment, but she wanted clarification.

"They outnumber us, and they have mages; we don't."

"The dead," Farmorl offered quietly, not wanting to spell out what he was really suggesting.

Dryana understood what he meant, though. "Where from?" She gave an expansive wave of her hand. "There might be a wreck I could find, but chances are the bodies will have been pulled apart and scattered across the seabed. Besides, they'll have to swim up a couple of miles to get to us and by that time we will have long ago passed by."

"Use the dead from any battle to fight on our side?" Farmorl offered. "You've done that before."

Dryana sighed. "That only works if we kill a lot of them faster than they kill us. Given their obvious advantages in magic and possible numbers, that seems unlikely."

"The weather," he offered.

"You mean the wind?" she replied.

Farmorl nodded. So Slinker had told his protege the story of how she had manipulated the winds once to give the Slayers an advantage in battle. The same thought had occurred to her.

"It might be worth a try and I don't see any other options," she agreed. "But I am not sure how much it will help us."

"How so?" he questioned.

"Last time the ships were fleeing, not pursuing. I becalmed the waters ahead of both of us, so it affected them more than us, allowing us to close the gap," she explained.

"So that was easy?" he queried.

"By comparison, maybe, but not easy; not even close to easy," she observed coldly. "The problem is the black ships are too close, and it's not magic, it is manipulating the weather. It is the difference between hitting with a mace and stabbing with a fine blade."

Farmorl looked over her shoulder. "Either way, we need to do something because the gap is shrinking."

Dryana did not answer. Instead she sat down and crossed her legs, facing the ship's direction of travel. Her eyes played across the sails in front of her. She muttered some words, barely audible and certainly to Farmorl unintelligible.

The wind grew stronger, filling the sails and pushing them forward. Some of the sails had not been fully patched after the ship's previous battle, the air whipped through them, and they gained less speed than should have been the case.

"Shal, you will have to adjust the angle on the sails. I am trying to manipulate the wind so it catches our canvas better than theirs, but it will take constant readjustment, especially with the sails still partially damaged."

The Nerlinean nodded his understanding and started to shout orders, berating his fellow sailors to move faster. Farmorl moved to the rail, and saw that the distance between the black ships and the Slayer junk had increased. He could see the enemy sailors rushing to adjust their sails. The weather manipulation that Dryana was using would increase the gap, but it would be a slow process. Would it be enough to dissuade the Kasem Navy from their pursuit? He did not know.

"Anything you need?" Farmorl asked. "I can get you a bucket if you want."

Dryana looked at him, annoyed. She understood the jibe. Magic users tended to vomit when using magic too aggressively or for too long.

"I'm a witch, not a wizard," she remined him. "The power of the goddess flows through me, not magic. The Gift does not create the same physical reaction in witches that mages experience, but the level of concentration required will drain me given time."

"So, what do we do when that happens?"

"Two things: first, we hope that they have given up before then or we have come up with another plan," Dryana answered.

"And the second?" he queried.

"Get me some cushions, so I have something soft to land on when I pass out." She grinned despite herself.

***

Farmorl mounted the steps as the grey light of dawn was slowly giving way to hints of sunshine. A thin curtain of drizzle filled the air as it had done all night. The sight that greeted him wrenched at his heart. Dryana sat where he had left her only two hours earlier. Her face was pale even by her standards, and dark shadows pulled at her eyes. Her sharp features seemed even sharper, almost as if she had been starved. Her eyes stared forward, bloodshot and exhausted.

She was surrounded by cushions soaked wet by the constant light rain. A grey blanket was wrapped around her shoulders; some protection against the weather. Farmorl said nothing, instead drawing out a fresh dry blanket from where it was stowed under his arm. He pulled the damp blanket off Dryana's shoulders. She shivered as the wind and rain caught her bare arms. He tossed it on a pile of half a dozen other blankets. Then he carefully, almost lovingly, wrapped the dry blanket around the Slayer witch. She shivered again, more at the change in temperature than for any other reason. He patted her lightly on the shoulder.

"The gap?" she croaked.

Farmorl stood up and looked out from the rail on the stern. The gap was larger, but still not big enough. She had stretched it out by sitting here all the previous day and through the night. Were she to stop it would close again. Now it would take several hours for the black ships to catch them; previously, they would have closed the gap in perhaps an hour. Still the Kasem bore down relentlessly on the Slayers. *What had the Company of Slayers ever done to anger them?* he wondered.

"It's larger, but they are still coming," he confirmed.

"At least that's something." Her parched voice was like sharp gravel.

"You want some water?" he asked.

"No, because then I'll have to pee," she said with a weary grin.

He laughed at that, raising a look of surprise from the sailors on the deck. A pall of fear had fallen over the ship. The sailors were quiet. Dread stalked them.

Farmorl squatted down in front of Dryana. For all her humour, she was teetering on the edge of collapse. He could see it in her face: her eyelids were starting to droop, and her shoulders gave involuntary stutters, as she fell asleep for just a second and then woke again. It was only a matter of time before she ran out of energy; likely a very little time.

"You are doing well," he declared, his tone aiming for comforting but coming out more patronizing than he had planned.

She favoured him with a withering gaze, but for a moment, just a moment, she was revitalized. He smiled despite their desperate situation. He took a cup of water and dipped his fingers in it before flicking it across the Slayer witch's face. A small drop trickled down her cheek, pooling at the corner of her mouth. She lapped at it greedily.

"You sure you don't want some water?" he asked again.

She gave the barest shake of her head.

He stood up and went back to looking at the pursuing ships.

Behind him, Dryana's head drooped, her chin touching her chest. She rallied one last time, a forlorn attempt to stay awake. Then she gave way to exhaustion and sleep. She

378

collapsed sideways to the deck and the soft cushions that surrounded her.

Farmorl did not hear her fall. For him the first indication that something had changed was that the drizzle had stopped. He looked back and saw his lover's collapsed form sprawled among the damp cushions. He surmised that the light rain had been a side effect of her manipulation of the weather. Perhaps a reflection of her sour mood at her exhaustion. He knelt down and placed his ear close to her mouth, listening and feeling for her breath. He felt it strong against his face. He pushed up and watched the up and down movement of her chest, confirming she was just sleeping.

He turned back to the following ships. Had the gap closed? He wasn't sure. Maybe imperceptibly. It would take their pursuers time – most of the day, possibly – but it would happen. Their only hope was for Dryana to recover in time. Looking down at the exhausted woman, that seemed a stretch. Farmorl shifted the sword at his hip as if preparing for battle, a fight that was hours away.

***

The fireball slammed into the rear of the vessel; sailors rushed with buckets to put out the flames as they scattered across the surface of the wood. Farmorl cursed as the rear sail and rigging caught. The desperate crew rushed to cut away the burning fabric before it could spread. It was still enough damage to slow the ship. Not that it would matter; it was now just a question of when, not if, they were caught.

The drizzle of the morning had given way to the warming sun of early afternoon. In that time, the gap between the Slayer junk had narrowed by more than half. Shal had been a constant presence, shouting orders to his sailors, using every trick he knew to keep from being caught. He had probably bought them an hour or more, but there was only so much that such actions could yield. The enemy was close enough now for an alternating rain of arrows and fireballs to be hitting the Slayer ship. The Slayer sailors had fired their own arrows in response, but it had no effect on slowing the pursuers; besides, supplies were running low. The Slayer ship was a merchantman, not a war ship, after all.

Farmorl looked around at the ship. The fires were out, but they were running out of water. The ship had used buckets of salt water to put out the fires, drawn up from the surrounding ocean, but they were now largely empty. They could drop the buckets over the side on ropes to refill them, but that would create a drag on the movement of the ship, slowing it and further closing the gap with the black ships, something they could not afford to do. They had stores of freshwater, but if they used them, what would they drink?

Shal approached Farmorl, berating exhausted sailors as he crossed the deck. He had re-taken full command since Dryana's collapse. She had been carried to the captain's cabin and laid upon the cot there. Even after five hours of sleep, she had shown no signs of waking. Farmorl had tried to gently rouse her an hour ago, but she had refused to come round.

"Could we put into shore?" Farmorl demanded of Shal.

He had been careful to phrase it as a question, but his tone was harsher than it should have been. Shal was in command, after all.

"Nothing along this section of coast, except fishing villages and small towns," the captain grunted.

He gestured towards the Nerlinean coast, which lay tantalizingly out of sight beyond the horizon. "Where is the Fleet?" muttered Farmorl, more to himself than anyone else.

"Big ocean," grunted Shal.

"Why are the Kasem so far south?" Farmorl queried.

Shal shrugged in response.

Another rain of arrows buzzed black across the sky. Sailors screamed as they found their mark. The enemy were closer, their missiles hitting the vessel from prow to stern, leaving few places for the crew to hide from their deadly rain.

Shal barked more orders, and sails were trimmed as the sailors tried to capture the maximum amount of wind. Farmorl had been impressed by the crew's efforts to maximize everything they could from the ship in terms of speed, yet it was simply delaying the inevitable.

"Ship ahoy!" the shout rang across the ship.

Farmorl fixed on the vessels behind him, and was confused for a moment. Of course there were ships in sight. They had been chasing them for a day and a night. Then he registered that the shout had come from the prow, not the stern. Shal was clearly more awake than Farmorl; he had already dashed to the front of the ship. Farmorl took off after him. Shal was staring out across the ocean, following where the sailor who had made the shout was pointing.

They could just make out a dark dot on the horizon. A sailor ran up, handing an eyeglass to Captain Chan. Farmorl fought down the urge to grab it. He watched while Shal focused the telescope on the ship on the horizon.

"What is it?" Farmorl demanded.

"I don't recognize it," Shal muttered angrily, thrusting the eyeglass into Farmorl's waiting hands.

It took a moment for Farmorl to register what he was seeing. It did not make sense. It was not an Imperial Fleet junk, or a junk of any type. Nor, thankfully, was it another of the black ships. It was a western vessel, so no wonder Shal had not recognized it. No such ship would normally be seen in the waters of the Farthest Ocean. That ship should not be here; its home was on the Nerlinean Ocean. It was a galleon, similar to the ships that Farmorl had accompanied on their journey to Port

Ren, but it looked larger, though it was hard to be sure at this distance. It was also moving impossibly fast.

He scanned the sails, looking for the signs of its allegiance, but the canvas was a solid white. He was thankful there was no gold P on red to indicate the Imperial Pandus Trading Company, but it could be another one of the Slayers' enemies. Were the black ships driving them towards this vessel? Perhaps they were completely unrelated to the Slayers and the black vessels? He could not make out the banner that flew high from its central mast, as the wind had wrapped it tight around the wood. Only blue and perhaps a hint of silver was visible.

Farmorl dropped the eyeglass, handing it back to the sailor who had initially brought it to them. It was not necessary; the oncoming ship was moving so fast it was now clearly visible with the naked eye. It was skipping across the ocean, its keel scything through the surface of the water, not resting upon it.

"A crown?" Farmorl observed to Shal.

The Nerlinean nodded his agreement.

If this was a trap there was no chance of escape, even if the sleeping Dryana was to come round.

More arrows thudded down onto the ship, followed by another pair of fireballs that caught the end of the Slayer junk. Farmorl ducked out of the way, narrowly avoiding another fall of arrows. Shal was not so lucky; one caught in his upper left arm. He cursed angrily at his bad luck, and snapped off the arrow, leaving the head embedded. He would have someone cut it out later if he survived that long.

"If they are still attacking us then maybe that ship is not with them," Farmorl suggested.

The injured Shal looked at him. "No idea," he muttered through teeth clenched against the pain.

The crown-driven ship had closed the distance already, thundering past the Slayer junk, with a gap of less than twenty feet. The banner unfurled in the wind, a silver griffin on a blue field. Staring up, Farmorl took a moment to fully understand what he was seeing.

The ship was from Kangorn.

The black ships had trimmed their sails, turning to port in a wide circle to slow their previous headlong rush. The focus of missiles and magic from the black ships now shifted to the ship from Kangorn. Arrows arced across the gap. Thirty feet above the ship, they exploded in flame, dropping as harmless cinders to the vessel below. They were followed by fiery orange globes. At the same distance out, they vaporized, hitting an invisible shield that turned to a blue light when impacted. They sprayed green and dissipated with no effect on the ship.

A figure strode down the deck of the Kangorn vessel, heading for the prow, tall and thin with sallow skin stretched tight over old bones. The last war mage of the Tancree mounted the forward deck and flung out his hands. White lightning danced from his fingers, covering the gap between him and the nearest black ship in moments. It crackled against the wards of the enemy vessel. Red light sprayed around the black ship as the magical barrier fought the incoming lightning. It turned a dark orange, then a lighter yellow. It exploded in a spray of white sparks as the lightning burst through, dancing across the ship and tearing apart people and ship alike. Ropes caught fire, followed by sails. Sailors wrapped in lightning screamed in agony as they were electrocuted.

Then it stopped. Slinker withdrew his hands and thrust them out again. More lightning flew across the ocean, hitting the second black ship. Its magical shield lasted even less time than the first ship, giving way almost immediately. White fire blitzed the rear of the vessel, blowing out wood from the stern. The Kangorn ship continued to close the gap, moving at speed. Slinker reset again and sent out blue bolts of light that punched holes through the side of the ship.

The black ships were turning fully now, trying to get away. The Kangorn vessel slowed their attack. Archers had come to the prow, joining Slinker, sending a hail of arrows into the fleeing vessels. Slinker sent another round of magical bolts thundering through the rear of one of the escaping ships.

Farmorl looked across the faces of the crew of the Slayer junk, where dread had been replaced with palpable relief. A great cheer erupted from his ship, with an answering shout from the Kangorn vessel. Farmorl fought back the urge to weep as tension rushed out of him. He tamped it down and with a grin on his face went to check on Dryana.

CHAPTER TWENTY-SIX – RESPITE

Dryana awoke bleary-eyed and tried to roll over. She nearly fell out of the cot. She cursed and remembered she was on a ship, rather than in her own bed. She had spent too much time recently sleeping on dry land and now she realized she had definitely not missed napping on a ship. She was exhausted; her body ached, and her legs and back were sore. She wondered if this was how mages felt all the time after using magic. There had been occasions when the use of her gift had reduced her to this level of weakness – on Syndion, when she had raised the army, and in the Temple of Thytha – but they were rarities. It had happened the last time she had manipulated the weather, so maybe it was related to that, though she did not remember it being this bad last time. Maybe it was just the act of sitting cross-legged and concentrating for hours that had done the damage.

She looked up and took in worried faces staring down at her. She must be dreaming. She squeezed her eyes closed and opened them again. They were still there, which made no sense.

"Slinker? Balinor?" she asked, unsure.

"Yes," Slinker replied.

"Obviously," chimed Balinor.

"You are real?" she questioned.

Balinor looked almost as confused as Dryana felt, and Slinker just chuckled.

She rubbed her eyes and sat up, swinging her legs around so they hung off the edge of the cot and dangled on the wood of the deck.

"You saved us?"

"Seemed like the thing to do," observed Slinker.

"Thank you," she mouthed quietly.

He patted her on the shoulder.

"Farmorl?" she asked. "Chan Shal, the crew?"

She added the latter, quickly realizing her concern for Farmorl might seem telling.

Slinker gave his leering grin; he had spotted it. "He's fine," he said. "And so are the others, mostly. Shal took an arrow in the arm. A large number of the crew were injured, and a few have died since you decided to take a nap."

She gave him a cold look at his last mocking observation and fought down the urge to childishly stick out her tongue.

"The black ships?"

"Gone," Slinker replied. "They fled after we arrived."

"When Slinker lashed them with magic," said Balinor with a grin.

"What did the Kasem want with us?" she wondered.

Slinker gave a shrug.

"No idea," replied Balinor. "I've never even met one of them."

"And what by the gods are you doing here?" Dryana shot back, turning on Balinor.

"State visit," he replied. "Thought I would come and see the Nerlinean Empire, as I've heard so much about it. I am Prince of Kangorn; I need to engage in foreign relations."

"I've seen the 'foreign relations'; she is very lovely," Slinker leered at Balinor.

"Why did you not tell us you were coming?" she asked. "You have mages?"

"It was a spur-of-the-moment thing. I heard you needed help against the Pandus," Balinor replied.

"What?" Dryana looked confused. "You must have left months ago."

"About a month," he confirmed.

"How?" she asked. "Oh! You have Ascrina's crown." She remembered the magical device that the Slayers had traded to Ascrina for a Lordship of Kangorn.

"It's *my* crown," the Prince of Kangorn replied, a little too defensively.

"Well, thanks," she replied. "Long way to come on the off chance we needed your help."

"What do you mean?" Balinor looked confused. "You asked for me to come. Your message."

A sense of dread permeated through Dryana. "What message?" she asked quietly.

"You sent a messenger, through our official network. He carried the black silk to confirm who he was," he replied.

"Balinor, it is wonderful to have you here, if only because you and Slinker have just saved my life and that of my crew, but I sent no message."

Balinor looked shocked. "That would mean our network has been compromised," he said, looking worried.

Dryana said nothing. Her eyes flicked from Slinker to Balinor, deciding what to say to her colleagues. It was possible, she supposed. The system that Pendian had developed was difficult to infiltrate, but no system would be truly foolproof. The more worrying possibility was that someone within the Company of Slayers had sent the message and attributed it to Dryana. Why? she wondered. A myriad of options surged through her mind. She chose not to say anything.

"So, you didn't send the message?" asked Balinor, seeking confirmation.

"She said that already," Slinker snapped.

Balinor looked more upset that he not actually been invited east than about the underlying issue of why.

"Maybe we should ask Pendian," observed Slinker quietly.

"Speak to him mind to mind as you mages do?" she asked.

"I was thinking more in person." Slinker's leering smile had a nasty edge.

Dryana swallowed.

"He's in Mahendra, and I have no intention of going back there to talk to him," she muttered. "Besides, if he is behind the deception, it will be on Sali's orders."

"Why would Saliana do it?" demanded a confused Balinor.

"She is still angry at you," answered Slinker.

"What? We've had barely any contact in the last five years since I became Prince of Kangorn," he replied.

"You thought that was because she was really busy?" asked Dryana, her voice dripping with sarcasm.

"No. I knew she was angry – that was obvious from the way she stormed into my hall and embarrassed me in front of my wife. But like I said, that was five years ago."

"And you thought Sali would just let it go?" chuckled Dryana.

"Long time to hold a grudge is all," Balinor observed with a slightly petulant tone.

"This is Sali we are talking about," grinned Dryana.

Slinker let out a throaty laugh at that, earning them both a look of annoyance from the Prince of Kangorn.

"Well, a problem for another day," declared Dryana, testing her tired legs against the rocking floor of the cabin and then pushing up from the cot. She winced as the red welts on her legs scraped against the wood of the bed's edge. She held the timber of the low ceiling and took a breath. The sleep had not fully dispelled the ache through her legs and back.

"What do you mean by that?" asked Balinor. "I am half a world from home, and we don't know why?"

"Yes, but an endless discussion will not change that," countered the Slayer witch.

Balinor looked like he might protest, but he held his tongue.

There was a knock on the cabin door and a woman stepped in.

"What in Jeddera's name is she doing here?" Dryana declared angrily, looking around for her short sword.

Slinker and Balinor looked confused.

"She is one of Balinor's servants," Slinker replied.

Dryana rubbed her eyes and looked at the beautiful woman in the doorway. She had soft brown skin and long black hair, and wore a tight-fitting dress of blue silk that reached just above the knee. She looked terrified at the Slayer's aggressive reaction to her appearance. The look of fear was enough to convince Dryana that she had been mistaken in her initial identification of the woman. Charlotte Halfnight-Pandus was not someone who would be so easily frightened by someone like Dryana. Other than that, the resemblance was uncanny: the servant was probably a touch taller, but in all other regards –

body shape, hair colour and face – she was a copy of the wererat woman.

Dryana moved closer, assessing the woman, who wilted under her penetrating gaze. Her eyes were cast down, making. her look less like Charlotte. She also looked a little less ratty around the nose than the Pandus girl.

"Who is she?" she demanded of Balinor.

"Shanti, my servant." Balinor sounded annoyed.

Dryana looked back at the Prince of Kangorn, taking in his irritated expression.

"Look up," she ordered the girl.

The servant looked up, meeting the Slayer's gaze, a note of defiance in her eyes.

Dryana took in the perfectly applied cosmetics and the expensive silk dress. *Oh, Balinor, you fool*, she thought.

"What do you want?" Dryana asked.

"I have prepared food, as my lord instructed," Shanti said quietly.

"Speak up, I can barely hear you," the Slayer mocked derisively.

"Enough, Dryana," Balinor interrupted. "You heard well enough."

He stepped forward, placing his arm protectively around Shanti. It was enough to confirm Dryana's suspicions. She gave Slinker a hard worried look. So, this was what the Tancree had meant by 'foreign relations'.

Slinker raised an amused eyebrow but said nothing in response.

"Slinker, if you used magic to attack the Kasem ships, then who is using the crown?" she asked, turning away from the girl and her protective prince.

"You don't think me capable of both at the same time?" he replied, a curl of his mouth indicated he was trying not to smile.

"Uncle," she said politely. Slinker was hard to read. She thought he was mocking her, but she could not be sure. "I have no doubt of your considerable abilities, but I am aware of only one mage who can operate a crown and cast at the same time."

Slinker gave a broad grin. "Balinor has mages with him."

"Mages plural?"

"Collyn and Tara," supplied Balinor. "It was Collyn who controlled the ship, while Slinker attacked the enemy."

"Good," said Dryana. "Can the Company of Slayers borrow Tara?"

"Why?"

"We need to get back to Port Ren. It will be quicker if we take your ship and use the crown," she replied.

"And this ship?" asked Slinker.

"Shal can take it back south at normal sail."

"And if the Kasem reappear?" the Tancree queried.

"It's unlikely; they will have headed north. I am assuming we are heading south?"

Slinker nodded to Dryana, giving confirmation of their direction of sail.

"Any remaining signs of continued pursuit?"

Slinker shook his head no.

"We can leave Farmorl and Tara with the ship. She can contact you, in the unlikely event they come under attack. We should now be far enough south to dissuade the Kasem from further pursuit. This far south, they will run an even greater risk of running into imperial patrols," she said.

Slinker said nothing. She was finding reasons for leaving the Slayer junk behind. He noted that she had similarly decided to leave Farmorl behind. He felt a momentary sadness that she seemed to be moving on from his young protege. It was her way, and Slinker had warned him, but he still felt for the boy; he knew how smitten Farmorl was with Dryana.

391

"You'll lend us the mage?" she demanded.

"Sure, but why the rush?" Balinor asked Slinker's question for both of them.

"We need to get to Port Ren. We have been betrayed. If I don't fix things, all Sali's planning could be for nothing. Besides…" she said.

"Besides?" asked Balinor.

"Besides, I have a fat man to kill."

CHAPTER TWENTY-SEVEN – THE TOMB

Night fell quickly on the steppe, especially as the season passed from autumn into early winter. A patter of rain, little more than drizzle, washed the riders' faces. In the dark and cold of the windswept grasslands, it made the four riders more miserable. Samarin had wanted to stop. She knew the steppe well and that night was closing in. Saliana had insisted they continue on, and when the dark had come upon them, she had held out her hand, creating from nowhere a magical light of brightest white. It sprayed out from the group, illuminating everything within fifty feet around them. Samarin found the whole thing discomfiting. Highlighting one's presence on the grasslands was never a good idea.

Despite the light, the cats the four rode had slowed to a walk from their normal headlong loping run. They had passed through the Solinad Gate a week past, seeing no sign of the hunters as they progressed south. There had been few signs of the slaughter of the great beasts in which Kyrian had participated. The Solinad Hunters had taken almost every scrap of meat and hide, and the steppe scavengers had taken anything left behind. Most of the smaller bones had been stripped from the animals, for use in clothing and tools. Only the larger bones, the great back bones and ribcages, marked the steppe, and most had collapsed flat to the ground and become obscured in the long grass.

For reasons neither Kyrian nor Samarin could truly understand, Saliana had insisted they cut south, almost to the edges of the grassland where it met the northern shore of the Nerlinean Ocean. Saliana had assured them it would be safer – something that Samarin privately concurred with as they would be passing through a portion of the steppe that was still dominated by the Fal'Gar. It might protect them from roving bands of Mourn, but risked bringing them into contact with tribes of Fal'Gar who would be interested to know why the niece of the Dumech'Di'Fal'Gar was travelling with the Count of Chazantria and two strangers. The Fal'Gar loyalty to their war leader was strong, but not absolute. As time passed, the pretence that they were many tribes rather than one people increasingly risked becoming a reality. There was always a chance that an ambitious local Fal'Gar chief might choose to waylay them to discover their purpose.

But there had been no need to worry. The steppe, empty at the best of times, had been strangely quiet. No signs of Fal'Gar tribes had been seen since they had approached the southern steppe. Even regular camping sites, near lakes, stone outcrops and the rare coppices, were all deserted. Samarin found it disconcerting. It was almost as if the population of the steppe had disappeared, which in truth it had – west towards the Mountain of the Moon to kneel before the Great Khan of the Mourn.

"That rocky outcrop there." Sali pointed a few hundred yards away.

"I can't see anything," moaned Kyrian. Unlike the other three with Gar blood, he could see nothing outside the bubble of light that Sali had created.

"Over there," Sali pointed in frustration, throwing out a line of light with her finger. It illuminated the rocks for a moment before dissipating.

"Looks okay," he grunted.

"We can push on further," Samarin suggested.

"Really," Kyrian shot her a glare. "You've been complaining that we should stop since before dusk."

"I don't know; doesn't look a great place to camp," offered Samarin.

"It looks fine to me," Saliana stated. She could see the rocks clearly, which Kyrian could not. "The stone will protect us from the wind and hide the fire."

"We are in a big light bubble, and you are worried about hiding a fire?" Samarin observed wearily. "I thought you wanted to press on."

"No," declared Sali. "Let's camp there."

"Sure," muttered Samarin.

Saliana gave her oradar a kick, causing it to spring forward towards the rocky outcrop, leaving the others struggling to catch up with the fast-disappearing light that guided their way.

***

Samarin's eyes fluttered open. She rolled over gently, patting her oradar, which rested next to her, whispering softly to persuade it to stay asleep. She looked over to Kyrian, who lay on his back, legs stretched out, face seemingly devoid of life. The snores that emitted from him told her he was fine. The sound was thunderous against the quiet darkness of the steppe. She could see the wrestler's own cat resting at a distance from its rider. The loud garrulous breaths that were emitting from the oradar made Samarin feel that the pair were better matched than either would acknowledge. She suppressed a chuckle.

She glanced over her shoulder, pushing herself up slightly so she could see beyond her own oradar, to where Rayllor and his snow oradar were curled up. She made a judgement of the time; it was hard with the sky still black. She relied on her body clock. She guessed it was two hours past midnight. Sali's watch would have started maybe an hour or so ago. Her sharp Gar eyes picked out the cloaked figure of the Slayer perched on a small rock in the shadow of the main outcrop. It was a good position at the far end, giving a clear view of most of the surrounding grasslands. A better view would have been gained by climbing on top of the outcrop, but that would have set her silhouette against the sky. It was unlikely to be an issue with the moons obscured by the cloud and rain, but still a sensible precaution. There was no chance of being spotted by a human in the pitch black, but the Gar and the Mourn were not so limited in their nighttime eyesight: the barest hint of light was enough for them to pick something out. The gain in terms of vision from taking up the high position would have been more than offset by the Slayer potentially giving away her presence.

The wind swept across the camp and Samarin shivered. She looked over at the small dung fire on which they had heated their food. It gave off a dull red glow. Personally, she would have preferred to have eaten cold rations to reduce the risk of discovery, but Sali had been insistent. She glanced at the Mistress of the Slayers again. She had not moved. Samarin had taken the first watch, before waking Sali and handing over to her. She had then commanded her body to sleep for about an hour before waking her. For once it had broadly obeyed her. In a couple of hours Sali should wake Kyrian. The final watch would be Kyrian's – the hours before and after dawn, when his human eyes were of more use. She might choose not to; she tended just to let him sleep. None of them yet trusted Rayllor enough to stand a watch for them.

Samarin decided she had at least a couple of hours before Sali woke Kyrian. It was worth the risk. She had to see it again. She could feel it calling to her. She pushed her kit up against the oradar, which growled in its sleep, then she tossed her blanket over it – enough she hoped, to look like a sleeping person. It might convince someone giving it a momentary glance, but no longer than that. There was nothing else she could do; it would have to suffice. She crouched low, using the oradar as cover. She sprinted across the open ground between her sleeping space and the rocky outcrop. It was only a few yards. She ducked down into the rocks and looked across the camp to the other end of the outcrop where Sali remained seated. The Slayer had made no movement, so the Gar was confident she had not been seen or heard.

Samarin ducked between two rocks at the front of the outcrop. It obscured her lower half and then she disappeared out of sight completely. Excitement got the better of her and she skipped down the grey cut steps concealed by the rock. They wound down in a carefully chiselled wide spiral staircase. A thin layer of dust had accumulated since Samarin's last visit, and her steps sent it wafting up in the air. She stopped for a second and fought back the urge to sneeze. She slowed her pace. The dark was oppressive. She could see a hint of blue light ahead, but the braziers surrounding the chamber had not come alight. She remembered there was a word of command. Cliphine had used it that time, but it was also taught to the Trendorns of the Fal'Dath and their heirs.

Samarin spoke a word, and the braziers blazed to life, the light varying between a pale blue and a sharp white. Whatever magic they contained did not require one being a mage to make it work. Was Cliphine a mage? Samarin did not know. She searched through the legends in her memory. She had the Gift of the Witch, but not that of magic, at least not in the stories the young Gar could remember. Until she had met Sali she would have declared that to hold both gifts was impossible. The gods would not be foolish enough to grant someone so much power, but then there was the Slayer.

She dismissed the woman from her mind and her eyes took in the cathedral-sized structure before her. The view captured only half its majesty, for a neatly carved and finished wall cut the chamber in two in front of her. A blue light seemed to dance across the patterns and sigils that covered the dividing wall. She sighed as she appreciated its beauty. She moved off the final step, almost gingerly, as if sensing a need to be cautious. She walked across the flagstones, stopping before the stone bier in its centre. She took in the crystal coffin that rested upon it. The resting place of Fenice, the eldest daughter of Cliphine, the Lady of the Crystal Ships. She touched her hand to it, feeling a sense of sympathy for the female Gar of legend, which made no sense for one long dead whom she had never met. Not even her ancestor, but indeed the enemy of her ancestors.

"You have a word in your mind."

Samarin started – she felt she had thought it, rather than heard it. She knew that was not true; she knew the voice. She turned silently towards the stairs. Standing on the lowest step, Saliana Slayer leaned against the unfinished stone of the cave wall rather than the neatly chiselled pillar of the spiral. Her cloak flowed around her; the hat she normally wore she held in her hands. Her sharp chiselled features and soft white-blonde hair made her look somehow more Garish in this place than was normally the case. It was then Samarin noticed that the blue-white light of the braziers had changed. She remembered that when she had come here with Cliphine the light had been softer: blue with a greenish tinge. Now it had changed again; the blue had been tinged with red, creating a purplish light that made the room darker. Sali's eyes were hard, her irises dark purple.

Samarin swallowed nervously. "You mean the word you use to command me," she offered. The Slayer could not know about the other word.

Saliana chuckled, and it lacked even the limited warmth it normally contained.

"You have a word in your mind; a word that wants to escape. You have held it, struggled with it for five years, that word," replied Saliana.

"I don't know…" began Samarin.

"Don't waste my time. Your grandmother told me you hold the word," Sali cut across the Fal'Gar's protests.

Samarin licked her lips. She looked over Sali's shoulder. Kyrian was walking down the steps, followed by Rayllor. They stopped behind Sali and watched the scene with interest.

"Stay on the stairs," said Sali quietly.

Kyrian nodded his agreement, not that Sali could see him.

"This place is sacred to the Fal'Gar," declared Samarin, trying to put as much anger and indignation into her voice as possible. "This is not a place for humans."

Kyrian gave a sigh. "I'm the only true human here and I'm too curious to miss this. Besides, I have seen a place like this before, though that was much bigger and full of soldiers. Who is in the coffin?"

"Tell him," commanded Sali.

"Fenice, the daughter of Cliphine," Samarin replied.

"So, a Syn'Dion'Gar or a Dal'Ri'Gar, possibly. Not a Fal'Gar at all," he replied seriously.

Sali was genuinely taken aback and turned to look at Kyrian in surprise.

"I listen when you and others waffle on about dead people and dead races," said Kyrian.

Sali gave him a smile, the first sign of warmth she had shown since entering the tomb. She turned back to Samarin. "The word?" she asked.

Samarin looked at Sali, her mind whirring.

"You can't make me," Samarin said. It came out more like the complaint of a petulant child, but that is not what the Fal'Gar meant. Sali could compel her to do virtually anything, but for some reason she was unable to force her to speak the word. It was nice to have some power again, some free will, thought Samarin.

"Why should I?"

"Why should you not?" replied Sali calmly.

"What is in it for me, for my people, if I do?"

"When did she last come here?" Sali asked Samarin.

"Who?"

"You know who, Samarin. Do not be obtuse, or we will be here all night," replied Sali.

Samarin felt so young compared to the woman in front of her, despite the fact that she was pretty certain she was the oldest person in the room and by some margin.

"Cliphine came here five years ago," she replied.

"Eight years early," purred Sali with an evil smile. "I really must have got to her. So, when do you think she will be here again? Every ten years is the norm. Have you got another five years before you see her or only three?"

Samarin licked her lips. The Slayer's face was hard to read, but the Fal'Gar suspected she was being mocked.

"Why does it matter to you?"

Sali laughed. "Not me, for you. How long until you bow and scrape to the Lady of the Crystal Ships again, and another ten years after that? Listening politely to the demands of your conqueror. Who will you teach to do the same? Your daughter, your niece, your granddaughter? Another six centuries of subservience."

"And what do you offer? War, death?"

"War is coming. The Great Khan of the Mourn will see to that; that cannot be changed. All that matters is will you be free or will you moulder in this crypt watching your people die slowly in the way the Ice Lords moulder away to nothing in their crystal towers?" Sali's tone was both angry and sad.

Samarin looked down at her feet, considering her options. Her grandmother had put her in this place. So had her uncle. Had this been what they intended? Did they know who this woman was? Did she? She looked up and made her decision.

She spoke the word.

She remembered the last time, the blue lights spiralling across the great double doors in the wall that divided the room. The groan of their opening, the sudden rush of ancient dust. The tomb of the dead Gar waiting beyond. But none of that happened.

Blinding white light blazed up from the floor, spilling upwards until it hit the ceiling of the cave far above, radiating back in a phosphorescent cascade of white rain. Saliana collapsed to one knee, grasping the bottom step to stop from falling into the light burning out from it. Her eyes bulged, and blood ran from them, curling down her cheeks and dripping from her chin. On the floor, Samarin was screaming as if on fire. She had coiled into a ball, grasped in the foetal position. She was sobbing and then screaming, trying to protect herself from the blazing light.

"Well played, Cliphine, well played," Sali muttered under her breath. She licked her lips, tasting the blood dripping from her eyes.

She pushed herself back to her feet. The pain was excruciating. She reached out, testing the light. It was magic, not witchcraft – that much she knew already, but feeling the power confirmed it. Cliphine had come alone, with guards but no mages; that was what Samarin's grandmother had told Saliana. That had been back before they had begun this journey. Sali had planned to compel the Trendorn Hildamar Mrignandor to tell her, but the Fal'Gar's chief witch had been remarkably willing to share what she knew with the Slayer. Her hatred of Cliphine had burned away her discretion. Cliphine's choice of word had opened the doors, but also primed the wards. She had come to this place to set a trap for Saliana Slayer. The wards were old, set centuries ago, was Sali's guess.

Cliphine should have brought Greldin of the Way with her and reset the power in the wards had she really wanted to stop Saliana, but Sali might have suspected a trap then. Cliphine had taken a calculated gamble, set a weaker trap that Saliana would walk into or risk her not taking the bait. Had she not been on the lowest step but on the floor itself then maybe Cliphine's gamble would have paid off.

This is going to hurt, Sali thought. She stepped out onto the blazing flagstone floor of the tomb. White light engulfed her, tearing at her, blazing through her. Every cell of her body was screaming in pain despite all the magic she had conjured up to protect herself. She reached into the light shining around her, feeling through the weaves of power. A static ward had to be set, placed; it had to draw power from somewhere, through a point in space. There was no mage to combat, no one to target, to unpick their weaves of magic. Instead, she followed the threads of power back to their source.

Eight, she counted, and she cursed. Who set so many wards to protect a place? Curving and twirling around each ward, neatly designed not to conflict. It was a work of genius; she would have acknowledged that had the pain not been burning through her. It confirmed what Saliana suspected – some of the power had leached out from the wards. She could see that they had been placed centuries before, the work of at least four mages of the first rank. Had they been set more recently, renewed when Cliphine had come here, she would have been overwhelmed by the power stored in them. Cliphine had not known how powerful Saliana was. She briefly considered using one of the orange crystals in her pouch. She wished she had three. No, she decided she could do this without them.

She found the first ward with her mind, a metal disc surrounding a blue-white crystal buried in the ceiling of the cave. She turned the disc in her mind and the power ebbed away slowly, like a flow of water being cut off when a tap is turned. She had found the second one and performed the same operation and then a third. Five remained: one more in the ceiling, four in the floor.

Sweat poured down her face. She had to keep up her own magical shield or she risked being burnt to a crisp. The wards had been elegantly designed and, she suspected, set deliberately to target her – or, more accurately, one such as her.

She watched the sobbing form of Samarin on the floor, her body alternating between writhing and clasping tight in a vain attempt to make the pain that racked her body go away. She had almost thrown a shield around the Fal'Gar woman, as Saliana needed her alive. That had to be the cleverest part of Cliphine's trap; or maybe it had been a creation of the mages who designed the wards. Had she followed her imperative to protect Samarin, the wards would have overwhelmed her. She would never have been able to keep two shields around different people under the barrage of the searing white light. She just had to hope she had guessed right and that Cliphine's fundamental kindness had trumped her ruthlessness. That or the Lady of the Crystal Ships felt some guilt for the penance she had inflicted on the Fal'Gar.

Saliana reached for the fourth ward in the ceiling with her mind. The closing of the first three had reduced the wave of power assaulting her, but that was more than offset by the exhaustion wrenching at her. She shut off the fourth and screamed.

Blue lightning crackled across the floor, slamming into her from three sides. She should have known it would not be that easy. She collapsed to one knee as lightning coursed into her. She looked up at the stairs where Kyrian was still seemingly unaffected by the blaze of magic coursing around the vast chamber. The Grey Folk lad had collapsed on the step behind him, his face white with terror. Kyrian watched her, his eyes questioning. He looked at her, and seemed about to move. She held up her hand to stop him. There was nothing he could do, and it was pointless for him to suffer for no reason.

Saliana struggled back to her feet, as blue lightning slammed into her. It became stronger, ricocheting around the chamber. The attack was increasing rather than decreasing. Saliana cursed in the ancient tongue, her face riven with rage and frustration. The white light of the floor continued to tear at her shield, seeking a way through. Saliana caught a bounce of blue lightning as it arrowed towards the stairs, deflecting it with a purple whip of light. It cascaded down the wall and hit the floor. She hoped it would dissipate, but instead it split, bouncing again, ramming into her shield as it continued its murderous path. The flashes of blue continued to build, splitting and merging, new ones flying unbidden from the wall. She had to stop this soon or it risked becoming exponential.

The lightning reverberated from the wall with the door arched over her and shot straight for Kyrian and Rayllor. She could not stop it; she was doing too much else. The Grey Folk boy's hands flung up, involuntarily creating a shield of bubbling orange light in front of him and Kyrian. The bolt hit it, bouncing up at a ninety-degree angle to hit the roof and turn back on itself. It slammed into Sali's own shield. It hit her like a charging huffrin, and she was thrown back against the wall that divided the chamber.

It made no sense, she thought, as she fought off more bolts. There was no way the boy was strong enough to stop it. It had flattened her so it should have cut through his magic with ease.

She realized her mistake. She had thought the magic was exponential, but magic was not exponential. Magic could not create magic: it was finite; in some places even scarce. How was it building in here?

"Cliphine, you cunning bitch." She gave her enemy a grudging smile of approval, though in truth the credit lay with the four mages who had designed this trap rather than the Lady of the Crystal Ships.

She looked up at the wall of the giant cave, her eyes stretching up across its surface to the ceiling. A glamour; it had to be. The bolts of energy continued to thud into her, the blaze from the floor unabated. She continued almost absentmindedly to deal with the incoming assault, which slammed unrelentingly into the glowing purple shield of energy that now surrounded her.

"How had her mages done it?" the Slayer mused out loud to herself.

A glamour was normally cast on the mages themself, so they could adjust their appearance. It could be maintained almost indefinitely with a relatively small expenditure of energy. To cast it on another thing or person would require you to stay close by to constantly feed power into it to prevent the glamour from fading and eventually dissipating. She was fairly certain that there was no Gar mage present, hiding quietly around a corner. The Syn'Dion'Gar might be a long-lived and patient people, but she doubted one of them would be willing to sit on the steppes for years doing nothing but maintaining an illusion.

The only explanation was that the Gar mages had somehow found a way of binding the glamour to an item, in the same way that the protective ward was bound to the devices in the floor and ceiling. Was that even possible? she wondered, batting away another barrage of attacks. She needed to work it out, and quickly; she was getting very tired.

A thought occurred to her, and Sali's gaze turned to the crystal coffin resting on the stone bier. *Oh, Cliphine, you cynical old hag*, she thought. *Could you really be that nasty?* For a moment she hoped so; it was going to be terrible if she was wrong.

She flung out her hand in the direction of the crystal coffin. Though the magic came from her voice not from her hand, the movement was more a declaration than a necessity. She let out a banshee wail that continued to climb, moving outside the hearing range of Kyrian on the stairs, still cowering behind Rayllor's shield. The Gar were not so lucky. The piercing sound whistled and screamed in their heads; better hearing was not an advantage today.

She found the correct modulation, using wizardry to amplify her voice. She used her hand to direct the sound wave, creating a focused blast. It shattered the coffin in two, splitting it across the stone bier on which it sat. The braziers of purple light went out, and the blue light that sprayed across the wall and door that guarded the tomb became dark. The white light blazing up from the floor continued. Sali cursed; she could feel her energy starting to ebb. She reached for the last four wards, painstakingly turning them off, so focused on the task that she could not see the chamber changing around her as the glamour dissipated. With the last of her energy, she switched off the final ward and collapsed to the flagstones, and the world went dark.

CHAPTER TWENTY-EIGHT — FAMILY

S aliana awoke to find someone shaking her shoulder. She opened her eyes and shrieked. "I'm blind!"

"Well, if you are, so are the rest of us," observed Kyrian sardonically.

The voice came from her right side, just above her. She reached out, feeling her way up until she felt a rough slab-like hand. Kyrian's hand. She had never welcomed someone's touch so much.

"I'm not blind?" she queried.

"We are in a cave with no light, and it seems none of us thought to bring anything to light a flame," he said.

"It's just dark?" she asked.

Usually there was some light, the barest hint that her eyes could use to see. In the total pitch black even her Gar blood could not help her.

"Did you hit your head?" he asked with a grin she could not see.

She gave him a foul look, which was fairly pointless given neither could see the other.

"Can you get back to the steps?" she asked.

"Well, I crawled to find you from them, which, with the benefit of hindsight, was fairly stupid, as I have no idea of how to get back," he replied.

"Great," Saliana grunted. "Samarin? Are you out there?"

"I'm here," came a weak whisper.

"Rayllor?"

The Grey Folk youth answered with a gold ball of light. He was sat on the lowest step of the stairs. Marvelling at what he had created, surprise and excitement lit his face as much as the golden light. The light from it bounced off the shining crystal of the walls, radiating across the lower part of the chamber.

"Neat trick," Sali observed.

She pushed herself to her feet. She took a breath and then, using both hands, palms facing each other, she performed a twisting motion. A ball of white light started to grow between her palms. She shifted them apart as it slowly got larger. When it was three times the size of her head, she removed her upper hand and used the lower hand to toss it up into the air. It floated in front of her face. The slightest bobbing motion could be observed, if one wanted to risk the pain of staring into the piercing light. Saliana swept her hand in front of it in a cutting motion. The ball split into three balls of equal size, which floated in the air. Beads of sweat were now running down her face. With a flick of a finger on her right hand, she sent one flying up to the ceiling. She sent the second flying up to the ceiling with a flick of her the finger on her left hand. The third she shifted so it hovered above the dark doors in the wall that split the chamber.

Light blazed across the chamber, so all the alcoves and crevices were visible. It was helped by the crystalline structure of most of the chamber that had now been revealed with the dispelling of the glamour. That was why the magic had bounced back. The crystal that the Syn'Dion'Gar used to build their ships could be enhanced with magic – that was what allowed the ships to sail below the oceans controlled by their mages. Here they had used it to reflect the magic, somehow creating a special resonance chamber to ensure that the magic was not diminished when it impacted against the crystal. It had created an impression of exponential power as more power was fed into the room and none left it. The glamour itself had come from the coffin, somehow bound into it.

Sali looked at Kyrian and gave a smile. But the smile disappeared as her stomach heaved and she vomited across the floor.

"That's what you get for showing off," grinned Kyrian.

She wiped her mouth clean on the back of her hand and straightened up, then bent over again as she heaved up her guts one more time.

"Take it easy," Kyrian suggested, his tone more mocking than concerned.

"Where is she?" Samarin's voice was timid.

She looked exhausted, her face grey and drawn, but she seemed to have no injury. Kyrian took in her appearance. It made no sense that she had been wrapped in burning white light, yet seemed not to have been physically harmed. However, the mental torment she had experienced was clear on her face.

"Who?" demanded Kyrian. He would ask why she was alive later.

"Fenice," she said quietly, pointing at the shattered coffin. She moved slowly towards it, gripping her chest at the effort.

Kyrian reconsidered his assessment. The energies that had racked her body had clearly had some effect.

"Her body was in there," Samarin said with certainty.

Kyrian looked in the remnants of the crystal coffin. Its opaque outer shell meant that nothing could have been seen from the outside until it was split in half. Now they could see either end from the riven centre. It was empty: no bones, no dust, no scrap of clothing, nothing to indicate it had ever contained anything, let alone a body.

"Nothing in here," Kyrian said with a shrug.

"Where is she?" Samarin was in tears. "She's been stolen."

"Samarin, she was never there," Saliana observed a touch coldly.

The Fal'Gar looked at the Slayer, her brain seemingly incapable of processing what she was hearing.

"Never?" she whispered.

"Never," Sali replied quietly.

"Six hundred years." It started as shocked quiet and ended in a raging scream. "More than six hundred years!" Samarin screamed again.

"What's the problem?" asked Kyrian quietly to Sali.

He watched as the Fal'Gar raged around the room in a very un-Garlike fashion, kicking the few things that would not hurt in the predominantly stone structure.

"For more than six hundred years the Fal'Gar have guarded the tomb of Fenice KalCliphine," said Sali quietly. "Their duty and their punishment. And yet she was never here."

Kyrian nodded. "So, what was the magic here to protect?"

"There is an army beyond those doors, an army of dead Fal'Gar," she explained.

"So, it was to imprison the army?"

"I think so," she replied.

"Why did she not do that on Syndion? There was no protection against us entering the tomb there?" he asked.

"We needed the word of power to open the doors," Saliana told him.

"And you had it, Sali, you as always, but then the word opened the door; here the word tried to kill us," he countered.

"I'm not sure: those behind the doors are not loyal to Cliphine, but those on Syndion are," she suggested.

Secretly, Saliana feared another possibility: that Cliphine had constructed this all as a trap for her. A desperate attempt to kill her. That there was nothing beyond the doors. She reached out with her mind, and the power of the witch so recently rediscovered flooded through her. Dark compared to the light of magic, but warm and protecting in comparison with the sharpness of wizardry. To experience both was to feel complete in a way she knew no other could really imagine. They were there – she could feel their restless bones – Salvarus and his army.

"Say the word," Saliana instructed Samarin.

The Fal'Gar looked at her as if the Slayer was crazy.

"You think that's wise?" queried Kyrian, though he appeared more amused than fearful.

"Do it," barked the Mistress of the Slayers.

Samarin was too weary to argue. She mumbled the word, but nothing happened.

"Maybe if you tried a little louder," advised Kyrian with a grin.

"Shut up," snapped Saliana peevishly.

That made Kyrian grin even more.

Sali reached out, trying to feel the magic in the room, particularly that which imbued the wall. She could feel the natural background power all around her, so familiar to her now that she rarely consciously appreciated it. It was more as if it was at a low level or there was an absence she would notice. She had never felt magic to be entirely absent, even in Las Ma where it was famously thin. Not surprisingly, Cliphine had chosen a magic-rich environment for the tomb to magnify the deadly effect of her trap. The magic was still present; Saliana could feel it seething through the air and the rock. It danced through the wall ahead of her, but the bound spell, which controlled the door and had very nearly killed her, was gone.

"The magic that operates the door is gone," she observed to Kyrian.

"And you can't replicate the effect?" he queried.

"I'm shattered."

He nodded politely; it was true that Saliana looked drained, sunken eyes ringed with black shadows, her skin stretched tight over her high cheekbones.

"Rayllor, you think you can do it?" He turned to the Gar now sitting tired on the steps.

"I can try," he offered in faltering Nerlinean.

The Grey Folk youth stood up and walked to the door. He reached out with his hand, using magic to draw the doors towards him. Nothing happened. He stopped, looking shamefaced at the Slayers.

"Try the other way," offered Saliana, miming the action with her hand in case he did not understand.

Rayllor redoubled his efforts. His hand stretched out and he pushed his magic forward, and the great stone doors shuddered, sending a thin shower of dust spraying across the floor.

"I'm sorry," he declared in his own tongue and sank to the floor, sweating.

"It's locked," observed Kyrian.

Saliana looked at him quizzically.

"You bring your lockpicks, bard?" He shot a grin at her, remembering the first time they had met.

"I have them," she replied, clearly not sharing his amusement. "But I doubt they'll be big enough for whatever lock that thing has. Besides, do you see a keyhole?"

Kyrian walked forward, giving Rayllor a reassuring tap on his shoulder as he stepped past the tired mage. He stood close to the door, staring at the split where the two double doors met. The gap between the two great stone monolithic panels was so tight as to be almost imperceptible. The wrestler ran his fingers along the line. The Gar were taller than humans – taller than him in most cases, as he was not short. He could see no indication of a bolt or a latch, but the gap was tight and with no light coming from the chamber on the other side, he doubted he would be able to see it anyway.

Taller than him, he mused.

He reached up to slightly above his head and felt around. Three holes at what would be Gar head height, just above his own. Calling them holes was being generous; they were small circular indentations in the rock. Kyrian put the ends of his three thick fingers on the holes. They were almost too big; the holes had been designed with the daintier fingers of the Gar in mind. Kyrian gave them a push. There was a click, and the recesses pushed inwards further.

Kyrian glanced cautiously at Saliana. He knew the next move was to turn it, but would it unlock the door or take his fingers off? Looking to Sali for reassurance, all he got was an uncertain shrug in return. He turned his hand sunwise, gritting his teeth. There was another click, and he could feel a lever move. He continued to turn his hand until he thought he had rotated the lever over and unlatched the door. He gave it a push, putting his shoulder behind it, expecting it to be a lot of mass to move. It swung in easier than he expected – good hinges, he thought – though it still needed some heft behind it to get it moving. Light spilled into the room from Saliana's balls of magic illumination, catching glints on metal.

He looked back to see Saliana inspecting the door.

"What's up?" he demanded.

"More a latch than a lock," she said, as if confirming his suspicion.

"Still found it," he said, slightly offended at the lack of appreciation for his efforts.

Sali walked over to the other door and inspected the handle that Kyrian had turned. She seemed uninterested in the yawning darkness beyond. Only a small bar of light had spilled into the room.

"I suppose it's a lock of sorts," she conceded grudgingly. "The system is buried in the rock and there is no countervailing system on this side."

Kyrian looked at her slightly perplexed.

"The door can only be opened from the outside."

"So, it's a prison?" he peered nervously into the dark. "What's in here?"

"Shall I show you?" Sali offered with a wicked grin.

She reached out her hand, stretching back into the antechamber that they had just left. She plucked two of the illuminated globes and drew them through the air to her. They stopped, bobbing either side of her shoulders. The outer chamber dimmed behind them as the single remaining sphere struggled to light the whole room. Shadows danced across the newly entered chamber, and light spilled across the floor, where white-wrapped bodies lay in neat ranks either side of a central path framed by two rows of columns. The light had caught on shards of alcidide armour strewn in scales across the floor of the tomb.

Saliana flung out her hands and the two balls of light sped across the hall rising to perhaps the twice the height of a man, until they stopped at the far end of the chamber. They rested either side of a stone throne carved out of the rock wall of the chamber itself. A series of four wide steps rose from the floor up to the rock-cut chair. On the throne rested a withered corpse, wrapped in dry grey flesh. A suit of shining alcidide with an ornate helmet enclosed it, a scimitar resting across his knees.

"Who is that?" Kyrian pointed down the hall at the warlord seated on his throne.

"Salvarus, Emperor of Fal'Dath, Dumech'Di'Fal'Gar," breathed Samarin quietly behind him.

Kyrian turned back to look at Samarin.

"I would like to know how you are so unscathed, given what I saw," he asked of the Fal'Gar woman.

"The trap was for me, not her. The magic that tortured her was to dissuade her from her actions, not to kill her. Had I not been present, chances are it would have let her escape to the stairs or simply the word would not have worked," muttered Sali, moving past the pair. She seemed absentminded, more focused on the throne at the end of the hall than their conversation.

So, we were tormented by magic because a woman from legend wanted to kill you, Saliana, thought Kyrian, but he chose not to say it.

He watched Sali's back as she strode down the hall, Samarin scampering after her. Kyrian let out a big sigh. Rayllor came up next to him and said something in the tongue of his people. The wrestler nodded wearily in agreement, not that he had any idea what the young Gar had just said.

Sali came to a stop at the bottom of the steps and looked up at the enthroned figure, just above her. She could not suppress the feelings that washed over her. Sadness, love, anger, fond memories that she was sure were not hers. She could feel the power of the Gift thundering through her. So like the magic that shared her body, but yet so different. They seemed to flow in two perfect separate streams within her, fearful that they might touch. Her confidence with magic was now fully realized or returned. She was not sure about the Gift; witchcraft was something new to her. Memories of how to use it flooded back; very ancient memories. She reached out, searching for the lingering spirit of the dead, doing it the way Dryana had described it.

"Salvarus," she pulsed in her mind, reaching out to the body in front of her.

There was no response, but she felt his mind seething, a raging torrent of pent-up power. She remembered when Dryana had used her to channel power during the battle on Syndion. She had got a moment of insight into the cold minds of the five undead commanders of the Gar. In comparison to what she felt from Salvarus, they had been warm and welcoming.

"Salvarus," Sali's mind demanded again. She felt a wall of hatred reflecting back. No response in her mind, no flicker from the corpse-statue.

"He will not hear you," Samarin said quietly.

Sali looked at the Fal'Gar witch.

"You are human," she explained. "And a Kanath to boot. It was Saska the Kanath High King who struck him down. Salvarus had little time for other races, especially Men. He had little enough time for most of the Gar except his own people. Whatever fear he had of your people, he lost when Elian the Great died."

"And yet he sits here imprisoned even in death," observed the Slayer coldly.

"You need Dryana," beamed Kyrian walking up behind them. "There were only a couple of thousand of them here, and she raised more than twice that on Syndion."

"Impossible," declared Samarin.

"You don't think you could do it?" Kyrian's tone was mocking.

"I don't know," she replied haltingly, unsure, her eyes cast down. Then she looked up, certainty filling her eyes. "Yes, I could do it. Should I show you?"

"No!" Sali's single word of command cut across the argument. "They are mine."

"These are not the Gar of Syndion. They will not come for a human, even for one with Gar blood," Samarin said with a hard smile.

"Salvarus," Sali's voice railed into all their minds, pushing with angry force. "You will do as I command."

"Powerful witch?" came the cold pulsating voice in all their minds. "You should have taken the descendant of my cousin up on her offer. Maybe I would leave my sleep for one of my own blood, no matter how thinned by time it has become, but not for a human such as you. Your power is tremendous, it screams at me, tears at me, but I am not Davyn KalEron. I am not a weak-minded fool to be commanded by the likes of you. I have centuries of hatred of your kind to block you out."

Davyn KalEron. Sali picked the name out from the undead Dumech's angry response. That was what Cliphine had called the undead general who had commanded the Gar of Syndion. How did he know that? What was it Dryana had once said? The dead cannot keep their secrets from a witch. Maybe it worked both ways. Maybe an undead as ancient, as powerful and as angry as Salvarus could see into her mind. She let out a cold laugh.

"Look again," Sali almost purred. "See what I am, Salvarus of Fal'Dath."

PRINCE OF SLAYERS

She felt his mind washing through her. Memories of her childhood came rushing back, of her parents, or more accurately the people she realized now had taken her in. Images of her being entrusted to them as a child, barely more than a baby, snatches of the past that she could never have remembered without the undead Salvarus rifling her mind. Then he was past them, back to older memories, things old and then ancient. They came to her sporadically in no particular order, events out of kilter, no sequence, no sense. Of her, but not her, riding on the steppe with her parents on the back of an oradar. A memory of drowning constantly, then of savage death upon death. Standing by the anvil in a smithy, hammer slamming again and again as he shaped the sword. She was him, but she did not know how. She grabbed at her power, both blue and grey. Witch and wizard combined in her, and she took hold of both streams and pulled them together. She pushed the undead Salvarus from her mind, shutting him out. She went further, stripping out the confusion in her mind, sorting memory after memory, life after life.

Now it made sense. Now she knew who she was for certain. She was Sali, she was Ara, she was so much more.

She flung out her arms as magic coursed across the chamber. The spells that Gar mages had entwined in the walls were reinvigorated. Light blazed around the arches of the chamber. The two globes that had previously provided illumination winked out of existence, surplus to requirements. A light wind conjured from nowhere blew across the chamber, lifting away the layer of grey dust accumulated on the white-shrouded corpses. The bodies started to shift. Slowly, the white wrappings were pushed away and the army of dead Fal'Gar started to rise to their feet. They had long lost their skin, being only bones now animated by witchcraft, with alcidide blades clutched in hands. Their armour, their bows, their spears – the wood, the bone and leather had long since rotted away. Scales of alcidide, arrowheads and spear points sparkled across the floor.

Rayllor's face was riven with fear. He yanked free his knife, though little good it would do him against the numbers that surrounded them. Kyrian patted him gently on the arm as if he might calm him.

"Is this you?" he demanded of Samarin.

She shook her head.

"Him?" he asked, nodding to the unmoving corpse in the chair. Kyrian loosed his flail from his belt. His wariness was starting to match Rayllor's building terror.

"It's her." Samarin spat the words, her eyes focused on Sali.

"Sali is a mage; she can't do this," Kyrian said, confused.

"Look around you, Kyrian," Samarin snapped back.

There was a scraping sound from above. Three of them looked up, though Saliana's eyes remained locked on Salvarus. There were cave-like openings high along either side of the chamber, only visible now after Saliana had restored the lights. Samarin had not really registered them on her first visit, five years before. Had she seen them she would have simply dismissed them as arches to support the roof. Skeletal beasts were climbing out of them. On first glance they looked like giant spiders and insects. The lack of flesh on their bones disguised what they were on first glance.

"Oradar," breathed Samarin. "They're cavalry."

The skeletal cats were slowly climbing down the outer walls of the chamber.

"You know who I am," Sali pulsed her thought into Salvarus's mind.

It was not a question.

"We have met before," she declared.

420

The undead dumech rose from his throne, his scimitar sweeping around to rest at his side. He loomed over Sali.

"I once called you daughter," the voice rang in all their heads.

"They are both long dead," said Sali coldly.

"She should have told me what you are," the warlord pulsed. He sounded wistful.

"Lied to by Cliphine," mused the Mistress of the Slayers. "That is among the least of her crimes against you."

"I should kill you," the warlord declared.

"Sit quiet here, Salvarus of Fal'Dath. I have what I came for," she replied.

She turned around, seemingly unconcerned by the armed warlord behind her. She nearly tripped over the kneeling form of Samarin. Sali bit back a curse and gave the Gar a harsh gaze. With her head bowed, Samarin could not really appreciate it.

"My Empress, Kinhilchazadan," she whispered.

"Get up, Samarin," Sali barked angrily. "You have no idea what you are talking about."

Saliana strode down the chamber back the way she had come. Rayllor and Samarin both raced to keep up. The skeletal figures of two thousand long-dead Fal'Gar and their oradar mounts moved in formation, following the Mistress of the Slayers through the doors.

Kyrian hefted his flail, watching the blazing figure in the glory of alcidide armour, helm and scimitar. Would he attack, he wondered? The creature seemed to be considering something. The Slayer slowly backed away, being careful not to take his eyes from the undead warrior, but also not to lose his footing as he made his way down the steps.

He stopped when he reached the floor of the chamber and looked back. He remembered the blazing light in the eyes of the five commanders on Syndion, but there was nothing similar in Salvarus's appearance. Had he not seen him stand and heard his voice in his head, Kyrian would have simply dismissed him as what he was: the corpse of a long-dead ruler.

"You not coming then?" the Slayer offered with a cheeky grin.

The head swivelled as if the long since decayed eyes were focusing on him.

Kyrian swallowed, briefly regretting his comment.

Salvarus turned and seated himself back on his throne, the scimitar returned to its resting place on his knees.

Kyrian stood looking at him for a number of minutes, waiting for something to happen. Then he thrust his flail back in his belt. He looked around him as the last of the undead Fal'Gar were filing out of the chamber. They had moved surprisingly fast given their numbers, he mused, or had he stared at the dead warrior longer than he had realized.

With a last glance at the seated warrior, Kyrian walked to the door of the chamber now empty of everyone except the pair.

"I couldn't do it," the voice of Salvarus pulsed in Kyrian's mind.

He stopped and looked back. The figure on the throne hadn't moved. Kyrian turned to leave.

"You understand? I loved both my daughters. I could not kill her." Salvarus' tone was oddly pleading, as if asking for forgiveness. It contrasted with his previous cold hard voice.

Was it just in his head? wondered Kyrian. Had he just imagined the difference in tone? Had he given it to the words?

"You will have to do it, no matter how much you love her. You must kill her," the voice rasped in Kyrian's mind.

Kyrian said nothing; thought nothing. He did not look back over his shoulder, he simply stepped through the doorway. The light winked out and the doors groaned shut behind him, leaving the long-dead Emperor of Fal'Dath alone in the dark of his tomb.

Chapter Twenty-Nine – A Deal

The Nerlinean man swore as his basket of reddish-pink fruit tumbled across the alleyway. Looking around to see who had barged into him, he saw a lithe pale-skinned girl with pitch-black hair already disappearing down the street.

"Bloody foreigners. Bloody Kanath," he muttered. The city was infested with them.

He turned around, coming to face a terrifying figure, stick thin, emaciated tight flesh, a faded leathery yellow in complexion so different to the soft light brown skin of his own face. He did not know what the creature was, but he shrank away from it in fear. Slinker Slayer tried his best polite smile. The effect of the Tancree's leering grin was not the reassurance that Slinker had intended. The young porter scrambled backwards, nearly knocking over a market stall behind him in his panic.

PRINCE OF SLAYERS

Slinker did not see it. He had already moved on, jostling down the crowded street, trying to keep up with the disappearing figure of Dryana. The four Company of Slayers soldiers that were supposed to protect her were trailing him rather than her, so were not much use in their assigned task. With the exception of the fruit vendor she had upended without realizing, she was able to slip between the people in the crowded street in a way that Slinker and his armoured companions could not. The Tancree had expected the crowds to melt away in the face of a group of obviously armed soldiers – a rarity in the streets of a Nerlinean city. It seemed that the opposite was true. Maybe they only moved for those in the armour of the Imperial Legions.

As she reached the crossroads, Dryana was completely unaware that her colleague and their guards were failing to keep up. She was too focused on her task to be concerned for them. They had been back in Port Ren for three days now and the anger that had been boiling since the attack in Mahendra had not even dropped to a simmer. She knew it was probably affecting her judgement, but she was past caring.

She turned left down the smaller side street, still wide enough for two huffrin-drawn carts to pass side by side. It was quieter than the main street, but far from empty of people. Her appearance was drawing wary gazes from the others. There had been a change, almost imperceptible to a Kanath but more noticeable to a Nerlinean. Nerlinean dress had given way to the kimonos of Amalanders. Small changes in architecture and artistry hinted at the switching of cultures. Dryana did not notice as she moved deeper into the Amaland district of Port Ren. She was searching for the street of the herbalists, although it wasn't called that.

In Kangorn there was only one such street and it bore the name of its resident merchants, but in Port Ren there were several. For all the Nerlinean Empire's multi-ethnic, multicultural nature, it was remarkable how separate some of its cultures could remain. The Amalanders, perhaps of all the empire's peoples, had successfully maintained their distinct identity. Living on a large island off the coast of the Nerlinean mainland helped. Another major factor was their refusal to acknowledge that they were even part of the empire. Rather, the Hadanan of Amaland, the island's ruler, simply happened to be the same person as the Emperor of Nerlinea. The complicated and hierarchical nature of Amaland society meant that while the Hadanan of Amaland had more power than the Emperor of Nerlinea in theory, in practice the result could be very different. The Hadanan was considered a god by the Amalanders, which would seemingly grant the incumbent supreme power. However, in practice, this godlike authority was dissipated by a series of political and military structures that circumscribed the Hadanan's authority, such that its weaker incumbents could be reduced to an almost entirely ceremonial role; more a chief priest than a ruling monarch. Nyandar, like many of the more muscular Emperors of Nerlinea, would no doubt clash with the Lords of Amaland at some point, but for now he had been largely uninterested in his island possession.

The insular nature of Amalanders did not mean that they were absent from elsewhere in the empire. They were a common sight in the ports of the east coast, but tended to live in close-knit communities, building up domination of a small portion of the city, which would become the Amalander Quarter. Port Ren had the largest such area in all the eastern ports – indeed in the whole of Nerlinea.

Dryana ducked down another street and then turned right into a wide boulevard. This one was lined with trees, which were looking decidedly worse for the searing heat and absence of water in which they found themselves. The two rows of trees had been planted to provide shade but were failing in that regard. Dryana looked back, suddenly remembering that

Slinker and her guards were supposed to be with her. They appeared around the corner behind her at a jog. Seeing her waiting they slowed to a walk and progressed up the avenue.

"Taking your time," she commented hotly. Sweat coursed down her face as the boiling sun beat down on them. Irritability had now joined her seething anger.

Slinker came to a stop next to her. He was breathing hard.

"Are you okay?" she asked, not sounding particularly concerned.

"Well, I'm old and it's really hot," he shot back. "You are not supposed to rush off."

"I'm not a child," she pouted, sounding younger than she was.

That and the smile of victory he gave her only annoyed her more.

"Oh, come on, we need to speak to this idiot," she declared.

She walked further down the street. As she approached, the smell of herbs wafted towards her. She fought down the urge to sneeze. The whole boulevard had been turned over to Amaland herbalists, but its width meant that it largely avoided the complicated stench that normally pervaded such streets. Closer to the shop, the telltale smell picked at her nose and eyes.

She stepped forward and rapped on the door. She received no response.

Slinker moved next to her and tried the handle, and the door swung inwards.

"It's a shop," he offered with a shrug.

Two guards muscled past Dryana, making cursory apologies. Slinker and Dryana followed them into the cool darkness of the shop, with the remaining two soldiers bringing up the rear. Dryana's eyes adjusted to the gloom of the shop. The paper shutters over the windows were closed and stained with brown patches, preventing much light coming in. A single copper brazier hung to one side of the shop from a long chain. It cast a stuttering orange glow across the room. A thin haze of smoke and steam filled the air, from various potion cauldrons that were simmering on low burners against one wall. Black stains of carbon marked the once white walls and Dryana marvelled that the place had not burnt to the ground long ago. A cloying collection of sharp smells joined the haze in attacking their senses: eyes watered and noses stung.

At the far end of the shop was a long narrow bar, obstructing the way to a door into a back room. An older Amaland man sat at a chair, such that his face barely poked across the bar. He was looking at them with unconcealed annoyance. Standing next to him was a muscular figure, heavily built; fat would have been a better word. There was a confidence about him that suggested he knew how to fight. A wrestler or a pit fighter, Dryana speculated. Did the Amalanders even have pit fighters? He squeezed his considerable form through the small gap at one end. He took position in front of them, dropping to a low fighting crouch. A wrestling stance, if an odd one, was Dryana's opinion – and given who her brother was, she knew better than most. The Slayer soldiers reached for their swords.

"No," declared the older man behind the counter, standing up.

The wrestler grunted acknowledgement, but did not change position or change his stance.

"You should not be here," the man spat angrily at Dryana.

The witch assessed the man. Shinmaku Chul was in his fifties, his hair still black through the use of dye. His features were sharp, with shrewd eyes penetrating through the gloom. His blue kimono was tied tight with a band of grey cloth to hold it in place. She had sent him messages each day for three days. He had brought her here by not responding to them.

"You've been ignoring my messages," she shot back. "Is that any way to treat your best supplier?"

The Amalander watched her warily. Chul was aware of the relative balance of forces in the room. Despite his obvious anger at the Slayers' presence, he knew he would need to choose his words carefully. Dryana started to circle the room, prodding at herbs. She lifted a ladle from one of the pots and took a sniff. Her nose wrinkled in discomfort, and she plopped it back.

"If the four soldiers and a Tancree war mage aren't intimidating me, a thin woman fingering my stock is hardly going to make much difference," the shopkeeper observed.

Dryana looked at him, trying and failing to read what he was thinking. She let out a sigh of frustration. "Did you get my messages?" she demanded. She sounded to herself more petulant than commanding, which annoyed her.

"Yes," came the cold response.

"All of them?"

"Yes," he replied.

"And you ignored them," she stated.

That garnered no response. He continued to look at her, his face betraying nothing.

She leant on the counter, staring into the shopkeeper's face, ignoring the giant bodyguard standing a short move away from her. Her head swung gently side to side in front of his face like a predator assessing its prey. All she got back was a blank, perhaps slightly wary, look.

"And you ignored them?"

"It was on my list to get to." The creep of the edges of his mouth suggested he was mocking her.

Dryana fought down the urge to slap him. This was not going to be solved by intimidation. She pushed herself away from the wooden bar between them and took a couple of steps back. The mood in the room seemed to cool, if only slightly. None of the fighters relaxed. Chul did not release his grip on the wooden cudgel concealed beneath the counter. He let out the breath he had been holding very gently – keen not to even hint at the fear he was feeling.

"I would have contacted you. You should not be here," he said quietly.

Dryana looked at him, continuing to assess. "When?" she asked.

"When the time was right," he replied.

"And you get to decide that?" she asked.

He shrugged, not wishing to have that particular argument.

She said nothing, waiting for an answer, letting the time stretch in front of them.

"You should not have come here," he announced, breaking the silence. "You are known, but your relationship with me is not. You have put me in danger."

Dryana kept the predatory face fixed on him. She did not care, she declared in her mind, but she was also annoyed. She had not even considered that when she had come bursting into his shop.

Chul had been the trader who had arranged the shipment of drun to Amaland. The shipment that, as far as she was aware, Fatboy did not know about. His network went far beyond his role as a herbalist. Chul, unlike the double-crossing Nerlinean, had paid on time and in full. She cursed herself for treating him as if Fatboy's betrayal somehow covered the Amalander as well.

"Maybe I am just here to buy a love potion?" she offered.

"I doubt very much someone as beautiful as you would need such a thing," he replied, giving the barest of smiles.

She grinned at the compliment.

"You still should not have come?" he observed.

"Well, we are here now. I suppose we can discuss business," Dryana said.

"What business is that? Drun? You have none, not until next year. Hardly a reason to demand a meeting now. Besides, your drun trade is done. Lan Xian has locked you out of the distribution in the coastal cities."

"How do you know?" Dryana asked.

"Mister Lan has been very vocal: no one is to do business with you – not drun, not legal goods, not livestock, not slaves," he replied.

"We don't trade slaves," Dryana muttered.

Chul shrugged; that was beside the point.

"No one will deal with you, sell to you, buy from you or *lend to you*." He emphasized the last.

"We are the Company of Slayers," her voice rang out in challenge.

"In Kangorn and Syndion maybe, even in Rastindor and the western ports perhaps, but not here in Port Ren. Here you are just merchants. The same is true in the other eastern ports, and certainly not in Halfnight."

"But Xian doesn't have the power..." Dryana stopped in mid-sentence, the name 'Halfnight' sinking in. A western port, not an eastern one, the port completely controlled by the Pandus family.

"It's not Xian, it's the Pandus?"

Chul nodded in confirmation.

"The Pandus does not have that power," she replied, but she did not sound sure.

The Amalander smiled at that but said nothing.

"They have threatened you?" she asked.

Chul laughed. "I am nothing to Xian and less than that to the Pandus. I doubt it would even have occurred to them. That was before you came barging into my shop, of course."

431

"Why now? Why move now?" Dryana mused to herself.

"Because you are exposed," Chul offered, answering the question despite its rhetorical nature.

"What would you know of it, shopkeeper?" she barked harshly.

Slinker gave her a hard look and a nod of disapproval.

"Sorry," she snapped.

Chul looked unoffended by Dryana's burst of petulance. "You would not have done a deal with me had I been a simple herbalist."

"So, you are still open to a deal?" the Slayer witch replied.

"You have no deal to do," he replied a touch sadly. "Maybe next autumn when you have dung and drun to trade. If you last that long."

"And you would risk the displeasure of Xian and the Pandus?" she asked.

"It is a year away," shrugged Chul. "If you are still here in a year, we can assess things then."

"You don't think we will be in control of the supply of the solinad dung the empire needs," she replied.

"You are not a merchant are you, war mage?" Chul changed the subject, addressing Slinker.

"No," answered Slinker cautiously. "I provide strength of arms, and strength in magic. Dryana here is the businesswoman."

Chul nodded. "No offence, but it is what I suspected."

"None taken," Slinker replied.

"Xian is telling everyone he has your gold, that you have no money and that no one will lend you any. That is the word on the street. I would suspect the Pandus are saying the same to every merchant, banker and noble," Chul said.

"We have money," Dryana replied through gritted teeth.

"Good for you," Chul said with an encouraging smile, which Dryana found deeply annoying. "But tell me, merchant of the Slayers, with no revenue coming in and money going out on wages, rents, taxes and bribes, how long will that last with no one willing to lend to you?"

Dryana had to concede he had a point. She could get more money from the west, but that would mean going on bended knee to Sali and Kyrian. It would be embarrassing when she had claimed to be self-financing, but that would not stop her doing it. Had the Pandus family assumed that the Slayers' structure was as adversarial as that of the Imperial Pandus Trading Company? She doubted that they had gone to all this trouble to simply fall down on a misassumption about how collegiate the Slayers could be when it was required. No, they would try and sink every ship bringing gold east to finance them. It wasn't a killing strike, it was squeezing the Slayers, weakening them ready for the coup de grace that would come later. She needed to get her gold back from Fatboy and she needed it fast.

"You know so much, Chul. Tell me, why now?" she asked him.

"How should I know? I know Lan Xian and the Pandus only by reputation. I have dealt with their agents, yes, but once or twice removed from the great people themselves."

"What does the street say?"

Chul looked at her cautiously. "Nothing," he said. "Though there was some talk about you Slayers when you first arrived."

"What talk?" she demanded haughtily.

"It was nothing," he said with a shrug.

"Tell me!"

"No one knew who the Company of Slayers were, but there was gossip that you had been enemies of the Pandus on the other side of the Nerlinean Ocean. That you had even killed one of their family. Everyone thought you would be snuffed out in moments. When you weren't, there was speculation. Some speculated that they feared your brother, but that was mainly women, who admired his tendency to walk around with his torso naked," he replied.

"Thank you for that image of my brother," Dryana interjected, pulling a revolted face. "And when I took over, it was because of what I did on Syndion?"

Chul look confused. "What happened on Syndion?"

"It doesn't matter," she snapped.

Scared of her brother's rippling muscles but not her ability to command the dead. This was just idle street talk; people finding reasons to explain things they did not understand for lack of the real facts.

"Of course, there was talk the Company of Slayers was protected," he continued.

Dryana looked at him oddly. "Protected? By who?"

"If it's true, you should know, not me," he laughed.

More idle gossip. She dismissed it.

"We apologize for disturbing you. Thank you for your thoughts." Dryana gave a sweep of her hands, ordering her guards out into the street. Slinker followed them out of the door. Dryana stopped in the doorway and looked back at Chul. He seemed confused by the suddenness with which she had finished the meeting.

"We'll deliver your next shipment in the late spring," she said and disappeared out into the sunlight.

"Spring?" Chul shouted after her. "That's impossible!"

CHAPTER THIRTY – THE TEA HOUSE

In the dark of the alleyway, the three hunkered in a doorway of a small wooden house and tried to look unobtrusive.

"I am not sure you should have come?" observed Slinker quietly to Dryana.

She shot him a filthy look. His comment also caused Balinor to raise his eyebrow.

"I think we need her; there are only three of us," the Prince of Kangorn observed.

"This is Nerlinea: there are no dead bodies for her to raise," Slinker whispered.

"Well, you and Balinor kill some people and we will be fine," she spat angrily.

"Still think we should have brought more troops or some mages," observed Balinor.

"We've had this debate," muttered Slinker.

To death, the Prince of Kangorn thought. They had spent several hours discussing whether they should take more support with them. Slinker had been most insistent it should be just him and two guards. Balinor had insisted he should be one of the guards. Dryana had decided she should be the other. Slinker, having insisted three was enough, now found himself encumbered with two of his colleagues that he not planned to take.

It was Dryana's plan – although to call it a plan was to dignify what she had suggested. Put broadly, she wanted them to stride into the House of the Four Stars, confront Fatboy, and demand their money back. His choice of headquarters had a number of things going for it. Firstly, there was only one way in and one way out, so unless he learned to fly Fatboy wasn't running away or, in his case, waddling. Secondly, it was well known that he kept the top floor for his exclusive use. So should the whole thing degenerate into violence, there should be a relatively limited number of witnesses to complain to the authorities. Not there was much risk of that, given the reputation of the House of the Four Stars and the part of town in which it was located. Slinker had hoped by leaving Dryana behind that the escalation into bloodshed would be avoided. The young woman seemed more focused on killing Fatboy than on retrieving their gold. He wasn't sure why she had taken it quite so personally. Maybe it was Fatboy's involvement in trying to have her killed; the young tended to be upset by such things. So many people had tried to kill Slinker that he had long ago stopped seeing it as anything other than a perverse form of flattery.

"Who's that?" Slinker pointed down the street.

A cloaked figure, hood drawn up, was proceeding down the street in the manner of someone trying to appear unobtrusive. Given that even the nights in Port Ren were warm and that the street was quiet, he stood out immediately. There was something familiar about his gait. Of course: Farmorl, he realized.

The young Slayer agent spotted them and dashed over.

"Gods, boy, could you be less subtle," the Tancree muttered.

"Sorry," Farmorl whispered.

"What are you doing here?" Slinker uttered in an angry whisper.

"I invited him," said Balinor, never taking his eyes off the tea house.

He was taking in each of the five storeys, built of wood and largely open to the air, a wooden rail surrounding the outside of each floor. A central square atrium ran from the ground to the top floor, and a railing protected anyone from falling from the upper floors into the open hole. Small iron braziers hung from the ceiling of each floor, blazing light across each level of the building and out into the small garden that surrounded it on all sides. The place bustled, a contrast with the quiet of the surrounding streets. The floors were packed with shouting and excited people. Balinor doubted that they were drinking tea. A light haze of tobacco smoke, probably laced with drun, emanated from the structure.

"Why did you invite him?" Slinker was keeping his obvious annoyance under control, but it was still clear in his whispered voice.

"We need more people," muttered Balinor.

"This isn't Kangorn: we can't just surround the place and slaughter everyone in it, knowing that the ineffectual local ruler will do nothing about it. We try that here and the Nerlineans will execute the lots of us," Slinker hissed.

"One more won't make a difference," the Prince of Kangorn shot back, ignoring Slinker's jibe at his own rule.

"How is he even here?" Dryana demanded.

Balinor looked sheepish and Slinker gave a grin.

"What do you mean?" Balinor tried to sound innocent.

"He's supposed to be on a ship back from Mahendra with your mage Tanya," Dryana said angrily.

"You mean Tara?" Balinor asked.

Dryana stared daggers at the Prince of Kangorn.

"How is he even here?" she repeated, looking around afraid that she had raised her voice too much.

"I stowed him away," Balinor offered with a shrug.

"You did what?" she wanted to screech but that was hardly an option.

"It was Slinker's idea. He said you really wanted him to come with us," Balinor replied.

Dryana fixed her adopted uncle with a frosty glare. The Tancree shrugged in response.

"I told you what I wanted him to do," she snapped to Balinor.

"Yes, but it was my ship – a Kangorn ship, not a Slayer one. Besides, Slinker said the boy would probably try and swim after us if I didn't help him," declared Balinor.

"Oh, stop arguing you two. What difference does it make? Shall we?" Slinker waved his hand towards the tea house.

"This discussion is not over," hissed Dryana, but it was too late; Balinor was already moving.

The four left the concealment of the shadows and strode down the street towards the tea house. They crossed into a small neatly kept garden. The carefully manicured moss lawn, in the Amaland style, was crossed by a wide gravel path, leading up to the short flight of wooden steps into the lowest floor of the wooden structure.

Balinor led the way, the most imposing of the Slayers in Kyrian's absence, especially when compared to the emaciated Slinker or the tiny Dryana who followed him. Farmorl followed the group, unsure what to expect.

PRINCE OF SLAYERS

The woman of middle years who seemed to act as the establishment's greeter moved to intercept them as they topped the steps. She was dressed now in a yellow housecoat. Dryana recognized her from the first time they had come here. If the woman realized who the Slayers were, she gave no indication. She bustled forward, trying ineffectually to block their path in the wide entranceway. Balinor brushed past just hard enough to push her out of the way and convince her not to interfere. He set off up the stairs, taking them two at a time.

You'll regret that, thought Dryana with an evil smile. She and Slinker had done this climb before, and continued at a more measured pace. Farmorl kept a step behind them, looking around him cautiously.

They passed through the three intervening storeys between the ground floor and the level Fatboy used for his headquarters. It was evening and each floor heaved with workers letting go after a hard day of work. Most were drinking something harder than tea, though it was hard to tell as they used the same porcelain bowls for both tea and rice wine. Dryana surmised this from the raucousness of the patrons, which seemed to increase with each floor. A cloying mix of tobacco and drun smoke permeated the air. At least in this house, the Nerlineans seemed unconcerned about enforcing their laws against hallucinogens. She looked for weapons, but saw nothing but the odd knife thrust into a cloth belt. Most patrons were dressed in loose trousers and shirts: the clothes of Nerlinean workers, not fighters.

Slinker took a moment one floor from the top to take a breath and stared venomously up at the stairway ahead: two more flights to go. Dryana and Farmorl waited with him for a moment, then the three set off again trying to catch up with Balinor.

They reached the last flight of stairs and threw themselves against the inner rail. A heavy-set Nerlinean man came barrelling down the last flight of wooden steps, tumbling head over heels before slamming into the outer railing of the stairway. There was a sickening crunch of wood, and for a moment it looked like it might give way, sending the man out into the void and the four-storey drop below. Instead, he just lay slumped against the railing, conscious, but dazed and bruised by his fall.

"Sorry!" Balinor shouted down the stairs sheepishly.

He had hit the man with a right hook to the stomach as he had reached the top floor, before grabbing the man by the shoulder, sending him flying down the stairs behind him. Now another guard was advancing on him. The Prince of Kangorn drew his sword and pointed it menacingly at the man, who backed off, raising his hands.

Dryana and the others reached the floor and took in the scene. There were more people here than her last visit: twenty in total, including the one that Balinor had just pitched down the stairs. They were dressed in similar clothes to the other patrons: loose-fitting trousers and shirts in soft cloth; no armour of any sort. Most carried blades, short swords or long knives that looked more like cleavers for cutting meat than weapons of war.

Everyone was standing now, though none had drawn their weapons yet. Lan Xian stood by the table in the corner furthest from the stairs, his beefy hands resting on the surface, an angry look on his face. To his left stood the thin-faced man that Dryana now knew worked for the Imperial Pandus Trading Company.

The guard with his hands up glanced over his shoulder, looking for Xian to give him an order. The barest of nods appeared to be enough. His hands dropped to his side, and he pulled from his cloth belt a wickedly sharp, monstrously large cleaver. He gave Balinor an evil grin. The Prince of Kangorn's face was stony as he dropped into a crouch ready to fight.

Slinker's right hand was thrust out. The attacker stopped as he was caught by a magical force, a look of surprise on his face as he struggled against invisible bonds. Then he was pulled into the air: not high – there was the roof to think of, after all – but just high enough that his feet were scrabbling and failing to touch the floor beneath him. The Tancree swept his hand across, and the man went with him. Torn through the air by wizardry, his shins cracked against the wood of the outer rail, leaving the guard hanging out in the open air. His arms and legs were pumping, and his face was a mask of panicked terror. His cleaver went spiralling from his hand, landing with a soft plunk on the moss below.

"We are not killing people yet," warned Dryana, her voice quiet but menacing.

"Shame," said Slinker with a smile.

He levitated the man further out into the air away from the tea house, building speed and rising him upwards in a sweeping angle. Then he flung him back like a pendulum. Slinker threw him through the outer rail of the tea house, sending him crashing through the hardwood and skating across the floor, slamming into tables and chairs as his hapless colleagues desperately flung themselves out of the way. He hit the inner rail, the one that surrounded the inside open atrium, and crashed through it out into a new space of open air. Slinker cursed. The figure was stopped in his plummeting fall and then tossed upwards and onto the deck of the upper floor, landing in a sprawled mess. Dryana thought he had been knocked unconscious but then she heard the small sobs coming from the prone form. She gave Slinker a reproving look.

"Been a while since I did that," he replied with a shrug.

She raised an eyebrow and then turned back to Fatboy.

The gang leader stood in front of them, his corpulent form covered in an unbecoming mass of yellow silk. His eyes were glassy. Dryana's gaze swung to the drun pipe the man had been smoking. It rested on the table in front of him, a small amount of smoke curling upward, before being blown away in the light breeze. Lan Xian's hands were clutching the table in front of him, his knuckles white. His face was angry but in an odd sort of way, as if the effect of the drun meant he could not quite convince his face to show rage. Dryana also noted the thin form of the Pandus representative, in a dark blue robe, slowly shifting himself behind Xian's impressive bulk.

"You owe me money, Xian," declared Dryana. "A lot of money."

The glassiness in his eyes seemed to fade a little and the anger in his face grew.

"Who are you to demand anything of me, girl?" he screamed, and flecks of spittle covered the gap between him and the Slayer.

She eyed him coldly. "You can pay me, Xian, or you can die here. Your choice," she offered harshly.

Fatboy's gaze swept across the men surrounding him. In his mind he had the Slayers heavily outnumbered, but the Pandus representative knew better; he was using Xian's body to shield him against the Slayers.

"Don't even think about it, Xian: you really don't have the advantage of numbers. We will kill half of you before you can blink. And then..." Dryana gave a chillingly evil smile. "And then you will really be in trouble."

"This is Port Ren, woman. You are nothing here," growled Xian. "I have the Pandus behind me."

"Quite literally," observed Dryana with a grin.

Xian looked behind him to see the quietly cowering figure of his patron's representative. He gave the man a look of disgust and turned back.

"You have played too much on reputation," he said, his voice low and menacing.

Here it comes, she thought.

442

"Kill them!" Xian barked to his men.

The words were barely out of his mouth when his bloated mass was lifted into the air. His feet pedalled space. Then he was flung sideways across the stretch of the tea house. He hit a group of four of his men, standing on the opposite side of the top floor. The wooden rail on the side of the building gave way and one of Xian's men was pitched off the side of the tea house, hitting the ground with a sickening crunch as the impact broke his back. Xian ended up on the floor, atop a pile of three of his subordinates.

Slinker stepped forward, his hands slipping into the main glove at the end of his fighting blades. They were worn in pairs, one on each arm. He moved like lightning, faster than any human. He covered the gap to the nearest gang member and slammed the point of the fighting blade up through the soft part behind the chin. The blade appeared out through the top of the hapless man's skull. Slinker wrenched it free, not stopping to check the man's fate. He spun on the next two approaching attackers, his blades whirling as fast as the eye could see. The first blade slashed across the new attacker's throat, and the second blade came in point first, plunging through the temple, carrying on through as Slinker ripped it out of the front of the man's skull.

The next attacker launched himself at the Tancree, barrelling him to the ground. The pair crashed through the wood of tables and chairs as the new opponent raised his cleaver to deliver the killing blow. Red lightning sprang from Slinker's fingers and the man screamed as magic tore at his body. He dropped his weapon and shook uncontrollably, lying prone on top of Slinker. Blood seeped from his eyes and ears and from his mouth. His white trousers and shirt started to turn red, darkening as more blood permeated them. It was as if his skin was no longer capable of holding him together. Slinker rolled the convulsing body off him and stood up. He looked down at the terrified face of the man as his body collapsed in a pool of blood.

He turned to survey the scene. Balinor stood over two dead men, forming a barrier in front of Dryana. Slinker wondered if such protectiveness was necessary anymore. Dryana could hold her own with the short sword she grasped in her hand. Even if her skills with a blade did not match those of the other Slayers, she should be alright against these amateurs.

Xian had got to his feet and scrabbled back to where most of his remaining men stood, on the far side of the room from the Slayers. A few stood closer, eyeing the Slayers warily but unwilling to join the attack. Xian looked pale, as if unsure how to proceed. What Slinker had done to his last opponent had given them pause. The Pandus agent was in the corner nearest Slinker now, trying to become one with the pillar that held up that part of the tea house. He was looking around desperately for an escape route, but on the top of a five-storey building with the only access being the stairs and four armed people blocking the way, there were few options. Farmorl stood at the top of the stairs, his gaze flitting between the fight and the stairway.

"Do we have to kill more of you?" Dryana asked. "Or is six enough?"

"Five," Xian replied, glancing at the bodies in front of him.

"Six," she repeated. "Your friend could not fly; he is dead."

Xian looked about his men, who seemed decidedly unwilling to attack. Loyalty among the criminals only went so far; certainly not past the point of death. Xian looked at the Pandus agent. The glassiness in his eyes had dissipated now, and he seemed to be asking something.

There was a thundering sound, the rumble of feet on wood. People were on the stairs.

"Dryana, we have a problem!" Farmorl shouted.

PRINCE OF SLAYERS

Then he flung himself to the ground. A fireball exploded out into the stairwell, slamming into the roof of the tea house. It scorched and blackened the roof where it dissipated. Farmorl was scooting along on his backside trying to get clear of what was coming.

Balinor ran to the central atrium and looked over the partially broken rail. The floors below were rapidly emptying. It seemed like everyone in the tea house was coming for them. They weren't just using the stairs: some were using the railings on the outside of the building and the inside of the atrium like ladders to climb up. He looked over towards Slinker.

"Slinker, behind you!" he roared.

Three men dropped over the rail, landing onto the platform. The first carried a pair of sticks. He whipped the first across the surprised Tancree's face, who felt his cheekbone go. The second came up under the arm, just missing the nerve centre in the armpit, but slamming against a rib instead. Slinker's eyes blazed. His hands never moved, but a line of invisible force blasted out, pitching the three attackers back over the rail. The Tancree collapsed to his knees, sweat pouring down his face. It saved his life as another fireball passed across his head, singeing his grey hair before spiralling out into the night air.

An enemy mage was moving across the floor. Slinker could pick him out; just a hint of ostentation in his light-fitting clothes gave him away. He was surrounded by a crowd of martial artists. Slinker cursed. He should have recognized them when he came in; the way they had sat, or held themselves. They carried wooden staffs short enough to use in the confined space, and others had pairs of sticks, like those with which he had just been attacked. They also held nunchaku; pairs of sticks held together with a chain. All weapons that were unlikely to acquire the ire of the imperial authorities, all explainable as having an alternative use, and all deadly in the hands of these trained specialists. Still, the priority was killing the mage.

445

"Slayers!" shouted Dryana across the increasing noise. "Kill them all, mages and leaders first!"

Slinker needed no such instruction; he was already walking forward, flinging gobs of blue light like lumps of mud at the assembled attackers. The mage threw up a shield, protecting the group, and the blue lumps impacted on a yellow umbra, sending up a cascade of green sparks as the two met. Slinker was getting closer. Now the mage would act, he knew. The fireball roared out, aiming straight for him. Slinker used his own magic to bat it away, slamming it into the roof above, which started to smoke. Slinker replied, flinging out his hand to send a bolt of blue lightning directly for the enemy mage. The enemy mage brought up his yellow shield in time, stopping the magical lightning, but it did not stop the metal throwing disc that flew hidden by the crackle of blue fire. It passed through the shield and slammed into the mage's face.

Slinker grinned: he had been taught to shield both the magical and the physical attack – the war mages of the Tancree had lived for combat. The human mage had not been so trained, and it had cost him his life. Slinker swooned slightly, as waves of nausea were starting to overwhelm him. Then the martial artists were on him. He blocked a rain of blows with his fighting blades, dodging flying fists and low kicks. There were so many he was forced back towards the rail, but luckily there were so many they were getting in each other's way, giving him a chance.

Dryana dodged behind Balinor as he slashed the chest of another attacker. She blocked one of Xian's men as he cut at her with a long knife and countered, catching him on his shoulder. He fell back slightly towards the central atrium, but then came on again, his blade slashing down towards the small woman in front of him. It hit flesh, but it wasn't hers. Instead, a man had imposed himself between the two, and the man was shocked not just because it was his friend, but because he had just seen the Prince of Kangorn kill him. The zombie turned to look at his former colleague and then rammed itself bodily into him. The desperate man hacked at the undead, but with no effect. Then he felt another pair of hands grab him from behind. Another zombie leered at him over his shoulder and headbutted him on the side of his face, smashing his nose in an eruption in blood. He screamed as the pair carried his struggling form to the atrium and tossed him over.

Farmorl had got to his feet in time to see Slinker strike down the mage. He stepped forward, hacking down at the nearest attacker with his blade. The man stepped in under Farmorl's grasp, catching his sword arm under the elbow and forcing his arm up. He brought his own elbow around in a slashing movement, cracking it into Farmorl's jaw. The Slayer agent grasped for consciousness, terrified he would black out. He staggered back and felt a foot hammer into his solar plexus as the man stepped into a side kick. He collapsed back against the rail and the man loomed over him. A blade plunged through the man's back and out his chest. A western sword, he thought, as the hot blood sprayed over him.

Balinor pulled his blade clear and pushed the dead man aside. He reached down and helped Farmorl off the rail.

"You've got a bloody sword, use it," he muttered angrily.

The Prince of Kangorn then turned to face his next opponent. He did not bring his sword from above his shoulder as Farmorl had been taught. Instead, he swung it low and from the side, cutting into the man's leading knee, sending him tumbling. In a western soldier it would have been protected by mail or similar, but not here in the east. The man collapsed as his knee gave way and Balinor thrust his blade into his chest, going through the solar plexus where it was softest. He wrenched it out and was onto the next person.

The top floor of the tea house was a scene of bedlam. Each attacker the Slayers cut down was reanimated as an undead fighter to join the Slayer's ranks, but each attacker was replaced by two more. They were thundering up the stairs and climbing up the wooden sides of the tea house. The wooden roof of the building had caught fire. Solid wood took time to burn, but with the help of a light breeze it was becoming a problem. The smoke remained minimal, but that was more thanks to the dry wood and the wind blowing it away across the city. It disguised the progress of the blaze. Dryana looked up, watching yellow and red flames licking across the large joists above her head. They were starting to blacken. Slowly but inexorably, other parts of the wood were catching. Aside from the increasing heat, Dryana knew it was only a matter of time before something gave way. They needed to get out before the building became their funeral pyre.

She needed to reach Fatboy and remove him from the situation permanently. She doubted it would dissuade the attackers, but anything that gave them pause had to make a difference. Besides, that was what the Slayers had come here to do. Well, at least that was what she had come to do.

Dryana was surrounded by a coterie of four zombies that she had raised, but they were in turn encircled by a much larger group of martial artists. The attackers were slowly battering away at the undead, trying to get through to the Slayer witch. It was ineffectual, but at the same time there was not much Dryana could do with the cadavers she controlled without opening herself up to assault. She glanced across at Lan Xian, who was now pressed into a corner on the other side of the atrium void, surrounded by his henchmen. His glance shifted nervously from the drop behind him, to the escalating fire above, and back to the maelstrom of combat between him and the stairway out of the building.

Dryana looked around. Where was Slinker? He was nearer the stairs, slashing and cutting at the mass of Nerlineans surrounding him. She watched as he hooked a punch into the side of one man, his fighting blade slashing through his opponent's stomach before the fist made contact. He pushed the man away and drove forward into another, batting away a long staff and jamming the point of the blade through the new enemy.

"Slinker!" screamed Dryana. "Xian – you need to clear me a path."

The Tancree looked up from the fight, narrowly dodging an incoming meat cleaver as he was distracted. Dryana was shocked; he looked exhausted. Slinker lifted his hand and a ball of blue flame blasted across the platform heading straight for Xian. The fat gangster flung himself to the floor, but others were less lucky. The searing flames might be blue but that made them no less deadly.

The smell of hot burning flesh filled Dryana's nose, but she ignored it; she needed to move. The zombies around her attacked outwards, using the gap Slinker had created, and they clawed and pulled at those still between Dryana and her prey. She dashed forward, aiming for the prone man on the floor. She jumped a tackle from one of his surviving guards and dropped directly onto Fatboy, jamming her sword two-handed into his great belly. Xian roared in rage and pain. A club-like slap slammed into the side of Dryana's face, but she held on tight to the blade and twisted. Blood burst upwards, soaking the raging woman. She wrenched it free and thrust it in again.

She was picked up by the shoulders and thrown clear of Xian, landing crumpled on a corpse lying on the floor. Then the man was on her. A fist hit her in the stomach, leaving her winded. Another fist barrelled down, aiming for her nose. She shifted her head, taking the hit straight on the forehead. It hurt like hell, but it minimized the damage. The man reared up, shaking his throbbing hand in anger, and then he grabbed for her throat.

"Bad move!" she gasped.

She grabbed his arms, flesh touching flesh. She had tried this once on a Samath, but he had been stronger than the human and she less knowledgeable. She drew out the man's life energy. The hand on her throat started to weaken. The man realized something was happening, but could not fathom what it was. He tried to move his other to grab her throat, but he was growing weaker and could not break her grasp. A look of panic crossed his face, and he tried to pull away.

"No," she hissed, dragging him closer.

His skin started to pull tight across his face, so he looked more like a Tancree than a human. He tried to scream, but only the barest yelp escaped his lips. Then his eyes rolled up in his head and he slumped dead, on top of the witch. She pushed him off with surprising ease and stood up. She swung her arms, feeling invigorated. Another mage had reached the top floor and was engaged in a magical duel with Slinker. Dryana looked at the pair. Normally she would have assumed that Slinker would triumph with ease, but it looked closer than that. It was unlikely that the mage was as powerful as the Slayer, but he was fresh and Slinker was exhausted. Dryana stared up at the roof and an evil grin passed across her face. She felt the wind and then called it harder, so it whipped through her hair, sending it spraying outwards. The wind curled and swept up strong enough to fan the flames, not put them out. The fire roared into ferocious life. There were screams and shouts from everyone as the fire licked around the uprights holding the roof. Globs of molten fire dropped from the ceiling – hot sap or burning lumps of paint, Dryana had no idea.

The enemy mage was carried down the stairs by the mass of fleeing people. Dryana watched as the Pandus agent made a desperate run for the stairs. Slinker grabbed him as he passed, catching the thin man by the collar of his robe. The Tancree drew him in close, maybe he said something – it was hard to tell – and then he thrust the man backwards, tossing him over the rail and out into the open air.

Dryana walked over. Slinker slumped into a chair. He looked shattered. He leaned forward and heaved over the floor. He sat back, wiping his face.

"You okay?" she asked, concern on her face.

He nodded slowly.

"Fire! Can you stop it?" demanded Balinor.

She looked at the Prince of Kangorn: his face was cut, and blood streamed from above his eye.

"No problem," she declared.

The wind whipped through the building, hard and strong. The flames dropped away for a moment and then roared back even stronger. Dryana looked up and panic crossed her face.

"A storm?" suggested Balinor.

"From where?" she asked desperately. "We need to get out of here. Help me with him."

She dragged Slinker to his feet; the Tancree was half asleep.

"I've got him."

Dryana looked over; Farmorl struggled over to them from where he had been leaning against the rail. She was thankful that he was alright, though sad about what had happened to his handsome face. His nose was broken, and he was in the early stages of forming a pair of black eyes. She hoped it would heal. She would do her best to fix it later.

The pair of them half carried the war mage to the top of the stairs, Balinor coming up behind. A pair of arrows flashed up the stairs as they approached. Farmorl screamed as one caught him in the arm and the other went wide. The four backed away from the field of fire. Another pair of arrows flashed by.

The fire continued to burn above their heads. The smoke was thickening, and the heat was becoming unbearable.

"Any ideas?" Balinor demanded.

Farmorl snapped the end of the arrow off and grunted – whether in pain or at Balinor's question it was hard to tell. Dryana looked at Balinor, her eyes showing fear bordering on panic. Slinker pushed her away, stepping out into the stair well, and lashed out with blue fire. It eviscerated the pair of archers. Slinker turned to the group with a broad and very un-Tancree smile. Then his eyes rolled up in his head and he pitched forward down the stairs.

He tumbled down the flight of steps, coming to a stop at the landing where the steps turned to follow the side of the building down, his fall broken by the bodies slumped there. The other three rushed after him and Farmorl dragged his mentor to his feet.

"Is he okay?" Dryana asked. Her face was creased with worry.

"I don't know," Farmorl answered. "I can't tell; we need to get him out of here."

There was a sickening crunching, snapping sound. The four watched as the centre of the roof gave in, crashing down through the atrium onto the lowest floor.

"No time to lose," stated Balinor, helping Farmorl with Slinker.

The pair dashed down the stairs, stumbling and slipping under the weight of the Tancree mage. Dryana brought up the rear, looking behind them in terror as lumps of burning wood dropped down from above.

The flaming wood that had dropped into the atrium had caught on the tables and chairs of the lowest floor and now the fire was coming up from below as well as from above. Carrying the unconscious form of Slinker they reached the lowest floor. The steps out of the tea house looked tantalizing close, only a matter of yards, but fire raged across the floor, blocking the way. They looked at each other, nodded and dashed through the flames.

The four tumbled down the stairs, out onto the mossy surface of the lawn. Farmorl was on fire. Dryana rolled him over and over, extinguishing the flames.

"Thanks," he breathed.

The pair staggered to their feet and ran to the street in front of the tea house. Balinor was halfway there already, dragging Slinker. He slumped down next to the Tancree's prone form. The three looked back at the burning tower behind them; the heat was unbelievable.

"Are we safe here?" asked Balinor, watching the roaring pyre in front of him.

"You think we should move back?" asked Dryana tiredly.

The top two floors of the building collapsed in on themselves, crashing into the atrium and turning the wooden structure into a giant bonfire.

"I think we're fine," mused Balinor with a grin.

Another lump of wood tumbled off the flaming pile and landed in front of them.

"Spoke too soon," he added sheepishly.

There was another sound. It took a moment for Dryana to register it over the roar and crack of the flames. Someone was clapping: a slow clap, mocking.

Dryana sat up and looked around. A woman was walking down the street. She was caught in the shadows of the night, but as she came closer Dryana recognized her, her brown face revealed by the light of the flames.

"Gods, you are wonderful. It is so rare to meet people who actually live up to their reputations," Srias Halfnight-Pandus offered politely.

Dryana's hand clasped the hilt of her short sword.

"Not a good idea, Slayer. You are not that fast and besides, that blade is mundane unless I miss my guess – oh, and no walking corpses are to come rampaging from the building or my people will fill you full of arrows," Srias said with a grin.

She stopped a few feet from them. Men and women were appearing from side streets. Some were those martial artists who had escaped the blazing building, their loose white clothing marked with grey smudges from the fire. Others were dressed in leather armour and carrying short swords or scimitars. Some wore the red uniforms of the Pandus; others had badges bearing the gold P on red of the Imperial Pandus Trading Company to indicate their allegiance. A man and woman stepped forward to flank Srias. They wore loose-fitting clothes, cloth trousers and short-sleeved shirts. Dryana recognized the man, his tousled hair and ash-stained face. It was the mage from the tea house, the one that Slinker had not killed. He looked tired, but his eyes focused tightly on the Company of Slayers, his hand held loosely in front of him ready to cast. The woman on the other side of Srias had the same look and similar stance. Another mage, concluded Dryana. The difference was she lacked the tiredness or dirt from the battle of the tea house. Instead, she was fresh and young. Dryana would not have placed her as much older than herself: a recent graduate from the Academy in Nerlon, she surmised. Her eyes contained a predatory look as she surveyed them, and a vicious grin touched the corners of her mouth.

The Slayer witch ignored them and crawled over to Slinker. She placed her head next to Slinker's, noting his shallow breaths. She gave a sigh of relief. She shook him, but he did not wake. She muttered a curse and pushed herself to her feet, making a barrier between Srias and the unconscious Tancree. Balinor was already on his feet, his back to the burning remnants of the tea house. His sword swung slowly from left to right as he took in the enemy surrounding him from three sides.

Only the roaring blaze to his rear prevented them from getting round behind him. Past the fire the Slayers could see Pandus soldiers cutting off that route to escape even if they could have got past the flames.

"You have my gold." Dryana made it a statement, not a question.

Srias laughed at that, a deep throaty sound that seemed incongruous with her lithe frame. "Oh, Dryana, you make me smile," the wererat replied. "I see why my daughter speaks so warmly of you. Almost so much she might forget you are our enemy. I, however, do not forget."

"I am Balinor of Kangorn."

Dryana looked at her colleague, performing a game attempt to use his status to give the Pandus pause. It was not like they had many options at this point.

"Oh, little prince," Srias said, her tone mocking. "You are nothing here. Your name will not save you. It may even give Nyandar the chance to reassert his authority over your recalcitrant island, if he can be bothered."

"Why did you wait?" demanded Dryana.

"I'm enjoying this. Why rush?" laughed Srias. "Gloating is one of the few perks one gets in life."

"No, I mean why did you wait so long to destroy us? We have been in Nerlinea, in the east, for five years. Why wait so long to confront us?"

Srias looked at Dryana, her gaze assessing as if she was unsure how to answer.

"It's tempting to give you a dismissive response. You were too small, too unimportant, but to diminish you would equally diminish the work we took in getting you here. In truth, you and yours have been marked for death since your brother first came here. We wanted what you stole from us first."

"The gold?" Dryana asked.

Srias nodded. "Not quite what you took from my cousin Antonnin, but close enough."

"Is that the only reason?"

"You are playing for time, witch." Srias gave them a predatory smile. "But I will indulge you. My grandfather was wary of you. He believed someone high up was protecting you. You know the Imperial Fleet was forbidden from taking the Isles of Syndion?"

Dryana did not. It never occurred to her that the Nerlinean Empire would be interested in the islands. She knew of the ancient army of the dead, something Srias did not, but then the Nerlineans were unlikely to know about it either. So, a simple decision not to invade the isles by the empire had been enough to persuade the Pandus to hold back. The last four years she had spent working and building the Company of Slayers here in Port Ren had been allowed by the Pandus, not despite them. At any time, they could have reached out and crushed them like bugs.

The dozen flaming corpses burst out from the fire, charging for Srias and the two mages. Dryana had to keep it to that number. Zombies were easier to animate than skeletons. Their recent deaths meant that were some residual memories of their existence, so you did not have to do all the work of persuading them to move and attack. For skeletons it was a more complex task, like making a doll dance. The problem was that, when they were on fire, there seemed to be reluctance on the part of the recently resurrected dead to do as commanded. It was the best Dryana could do to control a dozen of them. Still, it should be enough.

The female mage brought her hand back behind her head as if about to throw an invisible ball. She flung it forward, a line of searing white light exploding from it. It whipped through the zombie at one end of the line, passing it through him at chest height and slicing him in two. Then it moved onto the next and the next, cutting through all of them in only a second. The bodies did not collapse to the ground; instead, the white light seared upwards and downwards from where it had hit, consuming them. Each became a pillar of white fire, but only for a moment, until a large pile of ash dropped to the ground where each zombie had stood.

"Gods, what was that?" Dryana looked shocked.

She took small comfort that the female mage dropped to her knees and retched. Dryana looked up from the mage's discomfort to meet Srias' amused smile.

"It has been a long time since someone cast that spell."

The voice came from nowhere. It was soft and lilting, almost singsong.

Srias looked around, wariness filling her face for the first time. Dryana's eyes followed Srias searching for what she was looking for. A figure stepped from the shadows of a building on the other side of the street. He was thin, nearing seven feet in height, a Gar, with grey-white hair that hung past his shoulders. His white beard was neatly trimmed. Eyes that seemed to flit between dark blue and purple stared hard out of the darkness. He wore a long grey cloak despite the hot weather. As he moved out of the shadows it seemed to shimmer and change to a blazing silver that danced in the light of the fire. A gnarled wooden staff, capped with a blue jewel, was grasped loosely in confident hands. Greldin of the Way stepped into the gap between the Slayers and Srias.

"Not been much call for slaying the undead in recent years. Where did you learn it?" he asked the kneeling mage, his tone more curious teacher than angry wizard.

"The library of the university in Nerlon," the female mage said, pushing herself to her feet.

"The importance of education and study to supplement natural talent," he said with a benign grandfatherly smile.

The mage looked up into the Gar's face. His human-like smile was a lie. Cold, unhuman eyes stared back. She swallowed, backing away slightly.

"That took a lot out of you," Greldin observed quietly. "I would advise caution. The movement of the spell in the horizontal and vertical plains at the same time is quite stressing on the body of the caster."

The male mage shifted forward slightly, trying to get a better angle for whatever he planned.

Greldin raised an eyebrow. "You know who I am?" he asked.

The mage nodded.

"Know your limits, child," the Gar barked gruffly, his tone changing in a moment.

Both Pandus wizards twitched involuntarily in response.

"Well, I don't. Who the fuck are you?" demanded Srias.

Greldin looked at her, his eyes boring into her. He was met by the Pandus woman's equally implacable gaze.

"Time to go, wererat, before you make me angry," he said quietly.

Srias seethed in anger; the Pandus family were famously testy about their blood secret.

"You will be dying with them," she hissed.

Suddenly fire burned her. It was strongest on her hands and arms, as if she had placed them on a hot grill, but it was all over. A web of magical silver thread had enclosed her. It was touching her body and face in the lightest possible way. She tried to shy away from it but there was nowhere for her to go. It surrounded her like a set of clothes or a sack, but tightest around the arms and legs. She could feel the lines of silver searing her skin. If she tried to move her limbs the burning pain stopped her. Her eyes looked to her mages, trying to get their attention. She did not dare turn her head for fear of the thread cutting into her beautiful face. The pair were slowly backing away, leaving their hapless employer to her fate. Srias looked at Greldin waiting for a demand, waiting for anything. Purple eyes stared back. The only feeling she could read was boredom. Then she saw hope.

Three iribis riders cantered into the street. She saw her husband on the lead mount. She had never been so pleased to see Camlyn, Dumech of Haldorn. He was dressed in the leather cuirass and metal breast plate preferred by the legions raised in the west. A gladius hung at his belt. A crested helm enclosed his features. He was flanked by two others. To his left was Ko Quan, one of Nyandar's most powerful mages. The figure on the right she did not know, but he was dressed in the uniform of the emperor's personal guard, the Palace Legion. His ranking markings indicated he was an officer, a senior tribune. A blue and green robe was worn over scale mail armour. He looked so different from how Camlyn was dressed it was hard to believe both could claim to be part of the same army.

Srias gave a smile of victory, despite the pain that was racking her body. Then she heard it. Troops, hundreds of them, were appearing down the street, others racing in from side roads. All wore the blue and green of the Palace Legion. Wickerwork shields glued over with leather were clasped in one hand and a broad-bladed spear held in the other. Black horn and wood bows were strapped to their backs and a wide quiver of long arrows hung next to a sword on their belts. They were pushing up against the various Pandus employees surrounding the tea house, jostling and intimidating them. Already some were starting to slink away, the last members of Fatboy's gang leading the way.

"Husband," demanded Srias. "Will you rid me of this elf?"

Camlyn seemed not to hear his wife's furious request.

"You are ordered to disperse by imperial dictate. This district of the city is under strict curfew. Anyone still on its streets by the fiftieth drumbeat will be subject to summary execution!" Camlyn's voice echoed out across the buildings.

A legionary carrying a large drum hanging from his waist stepped forward and started a slow resolute drumbeat.

The Pandus employees needed no more encouragement, quickly scattering down side streets and alleyways. Camlyn dismounted and walked toward the Slayers, ignoring his wife and the Gar mage.

The drum hit ten beats.

"Why are you still here?" Camlyn asked.

Dryana looked up at him. "Slinker's injured; he's unconscious."

The Dumech of Haldorn shrugged. "If you are still here on the fiftieth beat you will be killed. Carry him, leave him, it makes no difference to me."

He turned on his heel so he was facing his wife.

"Greldin, release her," he ordered.

"No," Greldin replied.

Camlyn gave the Gar an angry glare, but it did not seem to change the Gar's stance.

Camlyn looked at the two mages on either side of his wife. They had slunk back but were still standing their ground. A group of maybe a dozen braver and more devoted Pandus agents were still in position behind Srias.

Camlyn looked them over coldly.

"Shoo!" He waved his hand dismissively at them.

They looked at him, surprised. He sighed.

"Archers!" he ordered.

A section of the palace guard carefully placed their shields and spears on the ground and unslung their bows and nocked arrows.

"Sorry," muttered the female mage to her employer.

The remaining Pandus employees melted away.

Srias stared angrily at her husband and then up the street where the Slayers were disappearing, with the slumped form of Slinker half carried, half dragged between the exhausted Farmorl and Balinor.

Dryana stopped at the end of the street. She wanted to see what happened next.

The drumbeat hit a thirty count.

"Dryana, come on," muttered Balinor.

She looked reluctantly down the street, catching Srias' eyes. The witch gave the wererat a big grin and then disappeared out of sight.

Srias was in too much pain to do much about the anger raging through her.

Camlyn looked around the streets and back at the burning teahouse; the fire was starting to die down.

"Husband, stop him," she demanded.

"Greldin, we will take it from here," he said forcefully.

"Why is it I don't trust you to restrain your wererat wife, Camlyn?" the Gar observed.

"I am a dumech of the Nerlinean Empire. You will address me correctly," Camlyn spat angrily.

Greldin of the Way looked at him impassively, perhaps mocking; the Gar were so hard to read, thought Camlyn.

Srias felt the threads of silver tighten. They slashed through the silk of her clothing, raising bloody welts across her naked skin, cutting her face and shoulders. Then they were gone.

She blinked. Where was that elf? She would tear him apart. He was standing a few yards away next to the ruined building. She went to move, but an arm blocked the way. Then Greldin was gone. Her wererat senses searched the dark, but he had simply disappeared.

She cursed and grabbed the arm blocking her.

461

"You let him do that to me, *to me*?" she screamed at her husband.

She fought down the urge to rend her husband limb from limb. She wanted to punish him as much as the Gar.

"Enough!" he shouted, grasping her.

She acquiesced. He was a strong man, but there was no way he was strong enough to control her unless she let him.

"Nyandar wants to see you," he told her harshly. "We will be lucky if any of our family get out of this alive."

Srias looked over at the two men still mounted on their iribis and back at her husband. She saw fear in his eyes. He wasn't really in command; they were.

"What's happened?"

"The Kasem," he answered angrily. "There is a line, Srias, even for one of your wealth and status, and you are far past it. They raided Mahendra, they took citizens as slaves, burnt ships of the Imperial Fleet."

She looked at him, doing her best to appear bewildered. "What is that to do with me?" she lied, feigning shock.

"He knows, Srias. You better have something more than straight denial or he'll execute all of us: you, me, and the children." He was seething.

"I know nothing," she declared.

"Well, you can explain that to the emperor when we get to Nerlon," he muttered, thrusting her angrily towards the waiting soldiers.

The drumbeat hit fifty.

CHAPTER THIRTY-ONE — REVENGE

The wind whipped at the braziers that lined each side of the high-ceilinged corridor. Charlotte walked along it, feeling claustrophobic; the corridor was not exactly narrow, just narrower than it should be. Also, the palace of the Prince of Kangorn was famous for its lack of windows, so little natural light spilled in. Besides, it was early evening in late autumn and the sun was rapidly dropping below the horizon. Soon the only light in these halls would be from the stuttering, choking metal braziers that were spaced evenly along each wall.

The palace was quiet, which Charlotte found slightly odd. Normally it bustled with servants and visitors. Under Prince Karden it had been barely used; he had preferred his small manor house at the other end of the palace gardens. The outer walls of the palace complex had been keenly guarded and visitors strictly monitored. That had changed when Ascrina and

Balinor had taken the throne. They had been much more active in the life of the Rock, seeking to encourage visitors, both cultural and commercial. The number of servants in the kitchens had increased and banquets were being held again.

The governing couple had also taken to calling council meetings to consult with their leading lords and officials. Others saw it as a refreshing change from the uninterested, bordering on neglectful, attitude of their predecessor. The noble houses enjoyed feeling included, even if they did not like the increased taxes that came with their involvement. It had given commercial advantage to the noble Houses that spent the most time on Kangorn and around their rulers. This favoured the likes of House Malkiel, House Redwind and House Tallyn and, of course, Charlotte Pandus herself.

The most favoured was Danzian of House Corinmount. He dominated the Bankers' Guild of the Rock, and some would argue the banking markets of the whole West. He was the prime lender to the Prince of Kangorn, a role in which he was heavily conflicted, given he was also the Chancellor of Kangorn. Unbelievably, the normally pragmatic and intelligent Danzian was blind to the obvious conflict that arose from his position. Charlotte could see it and she had been able to convince Ascrina of the existence of the conflict of interest. It was helped by self-interest – Danzian's insistence on keeping the princess's lavish spending firmly in check had not made him popular with her. A few weeks past Charlotte had managed to get the princess direct funding from her own family to sideline Danzian – permanently, she hoped. She needed to make the most of Prince Balinor's absence to persuade Lord Corinmount he was better off overseeing his business from High Ringstead or Dimchurch. Then, when Balinor got back, he would hopefully just go along with the situation – assuming he ever sobered up long enough to notice. The one advisor to the Princess Ascrina that Charlotte had not yet found a way to supplant was Lady Tallyn Hanath, the Gar former Captain of the Prince's Guard. Nevertheless, Charlotte was confident an opportunity would present itself and that she would grab it when it came. She would be Ascrina's main adviser if she was patient and, with the prince a drunk, that meant she could rule the Rock.

Her mind was focused on her dreams as she stepped into the great hall, and it took her moment to realize that she was not the first to arrive. In fact, she was among the last of those she would expect to be there. The hall was double height but narrower and shorter than would normally be the case in similar constructions. Buildings tended to be squeezed on Kangorn, even the prince's palace. The Palace of Kangorn had been built in the early days of the founding of the city some two hundred years ago. For a prince it was a poor building, but for a pirate captain it was an ambitious construction. Kangorn had been transitioning between the two roles when he had built his citadel. The fact it had been built more for defence than for comfort did not help.

At the end of the hall was a raised dais, built of wood with a line of steps up each side. On the dais rested two curule chairs that acted as thrones from which the prince and princess would dispense their decisions. Charlotte's nose wrinkled. There should be two chairs; one of the seats was missing. A single curule chair now rested centrally on the platform. She shrugged at the change. She would find out why later. She knew Balinor was away, so maybe Ascrina did not want to highlight her husband's absence.

Half a dozen people milled around the plain flagstone floor. No rushes, thought Charlotte. Winter was approaching, and it would have kept it warmer. She shivered. More Corinmount cost-cutting, she wondered. Rushes had to be brought in from abroad; Kangorn had no area to provide them. Something that in a Sevain castle would be commonplace became a luxury on Kangorn.

She looked across the faces of the assembled nobles and officials. No Lord Corinmount, she realized, and suppressed an evil smile of victory. She gave Tallyn Hanath a polite nod and the same to Lord Malkieth. The Gar was the only one openly armed, her alcidide rapier hanging at her side. The Prince and Princess did not trust the others sufficiently to carry weapons in their presence. Charlotte had handed in her own sword at the gatehouse, though two daggers remained hidden in her boots. She knew no attempt would be made to search her. Besides, this was Kangorn and everyone had a knife of some sort.

"Lord Redwind," she greeted the man politely.

Kaleb Redwind was among the more recent Lords of Kangorn. His grandfather had been ennobled by Prince Karden early in his reign, perhaps thirty years ago, replacing one of the founding families that had died out. They had been pirates and merchants, originally from Allakor, who, like so many before them had found a home and respectability on Kangorn. The Allakor blood shone through: Kaleb was tall, broad-shouldered and ruggedly handsome, at least if one liked men who looked like farmers. Red curly hair and an orange beard flecked with the occasional darker red meant he stood out. His charm and amusing tales had made him a firm favourite with both prince and princess.

Kaleb had been given the job of Warden of the Great Watchtower, an office that in theory gave him control of the city watch, the prison in the Great Watchtower, and made him responsible for the lookouts in the same tower. The problem was that the city watch, an innovation of Prince Sandon the First, had been abolished after his death over a century ago, and the cells in the watchtower had fallen out of use not long after. It was easier to fine criminals than imprison them, and for more serious offences permanent exile was an option. The most egregious offenders would be taken out by ship at night and quietly pitched into the chilly dark depths of the Nerlinean

Ocean. Still, the title and its stipend persisted, a way of rewarding a loyal supporter without them having to do any real work.

"So, you noticed the chair?" he said nodding down towards the dais.

"No," she lied and craned her neck theatrically to see. "Just the one, I note. I guess Prince Balinor has not yet returned."

"What do you think this is about?"

She shrugged in response. "Any sign of Lord Corinmount?" she asked, looking around.

"None, and he's normally the first here," Kaleb observed.

"Interesting," said Charlotte, suppressing a smile.

A servant near the main door cracked a wooden staff against the floor.

"Her highness, Ascrina of House Strabo, Princess of Kangorn and Warden of the Falcon Straits," the voice echoed around the chamber.

Ascrina strode into the hall, her dark blue velvet dress rustling as she moved. The assembled courtiers dropped into bows or curtsies depending on gender or dress. Charlotte went with a bow as she was wearing trousers and a loose blouse rather than a dress. Doing a curtsey in trousers looked ridiculous, at least in her mind. The Princess of Kangorn's gaze washed over the assembled councillors, more imperious than usual. Ascrina was still thin, if not the lithe thing she had been before bearing two children. Her chin was sharp, and her gaze had become more forbidding since she had taken the throne. She moved and acted with that sense of entitlement that only those who are born to rule can achieve. She was still young, a similar age to Charlotte, and for that matter, Dryana. It was why the three had become such close friends, at least for a time, before Dryana had left for Nerlinea.

JUSTIN WAINE

In Ascrina's wake trailed her shadow, the pale-skinned, dark-haired figure of Captain Sliva Droma. The commander of the Prince's Guard, the closest that the Rock had to a professional military, though increasingly she acted as a personal bodyguard to the princess herself. She was dressed head to foot in a coat of chainmail, the coif pulled down resting on her shoulders. Over it was worn a tabard of blue and silver, the griffin symbol of Kangorn stitched above her left breast. Unlike the others, except her predecessor Lady Tallyn, she was armed. Her weapon, a hand-and-a-half sword, rested in its scabbard on her left hip. It was long for her height, and she rested her hand on the scabbard just below the hilt to balance it forward to prevent it scraping on the flags.

The pair mounted the steps to the dais. Ascrina took a seat on the curule chair with the captain taking station behind her slightly off to one side, her left hand still clasping her scabbard. She pushed the blade slightly behind her, taking more of the weight of the heavy blade on her back rather than her hip. A servant scurried out of the small side door of the hall, down a short flight of steps and then up the wooden steps of the dais. He carried a crimson cushion on which rested a gold circlet. He stopped next to the princess and bowed. She plucked the crown from the cushion and then shooed him away. The assembled lords and ladies bowed again as she placed it on her head.

The councillors remained standing, as there was nowhere to sit. The round tables and chairs that normally filled the hall for banquets had been removed. The long table that usually rested on the dais for a banquet had been carried down and pushed up against one wall. No one thought to perch on that, for there was a reason behind the lack of furniture. Ascrina had decreed that such councils would take place standing, except for the ruler. She found things moved faster that way – if people were seated, they tended to speak for much longer.

468

"Welcome, my lords and ladies. Thank you for attending me at such short notice," said Ascrina, opening the meeting. "I apologize that I had to gather you, but a serious matter has come to our attention; one that impacts the integrity of Kangorn."

Charlotte fought hard to conceal the grin that desperately wanted to escape across her face. This was it, she thought; Ascrina had found the evidence she needed on Danzian Corinmount, or manufactured it. The man had probably fled already, hence his absence, voluntary exile better than being forced. It also removed from Ascrina the temptation to drop the man in the ocean, a desire that Charlotte would have actively encouraged. She was slightly surprised that Ascrina had not informed her of the plan before executing it, but the princess did like grandstanding, which probably explained why she was announcing it at this meeting.

"Our person has been violated," continued Ascrina.

There was an intake of breath from the assembled audience and a raised eyebrow from Charlotte.

"An act of lese majesty. One we believe loyal has seen fit to seduce our Prince-Consort Balinor and to force his lapse into adulterous ways," continued Ascrina.

Shocked cries of shame and doubt echoed in the room, although the effect was somewhat undermined by the lack of numbers in the hall. Charlotte joined in, carried away by the moment. Then she paused, a sickening feeling in her stomach, as her mind processed what had been said. Prince-Consort. Balinor was not consort; he was the prince, ruling jointly with Ascrina, and no one needed to force Balinor to be adulterous. Restraining him would have been more the task. Also, no one would believe that Balinor was sleeping with Danzian. Balinor would screw pretty much anything as long as it was female, and she doubted his interest extended beyond that. As for Danzian, who knew what he was interested in? The only thing she could imagine the man seducing was a chest of gold. This was not an attempt to remove Danzian, but someone else.

Charlotte felt a prick of cold metal at the back of her neck. Her ratty nose twitched. She turned slowly. The rapier point did not move, not even a quiver. It was no longer touching the top of her spinal cord, but resting on her artery on the side of her throat. Charlotte was not sure that was an improvement. She looked into the amused eyes of Tallyn Hanath, the one person in this room fast enough to keep up with her wererat speed. Against a human she would have risked moving, but not against the Gar. In her current human form, a steel sword would hurt less than it would a normal person, but the blade in the former captain's hand was alcidide. Tallyn could slash Charlotte's throat open whether she was in this shape or changed to her natural wererat form.

Charlotte shifted slowly back so she was facing Ascrina. She felt the point on the back of her neck, where she suspected it had broken the skin.

"I am very disappointed in you, my friend." Ascrina shook her head. "To have been betrayed by one's husband is terrible enough, but betrayal by one's closest friend makes the wound all the deeper."

"I didn't," Charlotte yelped.

The Pandus family rage was consuming. She wanted to scream and rant. She had never been near the man – a single drunken proposition by him that she had rejected. Her mind screamed at the unfairness, a reaction that only made it worse. The Pandus family traded on being unfair. She tried to wrench herself out of self-pity, but it just made her angrier. She could not clear the burning fire in her mind, and she needed to think clearly. Why was Ascrina doing this to her?

"I represent the Pandus," she managed to bark out angrily.

Was her trading house on fire, her mansion under assault? If so, who was commanding it? Droma, Hanath were here, Balinor not in the city. Who else did Ascrina have who could mount such an assault. Another of the noble houses could be leading it, but which one? Only Marcus Romanch came close to having the resources, and she would have known if he had returned to the city.

"Do you?" Ascrina tried to make it sound like a question, but it came with a confident tone that implied she knew the answer and it was not one she would like.

"My lady, the issue is with you, not your House. You seduced the Prince-Consort, not your family," came a familiar voice from the side door.

Charlotte's head swung round towards the door, and the rapier opened a thin bloody line along her neck. She gave Tallyn a look of venomous hatred. She watched as the thin urbane middle-aged man walked calmly down the stairs. His blue robes rustled across the floor, his thick gold chain of office still around his neck. Lord Danzian Corinmount, Chancellor of Kangorn, entered the room and gave Lady Pandus a polite smile.

"We are not savages, my lady. You will be given your chance to make your case in court. The Princess's argument is with you for your scandalous behaviour. We expect your family to understand the situation and act reasonably. They are more likely to be embarrassed by your actions than supportive of them. Espand Dani is more than certain that will be the case," Corinmount said politely.

Then Charlotte understood. *Charles, you bastard*, she screamed in her mind. She wanted to vocalize it but decided that would serve little purpose. Why had her uncle done this to her? He must have given guarantees to the Strabos that there would be no retaliation. When Karden had moved against Alorn Pandus he had done it with blood and fire and still used intermediaries to hide his actions. Did Ascrina really believe that she had slept with Balinor? She looked up at the Princess, but her face was unreadable.

Danzian stepped in front of the wererat. "Hands out," he instructed.

She thought about grabbing his throat and throttling him, but she could feel the rapier on her skin. She held her hands out. He produced a set of silver manacles from his robes. For a moment she feared they were actually pure silver; if they touched her skin they would burn. They could be steel, in which case she would be able to break the links. If they were silver, she would also be able to snap them if she could get past the searing pain of putting enough pressure on them. She wasn't sure she could.

"Shouldn't a servant be doing that?" she commented waspishly.

"It is my pleasure," said Danzian with an easy smile. "Besides these bangles are very valuable – chains of alcidide, specially forged."

Charlotte pulled away, but he snapped them on as she did. No, she could not break these chains. She felt them touch her skin. Alcidide lacked the searing pain of silver, but they irritated and itched, making her frustrated already. She wanted to scratch where they touched her skin. He produced another set of manacles and clapped them around her ankles. These went around her trousers, so they did not touch her naked skin.

"I am going to destroy you," she hissed into his face.

"Well, better luck at the second attempt," he smiled sweetly back her.

She glared at him angrily as he stepped away.

"Lady Hanath, please take Lady Pandus away. A prison cell has been prepared for her in the Great Watchtower. Lord Redbranch, as warden, you are now responsible for her until a trial can be arranged," declared Ascrina.

PRINCE OF SLAYERS

A squad of palace guards entered the hall and accompanied the three towards the main doors. Lord Redbranch seem bemused that his office now meant he had some work to do.

"I am deeply saddened by my husband's actions, and while I place most blame on the foul seductress, I cannot totally absolve him of his actions. So, I have come to a difficult decision," announced the Princess.

Charlotte stopped at the door. She wanted to hear this. One of the guards tried to push her out and looked surprised when the slight woman in front of him did not move. He went to push her again, but Tallyn indicated with a nod not to. *Let her listen*, her face said.

"As Princess Regnant of Kangorn, I, Ascrina Strabo, declare that I am divorcing my husband Balinor. I will seek a new consort who can support me in my rule. To secure the succession, I have decided to follow the Sevain custom of crowning the heir during the Prince's lifetime. Morianus Strabo, as my heir, will be crowned Prince of Kangorn," she finished.

The councillors gave a small cheer in response.

Charlotte looked at Tallyn. Crossing the Pandus was one thing, especially if Charles had cut a deal with the Strabos, but crossing the Company of Slayers required a whole different level of courage. She then looked down the hall at Danzian Corinmount. He met her gaze and smiled, a confidence in his face she had not expected to see. What did he know that she didn't?

This time she acquiesced to the shove from the guard as she was pushed out of the hall.

CHAPTER THIRTY-TWO — THE TENTS OF THE MOURN

Saliana pulled her oradar to a halt and rubbed the centre of its head in an affectionate manner. The cat purred contentedly. Rayllor was next, bringing his own mount to a stop just behind. Kyrian was the last to arrive; his recalcitrant mount had still not grown comfortable with a human on its back, despite all the months of journeying. Sali trotted her animal over to Kyrian's and rubbed the head of the great beast on which her fellow Slayer rode. It mewed happily like a kitten and quietened down.

"We made it," she said with a smile.

"Three weeks late," grunted Kyrian.

"Well, we are here now."

"Still think we should have brought the skeletons with us," Kyrian replied. "And Samarin."

They had first spied the Mountain of the Moon mid-morning on the previous day. Saliana had ordered the army of the ancestors to make camp. Not that the dead really made camp – they had no need to sleep and eat, after all. She had left Samarin in control of them. The Fal'Gar witch might have lacked the power to resurrect her antecedents, but she could maintain and control them. Saliana had even suggested to Samarin that, despite the Fal'Gar woman's uncertainty, she could have raised the army from the tomb. She had the naked power – she just lacked the self-belief. At least that was what the Mistress of the Slayers thought.

"Better to approach the Mourn without two thousand dead warriors to alarm them," she countered.

Kyrian thought about reviving the argument that they had had the previous day. The Great Khan of the Mourn might be willing to forgive their lateness if it came with an undead army. Kyrian feared that, without it, the Mourn ruler might choose to make an example of them, hanging them, or more likely impaling them, immediately in front of the camp as a lesson to others. Sali sailed on with her irritating confidence that suggested it would all be alright. Did she really have a plan for this encounter? He suspected she did, not that she would deign to share it with him.

"Looking at that I don't think even two thousand warriors would alarm him." Saliana nodded at the vista ahead of them.

The flat plain of the steppe stretched out in front of them, its rolling grasslands coming to a sudden stop as the Daldara Mountains reared up across the plain. In reality the plain graduated to low hills before the towering crags of the mountains behind, but the difference in height was so marked that it did not change the impression of flatness to sudden height. The mountains ran from the coast in the south in a wide arc disappearing into the north to plains of ice that no man could cross. In the south, they created the barrier between the Great Steppe and the Sevain principalities beyond. The fortress city of Hambledon blocked the main pass through to those lands. To the north, the mountains led to the Falcongate, a winding pass through the inhospitable crags, protected each side by giant towers. A combined force of Nerlinean legionaries and Fal'Gar cavalry had protected the Great Steppe from incursions. For beyond lay the Mourn Steppe, an inhospitable land of forest and barren waste that turned to freezing tundra in the north, and here the Mourn had been bottled up for centuries. Occasionally small parties had crossed the mountains from the Mourn Steppe to raid for slaves and booty in the Great Steppe using the lesser-known passes that a small group could navigate. Others had raided south through the thick forests that protected Allakor and Delenor. This had kept alive their fearful reputation but not provided any real threat to the kingdoms of Man and Gar. That had been before Lak Bok, a Mourn chieftain who had fought a bloody civil war to unite his people under his rule, had taken the Falcongate and conquered all the way to Nerlinea.

The greatest mountain in the whole range was ahead of them, with its frosted heights cloaked in cloud. It lay seventy miles north of Hambledon and several times that south of the Falcongate. Visible from nearly a hundred miles away, the Slayers felt they had nearly completed their journey for most of the last two days. Only now, in the shadow of the mountain, did they realize it was nearly finished. The Mountain of the Moon, in the language of the Sevains, but also in the tongues of the Mourn. It had been called that for so long no one was sure why. In truth, the whole mountain range could be described as the mountains of the moon. Daldara, for whom the mountains were named, was the Gar Goddess of the Moons.

PRINCE OF SLAYERS

To the Gar the tallest of the peaks had another name: Aman'Thy'Tharum, the Gathering of the Dead. Once, Daldara's people, the Dal'Ri'Gar, the Moon Elves, had called these peaks home, before Naron and his genocidal war against his neighbours. Here, below the Mountain of the Moon, an entire Gar people had gone down not just to defeat but to extinction. The only survivor, at least according to legend, had been Fenice, Trendorn of the Dal'Ri'Gar, the ancestor after whom Cliphine would later name her eldest daughter. She had escaped through the mountains to the forests of what was now Allakor. There, alone and close to dying, she had been found by a human, a Brinach. His name in the tongue of his people was Jedan. Through some witchcraft, the last of the Dal'Ri'Gar, driven to desperation at the death of her people, had found some way to conceive children with the human male. The eldest she named Jeddera, Dumech'Di'Dal'Ri'Gar and Ran-Dumech'Di'Gar. And so the half-elves had come into being.

Now, another army filled the plain below the mountain. Yurts and smaller tents filled the gap between the Slayers and the mountain, stretching out on either side for almost as far as the eye could see. The ragged totems of the Mourn fluttered in the breeze. A large wooden pole was ringed with three loops of metal and from them hung long tails of cloth in reds, purples and blues. Alongside them were the bronze standards of the Fal'Gar, dragon-headed trumpets on the end of thin steel poles. The steppe wind caught them, creating a keening sound as it whistled through them. Kyrian could see the human flags: the banners of the Count of Haydron, and his own, the banner of Chazantria, were present along with those of dozens of minor lordlings. The Count of Chazantria heaved a sigh of relief – at least Marcus had got his army here in time. Maybe that would temper the mood of the Great Khan, but somehow, he doubted it.

No rampart enclosed the camp, and no ditch as the Imperial Legions would have dug when on campaign. A large yurt stood closest to the Mountain of the Moon, sitting just below where the low hills in front of the mountain range rose. It was larger but not ostentatiously so than those of the other shelters that surrounded it, Kyrian suspected that was the Great Khan's tent. It was hard to tell; there appeared no attempt to administer the camp, let alone protect it. No main roads ran through it, and no obvious areas for storing supplies as he had seen in Sevain war camps. The overpowering smell that washed over the plain from the tent city further confirmed it. No attempt had been made to dig proper latrines or to guard against disease. Kyrian noted that the Sevains and in particular the Gar had made a better effort at administering their own areas, as thoroughfares had been left to move carts and people. Latrine ditches had been kept to the edge. Then further Mourn had arrived, dropping their yurts in spaces that the others had clearly intended to keep clear and surrounding the non-Mourn tents. He did not know why Sali had been so concerned about bringing two thousand undead here. They would have been no threat: the camp held tens of thousands of Mourn, Men and Gar, perhaps even hundreds of thousands. The only army capable of challenging this assembly was on the other side of the world. Great herds of adunel and huffrin also milled around the tent city.

"Are we waiting for something?" Rayllor asked in his heavily accented Nerlinean.

Kyrian eyed the young Gar beadily. Since the tomb, Rayllor had grown in confidence, enough to talk to the Slayers and even question their actions. Kyrian found this most annoying.

"For that," replied Sali.

Her gaze did not waver from the camp. She was watching a small group of riders leave the yurts, heading in their

478

direction. There were four of them: three mounted on hadan and one on an oradar. She picked out the leader, Harkon Lan, distinguished by his heavily scarred face and missing right eye, a herald of the Great Khan of the Mourn. She remembered watching him from a distance, the evening after the battle between Kyrian and the Count of Haydon. The herald had entered Kyrian's camp and demanded his attendance and that of others at this gathering. His sudden appearance had almost disrupted her own entrance to the camp that night. The other two Mourn with him she did not recognize. The fourth figure on the cat was Falthar Mrignandor, Chief of the Skyriders tribe of the Fal'Gar. His oradar was clearly desperate to stretch its legs and kept gambolling in front of the much slower hadan before its rider dragged it back. Its behaviour earned the Gar angry glares from the herald.

Harkon Lan pulled his hadan to a hard stop in front of the three.

"You are late?" he addressed his question to Kyrian.

"My men are here," the Slayer offered. His own hard look met Harkon's glare.

"It was you and your men that were summoned, Count of Chazantria. Your life is forfeit, your lands are forfeit, and if we did not need your men they would be forfeit too," he barked.

"I would see the Great Khan to make my case." Kyrian's tone was polite, but it had been a long ride, and he was struggling to keep his anger in check.

"You are nothing, man-thing. Who are you to demand an audience with the Great Khan?" the Mourn shot back.

Saliana took off her wide-brimmed hat and fanned her face, then hung it from the pommel of her saddle.

"It is my fault we are delayed; I would ask you to convey my apologies to the Great Khan and request that I can come to his tent to discuss the forthcoming campaign," she said politely.

The herald turned to look at her, incredulous. Anger seethed across his face. He pushed his hadan forward until it was nudging up against Sali's oradar.

Kyrian's hand moved to his flail, which he loosened from his belt.

"Who are you to demand anything?" the herald demanded.

Flecks of rancid spittle from the Mourn herald splashed Sali's face. Her icy glare never wavered, and that gave the Mourn a moment of pause.

"I am Aranarte KalElian KalJeddera, called Kinhilchazadan, and your master will want to see me," she declared.

The Mourn pulled back at the last name, a hint of fear on his face as if something deep in his subconsciousness tugged at him.

"You are not Gar," he replied. "Nor are you old enough to be the Falcon Empress or, for that matter, dead, though the last can be rectified." The herald gave an evil grin, his confidence returning.

Then something happened. Saliana's skin started to flow and shift, and her face seemed to change, becoming sharper and harder. Her alabaster skin paled to a luminescent white. The point on her ears sharpened and her cheek bones raised and changed their upward angle. A Gar of the Syn'Dion'Gar stared back at the Mourn herald. Then her appearance changed again, hair darkening from white-blonde to a lustrous brown, almost black, and her skin darkened to the tan complexion of the Fal'Gar. Then the ears began to round, the cheekbones changed to a more human angle, the skin faded, and the hair grew pale. Saliana Slayer, the Kanath woman with a hint of Gar blood, looked back at the herald.

"Glamour." The herald hawked and spat on the ground. "You are not her."

"You want to bet your life on it?" she asked with smile. "You have no idea what I am," she added, her tone turning harsh.

The herald looked at her. He seemed to be weighing things in his mind.

"I will ask for your meeting, but I will not recommend it. Go to your tents and await the Khan's pleasure," the herald instructed. He dragged his hadan around and galloped away, followed by his two outriders. Falthar remained on his oradar, watching them.

"I'm surprised he didn't arrest or confine us," observed Kyrian, tucking his flail back into his belt.

"Where are we going to go?" Saliana replied. "You want to keep Chazantria, and I want a meeting with the Great Khan. Neither happens if we leave."

"You are quiet, Falthar. No greeting," said Kyrian, looking at the Chief of the Skyriders.

The Dumech'Di'Fal'Gar looked at them and Kyrian realized he was actually angry, something that barely registered on the normally emotionless face of a Gar.

"Where is my niece?" he demanded. "You said you would return her."

"What? Sorry?" Kyrian was surprised by the vehemence of the question. "I mean, she's fine."

"She is a day's ride east," replied Sali, coming to Kyrian's rescue.

"Why is she not here?"

"She is looking after an army of two thousand Fal'Gar riders," explained Sali.

"You lie," Falthar snapped. "All the Fal'Gar are here. There are not a hundred riders left on the steppe, let alone two thousand."

"These ones are dead," said Sali. "I took them from the Tomb of Salvarus."

"Impossible."

"Not for Kinhi… Kinch…oh gods, how do you say it?" laughed Kyrian.

"Kinhilchazadan," supplied Sali with a grin.

"You are not the Falcon Empress. She died," Falthar said quietly.

"We shall see," replied Saliana.

"It is a dangerous game you play," he said cautiously. "Such a masquerade will offend my people. To the Sevains she is a bogeyman – something to warn children about. To the Mourn she is just another on a long list of Gar who have stood in their way. Claiming to be her will bring you nothing but trouble."

"As I said, we shall see. You plan to send someone east to check my story. When they speak to Samarin and report back maybe you will see things differently."

"Perhaps," the Fal'Gar conceded grudgingly.

"But send a witch," said Sali with a smile. "An army of dead can disconcert those who do not know the ways of life and death."

"I will send Hildamar," he said.

Sali nodded her agreement. "It will be a few days before Lak Bok will agree to see us, if only to assert his status. Long enough to confirm what we say. If we are lying, you can request our lives from your overlord. Now, do you know why we have been dragged here?" she asked.

"Hambledon," replied Falthar.

"What about it?" she asked.

"He wants to take it."

"It's only weeks from winter," Kyrian interjected in shock.

"Are you serious?" she asked.

"Very," replied the Fal'Gar. "The Mourn intend to besiege and take Hambledon."

"Why move against Hambledon now in winter. Why not wait until spring?" Saliana asked.

"A frozen steppe can be crossed as easily as a dry one," said Falthar with a shrug.

"It's not a steppe war, it's a siege. You need to move siege equipment, dig trenches, tunnel; not stuff you want to do when the ground is frozen. Besides, you would have to feed this army through the winter, and deal with disease and poor morale." Kyrian's military mind listed the problems.

"Well, that's the problem. Food," observed Falthar. "A disease has wracked the Mourn adunel herds, and the harvest in the Mourn Steppe, such as it is. Word is that the harvest failed. It is not clear: the Mourn are close-mouthed about the whole thing. By the time Lak Bok and his chiefs realized the problem, the harvest surplus from the Great Steppe had already been exported to Kangorn and beyond. Lak Bok is not doing this out of choice but out of necessity. He is facing civil war unless he can feed his people."

"He could seize the winter stores of Haydron and Chazantria," Kyrian replied. He looked worried.

"He might well do that, but it is easier to send you to battle against Hambledon. If the city falls, the rich Sevain principalities lie beyond. If the Haydroners and Chazantrians die in a failed attempt to take the city, then there are fewer to fight or rebel against them, if he has to seize their stores."

"You think the attack will be led by humans," replied Kyrian.

"And the Gar. We are not exempted from this," the Fal'Gar observed.

"He needs to take Hambledon…" said Saliana, lost in thought.

"You have an idea, a plan?" asked Kyrian.

She gave him a grin. "There may be a deal we can do."

CHAPTER THIRTY-THREE – THE GATES OF HAMBLEDON

The cushion that supported her back was hard by design. Saliana shifted a little, trying to get to a more comfortable position. It did not work. Now the cushion was stabbing into her lower back, and felt more like a wooden spike. She nudged Kyrian as she moved, drawing an amused look from her fellow Slayer. He wafted away the threads of smoke in the air so he could see her more clearly, then gave her a sour look. This had been her idea, after all.

The pair were seated in the Great Khan's yurt, clearly one used for audiences, as he had a separate one to actually sleep in. It was larger than Saliana had initially thought from a distance, not that it mattered much. The place was packed: Mourn lords, Fal'Gar chieftains and a few of the more senior human lords – Sevains from the western edge of the steppe and Havagians from the eastern end. The presence of so many in the already baking tent had turned the cloying heat she would normally expect inside a yurt up to an oven-like intensity. Sweat poured down her face and out down the crevices of her legs and chest. Nothing she did to alter her position improved the situation. She looked longingly at the tightly closed flaps of the main entrance. It was a forlorn hope: even on the rare occasions when it was opened briefly to let another huge sweating Mourn warrior into the yurt, the breeze barely reached her, only hinting at the freshness of the outside air she yearned for. Whatever memories she had of such a place, be they hers or someone else's, they did not make her feel any better.

Then there was the smell. Yurts had an odour that one endured, not enjoyed. The Fal'Gar tents were bad enough, but they were like a fresh flower meadow at the height of a Las Ma summer by comparison with the stench of the Mourn yurt. There was the smell from the animal dung that was used to heat it, but it was the rancid animal fat used to light it that really added to the stench. It was a solid lard pushed into small metal containers that hung from each of the rafters. It burnt with an orange-green flame and gave off a dark grey smoke that quickly thickened the air. Neither the humans or the Gar seemed to be enjoying it: eyes were rheumy, and there were frequent outbreaks of coughing. The Mourn, by comparison, treated the choking air with complete indifference.

Saliana was fuming. She had known the Khan would keep her waiting; that was to be expected, and she had guessed it would be three or four days. That suited her: it was enough time for the Fal'Gar to confirm Samarin's good health and that Saliana had indeed resurrected Salvarus' army. It had the desired effect when word came back, and the Fal'Gar had started to view her differently, treating her with a newfound respect. It was as she had hoped. By day five though, she was starting to worry that the Mourn Khan did not view her as holding the same importance. By day six, she was angry. That moved up to incandescent by day seven. Now, over a week later, she was at least sitting in his yurt as opposed to languishing in her own tent. She had not expected a private audience, but neither had she expected to be thrown in with some general council. Besides, she was sat now off to one side, barely able to see the enthroned Khan, blocked by a wooden support pole and the hulking forms of three rows of Mourn warriors in front of her.

Lak Bok, Great Khan of the Mourn, was not quite what Saliana had expected. He was short for a Mourn – taller than her, certainly, but she doubted he cleared seven feet in height like most of his people. He made up for it in bulk. He wasn't fat, just solid; nearly twice the width of Kyrian, with a hint of a belly as he sat in his silks. He had the wide forehead and heavy brows characteristic of the Mourn. Tiny black eyes stared out from his wide flat face, although Saliana was too far away to read anything in him. His skin was dark for a Mourn; it looked like the hard brown leather used for saddles. Rumour was that he originally came from one of the Mourn tribes far to the west. His lank black hair was turning grey, hanging in thin lengths past his small, pointed ears.

He sat on what Saliana thought of as a throne, though that was for the lack of a better word to describe it. There was a raised dais, only a foot in height, just enough to take the khan above the assembled crowd. On it was a wide, almost bed-sized, rectangular platform with a curving leg in each corner. At the short ends it curved up to provide something for the Khan to lean on. It was covered with a thick green cloth embroidered with gold thread and stitched onto the base and arms of the throne. The workmanship was very unlike the Mourn and she wondered where he had got it or who had made it.

PRINCE OF SLAYERS

The Great Khan did not lean against the side, as was clearly intended. Instead, he sat cross-legged in the very centre of his throne. He wore black leather trousers and a shirt of blue silk, covered with a furry sleeveless waistcoat, simply cut from the reversed skin of some animal and tied at the front with bone pegs. His clothing clashed, his nomadic heritage warring with his more recently accumulated power and wealth. Periodically, some servant or scribe, human or Mourn, would approach bearing a scroll. He would peruse it and then toss it back. He was centrally placed in the tent, his dais a little closer to the rear of the yurt than to the entrance that directly faced him. Between him and the back of the tent was a collection of Mourn shamans. They looked smaller and older than the other Mourn. Some walked with sticks, a sign of age or perhaps infirmity. Even the younger ones seemed to dress older to match their colleagues. Their clothing seemed from a different age, almost archaic: ragged cloth shirts over tattered leather trousers. A thick skin of partly treated adunel fur thrown around the shoulders. Charms of bone and wood hung around their necks from ear piercings and rattled against staffs.

Unarmoured and with no sign of a weapon close at hand, the Great Khan was not unprotected. Four of the largest Mourn that Saliana had ever seen stood at each corner. All of them cleared eight feet in height, giving an odd juxtaposition to their short lord and the raggedy shamans who sat close by. The guards wore long coats of black leather woven with metal scales painted black and burnished to a high sheen. They stood hands in front of them at chest height resting on the pommel of already drawn scimitars.

"My children," the Khan's voice was hard, almost a bark.

Saliana looked up, surprised. He was speaking Westerly, which she supposed made sense as it was the closest to a common language in the west.

"Thank you for attending upon me," he continued.

She watched those in the room. Some of the Mourn were struggling, but most seemed comfortable with their Khan's choice of language. The Havagians also seemed a little perplexed, though they could guess at what was being said given the number of Nerlinean words in Westerly and its underlying structure.

"We have sat under the Mountain of the Moon for longer than we expected. The tardiness of my eastern subjects is forgiven." The Mourn Khan's gaze moved over the faces of the nervous Havagians and onto the most recent Mourn arrivals, tribes that now ranged the eastern edge of the Great Steppe.

Saliana had to hide a smile; she had never seen Mourn cower before, but Lak Bok managed to make his own people do it.

"On the morrow, the army of the steppe will march to the gates of Hambledon and into the rich lands beyond."

A great shout filled the room: a roaring tone from among the Mourn, while the Fal'Gar beat their fists against their chests and whooped. The men of Chazantria and Haydron shouted their approval, though a few seemed less than happy that they would soon make war on their kin south of the mountains. The Havagians joined in last, picking it up from the mood of the room, rather than the Great Khan's words.

Lak Bok's gaze swung around the room, finally fixing on the humans clustered to his right.

"There is one among you who would speak to me; one who appears to be human, but claims to be a Fal'Gar of old. Where are you, Saliana Slayer?" he demanded.

Sali pushed herself up and navigated her way around the post in front of her. She pushed through the seated lines of Mourn chiefs, receiving disgruntled looks from them. She stepped into an open circle of space directly in front of the throne and gave the barest bow to the Great Khan. Her eyes met his, and for the first time in a long time she felt like prey facing a predator.

"So, this is the Prince of Slayers," he said.

Sali raised an eyebrow at that. Only Esselindanor, the High Lord of Kyth'Dath, had used that title. How did Lak Bok know it? She cast around, thinking for a moment that the ice elf might appear suddenly.

Lak Bok laughed. "He is not here."

"Who, your highness?"

"The Kyth'Gar you look for. He does not bow to me like his nomad kin – at least not yet. That does not mean he does not keep me informed when it serves him to buy favour," he replied.

"Mind to mind," Sali observed; it was the only way the news could have travelled ahead of them. She looked at the Mourn shamans.

"Not with an elf," he laughed. "My shamans will not countenance it; a hate from old times. No, there are other ways."

The Great Khan reached behind him and fished out a large thick leather glove and put it on his left fist. He reached forward under his throne and picked up a leather pouch. He raised his hand and whistled. A falcon previously perched with other birds of prey on a collection of stands whipped across the room. Its wings beat apart the thick smoke in the air. It landed on the leather glove of the Mourn Khan. He reached into the pouch and pulled out a thin strip of meat and fed it to the bird. He looked back at Sali.

"'Beware, Saliana, Prince of Slayers': simple and succinct, brought by falcon from camp to camp across the steppe. So should I be wary of you, Saliana?"

She shrugged in response.

"My shamans, especially the younger ones, say I should kill you," he continued.

"And the older, more experienced, ones?" she asked.

"They say we should not try," he replied with a smile.

"Why?"

"In case we fail. Even in the steppe we heard what happened in Las Ma," he said.

"I have a deal to offer you, Lak Bok," she said, hoping she had chosen her moment right.

The Great Khan eyed her beadily. He seemed unconcerned by her sudden familiarity.

"I rule here: I command, you obey," he said with a toothy smile.

"I have two thousand tutharum," she used the ancient Gar word for the undead. She knew that the Mourn would understand. "Fal'Gar, oradar riders, the calvary of Salvarus."

There was a murmuring in the room; the shaman seemed particularly discomfited.

"I know," the Khan replied with the barest glance at Falthar. "What is that to me? Is that why you can claim to be the Falcon Empress, despite being human and alive?"

"A simple ploy to intrigue you and persuade your herald to make my case for an audience. I did not know the reputation of Saliana Slayer had progressed so far," she said politely, giving the glowering herald seated a few feet from her a patronizing smile.

"Oh, your reputation is secure, Prince of Slayers," he said quietly.

One of the shamans, an elderly grey-haired Mourn, made even shorter by his crooked back, had leaned over the back of the throne and was whispering urgently to the Great Khan. Lak Bok looked annoyed and waved him away, narrowly missing the aged Mourn with his meaty hand.

"My advisers say the Mourn do not march with the dead," he observed.

"And they make such decisions." Sali's tone was mocking.

"Careful. You amuse me, and your reputation gives me pause, but there are limits on my patience," Lak Bok said coldly.

"My apologies, your highness," Sali did her best to sound genuine in her obeisance. "You marched with them once."

"That was a very long time ago."

"Then I have one other thing to offer you," Sali said.

She reached into her belt and drew out a single orange jewel, one of the two that Essel of Kyth'Dath had given her. She held it up, so it caught the light. It seemed to glow, blowing away the smoke in the air.

"What is…" Lak Bok started his comment but stopped. The shaman had reached over again and was speaking in rapid whispers.

The Great Khan nodded, his face serious. He looked back at Sali, thinking for a moment.

"Clear the tent. The Prince of Slayers and I have something to discuss."

***

Silar Baldwin dashed up the spiral staircase of the tower, his full-face helm clutched in his right hand. He pushed his way onto the battlement, smoothing down his tabard over his chainmail armour, a black sun on a yellow field. The bell was ringing incessantly, and he squeezed his eyes closed, trying to clear his head. He had drunk too much the previous night and was feeling the worse for it.

"Will you stop that?" he demanded.

The man-at-arms looked at the angry knight and stopped. Bells continued to ring out across the walls, but at least they were not going off right next to his head.

"You got a tie?" the knight snapped at the man-at arms.

The man looked perplexed at the question.

491

"A tie, a piece of leather, a band," the knight shouted.

"My lord, I'm here!" Silar's squire Bryn bustled into view from the spiral staircase.

The knight looked the fourteen-year-old up and down with barely disguised disgust. Seven years the boy had been his page and then his squire and still he would be late for his own funeral. The boy handed his master a thin leather strip, which the knight used to tie back his mane of long blond hair. The boy took out a comb and went to brush his master's voluminous beard.

"Not now," the Templar hissed.

More people were coming up the stairs. Another knight, this time in a green and silver tabard, appeared on the tower battlement.

"Silar," he greeted his friend.

"Alek."

Alek Tonday was a knight of the Prince of Hambledon. Silar Baldwin, by contrast, was a knight of the Temple of Caon, a priest as well as a warrior. For three centuries since its conquest, the Temple of Caon had sent knights to protect the walls of the great city of Hambledon, to guard against attack from the steppe. Normally it was a quiet posting, a chance to drink and become lax in one's religious duties. Hambledon was the greatest fortress of the north and virtually impregnable, at least when fully garrisoned. For as long as anyone could remember, nomadic tribes had raided merchant caravans as they approached the city across the steppe, requiring the knights of Hambledon to drive them off. More recently, the Mourn had taken to testing the city's defences, and the sounding of the alarm had become more frequent. That had taken the form of chasing in returning Sevain patrols, occasional barrages of arrows and magical assaults from Mourn shamans. They had not attempted an all-out attack. Even the Mourn were not that mad.

"Where is the prince?" demanded Silar.

"He went hunting," Alek replied.

"What, first thing in the morning?"

"It's nearly ten. You would know that if you actually managed to make morning services," Alek replied waspishly. "You are supposed to be a priest, for Caon's sake, and a Knight Commander of the Temple."

"No one has chastised me," Silar shot back.

"You are the senior priest in Hambledon; they would have to complain to Dimchurch," Alek chuckled. "So, what's behind the alarm?"

"That," Silar replied pointing out across the plain.

The city of Hambledon stood on the northern end of a wide pass through the Daldara Mountains. Slightly recessed from the two mountains at the far end, they rose precipitously from the valley floor into the clouds. Sharp and craggy, they were difficult to climb, like most of the mountain range. The city wall ran right up to the edge of the mountains, leaving a gap of only inches on either end before turning back down the valley and turning again to enclose the rear of the city.

Alek walked to the edge of the square tower and stared out through the arrow loop carved in the stone of the battlement.

"Mourn," he said.

"And Haydroners, Fal'Gar, and others I don't recognize."

"How can you see so clearly, Silar?" barked the other knight. "Where is my eyeglass?"

Another squire appeared and handed an eyeglass to the knight.

"Sorcery," muttered Silar, looking at the device.

"Science, you fool," replied Alek. "You know how the steel you wear was forged."

The Templar shrugged in the negative.

"Witchcraft!" Alek mocked, tapping his fellow knight's mail.

Alek held the telescope to his eye and swung it across the plain, taking in the assembled mass.

"I see scaling ladders, battering rams, grapples," he announced.

"Caon's teeth, why is the prince not here?" spat Silar. "He was told there was a gathering of Mourn three days' march away."

"He said that nomads could not take the city. He said they would be crazy to attack," replied Alek, dropping his eyeglass.

"Well, he was wrong," Silar observed, pointing at the army outside on the plain.

"True," said Alek more calmly. "But you heard what I said: they have no artillery, no siege engines, just the most basic of siege tools."

"Alek, there are still a quarter of a million Mourn, Men and Gar out there."

"Oh, don't exaggerate: a hundred thousand at most," Alek replied.

"That is still ten to one," observed Silar. "Enough to take it by storm."

Alek leaned over the parapet so he could observe the deep ditch in front of the outer wall. It was slowly filling with black pitch, bubbling and hissing.

"I'm worried about the Gar; they have mages," said Silar.

"So do the Mourn, maybe even some humans: heresy is rife among our northern cousins," Alek observed, still leaning out.

He watched the drawbridge being drawn up. The two mighty portcullises that stood at either end of the great gatehouse had been lowered when the enemy was sighted. The drawbridge took longer. It was the fortress's great weakness. The wood slammed against the stone of the wall. Plates of black stone were attached across the entire underside of the drawbridge. Despite its shuddering darkness, the stone seemed to writhe and curl. It was the same stone used in the Templars' black shields to block magic. As much was used to protect the gatehouse of Hambledon as in all the shields possessed by the Temple Knights.

"The drawbridge is up, so you can stop worrying about magic," smiled Alek.

"What about the walls?" asked Silar.

"There are wards in the walls from the days of the Kanath."

"Sorcery," declared Silar.

"Make your mind up, Si," Alek sighed.

"This fortress has fallen before," observed the Templar.

That was true enough, Alek would have to concede, but it was always to treachery and usually when the city and its environs were weakened. Neither was currently true. The fortress by its nature was nearly impossible to surround. The other passes through the mountains were only large enough for small groups to move through and only at considerable danger of rockslides and collapsing paths. The nearest pass was fifty miles southeast of Hambledon. They would know by now if an enemy was coming from behind, and it would not be in the numbers necessary to cut off the city.

"This is going to be a hard fight, Silar, if they are foolish enough to try and storm the walls, but messengers have been sent south. The Prince will be back soon, and reinforcements from the surrounding Earldoms will soon be here to support. By the time your brethren get here from Dimchurch, the nomads will have gone back to fighting each other. It always happens when they raid."

"That's not a raid, Alek, that's an army," muttered Silar.

"Oh Caon, you are unbearable when you have a hangover," Alek retorted, annoyance starting to displace his good humour.

"Sir, something is happening!" called one of the men at arms.

Alek looked out across the plain, bringing up his eyeglass. The army had drawn itself up in remarkably good formation for nomads. It had positioned itself just past the three-hundred-yard marker, out of longbow range. Not stupid, thought the knight. He watched as a figure in black with a wide-brimmed hat broke away from the group, riding forward on an oradar.

"Elf mage?" speculated Silar.

"Looks human through this," Alek countered.

"Don't be absurd, it's riding a cat."

Alek grunted agreement.

"It's going to target the gate; I love this bit. You remember five years back when three Mourn shamans tried it. They were vomiting and shitting for hours," laughed Silar.

"Lak Bok is testing our defences. He obviously hasn't told his new wizard," chuckled Alek.

Arrows were now landing around the cat-mounted mage. They burst into flame as they hit the wards protecting it, confirming to the knights on the battlements that this was indeed a magic wielder.

"I don't know why they bother?" observed Alek.

"Might get lucky. Besides, it tires them, doesn't it?"

Alek shrugged in response to Silar's question.

The mage was now standing up in the stirrups. She – Alek had decided it was a woman – had her left hand raised up in front of her. She seemed to be holding something in her fingers. She raised her right hand over her right shoulder and a blue light started to grow in it. Alek's mouth curled in disgust. The blue light beamed out from the hand and through whatever the woman was holding in her other hand. It changed to a bright luminescent green as it passed through the second hand. He had not seen it done like this before, but he knew the result. It would hit the gate, there would be a spray of light, maybe sparks, and then the mage would collapse. The light hit the underside of the drawbridge, the black stone seethed and hissed, but the beam did not dissipate. Instead, it continued to burn at the gate, hissing and fizzing.

"That's not right; that's impossible," Alek declared.

All the Sevain defenders were looking down at the gate. What they were seeing should not be possible. Fear gripped them. The enemy army remained eerily silent, probably equally surprised by what they were witnessing. Then, the black stone cracked with a sickening screaming, but still the beam continued, the stone shattering, scattering across the pitch-filled moat below. The wood of the drawn-up drawbridge exploded inward in a sea of green fire. When Alek looked down, it was gone.

He heard the shouts of surprise ring out among the men of Hambledon. Panic rippled across the wall, like a tangible force washing over it. He looked at Silar, who was staring in stunned silence at the shattered remains of the gate strewn across the plain. Alek's palms were sweating; he tried to rub them dry on his tabard, but it did no good. He cast around, searching for his leather gloves. They were stowed in his sword belt, but in his building alarm he did not think to check there. He had fought in several major battles, perhaps a dozen skirmishes. He knew he was no coward, he had faced fear and overcome it, but not this, not this all-engulfing terror.

The oradar rider tossed away what was in their left hand and rode a few yards further forward. She stretched out her right hand toward the gate. There was a sound of grinding metal and tearing stone. Then there was a crash as the far portcullis was torn through the stone tunnel of the gatehouse, becoming trapped against the outer portcullis facing the plain. It caught the men in the tunnel, crushing them between two grids of hard iron. Then the second portcullis gave way, as both were torn out and flung across the pitch-filled ditch.

Alek and Silar were running for the spiral stairs before the Mourn army had even started to move.

CHAPTER THIRTY-FOUR – THE ISLE OF THE TOWER

Greldin of the Way stepped out onto the top deck of the highest tower of the Crystal Ship. He had been born below the oceans, but he still loved to see the water tumble down the towers and the sides of the great vessels as they broke through the surface of the waters. The moons were full, which made the image all the more bewitching. He looked out across the open ocean to a storm-like squall ahead of him. For those few who had seen it, they would have known it never changed: the storm was always there. Not that many had; only the Syn'Dion'Gar came this far east across the Farthest Ocean or this far west across the Kraken's Wake, depending on where you started your voyage. The Tancree had tried it several times, failed, and now they were gone, almost.

The place gave him mixed feelings. He always came here with a heavy heart, but the power of the place filled him almost to bursting. So much magic. There were things that he could only do here. He reached out from the tower and drew a circle. A pillar of water exploded from the oceans, writhing up the side of the ship like some great serpent. It stopped in front of him, forming a flat platform. He stepped out onto the waterspout.

Daldara, Goddess of Magic, I love you, he thought.

The pillar of water carried him out across the ocean, twisting like a zephyr until he reached the front of the storm. A wave of his hand and the weather parted, and he continued on his journey unmolested by the maelstrom. Beyond lay a small island, bathed in moonlight. Rocky outcrops surrounded it, lapped gently by calm waters. The thundering ocean calmed by magic or the Gift or the will of the gods, he did not know. Even some secrets were beyond his knowledge. A stone arch stood at a break in the rock. A small flight of five steps ran from the water's edge up to the arch. Beyond it the stairway carried on as two more flights separated by a wide landing took approaching visitors up to a tower, if that was the right word. It was like an upturned bulbous glass vase, perhaps four storeys high, topped by a pointed round minaret of blazing white crystal. From it emanated a waving shield of pale blue light that ran from the top of the tower to the rocks of the shore. It undulated like soft lace caught in a breeze.

Greldin used the pillar of water to bring himself down to the steps at the waterside; only through the stone arch could the shield of blue light be avoided. He stepped off the ocean onto the white polished stone and looked nervously at the two figures guarding the gate: Gar in armour of alcidide, high helms in place, broadswords strapped to their backs, armoured hands clasped in front of them.

"Welcome, Greldin of the Way," the voices pulsed in his mind.

The mage brushed past them, saying nothing. The undead made him uncomfortable.

He walked up the stairs towards the ornate golden gateway that led to the crystalline tower beyond. Another pair of skeletal Gar guards stood either side of the entrance. It was the figure in front of them that gave him pause. It was a long time since he had seen this warrior.

"Is she okay?" he demanded.

"As far as I am aware," the undead warrior's voice pulsed in his mind.

"You worried me," said Greldin.

"Is it true? It has unlocked powers both blue and grey?" the voice tore in his mind.

"How do you know that?" asked Greldin.

"I'm a god," the undead Gar replied.

"It is possible, but we have a solution; Cliphine has a plan," the wizard declared, choosing not to offer his opinion on the warrior's claim to deity.

"If she lives?"

"You said she was okay," Greldin replied.

"Go to her now, but I will leave you something by the dock, in case you have need of it," the warrior declared in the wizard's mind.

"What?"

"You will know it when you see it. Now go to her."

Greldin slipped past the warrior and through the golden gate. The tower contained a single room on its ground floor. A large bed lay in the middle. A figure lay curled up under thin covers of soft cotton.

"Hello, Cliphine," he greeted the resting lady in the gentlest of voices.

JUSTIN WAINE

The sheet stirred and a face peered out. He hated this moment. The wizened figure stared back. Cliphine's shining skin had paled to a pallid grey, liver spots covered her flesh, lines cut her face. Her hair had lost its lustre and turned to the straw white of old age, of impending death. How many times had he done this? Why did he ask; he knew the answer. He remembered each of the four times. The beautiful woman he loved, riven and destroyed by age.

"No comment on my beauty," Cliphine's voice was a cracked whisper.

He shook his head mutely.

She smiled sadly. "Did you bring it?"

"Yes," he replied.

"And she survived?"

"Yes."

"I knew she would," cackled Cliphine.

"She is Lyrn Tutharum, a Trendorn of Death," observed Greldin.

"Give it to me," ordered Cliphine.

Greldin seemed unsure. Was this right? He had his doubts. His father had shared similar concerns before he had died so many centuries ago. He could not let her die; he loved her.

He reached into his robe and drew out a bone-white flute, the Illth'Di'Gar. He stepped forward and watched as Cliphine took off her thin shift and lay back on the bed. He placed the flute on her withered skin, resting it between her breasts. White light started to leak from it, then it seethed around the body, wrapping it gently in white streams. Then it blazed. She screamed. She grabbed the flute in both hands as white fire blazed across the room. Her body racked back and forth. She was raised above the bed, her body surrounded in white light. It cracked and crunched as if it was being pulled apart. Greldin ducked his gaze to avoid being blinded. The light blazed out.

He looked up at the lithe figure on the bed. Her pale white skin shone; her pert breasts were topped with perfect round nipples. Hard stomach. White hair luxuriant and blazing. Cliphine stood up and slipped off the bed. She walked toward the mirror and admired her naked form in the reflective glass.

"I almost waited too long. Each time the ageing comes on me quicker than the last. I went from a body of middle years to old age in six months," she stated quietly, more to herself than Greldin.

"Forty-two years," said Greldin.

"Pardon?"

"Since we last drew the power of the flute."

She nodded.

"Seventy-six years the time before that, a century before that, a hundred and nineteen years before that," observed Greldin.

"Your point?" she demanded.

"You are not just ageing faster at the end; each time you use the flute the years it gives you are fewer. Without the power of a Lyrn Tutharum to renew you, it might not have worked at all."

"I realize that," she answered testily.

"Do you? A simple witch would not have been enough: it needed the power only a Death Lord could generate to bring you back this time. Without the Slayer girl you would be dead."

She turned to look at him.

He cast his eyes down to avoid looking at her naked beauty as much as he wanted to. "Do you want to put some clothes on?" he muttered.

She looked again at her beautiful form in the mirror. "No, I'm good," she said with an evil smile.

"Is there a solution?" asked Greldin.

"To what?"

"This might be your last life, Cliphine," he observed.

"I think I may have a solution to that."

"The girl?"

"You will know when you need to."

"You keep too many secrets, Cliphine."

"The boy, Nyandar. Did he receive the obeisance he so craved?" she asked, changing the subject.

He nodded.

"And the Emperor of Nerlinea thinks it was his idea?"

Greldin nodded again, this time with a small smile.

"Ran'Dumech'Di'Gar, soldiers, nothing changes," she laughed. "And Ara?" she asked.

"She is not your daughter, Cliphine. She is called Saliana Slayer now," he observed a touch coldly.

"She was once," the Lady of the Crystal Ships replied.

Greldin sighed. He had had this argument too many times to bother having it again.

"Saliana Slayer has gone to the Great Steppe; she has triggered the wards on the Tomb of Salvarus."

"And it didn't kill her? You are slipping, Greldin."

He ignored that. "Our spies report she is with the Mourn Khan."

"Spies? You mean Essel, that duplicitous…" Cliphine left her thought unfinished.

"Among others," Greldin replied.

"Blue and grey. It is a long time since he had both," Cliphine mused.

"He? You mean she?"

"Don't be difficult," she pouted.

She tossed her hair back, showing off her breasts and hips.

"You must return and protect the witch," she ordered Greldin.

"Which witch?" he answered with an amused grin, switching language to Westerly so the joke worked.

"Very good," sighed the Lady of the Crystal Ships. "The Slayer witch. What is she called; Dryana? Samarin is with Ara. She can protect her."

"Are you coming with me?" he asked.

"No, I have things to finish here. We are winning so far, but Ara will be making her own plans. There will be something coming to bite us," replied Cliphine.

"Saliana," stated Greldin.

"Pardon?"

"She is not your daughter. You let too much emotion into this. She is Saliana Slayer. Aranarte is long gone."

The Lady of the Crystal Ships knelt down in front of the wizard and looked up him. He stared down at her, eyes playing across the pout of her lips, the white skin of her shoulders, the nakedness of her breasts. Words fled as he felt the blood burning in him. She picked up the flute and, standing up, handed it to him.

"Take this back to Nyandar. It is his, after all." She turned away and walked off to the other side of the room.

"You are beautiful, Cliphine," breathed Greldin quietly.

He gave a bow to her retreating figure and left.

He walked down the stairs, passing through the stone tunnel to the final steps before the ocean. On the second to last step, just above where the ocean lapped across the rock-cut stairs, rested a sword. It was a broadsword, nearly five foot in length from the tip of the blade to the pommel of the hilt. Hard to wield. Greldin drew the sword and marvelled at its alcidide blade. It was light despite its size and perfectly balanced. He admired the fine wire binding of the hilt; it looked like gold, but he knew it was not. At the end of the hilt was a jewel, a stone of milky orange. The pattern on its surface changed as the white lines writhed and spun against the orange background. He looked at the word written on the blade picked out in the long-forgotten runes of the old north. The word they spelled was not in that tongue or in the language of the Gar. Instead, it was an archaic form of Kanath. It said one word: Othrys. Or, as others called it: the Summersword.

***

The late spring sun blazed down over Port Ren. Dryana felt it warm her skin, which despite all the sun stubbornly resisted tanning. The wind blew up, whipping her black silks around her. She enjoyed the momentary breeze. It was going to be a long hot summer, she suspected. She watched the two ships slowly berth against the harbour. Sea-going junks: the perfect ships for the rigours of trade on the Farthest Ocean.

"My Lady Dryana," came a soft voice to her left.

She turned and put on her best smile. "Custom Officer Shan. How is my favourite port official?"

"Well, my lady," he replied. "You?"

"Enjoying the sun," she replied politely.

She reached into her silks, produced a red envelope and handed it to him.

"Thank you." He gave a small nod of thanks.

He turned to leave.

"No inspection?" she queried.

Not that the man did the work; that he left to his slaves.

He raised an eyebrow. "Those ships?"

"Early harvest grain ships from Mahendra," she supplied, catching his meaning.

"No need," he chuckled. "The de Trovilles have lumber ships in from the Southern Kingdoms; my staff are busy checking those. Besides, if I get done early, I can go fishing."

She nodded politely. "Good luck. I hope you catch something."

PRINCE OF SLAYERS – CAST OF CHARACTERS

The five Slayers.
Saliana Slayer, Mistress of the Company of Slayers. A Kanath bard and mage, with possible Gar ancestry. High Lady of the Isles of Syndion

Kyrian Slayer, Military Commander of the Company of Slayers. Count of Chazantria. A former wrestler, a Kanath, older brother of Dryana

Slinker Slayer, Spymaster of the Company of Slayers. A Tancree war mage. Once a member of their ruling caste, now a fugitive from the Samath

Dryana Slayer, Head of the Company of Slayers' operations in the east. A Kanath witch and necromancer. Younger sister of Kyrian

JUSTIN WAINE

Balinor Strabo-Slayer, a partner in the Company of Slayers. Prince of Kangorn and Warden of the Falcon Strait. A former slave of unknown ancestry

Other characters:
Marcus Romanch, a Kangorner, Lord of Kangorn and Chazantria
Falthar Mrignandor, a Gar, Dumech'Di'Fal'Gar and Chief of the Skyriders
Radnor Callico, a Sevain, Count of Haydron
Harkon Lan, a Mourn, a Herald of the Great Khan
Lak Bok, a Mourn, Great Khan of the Mourn, Overlord of the Great and Mourn Steppes, Conqueror of Havagia
Morianus Strabo-Slayer, a prince of Kangorn, son of Balinor and Ascrina
Ascrina Strabo, Princess of Kangorn and Warden of the Falcon Strait, wife of Balinor
Alisha Strabo-Slayer, a princess of Kangorn, daughter of Balinor and Ascrina
Sliva Droma, a Kangorner, Captain of the Palace Guard of the Prince of Kangorn
Kolith Shardath, Samath Ambassador to Kangorn
Farmorl, a Nerlinean, an employee of the Company of Slayers
Caldimor Mrignandor, a Gar, wife of Falthar
Hildamar Mrignandor, a Gar, Trendorn'Di'Fal'Dath
Samarin Mrignandor, a Gar priestess
Cliphine KalElian KalJeddera, a Gar, ruler of the Syn'Dion'Gar and religious leader of all the Gar, known colloquially as the Lady of the Crystal Ships
Amdon, a Solinad Hunter
Lan Xian, a Nerlinean merchant and criminal
Nyandar KalElian KalJeddera, ninth of the name, Emperor of Nerlinea, Hadanan of Amaland

PRINCE OF SLAYERS

Camlyn Halfnight, a Nerlinean, Dumech of Haldorn and Lord of Halfnight, husband of Srias, father of Charlotte and Alphion

Srias Halfnight Pandus, a Nerlinean, operational head of the eastern part of the Imperial Pandus Trading Company, Camlyn's wife, Charles' sister and Charlotte's mother

Charlotte Halfnight Pandus, a Nerlinean, Lady of Kangorn

Zem Pandus, a Nerlinean, titular head of the Imperial Pandus Trading Company, grandfather of Srias and Charles, great grandfather of Charlotte

Pu Zin, a Nerlinean, Dumech of Ren

Anudin KalElian KalJeddera, a Prince of Nerlinea, Dumech of Las Ma

Samantha KalElian KalJeddera, a Kanath, eldest surviving daughter of the Duke of Las Ma, wife of Anudin

Syndanor KalElian KalJeddera, a Gar, Dumech'Di'Syn'Dion'Gar, a descendant of Cliphine

Greldin of the Way, a Gar, a priest of the Syn'Dion'Gar and mage

Talnan, a Solinad Hunter

Yana, a Solinad Hunter

Karn, a Solinad Hunter

Danzian Corinmount, a Kangorner, a banker and Lord of Kangorn

Pendian Sar, a Kanath, agent of the Company of Slayers and former mage of the Order of Dawn

Shanti, a Nerlinean, a tavern worker

Kcillit Taydas of Clan Tiramor, a Gar of the Debion'Gar

Darinya Hellithan of Clan Tiramor, a Gar of the Debion'Gar

Koman Hellithan of Clan Tiramor, a Gar of the Debion'Gar

Sconya Teldinar, Trendorn'Di'Debion'Gar

Hynin, one of the Grey Folk

Pynathin, a Gar of the Kyth'Gar, daughter of Esselindanor

Esselindanor, a Gar of the Kyth'Gar, a High Lord of Kyth'Dath and father of Pynathin

Tandral, a human from the Southern Kingdoms, Slayer Chancellor of the Isles of Syndion

Kanjar Hoey, a Kangorner, merchant

Charles Pandus, a Nerlinean, a merchant of the Imperial Pandus Trading Company

Espand Dani, a Nerlinean, an agent of the Imperial Pandus Trading Company

Tallyn Hanath, a Gar, Lady of Kangorn, former Captain of the Prince's Guard on Kangorn

Chan Shal, a Nerlinean, a ship's captain in the Company of Slayers

Collyn, a Nerlinean, court magician to the Prince of Kangorn

Tara, a Kanath, court magician to the Prince of Kangorn

Salvarus Mrignandor, Emperor of Fal'Dath, Dumech'Di'Fal'Gar

Shinmaku Chul, an Amalander, a herbalist

Ko Quan, a Nerlinean, a mage of the imperial court

Lord Kaleb Redbranch, Lord of Kangorn and Warden of the Great Watchtower

Silar Baldwin, a Sevain, Knight Commander of the Temple of Caon stationed at Hambledon

Bryn, a Sevain, squire of the Temple of Caon, in the service of Silar Baldwin

Alek Tonday, a Sevain, a knight in the service of the Prince of Hambledon

GLOSSARY

Geography
Galvia, the planet on which events take place.
The West, the lands lying to the west of the Nerlinean Ocean and the Great Steppe.
The East, the lands lying to the east of the Nerlinean Ocean and the Great Steppe.

A Selection of the Races of Galvia
Ananrorers, a race of humans, fair-skinned, brown-haired, close cousins of the Kanath, largely found on the Isle of Anaror.
Brinach, a race of humans, fair-skinned, dark of hair and eye, the most ancient of the human peoples in the west. Ancestral enemies of the Kanath. Reduced to a few small tribes living in forests. Servants of the Sevains in the lands in which they live.
Gar, a non-human people, human-like but taller and thinner, with pointed ears. Renowned for their magical skills and

artistry. Closely allied with the Nerlineans and the Kanath in times past. Originally split into seven different tribes (see below).

Kanath, a race of humans, fair-skinned, dark of hair and eye. Largely subjugated and increasingly integrated with the Sevains. Kanath under Sevain rule follow the one-god, Caon. Kanath that are still independent follow the old pagan faith.

Mourn, a non-human people, reaching seven feet in height and the width of two normal humans. Skin the colour of brown leather, with dark hair, beady eyes and pointed ears.

Nerlineans, a race of humans, originally of light brown complexion, with dark hair, increasingly a term used to describe the citizenry of the multi-ethnic Nerlinean Empire rather than a particular racial group. They follow the same gods as the Gar.

Samath, a non-human people, tall, heavily built with scaly skin in mottled greens, browns and dark blues. Originally slaves to the Gar. Often called Lizardmen by the other races.

Sevains, a race of fair-skinned, light-haired humans. Originally from the Great Steppe, they migrated south, subjugating the Kanath. Followers of the one-god, Caon.

Solinad Hunters, a human people from the Great Steppe, light-brown-skinned and dark-haired.

Southern Kingdomers, a race of humans, dark-skinned and dark-haired.

Tancree, a non-human people, tall but thin to the point of being emaciated, skin the colour of old dried parchment. A war with the Samath has driven them to the point of extinction.

The Tribes of the Gar
Aman'thy'Gar: the formal name of all the Gar, literally the Gathering of the People.

PRINCE OF SLAYERS

Tribe: *Dal'Ri'Gar* – the People of the Moon
Land controlled: None – extinct
Other names: The Children of Daldara, the Moon Elves
Tribe: *Debion'Gar* – the People of the Desert
Land controlled: the Deserts of Debion
Subjects to the Emperor of Nerlinea
Other names: The Desert Elves
Tribe: *Den'Sar'Gar* – the People of the Far Mountains
Land controlled: None – extinct
Other names: The Children of Naron, the Elves of the
Mountain, the Dark People
Tribe: *Fal'Gar* – the People of the Falcon
Land controlled: Formerly the Empire of Fal'Dath, comprising
most of the Great Steppe, lost to the Mourn Conquest
Other names: The Falcon Elves, the Lords of the Steppe
Tribe: *Kyth'Gar* – the People of Ice
Land controlled: Kyth'Dath
Other names: The Ice Lords, the Ice Elves, the Guardians
Tribe: *Quil'Gar* – the People of Fire
Land controlled: Quil'Dath
Reluctant subjects of the Emperor of Nerlinea
Other names: The Builders, the Fire Elves
Tribe: *Syn'Dion'Gar* – the People of the Summer Dawn
Land controlled: None; they live below the oceans on the
Crystal Ships
Other names: The Shining Ones, the Gar of the Crystal Ships,
the Sea Elves

Lands of the West
Allakor, a Sevain city and principality, a Kanath earldom that
became Sevain through religious conversion and marriage
rather than through conquest. Not considered proper Sevains
by some of the northern Sevain principalities.

Chazantria, a Sevain County in the west of the Great Steppe formerly considered part of the County of Haydron.

Dimchurch, a Sevain city ruled by the Temple of Caon, who control the surrounding territory as temporal rulers.

Fartowers, a city ruled by the Order of Dawn, which controls the island of Anaror.

Hambledon, a Sevain principality and city, ruled by the Prince of Hambledon, conquered from the Kanath.

Haydron, a city and county on the southern fringes of the Steppe, ethnically a Sevain people who stayed on the Steppe rather than migrating south. Now subject to the Mourn Khan.

High Ringstead, a Sevain principality and city, ruled by the Lord of High Ringstead, conquered from the Kanath.

Kangorn, an island city, known as the Rock. It serves as the key merchant trading hub between East and West and the Great Steppe. Founded two hundred years earlier by a Nerlinean pirate called Kangorn and his twenty captains. Ruled by Princess Ascrina and Prince Balinor, it is a cosmopolitan mix of Nerlineans, Kanath and Sevains, most of whom consider themselves Kangorners irrespective of ancestry.

Las Ma, a former Kanath dukedom and city, now conquered and split between the Samath and the Setsonians.

Setsonia, a Sevain city and principality, the largest and richest of all the Sevain principalities, ruled by the Prince of Setsonia.

Lands of the East and South

Amaland, an island kingdom ruled by the Empire of Nerlinea through a personal union rather than conquest.

Graci Isles, a group of islands off the east coast of Nerlinea, once part of the Empire of Kasem.

Havagia, formerly a Dumechate of Nerlinea, recently conquered by the Mourn Horde.

PRINCE OF SLAYERS

Kalygon, a kingdom to the North of Nerlinea and Quil'Dath, once part of the Empire of Kasem.

Kasem, a kingdom to the North of Kalygon, once the centre of a much larger empire.

Narazgon, a dumechate of the Nerlinean Empire, largely unpopulated.

Nerlinea, a large empire dominating most of the East. Ruled by an emperor, it is the dominant economic and military power on Galvia. It is split into dumechates ruled by a dumech, a Gar word meaning 'war leader'; also the root for the Kanath word 'duke'.

Quil'Dath, a Gar dumechate, north of Nerlinea, considered a vassal of the Nerlinean Empire, though occasionally in conflict with it.

Ravangia, an island dumechate of the Nerlinean Empire in the far north of the Farthest Ocean, famous for its peculiar microclimate. Once part of the Empire of Kasem.

Samathitir, the land of the Samath, comprising a large territory south of the Nerlinean Empire and a number of island chains in the west conquered from the Tancree.

Southern Kingdoms, a group of constantly changing kingdoms, used as buffer states between the Dumechate of Narazgon and Samathitir.

Syndion, an island chain once the home of the Syn'Dion'Gar before they moved to live below the waves. Backistri is the largest island.

Companies and Religious orders
Company de Troville, originally a Kanath merchant trading company that relocated to the Nerlinean Empire following the Sevain invasions. The third largest of the Nerlinean merchant trading companies.

House Caldric, the oldest and second largest of the Nerlinean merchant trading companies, now surpassed in size by the Imperial Pandus Trading Company.

The Imperial Pandus Trading Company, the largest and richest of the Nerlinean merchant trading companies.

The Merchants' Guild of Kangorn, a trading guild comprising the ships of the Prince of Kangorn and three of the richest noble houses. It also supports the merchant activities of other lords and citizens of Kangorn in return for a fee.

Nerlinean Imperial Fleet, the naval forces of the Nerlinean Empire. In the West they are very far from Imperial control, with their ships often acting with a wide latitude to interpret the empire's wishes.

Old Faith or Old Religion, a term used by Sevains and some others to describe the pantheistic religious beliefs of the Kanath prior to the Sevain conquest. Sometimes used to include all those who follow pantheistic beliefs, including the Gar and the Nerlineans.

The Order of Dawn, an order of wizards, survivors of the destruction of the magical College of Krena during the Sevain invasions. They fled to the isle of Anaror with other Kanath, establishing a new College of Magic at Fartowers.

The Temple of Caon, the controlling entity behind the Sevain monotheistic religion. The Temple comprises a priesthood led by an order of knights under the overall command of the Grandmaster of the Temple.

Gods and Goddesses

Caon, the Onegod, monotheistic god of the Sevains.

Casala, Kanath goddess of night.

Cragon KalShon, the Ravenlord, Deathbringer, Gar and Nerlinean god of autumn and death.

Daldara, Lady of the Moons, the threefold goddess, Gar and Nerlinean goddess of magic.

Jeddera, the Summersword, Lord of Morning, Captain of the Ravenscar, deified Nerlinean Emperor, god of summer and seafarers to the Nerlineans and Gar. God of magic and battle to the Kanath.

Julyiana, Kanath goddess of sky and birds. An earth goddess.

Kay, Coldheart, Sleeper, sister-wife of Cragon KalShon, Gar and Nerlinean goddess of winter.

Lynidine, of earth and oceans, Queen of the Harvest. Kanath mother goddess, responsible for both land and sea.

Nordian, the seafarer, Kanath god of sailors and ships.

Paschen, the forgotten god, Dawnbringer, Gar and Nerlinean god of summer cast down by Jeddera.

Rasmanor, the Hunter, Lord of the Dance, The Horned One. Gar and Nerlinean god of the hunt and the forest.

Sargon, the Thunderer, First of the Dragon Lords of Old, the Dragon King, Kanath god of thunder, the rains and war. Also worshipped by the Brinach and some Gar.

Sidarra, Mistress of the Rains, Gar and Nerlinean goddess of spring and fertility.

Tempor, Lord of Time, Kanath god of time and death, father of the Kanath gods.

The Adversary, not a god more a force of nature representing entropy and chaos. The Sevains believe that through Caon they can hold this force at bay.

The Mad One, Kanath god representing turmoil and destruction.

Thytha, the Great Mother, also called Shon, Galvia and Mother Earth. Gar and Nerlinean goddess of the earth.

Other terms

Alak, a white alcoholic beverage made by the steppe peoples.

Alcidide, a rare metal believed to have magical properties. It is used by humans to alloy with other precious metals to create the crowns used to control ships. The Gar combine it with iron to create weapons and armour immune to rust.

Amanthagan, A Nerlinean ceremony of obeisance to the emperor; also a place at which the ceremony takes place.

Aureus, Nerlinean currency minted in gold.

Crown, a magical device that allows a human wizard to manoeuvre a ship single-handed.

Houses of Kangorn

The Princes of Kangorn
House Strabo-Slayer

The Surviving Original Houses
House Romanch, the first Lord of Kangorn
House Winterborn, the second Lord of Kangorn
House Makin, the third Lord of Kangorn
House Mandin, the fourth Lord of Kangorn
House Daldin, the fifth Lord of Kangorn
House Kirkdun, the sixth Lord of Kangorn
House Watkin, the seventh Lady of Kangorn
House Hiller, the eight Lord of Kangorn
House Chanda, the ninth Lord of Kangorn

The New Houses
House Malkiel, the tenth Lord of Kangorn
House Tymandor, the eleventh Lady of Kangorn

JUSTIN WAINE

House Masterly, the twelfth Lord of Kangorn
House Brondin, the thirteenth Lord of Kangorn
House Brewer, the fourteenth Lord of Kangorn
House Redwind, the fifteenth Lady of Kangorn
House Corinmount, the sixteenth Lord of Kangorn
House Tallyn, the seventeenth Lady of Kangorn
House Halfnight-Pandus, the eighteenth Lady of Kangorn
House Slayer, the nineteenth Lady of Kangorn
Vacant, the twentieth Lord or Lady of Kangorn

ABOUT THE AUTHOR

Justin Waine has been writing fantasy novels for almost as long as he has been reading them. Having spent the last two decades working in the investment industry he decided he really should get around to publishing some of them. He is the author of The Company of Slayers series and The Kylnnar War Saga. When not writing he spends his time training and teaching martial arts.

DID YOU LIKE IT?

So, you have made it this far. Either you liked it, or you pushed through to the end. Either way I would love to hear what you think of my work. Please rate and review on Amazon, Goodreads or your platform of choice. Also don't forget to tell your family, friends, enemies and random strangers on the street about my books.

You can follow me on Amazon or on Instagram at justinwaineauthor to stay updated on forthcoming books and events. You can also keep up to date via the Epsom Fantasy Press Limited website.

www.epsomfantasypress.co.uk